Praise for
The Movement

"While more narratively complex than its predecessor, The Movement is in many ways more inviting, right down to the helpful footnotes explaining the nuances of backstories"
—*Booklife (Publisher's weekly)*

"The plot unfolds via multiple first-person perspectives in multiple timelines, sometimes recapping the same incidents from different points of view"
—*Kirkus Reviews*

"Avi Datta has once again crafted a mesmerizing tale in The Movement. It is a layered tale that will linger in conscious thoughts for some time"
—*Steven Robson for* **Readers' Favorite**

"The Movement is another tense and thrill-packed install-ment in Datta's innovative science fiction series"
—*San Francisco Book Review*

"A stellar addition to the Time Corrector Series"
—*Pikasho Deka for* **Readers' Favorite**

"Datta handles the utterly intricate structure of the plot, which includes the multiple storylines alternating between different timelines and several characters' first-person perspectives"
—*Prairies Book Review*

"The emotion in his words allowed me to experience his wonderfully developed cast's feelings"
—*Keith Mbuya for* **Readers' Favorite**

THE MOVEMENT

TIME CORRECTOR SERIES BOOK 2

AVI DATTA

Edited, designed and distributed by Bublish, Inc.

ISBN: 978-1-64704-629-3 (Paperback)

ACKNOWLEDGMENTS

THESE PAGES ARE JUST AN attempt to connect with memories of a past life that may happen in the future—Avi Datta

I am eternally thankful to the Bublish team for translating this work into a final product.

Note to my readers

While *The Winding* was narrated using Vincent's singular point of view (POV), *The Movement,* despite being predominantly Vincent's story, includes close to a dozen POVs. That made the book slightly longer. But, trust me, it will be worth your time.

Right in the middle of my writing, I spent three months in Japan, working as a visiting Professor at Hitotsubashi University. I visited the places that are mentioned in the book. I tried to unlock Vincent's fascination with Japan too. Did I succeed? I don't know.

I am grateful to everyone who chose to pick a copy of The Winding. Because if you did not, I would not write this.

So, where are we? At the end of Book 1, we saw Vincent and Emika meet outside their house, which was removed from reality (Chapter 19—Today [finale]). So, did they actually meet? Or was it a figment of Vincent's imagination? Or was it both? In the last chapter, we saw Vincent's act of extraction made someone return (Chapter 20—Found You!). Someone who, according to Vince, is synonymous with life itself. But how? Is it all too simple? Let's find out. (Please pay close attention to the dates on each section, as the story is not entirely linear)—Avi Datta

You can reach me at Web- https://avi-datta.com/, Instagram- @avimanyu.datta; Twitter-@avimanyu_datta; Facebook- authoravidatta

Also, by the same author
The Winding—Time Corrector Series Book 1

CONTENTS

CHAPTER 1

REVELATION—STAGE 2

"Don't you die on me."
—Vincent

April 13, 2027

Vincent

SHE DOESN'T HAVE A LOT of time. I can hear myself gasping—every single whiffling note. I can't lose her. My heart is thumping through my rib cage. It has had enough. My only hope is Philip rescuing us in his NASA-collaborated DoD supersonic aircraft, the X60. They're close. They must be.

It's 11:30 a.m., according to her blood-soaked wristwatch. I can't see mine; my hands are busy tightly pressing my jacket over her wounds. Her blood is still leaking through it, reaching my hands, turning them red. The intreton in my bloodstream has healed my wounds. I can't even tell her flesh from the intreton attached to the tip of the spike Vandal used to strike us.

As I look into her eyes, my tears make her face hazy. "Don't you die on me," I growl, shaking her. I have made an impenetrable shell of crystalized intreton around us. We are invisible to the world—but not to Vandal. I didn't even create the intreton case with sparks, like last time. I just thought of it, and it formed. But how? How did my whole body emit sparks? Is this the power the future me had warned me about? Or is there more?

Vandal, encased in his two-story, manned Jaeger, knocks the wall of the intreton shell with his ten-foot, thorned flail. The blast from his flail pierces through my ears, hurting my head. I want to cover my ears, but I can't. I have to keep pressing her wounds. The high-pitched ringing has conquered my eardrums and is ratcheting around every corner of my head. My skin crawls and shivers to the screech of his flail on the paved road. I squeeze my eyes shut. That's all I can do. I can't close my ears—my hands are busy trying to keep her alive.

Suddenly, Vandal stops. Why? What's that sound? I look up, seeing the X60. I exhale in relief. She'll live.

Why couldn't I untangle Vandal's identity earlier? I could have stopped the death . . . it hasn't even been a month since Vandal murdered ....Fuck, I can't even face that reality, that he is gone. We are barely fifty feet from my shattered G-Wagon, smashed against the guardrails. The batteries are steadily catching fire. I need to get out of here before the authorities start looking for us. The blinking blue and red lights and their accompanying sirens are getting closer to me with every tick of my 36,000 vibrations per hour wristwatch.

Why is it taking so long for Philip to pull us out? I shout at my phone, resting in my jacket pocket. "Ludwig, connect me with Philip."

"Vince?"

"Hurry. She's bleeding out."

"Almost there. I'm hovering above you. My men have blocked the road from the police. You are invisible to the outside world, right?"

My voice quivers. "Yes. Is Dr. Lee ready?"

"Yes. You're doing great. We will get you out."

"I can't lose her."

She opens her heavy eyes. I touch her cheek as tears stream down my own. "We will survive this."

She lifts her hand and touches my face. Tears pour out of her eyes as she mumbles through her trembling lips, *"Anata o aishiteimasu."*[1]

Why is she telling me this now? After walking away? I cradle her head against the nook of my neck and shut my eyes. "Shhh. *Boku mo itsumo.*"[2] These can't be her final words. Kissing her head, I ask, "Why did you throw yourself like that?"

She whispers, "I'll keep doing it." Her breathing slows. "Because you're my . . ." Her eyelids get heavy, yet there is that unmistakable smile. She slowly closes her eyes. I feel my pulse racing in my shaking hands.

Swallowing hard, I shake her. "Open your eyes. Wake up! Wake up!" I put my ear against her heart—still beating.

What do you mean you will keep doing it? Why did Vandal choose this moment to attack me? Were you the target? He knows hurting you will inflict the most pain on me. That's it; there is only one way to stop this from happening in the future. I have to change your reality and erase Vince from your life once and for all. I'll set this right. No one will come after you if we never meet. And you wouldn't have the urge to save me. But before that, I must shield my house with intreton. Even if the core selects the path of least resistance, my actions might change the reality of those in my house now; they are connected to you.

I'll rip Vandal from his forty-foot Jaeger, and he will beg for his death. Blood rushes to my head.

There are some lines one must not cross with me. Vandal, you won't dare cross another line after today.

I clench my jaws, gritting my teeth.

You're done, motherfucker.

Gripping her tightly in my arms, I scream at the top of my lungs, "She will live!"

Her hand against my cheek, she murmurs, "Let me go, Vince. I got my minute with you."

Frantic, I declare, "Never."

This world makes no sense without you in it.

The intreton shell shakes as it topples. What now? The ground beneath us disappears, and Philip's skyhook pulls us out.

---

[1]   I love you.

[2]   Me, too, always.

CHAPTER 2

ORIGAMI

"Goodbye, Vincent. Goodbye, Hulk."
—Emika

September 2026

Emika

ITTLE NOZO IS SUCKING MY finger. Is she hungry? She is just a few hours old; it's November 15, 2024. She opens her eyes, which are identical to her father's. They are all I have of him. I look around the room and see the doorknob turning.

It's him!

I never thought I'd see him again. He walks over to me, takes out his pocket square, and wipes my tears. Then, he takes the baby from my arms. She grabs his finger, then falls asleep with a whimper. He kisses her forehead and looks at me with those twinkling, blue-green eyes. When he raises his eyebrows, I know he is asking for the baby's name.

I blink. "Nozomi . . . it means . . ."

Putting Nozo back into my arms, he says, "I know. Hope." He kisses my forehead and runs a hand over my hair.

Locking my eyes with his, I touch his hand on my head. My voice trembles. "You're the dad."

He removes some strands of hair from my face and tucks them behind my ears, whispering, "I know."

I touch his face. "I am sorry for breaking up with you and letting someone else take your place. I did not want to impose, so I didn't stay on August 15."

He runs his hand tenderly over my head again. "You are never an imposition. Just hang in there. When the petals fall, I'll be back home—just a day for me but a little longer for you."

The room changes. I am now sitting in the living room of what used to be our home. The cherry trees in the backyard have blossomed, and the petals slowly fall to the ground, like the notes of Handel's Passacaglia, creating a snowstorm of flowers—*hanafubuki*. Looking at the living room clock, the date is April 15, 2027. There are slightly blurry faces all around in the living room. There is Hulk! And Nozomi is older. Her father comes and sits next to me, taking my hands and kissing them. Then, he stares at me with his stinging eyes.

"So, Emi, are we still a work in progress with beautiful potential?"

I smile. "We are more."

"Then would you terribly mind—?"

As I am about to touch him, he starts to disappear. So does Hulk, the home we built—all gone as the sound of "Clair de Lune" blares through my head.

That's my 5:30 a.m. alarm—time to feed Nozomi. Rubbing my eyes, I wipe off the dream. Will there ever be a day when it will be the same alarm but on his phone? When I wrap my arms around him and ask him to sleep some more?

Snap out of it, Emika. It's been too long, and you left him, remember? You have a long flight tomorrow and lots to pack.

I yawn, stretch my arms, remove the comforter, and leave the bed. But how can I avoid him for the entire week? This year, the whole AI conference is about him. Do I really *want* to avoid him?

As the attendee stretches out her arms, Nozomi digs her face deeper into my shoulders. I scoop out her head and look at her frowning face. Kissing her tiny nose, I stretch my eyes wide. "They have Legos." Smiling ear to ear, I promise, "Ice cream later?"

She clenches my collar, widens her blue-green eyes, and tilts her head. "Choco i-kim?"

I pull her close again. "Whatever you want." *Anything for those eyes, anything for your smile.*

She finally leaves with the attendee, resting her head on the woman's shoulder and staring at me as they go. Keeping my Ghurka bag on the floor, I sit on a gray sofa, waiting to be called. The curved OLED TV is perpendicular to me, about ten feet away, on top of the fireplace. They are featuring some K-pop band touring the UK. I rub my arms.

Why is it so cold in here?

(A memory fragment)

Vincent took off his mustard, burgundy-striped cashmere scarf and wrapped it around my neck, pulling me closer as he did so. "Is it warm?"

I touched the scarf, smiled, and dabbed my eyes with his pocket square. "*Atatakaidesu.*"

(Back to reality)

What memory is this? It never happened, but it feels so real. Why?

The loud jingle of breaking news jolts me back to reality and brings my attention to the TV in the waiting room.

"This is Trisha Ingram, bringing you the latest updates. Philip Nardin's net worth crossed two trillion USD after he successfully built his intreton-C-powered supersonic X60 for the Department of Defense in collaboration with NASA. In other news, the world is in disarray as Vandal continues to expose every vulnerability of our digital infrastructure. After the attack on JPX, he caused a head-on collision in Haneda airspace between Flight 667 and Flight 3078. Japan has closed its Kansai, Narita, Chubu, Haneda, and Osaka airports until further notice. There are still restrictions in Singapore, Hong Kong, and Shanghai. The global AI conference starts in two days, and the world is holding its breath, eager to see Quantum World's new invention, the Neurolink. We have the CEO and chief inventor at Quantum World, Dr. Vincent Abajian."

As the camera shifts toward him, I can't move my eyes from the screen. His image is plastered on every digital billboard in central London, the back page of *AI Quarterly,* and occasionally on TV. The brilliance of his mind exudes from his penetrating eyes. He looks sexy, with a full beard with hints of gray.

Trisha asks, "Is it wise to launch Neurolink in two days amid a crisis? Wouldn't your customers want assurance of security?"

Vincent takes off his glasses, wipes them with his pocket square, then puts them back on and looks at the interviewer. He asks in his seductive accent, "How fluent is your English?"

I knew he would say something snarky. That accent hints at the perfect notes of someone raised in Switzerland and who went to college in the UK and US. I could listen to him talk all day.

Trisha shrugs. "I'm a native speaker."

Vincent scoffs. "So, you should know the difference between showcasing and launching." Leaning forward, knocking on the desk, he clarifies, "We will be showcasing the product in a couple of days. We will beta test in early April 2027 and launch it in late April next year." He looks at the camera and smiles. "Our customers and their information security are our top priority."

Trisha leans toward Vincent. "What about Vandal?"

Staring at the camera, Vincent smirks. "He can't hack our network."

And the segment ends.

That's the arrogant Vincent the world sees, not the kind, sweet one I knew. The one who continued to love me, despite my blunders. Did he move to a different house? He must have. The old one is stained with memories of me.

An attendant comes forward. "Dr. Amari? Dr. Mishkin will see you now."

As I walk in, Dr. Mishkin is ready with her notebook, her eyeglasses hanging from a chord. Smiling, she points at the sofa. "Sit."

"Thanks." After sitting, I take out a Rubik's Cube and two pieces of origami paper from my bag. A box of tissues and a water bottle are aptly placed on the side table next to the sofa.

She puts on her rimless glasses and holds her pen over her notebook, staring at me. "Go on."

With my eyes fixed on solving the Rubik's Cube, I admit, "I don't know if I can face him."

She leans forward and squints. "Vincent?"

On to the last three colors of the cube, I shrug. "Yes." Isn't that why I always come here? And solve the Rubik's Cube and make shapes from origami papers?

"Why do you need to face him?"

I put the Rubik's Cube on the side table and start folding the first origami. Color—red. "It's the Annual Global AI Conference, which Vincent and his team hardly attend. But this year's highlight will be Vincent's team showcasing their signature helmet called The Mind and something called the Neurolink." Taking the water bottle from the side table, I take a sip and gather my thoughts. "My old colleagues—Ravi, Anna, and Chris—will also be there."

Dr. Mishkin squints. "So?"

I fetch a few tissues and dab my eyes with them. "The products are based on patents I have with him." My lips tremble. "I also had papers with him, but he removed himself as a co-author because . . ." I can't seem to find the words; my throat is dry. Lifting the water bottle to my lips, I take a few more sips.

Leaning closer, Dr. Mishkin touches my hand. "What's on your—?"

"You know . . ." I interject before she can finish her question.

Dr. Mishkin presses her lips together, then says, "I need to hear it."

I lift my eyes from the folded tissue in my hand. "I thought he moved on. Why else would he write a terse text in April 2024? So, I turned down the offer at Nardin Robotics on August 15, returned his violin, and came back. I still have his jacket and the photo." Sniffling, I confess, "I couldn't give those back."

Dr. Mishkin pushes her glasses higher up her nose. "What happened afterward?"

I rap my knuckles on my knee. "Damn it, you know," I say, pointing at her notes. "It's all there."

She remains silent as she stares at me intently, knowing I will give in because I have this incessant compulsion to talk about Vincent.

Exhaling in defeat, I glare at her. "All right, you win." I close my eyes, and tears pour out of them. "I wish I'd checked my voicemail earlier."

"And when did you check it?"

I take more tissues. "December 15—four months and two days late." Taking a deep breath, I continue, "Eight months since Vincent's Senate hearing on April 2024 and four months since I turned down the offer from Nardin Robotics." My voice quivers. "Four months since I left his house after putting the violin by his door, without even a note."

(December 15, 2024)

Nozo just turned a month old, and I received my replacement phone. While transferring data from the old one, I noticed an old voicemail I hadn't checked. It was dated August 13, 2024, and it was from Vincent.

"Hi, Emi. I'm wary of moving past you, and I can't lie to myself anymore. I'm surrounded by objects that tease me of our brief time together and what we could have been. Now, I'm sitting with a cup of Genmaicha tea and watching the rain splash against the window. I can see the mountains and the lake through the rain and how everything changes as soon as the lightning strikes. Yesterday, it was sunny, and the golden light touched the snowcapped mountains, the hill, the trees, the grass." He paused. "Hey, you know the bellflowers never bloomed in spring, but they did yesterday. The setting sun shone on them, and it was gorgeous how the light danced around them. I could almost picture you picking them and placing the flowers all over our home. Yes, our home. I know the conflicts in your mind. But I think you may get some clarity tomorrow morning. And after that, if you feel we are still a work in progress with beautiful potential, I will be waiting for you. And Emi . . . I love you."

He had never said those words to me before, though his eyes had often revealed his feelings. If I had heard them four months back, I would have taken the job at Nardin Robotics. Had he also left a voicemail on my US number? I ran to my bedstand and fished out my US phone from the drawer. The home screen was a photo of me kissing Vincent's cheek while making a horn-shaped victory sign with my hand behind his head. We were in our pajamas, in our bedroom, and he had the most adorable sleepyhead hair, with Hulk on his lap. And there it was, another voicemail from February 16, 2024.

"I know you won't check this message. Whatever happens to me, just know that I love you."

That had been just a day before I'd broken up with him.

I wouldn't have, Vince, if I had listened to it.

I listened to both voicemails over a hundred times. Pacing around the apartment, I rehearsed every word I'd say. I even wrote it down.

Vince, I love you. Can I come back? I packed all my stuff like I promised I would on February 14. I don't care if I moved too quickly. But I don't want to waste another day without you.[3] I also have a lovely surprise for you.

Only four months back, outside his house, when I'd rejected the offer from Nardin Robotics, I'd decided not to call him. Ever. Now, that oath meant nothing.

I ran to Nozo's crib, picked up my sleepy baby, and whispered, "Guess what? We're going to see Papha!"

---

[3]   She said the same to him at the reality crossroads, where she returned to Vincent. Chapter 19 of The Winding (Time Corrector Book 1)

I put her back in the crib, switched the mason jar lights from the ceiling, and watered all the plants. The warm, yellow lights contrasted with the setting sun, and the slow dripping of snow visible outside the window created the perfect ambiance. After putting Vincent's chambray jacket on—I wanted to feel his hug before calling him—I danced back to my cell phone. Sitting on the floor with the phone, I dialed Vincent's number and put it on speaker. I bit my nails and wondered if he would say, "Hello?" or "Emi?"

But my eyes got stuck to the phone when all I heard was, "The number you have dialed has been disconnected."

My heart stopped, and my hands shook. I turned my phone off and back on. Then, I checked the SIM card and the battery. Everything was working. I dialed again, getting the same response. I paused and assembled my thoughts. Out of desperation, I called Anna.

After three seconds, the response was the same. I tried Ravi and Chris. All disconnected. Couldn't I make international calls? I dialed my parents' number in Kyoto.

"*Emi-chan*," my mother answered before I hung up.

Panicking, I started wheezing. Pressing my palm against my thumping heart, I crawled on all fours. Why hadn't I checked the voicemail earlier? I'd had four months. Could I use a landline to call? After checking on Nozo, I went downstairs to my landlady's apartment. I couldn't even hear the squeaky floor under my heavy breathing.

I banged on her door. "Ms. Baker, are you home?"

Please answer.

She opened the door, looked at me, and covered her mouth. "What's wrong, love?" she asked, pulling me in and steering me to a chair. "Another fight with Markus?"

Getting straight to the point, I asked, "Can I use your landline to make an international call?" I clasped my hand together. "I'll pay you."

She kissed my joined hands, shut her eyes, and shook her head. "Don't ever say that. You're like my daughter."

I knew it was pointless. There was nothing a landline could do that my cell could not. But I still dialed all their numbers, starting with Anna and then moving to Chris, Ravi, and Vincent—alphabetically, as Vincent would have done. When I dialed Chris's number, I knew I should stop dreaming of a life with Vincent. After all, I'd been the one to discard it. And I had to be okay with the consequences. I shut my eyes, picturing the last time I'd seen him, in the airport.

Then, I put a smile on my face to distract from my wet eyes. I bowed. "Thank you, Ms. Baker."

She came close and touched my hands. "You okay, love?"

My lips trembled as I spoke. "I have to be. I have a little one to raise."

I climbed upstairs and went to Nozo's crib. Her eyes were open, and she giggled, struggling to get out of her cotton wrap. No, Vincent could not be mine, but I had proof of what he was to me. And no amount of changing phone numbers could take that away from me. I stared into her eyes—his eyes. She smiled, and that was his smile.

I picked her up and nuzzled my nose against her tummy. "I love you, baby. And you are all mine."

Going to my desk, I opened my laptop, googled Vincent and his three musketeers, and clicked on the LinkedIn site. What used to be their profile was now a page one could only follow. I followed all four of them. The pages were all professionally managed, with no option to message them. I didn't know why or when they did it. All I knew was that I should have checked the voicemail earlier.

✻

(Back to the present)

I turn to Dr. Mishkin. My first origami has transformed into a red robin. Picking up the bottle, I drink half the water and then wipe my face with a tissue. I take the second paper into my hands and begin to fold it. Color—white.

Sighing, I continue, "So, I diverted my attention to Nozo while battling disapproval from my father for having a fatherless child."

Dr. Mishkin squints. "Disapproval?"

The disappointments never end with you, Papha. I couldn't be a pianist or a violinist. I dated the wrong guys, and now, I am a single mother.

Wiping my eyes, I force a smile. "Nothing. Some other time."

Tilting her head, Dr. Mishkin asks, "So, you never tried contacting your ex-colleagues?"

As my origami takes the shape of a puppy, I smile and run my fingers on its face.

Hi, Hulky. Remember Mum?

I look up at Dr. Mishkin. "No. I kept myself deliberately busy with Nozo and my job. But I often think of a life with Vince, Nozo, and Hulk, in a place I once called home." I wipe my eyes and shrug. "Just wishful thinking—a fairy tale."

Shaking her head, Dr. Mishkin shuts her notebook. "Let's come back to reality, then. Vincent may have moved on. So, why don't we look at things that occupy your life—Nozo, your job . . ." Clearing her throat, she stares into my eyes and adds, "And Markus?"

I put the folded origami next to the Rubik's Cube on the side table. "What about him?"

"Isn't he there for you? You've told me he also loves Nozomi."

"Mark and I were in a relationship, yes," I say, crossing my legs together. "He helped me through a lot, during my pregnancy and even after Nozo was born." I exhale slowly. "Whenever I even have"—I bring my thumb and index finger together—"the slightest inclination to revive what we had . . . it all disappears when I look into Nozo's eyes. All I think of is Vince and what we could have been." I lean forward and defend, "It's not fair to Markus for me to be in a relationship with him while carrying a torch for Vincent. He deserves better." Swallowing, I confess, "Though he is attractive, I will be more than happy if he seeks joy elsewhere."

Dr. Mishkin takes off her glasses. "And you've been clear with Markus? Because he may feel used."

Staring blankly at the coffee table, I say, "In bits, yes. But at times, he gets weak and tries to touch me." Looking into Dr. Mishin's piercing eyes, I cut a broken smile. "I get weak, too . . . I want to succumb, too. But I don't want to give him false hope."

She puts her glasses back on and crosses her legs. "If you see Vincent at this conference, will you tell him about Nozomi?"

Sniffling, I laugh sardonically. "Wouldn't that be great? And he'd be like, 'First, you treat me like shit, and now, when I am a billionaire, suddenly, I fathered your child?'"

Dr. Miskin squints. "Is that your truest interpretation of Vincent?"

I drink the rest of the water. Sighing, I concede, "No. Deep down under the blanket of arrogance hides an incredibly kind and unquestionably moral human." Wiping my tears, I admit, "That's my Vince." Suddenly, I feel breathless. "What do I do?" I ask. "What should I tell him if I meet him?"

Leaning forward, Dr. Mishkin says, "That's for you to decide." She touches my hand. "Just don't rush to a conclusion if you see anything out of the ordinary."

I collect my cube and origami figures and stand up. "Thank you for your time."

She smiles. "Good luck with your travels."

Leaving, I rush to the playroom. Nozo is squinting her eyes as she figures out the last two pieces of the Lego Home Alone house. The other older kids, and the attendants, have their jaws wide open.

Placing the pieces, she brushes her tiny palms off and announces, "Done."

My heart flutters with joy as I drop to my knees and clap. "*Sugoi, Nozo-chan*," I cheer.

With her tiny feet, she walks over and hugs me. Then, she points at my bag. "What did you make me?"

I take out the two origamis, and her eyes widen. She stretches her chubby arms. "A doggie and birdie. Gimme now."

I kiss her soft cheek. "*Nozo-chan*, what do we say?"

She pouts. "Please, *Kudasai*."

I point at the two folded papers. "What do we call a dog and a bird in *Nihon go*?"

Growing impatient, she puffs her plump cheeks. "*Inu to tori*."

"Good girl." I hand her the two folded papers. I hug her tightly. "*Watashi no ai. Watashi no Nozomi*."[4]

As soon as I enter my apartment building, Ms. Baker comes forward. "He is upstairs, waiting. You might as well give him a key."

I reorient my tote on my shoulder while holding a sleepy Nozo in my other arm. Smiling, I shrug. "I'll think about it."

---

4   My love. My Nozomi (Hope).

Climbing the stairs, I see Markus waiting by the door. He looks up and jerks his head to move the flop of hair covering his left eye. "I saw your text and got her favorite chocolate ice cream," he says, smiling.

Nozo throws her arms in the air at the sight of him. "Ma-kus," she says, her eyes gleaming.

He takes Nozo from my arms and kisses her as I open my five-hundred-square-foot apartment. Markus tucks Nozo into her crib and puts the ice cream in the freezer. Then, he turns to me. "All packed?"

I point at my luggage. "Almost. You?"

He loosens his necktie, runs his fingers through his blond hair, and sits on the sofa. He sighs. "Yes, but you will be in premium economy, unlike me." Leaning forward, he rubs his hands together. "The conference arranged babysitting services for all the children."

"Wow." I sit next to him and ask, "But why can't you travel premium economy?"

He scoffs. "You're the scientist. I'm just the media guy."

"I see." Maybe, I will upgrade his seats. I fish out the origami dog and bird from my bag and gently place them into a woven storage basket. It's eight cubic feet, but it's overflowing with dogs, cats, boats, birds, planes, and toads—each testimony to hours of therapy dealing with only one subject: Vincent.

Markus looks at the box and frowns. Raising his brows, he asks, "What new things have you learned from Dr. Mishkin today?"

A few strands of hair fall in my eyes. He leans toward me and tries to tuck my hair behind my ears, as he did in the past. I stop his hand and raise my finger.

"I am still not ready," I say.

Standing up, he glares at me. "And you will never be." Pointing at the origamis, he says, "You think that billionaire will care about you and Nozo?"

I remain sitting. "You know nothing about him. He's Nozo's father."

"Wow!" Markus sneers. "Where was he when you delivered? When Nozo spoke her first words and called you Mum? Or when she took her first steps?" Pointing at himself, he asks, "Who was with you?"

I feel my nostrils flare. Raising my voice, I point toward Nozo's crib. "He doesn't know she exists. And she is not your child."

His face turns red, and the veins in his forehead bulge. "I missed it by, what, a week?"

I hiss, "Shut up." Pointing at the door, I order, "Get out! Before I say something, I'd regret."

Throwing the door open, Markus storms out.

I'm so sorry. I wish we hadn't made those promises before discovering my pregnancy or my interview with Nardin Robotics. Or before looking at those beautiful eyes of Nozo's.

"Mum, Mum," cries Nozo. The door slamming must've woken her up.

I rush to her crib and pick her up. "Yes, baby?"

She hugs me. "Is Ma-kus my papha?"

I bring her head in front of me. "No, he is not." *Do we fight like a couple now?*

She tilts her head and rubs at the tears on my cheeks. "Who is my papha?"

"He is in America," I whisper.

Her eyes widen. "We are going to America?"

"*Hai* . . . tomorrow."

I place her head against my neck and rock her.

Would it be that bad, Nozo, if it were just you and me? Am I not enough? I would have told your dad about you if things had happened differently in February and April 2024.

(February 17, 2024)

I wiped my tears, gathered courage, and spoke into the phone.

"You're stuck deciphering some theories surrounding a violin. The secret was not the violin. It was far more sentient. A genius like you should have figured it out. In a way, it's good you didn't. Anyway, take care, Vince. Have a great life. *Wakare!*"

I hung up on my Vince! How could I? Even I couldn't believe what I'd told him. I stared at my cell phone in disbelief. He was kind and patient and everything I hoped for. But, at that moment, I felt relief. I did not know any better. It almost seemed like I had no control over my impulses.

I went to the bathroom and, running my hands over the faucet counter, swiped everything on the floor. Breathing hard, I sat on the floor.

It serves you right. The violin was not a fix to my headaches—you were. I heard your voice, the voice that asked me to find you. But to you, I was just a fragment of Akane. Was it so wrong to ask for a greater role in your struggles? I am not Ravi, Anna, or Chris. You never saw me as a partner . . . if you had, then you wouldn't have concealed anything. I hate you. I wish I had never met you. I will not shed a tear for you.

I moved into crawling position, readying to get up off the floor. My tears dripped on the tile.

I am done with you, Vincent Abajian. I know what sleeps beneath the genius—a self-centered jerk stuck in his childhood with Akane.

I grabbed my cell phone and texted Markus.

Me: Hey.

Markus: What's up?

Me: Can you come? I need to talk to someone.

Markus came, and we talked all night. He convinced me that Vincent had pushed me away, and I was better off without him. Though he had said what I wanted to hear, I was still easily persuaded. I fell asleep on his lap, wearing Vincent's chambray jacket, while Markus ran his heavy, tender hands over my face and hair.

(April 13–April 30, 2024)

I wrapped myself in Markus's shirt as he brought me breakfast in bed in his apartment bedroom.

Vince, you were better at cooking, but you were too stubborn about eating on the bed. See, I've moved on from you.

It'd been almost two months for Markus and me. Karaoke, weekend trips, backpacking to Scotland, Portugal, and Spain, and those cozy nights by the fireplace. Vincent wouldn't even backpack; he had to travel first class. He wouldn't karaoke, even if my life depended on it.

Pushing my hair behind my ears, tickling my neck, Markus said, "Stay here for the weekend." He insisted, "Why do you need to watch the Senate hearing? Aren't you over him?"

I wrapped my arms around his neck and nuzzled his nose. "Just want to know why he kept all the secrets." Running my fingers through his straight, blond hair, I assured him, "I am over him. It's like Vince, and I never happened."

"Then why do you still keep his chambray jacket, the violin, the pocket square, and the photograph of you, him, and his dog?" he asked, furrowing his brows.

I kissed his lips. "I will mail those back. Promise."

Shaking his head, Markus didn't look convinced.

"How about I move in with you here at the end of the month?" Pulling his hair, I bit his lips gently. "Will that assure you?"

He pulled me close and kissed me. "I love you."

I didn't know why I couldn't reply.

I returned to my apartment just in time, on April 13, 2024, to watch Vincent live. I was looking for some validation to justify my breaking up with Vincent over the phone, knowing it had been wrong of me. But I didn't want to be vulnerable before Markus.

I switched on the TV. Then, I squinted at Vincent as he raised his right arm. My jaw dropped. How could that be Vince? Was he sick? His cheeks were sunken, and his shoulders were drooping.[5] A full beard replaced the Balbo and Anchor. Why was his impeccably cut suit sagging? I bit my bottom lip as tears filled my eyes. Had I left him when he was sick? How could I? What rage had blinded me? Who are those people sitting next to him? Lawyers? That many? Why are the senators grilling him like this? How would he know where Philip was? Why don't they stop?

I felt the blood rush to my head as I yelled at the TV, "Stop! Please leave him alone. Can't you see how frail he is?" The camera moved and zoomed in on Vincent.

How many nights since you last slept? Your eyes look ferocious, despite the dark circles.

---

[5]   Vincent was struggling with mastering his powers and was losing weight. It is explained in Chapters 13, 14, 15, and 16 of *The Winding* (Book 1).

I wanted to pull his head against my shoulder, switch off all his alarms, and sleep.

Someone asked, "Do you think Mr. Nardin has anything to do with the assassination of Dick Graham?"

How could he know that? Please let him be.

Vincent's eyes looked bloodshot, though he kept sneering at the politicians.

One senator pointed the finger at him. "Dr. Abajian, please wipe that smirk off your face and answer the question."

Why would he? He is brighter than all of you put together.

I tried to blink away my tears, but they just trickled down my cheeks.

Leaning forward, Vincent said, "Yes. And your time is bought by the lobbyist who represents weapon manufacturers. Your intention isn't to find Philip. Now that Lombard is dissolved, you're showcasing your resolve to find a new employer—a new DoD contractor interested in weaponizing intreton. And, in return, you will get our mansions, yachts, and more money in your Swiss accounts."

He took some folded papers from his jacket pocket and put them on the table. Then, he said, "Dick Graham was just the tip of the iceberg. If one carefully looks at who funds your campaigns and can hack into your private routers, they'd know how loyal you truly are to the people you're supposed to serve." He pointed at the senators. "I'm talking to you two, McCarthy and Franks. Haven't you received five million from Lombard to vote in their favor, which shows their intreton-container is as good as Nardin's? The evidence will be in print tomorrow. I have the account numbers with me."

Taking some tissues from the box on the side table, I buried my face in them. Feeling a cold draft over my neck and shoulders, I wrapped myself in Vincent's chambray jacket, holding on to the lapel.

You were going through so much . . . you did everything to protect me, Ravi, Anna, and Chris. Markus was wrong. You did not push me away. I shoved you while you begged for my patience.

My shoulders shook as I cried.

I accused you of cheating. In return, you booked a whole box at the concert. I called you names that night.[6] *And then, I cheated on you. I even took Brad to your dinner party, flaunting how quickly I got over you. That day, I saw the pain in your eyes, though you tried to hide it beneath the excitement of your pathbreaking invention. Yet, I still kept inviting Brad to my townhome. Still, you took me home the day before my flight and cooked my favorite meal—omurice.*

I stared into my shaking hands.

Look what I did. I broke up over the phone and invited Markus over right after. How could I move on so quickly? I don't deserve you.

I couldn't bear to watch the hearing, but maybe it was the last time I could see him. So, I plowed through, seeing the rage and pain behind his eyes.

I was worse than those senators who are grilling you. Will you ever forgive me?
I texted Anna.

Me:	Hi.
Anna:	What?
Me:	I have wronged Vince.
Anna:	No shit.
Me:	I'm watching the hearing. He looks so frail.
Anna:	What do you want?
Me:	Can he forgive me? Is there any hope for us?
Anna:	He has forgiven your rudeness and all your indiscretions. You were his home, and you shattered it. He is trying to reassemble and wants to move out of the uni. Let him be busy, start fresh, and bury himself in work—we will pick him up if he falls. I think you did enough.
Me:	I see.
Anna:	We all loved you. You broke the heart of someone who means a lot to me and everyone else.

---

[6]　Chapter 13 of *The Winding* (Book 1). Vince and Emika had a huge fight following a concert night. Emika called Vincent an "apathetic, rich, spoiled brat."

> You left him in a worse state than when Elise
> died. Leave him be. Please.[7]

Anna was right. I remained in bed all Saturday and Sunday, wearing Vincent's jacket. Markus kept calling me, and I kept ignoring him.

The following Monday, April 15, 2024, I went to work, as usual. My thoughts were gloomier than the weather in London. Around noon, my phone beeped for a video message. My whole demeanor brightened at the name of the sender.

Vince!

The text read, "*Hanafubuki*: Keeping my promise." It was a four-minute-long video of the cherry blossoms in our home's backyard. In the background, he put on Aoi Teshima's song "*Haru no Kaze*."[8] Hulk ran around like a happy puppy, a floating cloud chasing the slow-falling blossoms. Vincent was not in the video, but he remembered my request, which I had made on the same day I flaunted Brad in front of him. Was there still hope? I wanted to somehow crawl inside the phone screen to the place I'd once called home. I stared at my hands, hoping to find his. Suddenly, the gloom was gone. Sun peeked through the clouds over London, and I felt goosebumps and curled my toes. I drank some water, trying to calm myself and lower my heartbeat. As I wrote my response, memories from our home came rushing in.

Me: *Arigatō*, Vince. The song perfectly complements the video. It reminded me of our conversations when I discovered you were an artist. You know, the one in which you talked about language barriers and music. Saw you at the Senate hearing. I understand what you were going through and why you concealed everything from me. I'm so sorry. I hope one day, you will forgive me.

What will you write back? Will you ask me to come back? If you do, I would. I would tell you everything about Markus. Would you forgive me one last time?

I began to dream of restarting our life, working together, waking up next to him, mischievously delaying his alarm. I would do everything right.

---

[7] In Chapter 16 of *The Winding* (Book 1), Anna wanted to share this text with Vincent.

[8] Spring Breeze.

Maybe I'll let you have a Reuben.

Looking up, I tapped my chin.

On second thought, no.

The phone beeped. I shut my eyes, my heart fluttering with anticipation. I opened the message, and the cloud covered the sunny sky again. My heart stopped. I read it. Then, I reread it. I scrolled to see if that was all he had written.

Maybe he will write more. Let's wait.

I waited one hour, simply staring at the phone. My longest dream ended. I reread his message one last time. All he wrote was, "You're welcome. Good to know."[9]

That's all? Why were you so terse? What was I hoping for? You groveling?

Although I hadn't eaten lunch yet, I felt a tightness in my stomach, as if my organs were trying to come out. I ran to the restroom and threw up.

When I came back, Markus was waiting by my desk. Rubbing my back, he asked, "Hey, you okay?"

I closed my eyes and nodded. "Perfect."

He checked if anyone was watching, then put his hand on my shoulder and kissed me behind my ear. "Want to go to lunch with me?" he whispered.

My throat was dry. I swallowed. "Not today. Please."

Rubbing my back, he assured me, "I'm with you no matter what."

"Thanks."

"I love you."

I hesitated. "Me too."

I'm sorry, Markus; you deserved better.

I felt sick, and on April 21, I found out I was pregnant.

"Do you want to know the date of conception?" the doctor asked.

"Sure." I shrugged but crossed my fingers.

---

[9]   *The Winding* (Book 1) reveals that Vincent already knew how Emika was split between what she wanted and what the Akane in her wanted. So, he did not want to add to the confusion by revealing what he felt. But about four months later, on August 13, he broke his oath and left her a voicemail—The one Emika spoke about to her shrink.

Please don't let it be Brad's; he was so dumb. His IQ was lower than a room temperature—in Celsius. Wow! I sound like Vince. The child cannot be Vince's. He wants to move on. I hope it's Mark's. He's not the brightest, but I'll take it. Yes, it must be Mark's.

I wanted certainty.

The doctor confirmed, "It's between February 12 and 15."

Time stopped. I could hear every beat of my heart. My palms began to sweat as I recalled only one unprotected encounter between those days—February 14, at our home. No, Vincent's house. My hands shook.

What do I do now? Should I keep the child? I cannot discard the only symbol of what Vincent meant to me.

A week later, I wrote a text. "Hey, Vince! Just so you know, there is a little baby inside my belly. It is yours too." I didn't have the heart to send it.

It was not fair to Markus that I was with him while still in love with Vincent. "The baby is Vincent's," I told him when I went to his place to tell him the news.

He stared at me with his loving blue eyes and said, "So? When I said I am all in, I meant it."

I touched his shoulder. "I need to rethink our moving in together."

He kissed my hand. "Take all the time you need."

(Back to the present)

Markus wasn't even surprised when I revealed Vincent was the father. I wonder why.

"Mum, Mum," I hear Nozo whimpering. I leave everything and pick her up from the crib.

"What do you want?" I ask, looking into her sleepy eyes.

Yawning, she asks, "Can you sing?"

I kiss her forehead. "What song?"

Stretching her eyes wide, she says, "*Haru no Kaze.*"

Resting her head on my shoulder, I rock her and start humming Aoi Teshima's "Spring Breeze" as tears fall down my cheeks. Every time this song enters my mind, I think of Vincent's video.[10]

Putting Nozo to sleep, I pick up Vincent's chambray jacket. I bring my nose to it, then fold it and pack it in my luggage. This is a bit of Vincent I carry with me all the time. I should not have broken up with him. What was so wrong with my mind that I didn't have this simple clarity? A clarity I felt on August 14, 2024.

✺

(August 14–15, 2024)

I woke up feeling fresh; I heard the birds chirp and the leaves shake. That night, I'd had the strangest and longest dream of standing beneath the perfect cherry blossoms in the backyard of our home. Smiling, Vincent had said, "You're free. Now, live your life."

As I brushed my teeth, my eyes were glued to the mirror. The mole above my lip was gone. How? I kept touching the place where it had been. There wasn't even a mark. My phone rang, and it was a call from Nardin Robotics, seeing if I'd be interested in interviewing to lead their memory transfer division. My main job would be supervising the hardware and interface design of a two-way consciousness transfer invented by Vincent and my old colleagues.

My heart drummed with joy; I would see Vincent again. The salary was four times what I made in London, and they sent me a first-class ticket for the interview. Markus dropped me off at the airport. He knew I might not come back, but he acted happy for me—smiling despite his moist eyes. I felt sorry for him, but I wanted him to move on. So, I didn't look back.

On August 15, I had the perfect interview with Nardin Robotics. But my soul was dying to see Vincent. My heart fluttered as I Ubered to 100

---

[10] This is the scene that Vincent saw on August 13, 2024 through the spark in his hand. He left Emika a voicemail, then entered the core and extracted Akane from her. It's the same voicemail Emika listened to on December 15 in Chapter 17 of *The Winding* (Book 1).

Summit Drive, our home, at 7:30 p.m. I wanted to surprise him. Tears welled in my eyes, and a smile stretched my lips as I rang the doorbell. No one answered, so I walked around the property.

Where are you?

I waited for him. Suddenly, I remembered what Anna had texted me: that the damage I'd done was enough. I should not impose myself or this child on him. Maybe my absence was best for him. If I accepted this job, then I would keep running into him. I did not want to reopen the wounds I had inflicted. I should not get in the way of his moving on. It was the least I could do for him—the gift of my absence. I would free Vincent of me. I would never call him.

I wish you the best in every world.

I called Nardin Robotics. "Thank you so much, but I'll continue to work with Turing Labs. No, no, it's not the salary. It's more personal."

I looked at my wristwatch—the Cartier Vincent had gifted me. Why was it stuck at 7:30 p.m.? It didn't have a second hand, so I brought it to my ear to hear its ticking. It sounded different—like a whoosh. I started to wind it, and tears dripped onto my hands.

It's just winding a watch, but it felt so warm when you held my wrist and did it for me.

According to my cell phone, it was 7:45 p.m. I sat on the bench next to the fully bloomed bellflowers sparkling in the evening sky. I looked down at my belly and rubbed it.

"Hey, baby, this could have been your home. I picked it. I hope you can meet your wonderful father and Hulk one day. Hey, that's a nice name—Hope. That will be your name—Nozomi." I could not keep my shoulders from shaking and my lips from trembling. I knew that was the last time I would see that house. I knew I was leaving behind all the dreams I had forged.

My hands shook as I put the violin case by the front door.

I don't deserve this violin. This is your soul, proof of who you are underneath. I was wrong to think you were stuck in your childhood with Akane. You parted with it just to encourage me to play.

I swallowed hard.

And look how I repaid you. I wouldn't be able to earn your love back. Maybe one day, you could forgive me.

I opened the case one more time to touch Vincent's pocket square, bringing it to my nose.

I won't stain it with my tears anymore.

Putting the pocket square back, I shut the case.

I'll always love you.

I touched my belly.

A part of you will forever be with me.

I walked toward the front window and peeped into the home we'd built. Then, I kissed the door.

"Goodbye, Vincent. Goodbye, Hulk."

Goodbye, home. Goodbye, life.

I kept his chambray jacket and the photo of him, Hulk, and me.

You won't miss the jacket, and the photograph will only remind you of the pain I caused.

My Uber showed up, and I got in. "Airport, please."

The driver turned to look at me over his shoulder. "Are you okay, ma'am?"

Looking at the rearview mirror, I faked a smile. "Just allergies."

Wiping my tears, I turned back to see our home disappearing into the cascading evergreens. "See you later, Vince." And just like that, my watch reoriented itself to match the cell phone time—7:55 p.m.

What was that?

As I shut my eyes, a shimmering image of Vincent appeared before me, standing by the main door to his house—our home. He was holding Akane's violin, and a scarf was wrapped around his neck. Smiling, he said, "You're free from Akane. Now, live your life, free from me. Goodbye, Emi."

Beyond Vincent, I saw myself wrapped in the same scarf inside the house. I stretched my hand out to touch him, only to realize I was in my Uber and had departed from Summit Drive. I could feel myself splitting into three—one inside this car, leaving everything I held dear; another part of me wishing to stay a bit longer, to see my Vince and Hulk one last time; and the last one, the most prominent one, longing for a life where Vincent, Hulk, Nozo, and I would be together for the remaining days of my life.

(August 17, 2024—Gallery rooftop, London)

Holding Mark's large hands, I confessed, "Sorry. I know how you feel about me." Pressing his fingers, I stressed, "I want to feel the same. But Vince is still in my mind, in my heart."

Clenching his jaw, he asked, "Why did you come back, then?"

I stared blankly at the pigeons flying over Trafalgar Square. "It's complicated."

Markus scoffed. "I get it." Then, he pointed at my belly. "I guess Vincent didn't want anything to do with her?"

I was grasping for straws to defend my Vince. "No! Vince doesn't know about Nozo," I said. My voice quavered. "I did not even meet him."

He gulped his tea down. "Stop defending him," he ordered.

"More tea, sir?" inquired our waiter.

Markus shook his head. "No, we are done." He stared into my eyes and declared, "I will be with you no matter what." Then, he sneered, "Unlike your Vince."

(Back to the present)

Markus was kind, supportive, and everything I could hope for. He was with me through my doctor's visits, Nozo's birth, and beyond. I wanted to reciprocate Markus's feelings. But on November 15, when I looked into my Nozo's eyes, even that thought of Vincent made me feel like I was cheating on Markus.

Yet, Markus never understood. With time, he became impatient. He started making remarks like, "Just once, for old time's sake? What do you think Vince is doing right now—longing for you?"

I couldn't get over Markus's fatal flaw; he was not Vincent.

Now, my shoulders are shaking.

I'm so sorry, Vince. I wish I had seen your interview on What's Tonight? *on August 15, when you said your love was unrequited. I would have waited for you as you drove back from Seattle. I wish I had checked your voicemail the day you sent it and not waited till December 15. If I had, I wouldn't have come back to London. I should have called you at least once between August 15 and December 15.*

But his voicemail dated August 13. I felt free and fresh on August 14, and I went on the job interview on August 15. Are all these coincidences? What about the watch suddenly stopping and then resetting to the correct time? Should I ask him if I get the chance? How could I, with the media circus that will surround him? And beyond that are Ravi, Chris, and finally, Anna, his closest confidant. She has the right to hate me. I would hate myself if I were Anna. I take a deep breath and shut my eyes to stop my tears from falling.

I wish I could hold your hand one more time.

And why don't I get any news alerts relating to Vincent on my cell? He's synonymous with AI, so he should always appear based on my preferences.

CHAPTER 3

DOPPIO

"He's a limited-edition man."
—*Emika*

September 2026

Emika

HAVE SECURED NOZO TO THE seat next to me. People move by us in the lane as they board. An elderly woman stops by our row. Is she Nozo's neighbor? Her smile reaches her ears. Pointing at Nozo but looking at me, she asks, "Yours?"

Touching Nozo's chest, I bite my lips to hide the tremble. Then, I look up at the American lady. "Yes, all mine."

Widening her eyes, the lady touches her cheeks. "So precious."

My heart flutters. "Thank you so much."

Looking over her shoulder, the lady realizes she's blocking the traffic and moves on. The ones behind her soon discover why the lady stopped once they lay their eyes on Nozo. I'm biased, but there isn't a baby as cute as my Nozo on this planet. She is simply the most Kawaii. I kiss her forehead and her cheeks.

Stretching her arms, Nozo points at my cell phone. "Gimme *Sobo* and *Sofu*." She looks at my lowered eyebrows. Pouting, she adds, "*Kudasai*."

I run my hand across her head. "It's late in Japan. And we shouldn't make calls from a plane."

Crossing her arms, she sulks. Then, pointing at the empty seat next to her, she demands, "I want Ma-kus."

Gently holding her hands, I say, "Markus is in the back."

"*Naze?*" she asks, frowning.

I sigh. "He was naughty."

Scrunching her eyebrows and shaking her head, she declares, "Naughty is bad."

"High five to that," I say, lifting my hand. Nozo's tiny, chubby fingers touch my palm. I gently grab her soft hand and sniffle. It happens often because it's like touching a part of Vincent.

Raising her brows, Nozo asks, "Mum, Papha *mo* naughty *desu ka?*"[11]

My shoulders shake at her question, and I cover my mouth. Musing on Nozo's existence and the last night I had with her father, I react with one lifted shoulder and a smile. "Um . . . sometimes." Raising my finger, I wink. "But different naughty."

After the airplane reaches the designated altitude, Nozo turns to me. Widening her eyes, she orders, "Tell me Hulky story."

I kiss Nozo's head. "Okay, so there was this puppy, Hulky." Then, I rub my hands, pretending it's cold, and pout my lips. "He lived in a cage, all alone and cold."

Shaking her arms impatiently, she says, "Vincent, Vincent?"

I gently poke her cheek. "So, one day, a kind man, Vincent, stumbles upon Hulky and takes him home."

"Then, then?"

---

[11]   Is Papha also naughty?

I respond while wiping her nose and checking how tight her chair is secured to the seat. "Then, Hulky and Vincent become the best of friends. But Vincent was lonely sometimes, so a girl came into his life one day. They fall in love." I spread my arms. "Vincent, Hulky, and the girl move into a castle with fifteen cherry trees."

Nozo leans forward and then turns her head to look at me. "Like *Sobo* and *Sofu*'s house?"

The plane starts jerking as we enter an air pocket. I push Nozo back against her seat and respond, "Bigger and prettier. And then, one day, Vincent and the girl have a cute baby. Together, all four of them live happily. And during blossom season, the baby and Hulky run around the cherry trees. Vincent and the girl sit by a tree and laugh until the end of time."

Wiping my eyes, I check on Nozo. She is asleep, holding my left index finger with her tiny, chubby right hand. I sigh with relief; I don't want her to feel my voice shudder. I kiss her forehead and wipe the drool from her lips and chin.

I scrunch my nose as I open the airline food box. This is food? Only an airline can manage a simultaneous mixture of overcooked and undercooked rice. And this slimy thing is tuna?

Staring at the empty seat next to Nozo, I sigh. Mark didn't even try to come to occupy it. If he had apologized, then I would have upgraded his ticket. He could have distracted me from going back and forth in my thoughts. He might cool down when we land.

We are now flying over the Cascades. Those snowcapped peaks bring a lot of mixed memories of Vincent and me. We first gazed at them from my townhome, then from the restaurant, Chez-Giraud, and later, from the backyard of our home. If he still has the house, I would like to visit it, at least one last time. I'm sure he has thrown out everything that reminded him of me. Has he furnished the main bedroom?

Some of my memories of leaving the violin are mixed up and fragmented. It's as if there is an alternate version of the truth—almost like someone robbed my memories and actions that didn't exist in the first place.

(2011—Oxford)

I remembered playing Ravel's Sonata No. 2 for violin and piano. I was playing the violin, and Benji was on the piano. Halfway into the sonata, *Chichi*
raised his hand and said, "Stop." He rushed toward Benji. Pointing at Benji's
fingers and glaring into his eyes, *Chichi* derided, "You call yourself a pianist?" Then, he stared at me. "A drum-playing monkey toy sounds better."
He snapped at Benji. "Stop using my daughter for my music connections."

He then pulled me by my hand. "Stop dishonoring me by dating entitled opportunists." Every invited guest leaned back in shock. Some had their
hands over their mouth. Others stared at us with wide eyes and raised brows.

Despite his rudeness, Papha had seen through Benji's intentions. He
broke up with me soon after. Mum—well, she was silent. Her quivering
lips never uttered a word. Maybe she, too, saw through Benji. And who
would speak over maestro Hiroshi Amari—the winner of the Chopin
Competition at age eighteen? When he was a pianist, the conductors were
terrified. When he was the conductor, the first chair trembled.

(Back to the present)

That's how it happened. But sometimes, I think Benji left me because I
struggled to play Zigeunerweisen. Why would I believe that? I had mastered that piece by the time I was twelve. Or had I? I shut my eyes tight
and massage my temple. Which story did I tell Vince? And why is it that
something that didn't happen seems natural? After that incident with Benji,
I stopped playing violin altogether until Vincent gifted me Akane's violin
on my thirty-second birthday. I never played it for him.

In 2014, I saw Vincent at a conference in Tokyo and decided to pursue
the mathematics of AI. Was it the topic that piqued my interest, or was it
him? And then, when I met him in 2023, I fell madly in love. But then, why
did I keep shuttling between my townhome and our home? What stopped
me from moving in with Vince? It was almost like someone else was in my
mind. I have such fractured childhood memories that I can't piece them

together. I faintly remember practicing classical piano with Papha. I loved the piano and knew the piano notes by heart, yet I still struggled to reproduce the sound. Why did I give up piano and choose violin? Which reality is real? Which one does Vincent know? Who did this to me?

I press my temples again. The plane's intercom beeps.

"We will be landing shortly at Seattle Tacoma International Airport. Please ensure all your items are securely stowed in the overhead compartments or under your seat. Please turn off your cell phones and fasten your seat belts."

Nozo opens her eyes and starts to crumple her lips. Before the cries can follow, I insert a feeding bottle into her mouth.

"*Dōzo, Nozo-chan.*" She shuts her eyes, and I kiss her head. "Good girl."

We are here, Vince.

(Hyatt concierge desk)

"What are their credentials?"

Handing me the keycard, the concierge blinks and says, "They are PhD students in child psychology. Please be assured, Dr. Amari, that we will ensure your daughter is safe and calm. You will have the cell phone number of the babysitter. The service comes with a camera feed you can sync to your cell phone using our hotel app."

(Convention center)

After setting up the stall, I straightened my sleeves and put on my gray suit jacket.

What's the point of these stalls? No one ever comes, and the ones who do are morbidly stupid. Last year, one bloke asked if Alan Turing was the CEO of Turing Labs.

Across from our stall, I see a young woman struggling to set up a projector in the Quantum World stall. I turn to Markus. "Be right back."

He scoffs. "Sure. Don't forget to leave your resume with them."

Waving my hand at him dismissively, I walk to the stall. Leaning down, I see the girl blankly staring at cables. She is panic-stricken, and her forehead is peppered with sweat. Her hair is dyed brown, but the roots are blonde.

Tucking my hair behind my ears, I ask, "You need help?"

She is breathing hard as she adjusts her glasses and looks up at me. "Could you please? Dr. Calimaris will fire me." Her eyes are wide with fear.

That's awkward. Why does she assume I'd know who Dr. Calimaris is? I know that's Anna, but this girl has no way of knowing it. I take the cables from her hand and help her stand.

"What do you want these for?" I ask.

Coming closer to me, she explains, "Dr. Calimaris said I need to livestream Dr. Abajian's presentation"—she points to the wall across from the hall—"and project them on the two screens, each attached to a dedicated projector." Her breath reeks of cinnamon candy.

I tilt my head and squint. "And the problem is?"

She panics, crumpling her brows and biting her nails. "I forgot the HDMI splitters to connect this laptop to the projectors." She slaps her forehead. "Little shit, Frida."

I lift my shoulder. "That's it?" I turn toward our stall. "Hey, Markus, do we have HDMI splitters?"

After I connect the projectors, the girl remembers how to breathe. "I'm Frida Chaturvedi. I have been with Quantum World for six months."

I've traveled a bit, and there's no hint of Chaturvedi in you. Are you adopted?

I smile. "Pleased to meet you. I'm Emika Amari. So, why do you need to project the presentation?"

She shakes her head. "Registration numbers have exceeded the auditorium capacity. Dr. Calamaris said, this way, we can avoid a panic."

"Can I call you Frida? You can call me Emika."

She shrugs. "Sure, Emika."

I touch her shoulder reassuringly. "Dr. Calimaris wouldn't have fired you."

Her eyes grow wide in fear. "You don't know her. Unlike the other two—Dr. Bose and Dr. Washington—she is a demon."

Without thinking, I blurt, "What about Vince—I mean, Ahem! Dr. Abajian?"

Frida lifts her eyes. "Um . . . he mostly keeps to himself and a tight circle." Her eyes twinkle. "But he makes sure all the employees are happy."

"How?"

She spreads her hands in front of her. "Everything is paid for—lunch, dinner, on-staff doctors, medical bills that insurance won't pay, day care, pet care, dry cleaning." She pauses, catching her breath. "We have a grocery store, sushi bar, ramen stall on campus. We only work four days a week." Looking beyond me, she goes on, raising her voice. "At times, we volunteer for Dr. Abajian in his orphanage-cum-boarding school. Sometimes, he cooks, cleans, and teaches the kids." Smiling, she stresses, "The kids *adore* Dr. Abajian."

Was she staring at Markus to make a point? I am overthinking. Orphanage and boarding school? Of course, the media wouldn't concentrate on that. I need to find out more about it.

Tilting my head, I ask, "Does Hulk accompany him?"

Shaking her arms, she exclaims, "Oh my gosh, he is adorable." Then, she stops and squints through her glasses at me. "Wait, you know Hulk?" She looks up and snaps her fingers. "That name, Emika Amari . . . I have read it somewhere." Shutting her eyes tight, she mutters, "Where? Where?" She slaps her forehead. "Little shit, Frida, think."

I place my hands on her arms. "Relax. Your firm was founded on a two-way transfer of consciousness patent with three co-inventors. That patent cites two other patents co-invented by three original gangsters, plus one extra person. Look it up." Turning back, I walk back to my station.

In seconds, Frida catches up to me and touches my hand. "Forgive me, Dr. Amari. I just couldn't make the connection."

"It's okay. Don't beat yourself up."

She reaches for her bag. "Let me repay you. I have one extra pass for the exclusive invite-only post-showcase presentation dinner party that Quantum World is throwing." She clasps her hands. "Please."

This is my only way to circumvent the press and maybe talk with Vincent. Grabbing the pass with my thumb and index finger, I wink. "Sure!"

Frida looks at her cell phone. "They will be coming in any time. Want to have a peek?"

"Definitely." I turn to Markus. "C'mon, Markus."

(Entrance to the convention center)

The entrance is flooded with the press. Reporters say the same thing in their cameras in English, French, Spanish, German, Japanese, Mandarin, and Hindi.

"We are moments away from the showcasing of the Neurolink." Suddenly, everyone is in a rush to get to the door. "They are here." The squeaks, the patter, the knocks of the shoes, and the camera clicks all become one as a single car pulls in.

I poke my elbow into Markus's side while pointing at the car.

He smiles, jerking his head to flick his hair out of his eyes. "Bentley Mulsanne."

You look cute when you flick your hair like that. Did I ever tell you?

Subconsciously, I hold Markus's left arm with my right hand. Smiling, he grips it softly.

A hotel staff member opens the door. A tanned leg comes out of the Bentley, and the hotel staff member helps arrange her dress as she emerges. That's Tabi in the red dress. Is she with Vincent now? From the other side of the car emerges a tall man with a full afro—Chris—clad in a white tuxedo jacket and black trousers. The two hold hands and enter the hotel reception area. So, Tabi is with Chris? And I had blamed Vincent for seeing her behind my back.

Five camera crews circle around Chris and Tabi. One pushes past the others and intercepts the couple in their tracks.

"We have Dr. Chris Washington, CFO, and Ms. Tabitha Bishara, Director of Media at Quantum World. Dr. Washington, what can you tell us about Neurolink?"

Tabi pulls Chris toward her and whispers as he nods and smiles. Then, he looks at the reporter. "Well, why don't we wait for thirty more minutes? All I can say is"—he contracts his fingers and makes an explosive fist bump—"Vincent will blow your mind."

The two turn toward the door as another Bentley pulls in. The staff member once again runs toward the car. A couple emerges first. Maddy looks beautiful in a green dress as she holds Ravi's hand. Ravi is wearing a black tux, and, like Vincent, he has a full beard now. Like a younger sibling idolizing his older one, Ravi always imitated Vincent. Opening the other door of the Bentley is a long-haired blonde limping while trying to hold the skirt of her dress. Anna. Shaking his head, Ravi holds Anna's clutch while she straightens her dress. Ravi is such a gentleman. He loved me like a little sister.

A reporter weaves through the crowd and intercepts the trio. "We have COO, Dr. Anastasia Calimaris, and Chief Research Officer, Dr. Ravi Bose. Expectations are high, as you've become the most valued company before an IPO. Are you nervous?" She puts the mic in the middle of Ravi and Anna.

Ravi leans forward. "We would be if we didn't trust our research."

Anna moves closer and snatches the mic. "Hey, you wanna know about Neurolink? Just wait." Then, she faces the camera. "And Vince, get your ass in here." Scrunching her face, she hands the mic over to the reporter.

Raising his brows, Markus remarks, "She is a delight."

I smile. "No one loves Vincent the way she does." She hasn't changed a bit. Is Vincent the same?

My old colleagues, plus Maddy and Tabi, all pose for photographs. Most photographers still look outside the door, waiting for the man of the hour to arrive. I can't blame them.

An engine's explosive popping and blistering gets louder and dies as a red sports car stops at the main entrance. I look up at Markus. He looks down, straight into my eyes, and smiles.

"Pagani Huayra." Squinting at the car, he remarks, "It's a limited-edition car."

I let go of Mark's hand. "He's a limited-edition man."

Lifting his empty hand, Markus smirks.

Vincent's car door opens like a batwing. The first thing I see is his left leg, then his left arm. I can feel every beat of my heart as Vincent leaves his car and countless camera crews surround him. One can't ignore the light that exudes from Vincent. The lights in the hall decided to shine on him, or he somehow became celestial. Even his blue tuxedo seems to glow. A cameraman is instructing him on something. Waving his hand in dismissal, he walks toward his team.

Markus taps on my shoulder. "What was that about?"

"He doesn't like to pose." I roll my eyes. "What a joy it was to take selfies with him." What wouldn't I give to get a minute of that frustration back? But there may be no room for Nozo and me in his new world. Is the old Vince—the sensitive, synesthetic, vulnerable one—hidden somewhere?

As he walks in, Anna hugs him for a long time, and they whisper to each other. He then shakes Ravi's hand, followed by Chris's, before hugging Maddy and kissing Tabi's forehead. I wish I had that kind of a team at Turing. Then, he surveys the room. His eyes stop. Is he looking at me?

Markus brings his lips close to my ear. "Is he looking at you?"

Shaking his head, Vincent surrenders himself to the reporters. One reporter holds a mic out to him. "What can you tell us about Neurolink?"

He tilts his head and smiles. "You'll just have to wait half an hour. Else I will have to say the same thing twice. I hate that."

Another reporter interjects, "Will you delay your launch because of Vandal? Do you have any message for him?"

When Vincent walks toward the reporter, Tabi blocks him and whispers something. He gently nudges her aside, takes the mic from the reporter, and looks around. "I won't delay anything. And I have one message for Vandal: why don't you drop your mask and face me?"

One journalist shouts from the back of the crowd, "Is there a Mrs. Abajian on the horizon?"

Vincent shuts his eyes, breathes in, and smiles. "It's not a mathematical improbability." Then, he turns in the direction of the journalist. "But more importantly, it's none of your fucking business."

Mark scoffs. "Great influence for Nozo, right?"

I wave my hand, dismissing his remark. Vincent and his team get escorted backstage, Tabi ruffling his hair and Anna holding his hand. We head toward the auditorium.

Everyone is pushing each other while shoving themselves into the arena, while the ushers constantly remind, "Please form a single file line."

Microsoft, Oracle, Apple, Google, Amazon, and Tesla have over thirty delegates. Then, the press—NY Times, The Tribune, The Washinton Post. Research heads from MIT, Caltech, Stanford, and Carnegie Mellon. Now, it's our turn. Markus and I look back. There are people as far as my eyes can see. They are all waiting to see Vince.

(Arena)

"I'm sure we will find two empty seats next to each other," Markus assures me as I move for the first empty seat I see. He points at a couple of seats in the next row. "There."

We sit. Markus nudges my hand. "You like the seats? The view?"

Bringing my finger to my lips, I say, "Shhh. Let me enjoy this."

Markus scowls at my rudeness.

The room darkens, and a woman's voice informs us in five languages—English, Spanish, Mandarin, Japanese, and Hindi—"Please silence your cell phones and enter a new world."

Projections of constellations appear all over the ceiling and walls. Two sets of lights project on the opposite end of the stage. One shines on a pianist dressed like Chopin playing Nocturne, Op. 9, No. 2, and the other is dressed as Van Gogh's painting *The Starry Night*. As the Chopin look-alike hits the last note, another light targets the center of the stage. Slowly, Vincent emerges from under the stage—first his head, then his entire body—and walks up front, passing a barstool with a water bottle. Every other audience member takes out their cell phone and records the event.

Vincent bows before the pianist and the artist, and they bow back. He then adjusts his mouthpiece and points his arms to all of us.

"Have you ever wished you could play or paint like that?" he asks.

"Yes!" everyone shouts, making the walls boom.

Vincent tilts his head. "But you feel discouraged when you realize how difficult it is to master the fundamentals." He then snaps his fingers and widens his eyes. "It doesn't have to be like that."

Another light shines on a socialite-cum-model, dressed in an elegant white dress, who walks toward Vincent, holding the signature, yet-to-be-released memory transfer helmet Nardin Robotics is making for Quantum World. I was the one to oversee the design and production of those helmets. Stupid, stupid me. Vincent takes the red helmet from the model and kisses her on the cheek. What are they whispering to each other? He points at the shiny red helmet and looks at us as she leaves.

The screen focuses on his piercing, green-blue eyes as he says, "This is our signature memory transfer helmet." Holding the helmet with his left hand, Vincent spreads his right arm and asks, "What do you call this?"

The walls again boom as everyone screams, "The Mind!"

Vincent nods while holding The Mind parallel to the ground. "You're a beautiful crowd." He then takes another step forward. "When you buy this, you can choose an array of talents and skills as an upgrade. You don't have to send it back to us. It will all be done remotely using what we call the Neurolink. Does that answer your questions?"

I cover my ears as a section of the crowd chants, "Neurolink," while others either whistle or applaud. After putting the helmet on the floor, Vincent throws his hands in the air and pushes them down as the crowd quiets down. Wow!

"Did you see that, Markus?" I ask, uncovering my ears and turning to my left, but Markus is gone.

What the hell? Why make me sit next to you if you had to leave?

Vincent continues, "I'm not telling you that you will wake up and magically play the piano like Lang Lang or paint like Dali. But the fundamentals can be codified into your brains." He pauses, walks to the barstool, and takes a sip from the water bottle.

Then, he gives the crowd another smile. "Ladies and gentlemen, we at Quantum World are building a more humane AI, where humans and robots complement rather than compete. Imagine the billions you can save on training new employees." He holds up a hand. "There are some risks involved." His voice gets somber as he continues, "Someone can hack into the system and upload programs like mind control for our customers. Firms, nations, and governments can use this to create compliance, thereby taking away our free will."

The camera zooms in on his face. "That's why we are working on an encryption system that utilizes your biometrics to confirm any uploads. And unless we are ready with that, we won't release this product. Because we cannot build a better world without you."

He squats and spreads his arms, encompassing all of us. Then, he stands again. "Are you with me?"

The whole auditorium blasts, "Yes!"

Vincent places his hands at the back of his ears. "I can't hear you! Are you with me?"

The gallery walls shake as they all yell, "Yes!"

He bows. "Thank you so much, ladies and gentlemen. You're awesome. Those registered for the event will get a sign-up sheet for our newsletter. You can even place your order and receive a developer discount."

Someone from the crowd shouts, "How much do we pay now?"

Vincent adjusts his mic. "You pay nothing till we ship, sir. We are not Tesla."

(Exclusive dinner)

Am I really going to meet Vince? My heart drums, and my palms sweat as Frida, standing next to the enormous TV, points me to a table.

"That's the table for the founders. Have a nice time with your old friends." Then, she takes my hand. "Thank you again, and it was great to meet you."

I hug her. "The pleasure was all mine." Then, I notice she is carrying a ball—soccer, volleyball, basketball, or a globe—inside a Jute bag, with the opening partially tied. Pointing at it, I ask, "What's that?"

Waving her hand in dismissal, she smiles. "It's nothing. Enjoy the dinner." She then turns and leaves the room in a rush while looking everywhere. Wasn't she supposed to have dinner, too? Strange girl. Her breath of cinnamon candy overpowers everything. The TV is showcasing commercials on Neurolink and Quantum World in a loop.

As I walk about fifty feet from the TV toward the center table, I see people posing with Vincent to take selfies. His eyes look heavy, but he keeps smiling nonetheless. Maddy is the only one sitting. The rest are all busy talking to journalists and attendees.

Ravi takes a deep breath, wipes his forehead, mutters, "Phew," and sits next to Maddy. On my left, I see Chris heading for the table. Stretching my arm out, I tap his shoulder.

As soon as he turns back, his eyes go wide. "Oh. My. God." Then, he wraps his massive arms around me, and my arms are too squished to hug him back. Rocking me sideways, he says, "It's good to see you." Then, he releases me and touches my shoulders, asking, "How have you been?" He points at the dinner table. "Please join us." As a waiter passes by, Chris says to him, "We need an extra chair. And a serving of sea bass."

Bringing my hand to my lips in surprise, I ask, "You remember?"

He touches his heart. "Of course. Our fish- and egg-eating vegetarian sister." Then, he hugs me again.

Why on earth did I leave this team? As we walk toward the table, I see Anna glaring at the selfie-hungry socialites. "How about we do this after dinner?" She pulls the chair from Vincent's right, then turns to Tabi, seated to the left of Vincent. "How the fuck can you tolerate these shameless social media people?" she asks.

Tabi sighs. "I don't." Then, she puffs an inhaler in her mouth three times.

Pointing at me, Chris reveals, "Guys, look who I found."

Ravi springs out of his chair and hugs me. "So good to see you." His eyes get moist as he places his hands on my arms, and his voice quavers as he asks, "How have you been?" He then kisses my forehead.

Before I can respond, Maddy stands up. "You may not remember me, but we met at Vincent's house."

"I remember, Maddy." I recall every single detail from that night. Every blunder I made.

Tabi stretches her arm across the table. "We met only once."

I shake her hand. "We did."

Everyone goes silent as Anna turns to me. She clicks her tongue, flares her nostrils, and glares. "Nice to see you."

"Likewise, Anna."

Vincent takes his seat and looks at me. My heart pounds, and my palms sweat as I dread he'll ask me to leave the table.

No, you are not like that. You won't make a scene.

I am about to lift my hand and wave my fingers, but he speaks up.

Squinting, pointing at me, he asks, "Who do we have here?"

My heart stops. *Seriously? Don't you remember me? Is this place not well-lit? Are you being sarcastic?*

Anna grabs Vincent's right arm quickly. "That's Emika. She was a post-doc researcher at the uni. She was also on two patents we cited."

Everyone is staring at Vincent to see how he reacts. Smiling, he looks at me. "Ah! Forgive me. You must be brilliant. Why didn't you work for us? We can exceed any salary and stock options." Pointing at Anna, he smirks. "Did she scare you?"

Anna rolls her eyes. "Idiot." Then, Vincent leans closer to her, and they start whispering back and forth.

I keep staring at Vincent. *Do you not know who I am? I would take your hatred over this indifference. This can't be amnesia. You remember everyone else.*

The server brings us food, and everyone except Vincent digs in. He picks up the steak and shows it to Anna. "They call this Wagyu?"

Anna rubs his shoulder and chides, "Don't be obnoxious. You had a long day."

Vincent drapes his arm on the back of Anna's chair. "Okay, Mom."

He takes out his cell phone, squints at the screen, and then smiles. He types something and shows it to Anna. She takes his cell phone, possibly to change something he typed. Vincent rolls his eyes as Tabi leans over for a peek. She covers her mouth with her hand and giggles.

Can't you even glance at me? Hello, it's me, Emika—the one you couldn't keep your hands off. Ring a bell? What's so fascinating about the cell phone that you can't stop smiling? I was your world. Why are you so indifferent? Is it because you are a billionaire now?

I look around at my colleagues. I'm just a stranger sharing a table with them—a shameless beggar waiting to be thrown out. But I can't be rude to Chris since he did invite me to the table. I pick up my fork and begin to dig in, subtly taking the napkin from my lap and wiping my eyes. This was a colossal mistake.

I feel a warm touch on my left hand. My breathing gets ragged as Ravi assures me, "It's complicated, and it's not what you think."

Then what is it? I turn to Vincent, and suddenly, his cuff glows with a tinge of green-blue light. Lifting his cuff, he shakes his head and clicks his tongue in disgust. He turns to Anna.

"Be right back."

"What? You need food."

Ignoring her, he leaves the table.

The TV program switches to CNN.

"Breaking news. We have live footage of a FedEx freight plane heading straight toward the Seattle Needle. The Air Force has already been deployed.'"

The eyes of every single dinner attendee are now fixed on the TV. Many take out their cell phones, desperately trying to reach their families. Chris, Ravi, Tabi, Maddy, and Anna leave the table to get closer to the TV. My heart pounds only one word in my head—Nozo.

I reach for my cell phone with shaking hands and call the babysitter. "Can you take her to safety, please?"

"We are already in the lobby, ma'am. She is fast asleep. Don't worry."

"I'll be right there."

I don't care about this dinner anymore. As I am about to leave the room, everyone's eyes are fixed on the TV, and they start buzzing with shock.

"What?"

"Wow! How did that happen?"

I look at the screen and see the entire plane engulfed by a ginormous light funnel that looks a lot like the simulated models of time turbulence.

Then, the screen switches back to the studio camera. The presenter touches his earpiece. "We have not seen anything like this before. We are getting reports that the freight plane is back in the hangar. What just happened? Stay tuned as we have Professor of Quantum Mechanics—"

The TV blacks out, and the entire dining hall also goes black. The whole crowd goes silent for a second, then the panic begins.

"What the fuck?"

"Are we under attack?"

"Anyone has a lighter?"

The room lights up with flashlights from some cell phones while people shout.

"I don't have enough charge on my phone."

"I can't call my wife."

"There is no bar on my cell phone."

I hear cars outside the convention center honking. What's happening? I keep calling the babysitter, hoping to connect, even without bars.

Why did I come here? How is my Nozo? God, I need nothing else, just her.

And then, just like that, the lights come back on.

The TV comes back on, resuming with fitting commercials: "With Nardin ceramic-oxide-electrolytes, you will never lose power."

Perfect product placement timing. I sit down, exhaling in relief. I'd thought I'd lose everything; my Nozo is everything. The others sit as well, and dinner service resumes. A waitress pours us more champagne.

Anna turns to Ravi and Chris. "Vince leaves, and this happens."

Chris rolls his eyes at Anna. "Your point?"

"I think he made the plane disappear," Anna says, snapping her fingers.

Chris almost chokes on his champagne. "That's a stretch." He kisses Tabi's hand. "You think Anna is way off?"

She lifts her shoulder. "I'm not taking any sides. Vince warned me."

Anna looks at me, curls her lips, and turns to Tabi. "Do you think Ravi, Chris, and I are sycophants to Vincent?"[12]

"What?" Tabi squints.

Ravi touches my wrist and whispers, "Sorry." He then points at Anna and snaps his long, thin fingers, flaring his nostrils. "Cheap shot."

Chris stares straight at Anna and agrees. "Absolutely."

Even knowing I referred to them as sycophants in a fight with Vincent, are these two defending me? So, Vincent spilled the beans? Why wouldn't he? I cheated.

Frowning, Anna throws her napkin at Ravi. She then lifts her middle finger. "Fuck you both."

Ravi imitates her gesture. "Fuck you."

"Stop it." Maddy grabs Ravi's middle finger and glares at him. "Act your age."

"She started it," Ravi says, pointing at Anna.

Shaking her head, her eyes wide, Maddy says, "Unfuckingbelieveable. Are you five?"

Tabi's shoulders are shaking with laughter.

"You three, apologize to each other," Maddy orders, snapping her fingers.

"I'm sorry," they all sing in chorus.

---

[12] In Chapter 13 of *The Winding* (Book 1), Vince and Emika had a huge fight following a concert night. Emika called Vincent an "apathetic, rich, spoiled brat." Then, she said Anna, Chris, and Ravi were nothing more than his sycophants.

Maddy turns to Anna. "And?"

Anna looks at me and pouts. "Sorry."

I force a smile. "I'm sorry, too." This camaraderie, no matter how verbally violent, has an inexplicable warmth. At times, Vincent and I would simply watch them fight. And, at the last moment, Vincent would say, "That's enough."

I let it all go. I'm a stranger to this world today, and I shouldn't infringe on their perfect, Emika-free reality. I stand up while they are engrossed in their conversation.

"Thank you for dinner." I bow. "I wish you all the best."

They all smile. Chris waves his hand. "See you later."

Touching my hand, Ravi says, "Stay in touch."

How? Through professionally managed social media accounts? And that guy who just left . . . he is not the Vincent I knew. I turn toward the door, wiping my eyes with my jacket sleeve. Someone grabs my left arm. I turn around. Anna? She is looking at me through wet eyes.

Her voice quavers. "That's it? You leave without even a hug? A goodbye? Like last time?" She touches my face and kisses my cheek. "Let me at least look at you." Then, she pulls me in and hugs me. "Why did you leave us? We loved you so much."

My tears fall on her bare shoulders. "I don't know. But you all changed numbers. Why did Vincent leave the dinner? How could he ignore me?"

She pulls back but keeps holding my shoulders. "Tabi made us do all that 'change your number and professional account' shit." She points at the door and says, "Vincent often leaves to blow off steam." She pauses. "There is a café across the street. Tomorrow, eleven o'clock? We owe you an explanation."

"I'll be there."

(Hyatt)

As I cross the road, all I can think of is Nozo. I can't hear the cars, buses, or emergency vehicles. I take the elevator and open my door.

"Are you okay, ma'am?" asks the babysitter.

I tilt my head and fake a smile. "Never better."

Markus was right; billionaires don't care about us. I was wrong to think Vincent was any different. I dig my face in my Nozo's chest. It's okay if she wakes up.

We don't belong here, Nozo-chan. *You and I are perfectly fine in our modest world.*

Nozo grabs my hair with her tiny hands. "You crying? *Naze?*"

I kiss her head. "I love you." I kiss her tiny nose. "I love you." I kiss both her cheeks. "I love you." I kiss her chin. "I love you." I kiss her tummy. "I love you."

I tickle her, and she laughs. I look into her eyes. Shutting my own, I let my tears trickle down.

You may have your dad's eyes, but you're mine. All mine. It's just you and me, and that's perfect. I was wrong, thinking there could be more.

(The following day—Across the road from the café)

Anna

Chris is about to press the walk button on the stop light post. I stop his hand. "Wait."

He turns to me. "What?"

"She is already waiting." I point at the café across the street. "Should we simply let her waltz into Vincent's life again?"

Ravi pulls my shoulder and moves me away from the other pedestrians. "Waltz? I thought we were just talking. How can she waltz, given Vincent's current station?"

The three of us move toward the corner of a newspaper stand. I lift my finger. "She doesn't know the situation. What if she rocks the boat?"

Shrugging, Ravi asks, "What do you mean?"

Chris touches Ravi's shoulder. "In fifteen months, Vincent scared away three investors, and all we had was Richard Nicklas and Pat Kovac."

"It's different now. We have ten billion from Japan." Ravi pauses, catches his breath, and raises his eyebrows. Maybe now the idealist realizes what I was hinting at. Shaking his head in disgust, he asks, "Is that what you guys think of her? That she will withdraw funding because Vincent had a relationship?"

Squeezing Ravi's arm, Chris growls, "Emika isn't a mere relationship."

Ponting at the café where Emika is sitting, Ravi looks at Chris and me. "She could have moved on. We don't know what she has been through." He touches his chest. "She is our Emika, remember?"

Clenching his jaw, Chris argues, "Moved on? Did you see her face last night?"

Ravi scoffs at Chris. "Tabi will be so delighted to see this avatar of yours."

Chris lifts his finger at Ravi. "Hey, leave her out of this." The veins on his forehead bulge.

I take a deep breath. "Are we done, gentlemen? Now, let's walk into the café and shoo our little sister away in the most dignified manner. Remember, she chose to leave us in the first place."

(Café)

Emika

This is my second doppio, yet I'm still drowsy. I stayed up all night, staring at my Nozo. She is now with Markus, sightseeing. At least someone should have some fun during this sham of a visit.

"I thought you prefer tea?" Ravi pulls out a chair and sits opposite me. Anna takes the seat on his right, and Chris takes the one on his left.

Chris takes my shaky hands in his. "We didn't get a chance to talk last night."

Ravi narrows his eyes at Chris and slowly shakes his head in disbelief. *What's going on?*

I smile, shrug, and swallow back my tears. "Couldn't he at least look at me?" I ask, looking at Anna.

Chris hands me a napkin. At the same time, Anna grabs my left hand. Taking a breath, she reveals, "He doesn't know who you are."

Through my tears and constricted throat, all I can manage in a shrill, trembling voice is, "What?"

Anna squeezes my hand. "I got a call from Philip Nardin on Vince's birthday in 2024. The three of us rushed to Vince's house." She looks into my eyes and nods. "Yeah, the same one. He still lives there. We found that he was attended by one Dr. Andy Lee. Tabi, Edward, and Philip Nardin were also there." Anna grabs a napkin and wipes her eyes.

While Anna is struggling for words, Ravi leans forward. "Vince was unconscious, and when he finally woke up, his mind was foggy—especially about you, the house, everything between you. And we don't know why. We don't even know why he was unconscious. Philip won't tell us."

This story makes no sense. I press my lips together and nod. "And you never thought of bringing me up to him?"

Chris takes my other hand in both of his. "We debated. But we thought you moved on. And Vince needed to put all his effort into our business. We let bygones be bygones."

So, that's it? Their explanations are so rehearsed. They thought I wouldn't notice it. But why? How am I a risk to Vince? What are they protecting?

Get back to your life, Emika. Stop dreaming and face reality.

The door to the café opens, and Markus comes through, pushing Nozo's stroller. He places the stroller, carrying my life, next to me.

Jerking his head, he says, "She won't go sightseeing. She just wants her mum." All the gloom suddenly disappears as I see my Nozo.

I point at Mark's bandaged nose. "I don't believe there was a stampede in a two-minute blackout. Let's take you to a doctor."

He shrugs. "I'm fine." Then, he points to the door. "Hey, can I go sightseeing alone?"

I shrug. "Go ahead." Pointing at his nose, I assert, "But doctor first."

After kissing Nozo's hair, Markus leaves.

Ravi, Anna, and Chris lean toward the stroller. Smiling, Chris admits, "She's a doll."

As I pick my Nozo up, Anna stretches out her arms. "Can I?" I hand her over. Holding her, Anna glances at me. "When did this happen?"

"November 15, 2024."

Anna clicks her tongue and wiggles her eyebrows at Ravi and Chris. She probably thinks I'm a slut who slept around as soon as I landed in London.

Ravi's eyes get moist. Smiling, he asks, "What's her name?"

"Nozo, short for Nozomi."

Anna tilts her head at Nozo and looks at her. "Hello, Nozo. I'm Anna, your mom's . . ." She trails off as she stares into Nozo's eyes, then turns to Ravi and Chris. "Look at those eyes." Anna's eyes widen, and she bites her lip as she turns to me. Her voice quavers. "Is she—?"

I nod. "Yes." Blinking back my tears, I clarify, "I need nothing from him." I touch Nozo's soft shoulder and stress, "She is all mine."

Anna looks at Nozo again. Closing her eyes, Anna kisses her forehead. "You're so precious. We are your mom's friends from America."

Nozo tilts her head and says, "A-m-e-r-i-ka?" Widening her large eyes, she asks, "You know Papha?"

I knock on the table. "Nozo, no."

"It's okay," Anna says to me. As she looks at Nozo, her lips begin to tremble. "Do I know your papha?" Tears well in her eyes as she turns to Chris and Ravi. "Guys, she is asking if I know her papha?" She sniffles. "I'll be back," she says, placing Nozo in my arms. She leaves the café.

Pushing his hands against the table, Ravi stands up. Turning to me, he says, "Excuse me. Let me check on Anna."

(Outside the café)

Anna

I can't stop pacing. Fuck. Fuck. Fuck. This can't be happening. I must do what's best for the company. But I owe everything to Vincent. What if, one day, he remembers everything and finds out about his daughter? What would I say? That I didn't know? I can't lie to those trusting eyes.

That little one has exactly the same eyes. And the way she asked if I knew her father . . . Only two or three people know her father better than I do. What am I doing? Emika did nothing wrong. What the fuck was I thinking, shooing her like she was a critter? She was once the life of our lab. She brought a smile back to Vincent's lips. Whatever she did, she must have her reasons. She is the girl Vincent once loved. Maybe he still does but doesn't realize it. This is not my decision to make. It's theirs. But I won't reveal everything to Emika.

I snap my fingers.

Yes, Emika, we will hear you. But you will feel what Vincent felt on January 7, 2024.

I clench my jaw and form a fist. Turning, I bump into someone. "Ravi?"

Placing his hands on my shoulders, his eyes wide, he asks, "What do we do now?"

I poke my finger into his chest. "I'm gonna make some decisions. You and Chris will back me up. Let's go in."

❋

(Café)

<u>Emika</u>

Chris stretches his arms out. "Can I hold her?"

His enormous palms engulf Nozo's torso. Nuzzling his nose against hers, Chris asks, "Who is the cutest?"

Nozo tilts her head. "Who?"

"Nozo." Chris touches her little nose. "And who is Mum's favorite?"

Nozo tilts her head in the other direction. "Nozo?"

Chris kisses her forehead, and Nozo grabs his afro. "Who is Uncle Chris's favorite?"

Pulling Chris's afro, Nozo says, "Nozo?"

Then, Chris turns to me. Looking into my eyes and pressing his lips, he says, "I'm so sorry."

"Huh?" I ask.

Anna and Ravi storm in. After they take their seats, Ravi starts to play peekaboo with Nozo. "What's your itinerary?" asks Anna.

I collect Nozo from Chris and place her in the stroller. "I'll fly back tomorrow." My lips tremble as I touch Anna's hand and assure her, "I'll never bother you guys again. Promise." I sniffle, then fake a smile.

Anna touches my shoulder. "Just shut up and cancel your flight."

"I have to report to work."

"What work?" She tilts her head and smiles. "I thought you were Associate Head of R&D, assisting Ravi in burning through our cash reserves." Snapping her fingers at Ravi, she asks, "You have a problem with that?"

Looking at me, Ravi admits, "I'd love to have her back."

"Me, too," adds Chris.

I push my hair behind my ears. "What if Vince says no?" I ask.

Anna lowers her eyebrows and leans her head toward mine. "I'd like to see him try," she says, imitating Vincent. She then moves her index finger like a chopper propeller. "Pack up. We are gonna go see Philip Nardin. I'm sure he knows more than he's revealed."

Why this sudden change? Is it because of Nozo? Must be. And why am I not resisting? What do I do with my stuff in London? Don't I need to give notice to Turing?

Anna touches my shoulder. "Don't worry. We will take care of the logistics. We will buy you out if necessary."

Then, she wipes my tears with her thumbs. "Vincent hasn't entirely forgotten you. You still appear in his dreams, but he doesn't know it's Emika or who Emika is yet."

I admit, "Mr. Nardin once offered me a job. I was in town on August 15, 2024."

"And you didn't tell us?" Ravi frowns.

Clasping my hands together, I implore, "I'm sorry. It's a long story."

CHAPTER 4

MEMORIES—EPISODE 1

"After the extraction, the core had to readjust the past to justify Vincent's action."
—Philip

September 2026—Philip's house

Philip

THE WOODY NOTES FROM THE Mizunara cask, where the Yamazaki 55 was aged, transform into a smoky bouquet, tantalize my tongue, and travel through my esophagus.

Shutting my eyes, breathing deeply in satisfaction, I conclude, "Freeing Emika from Akane was the single most selfless act of love a time corrector has ever done."

If my calculations are correct, Vince, you will surpass that act . . . very soon.

I look around the room. Anna, Ravi, and Chris have their jaws wide open, and the whites of their eyes are visible around their irises. Emika's eyes are all red; her tears, while encased, are ready to erupt as soon as she blinks. Her lips are trembling, despite her attempt to press them together tightly.

Wiping her eyes with a tissue, she asks, "So, my feeling of clarity on August 14 was his doing?"

"Yes. He freed you at the risk of you forgetting him."

Pointing at Emika, Anna asks, "Then why does she still feel for Vincent?"

Leaning back, I exhale. "Yes, Akane inside Emika initiated contact with Vincent." Turning to Emika, I raise my brows. "But the feelings spilled from Akane to Emika." Staring into the amber hue of my whiskey, I divulge, "And then, those feelings became Emika's alone." Swirling the golden liquid, I say, "Vincent expected Emika's clarity would make her forget him." Then, I look at Emika and smile. "But the effect was just the opposite, correct? Your feelings for Vince deepened?"

"Yes," she croaks.

Moving my eyes from Emika to everyone else, I ask, "More tea? Whiskey?"

As I stand up to pour tea for Emika and Ravi, Emika takes the pot from me, insisting, "Let me, Mr. Nardin."

"Thanks." Touching her hand, I say, "It's Philip."

"Okay."

Edward fills Anna's and Chris's whiskey glasses, puts the bottle on the table next to me, and then sits back with Nozo and Tabi twelve yards away. Every time Nozo achieves a feat with the Legos, Tabi and Edward clap and cheer. And Nozo will walk toward them on her tiny feet and hug them. Occasionally, she will also kiss both of them. Such a sweet girl. Emika did a fantastic job with little or no help while battling memories from someone else's childhood and fractured reality.

I am sorry, Emika, for what happened to you.

Ravi touches Emika's hand. "It's the same for Vincent." After sipping the tea in his cup, he reveals, "I think it was a couple of days after the Senate hearing . . ." He looks at Chris and Anna for verification. When Anna nods, Ravi continues, "When Vincent said that he initially looked for Akane in you but that he ultimately fell in love with just you."

Emika tucks her hair behind her ears. "But he was so terse in his text," she says, raising her brows.

Chris leans toward Emika. "He did not want to add to your conflicts." Unconvinced, Emika looks at me. "And then, he leaves a loving voicemail after four months?"

Sighing, I stare at Emika. "Even the most intelligent beings are driven by emotions." Taking a deep breath, I say, "He was conflicted . . . he wanted to free you, but also couldn't imagine a life without you." I stress, "That's why I asked my robotics division to hire you." Looking down, I swirl my glass of Suntory's finest, admitting, "If anyone deserved a chance with Akane-free Emika, it'd be Vince." I scoff. "But you rejected the offer and went back to London." I move my eyes back to Emika's. "I saw you leave. Then, I saw Vincent return from that talk show. I saw it on his face—the expression of failed love and imminent solitude. Yet, there wasn't a tear in his eye. He smiled and entered his empty house . . ." I swallow hard. "His empty life."

Emika's eyes can't hold the tears flowing down her cheeks. I walk over to her, hand her a box of tissues, and touch her shaking shoulder.

Yes, maybe you deserve a chance with Vincent.

Her voice is muffled through a pile of tissues as she speaks, "I have disjointed memories of staying with him here. Even though I went back to London."

Anna waves her hand. "Must be a dream." Then, she looks at me as I take my seat. "So, how did Vincent lose his memories?"

"Ah." I point at Emika while looking at Anna. "Those are not just dreams; they are linked with Vincent's memory loss." I turn to Emika. "On August 15, when you decided to leave for London, did a part of you choose to stay back and be with Vincent?"

She looks down and inhales deeply. "I did," she says, sniffling. "I still do."

"When Vincent created the turbulence for the extraction, he accidentally enveloped his property under intreton, divorcing it from a singular reality." Bringing my hands close together, I explain, "It was an intersection of realities, where all the things you thought you should have told Vincent actually happened." Staring at Emika, I sigh. "I was outside Vince's property when I saw you leave, so I couldn't sense the intreton. Not until two weeks later, on Vincent's forty-first birthday."

Little Nozo yells, "Mum, *mite.*"[13] She points at her Lego accomplishment while looking at Emika with those large, inquisitive, Turkish-blue eyes.

With our eyes wide with astonishment, we all stare at little Nozo. A girl, barely two, almost finished constructing Big Ben and Parliament.

Emika says to her, "Finish it, and I'll be there." Then, she looks at us and smiles. "Brilliant, like her dad."

Ravi touches Emika's hand. "The mom is equally guilty."

Emika gives him a weak smile.

Waving her hands impatiently, Anna asks, "So, Vincent turns forty-one . . . and? Could we continue, please?"

I give Anna a stern look. "I am getting there." Scanning their faces, I continue, "Vince came to race me. After the race, I asked about his life, and he said something utterly strange. He said that he was living the perfect life with Emika."

Tilting her head, Anna scrunches her face. "The fuck?"

I point my finger at Emika. "I knew you were in London. Suspecting something was wrong, I fetched Edward, Tabi, and Dr. Lee and followed Vincent to his house." I tap on my A. Lange & Söhne Tourbillon perpetual calendar. "Around the edge of his property, this stopped."

Bringing her hands to her mouth, Emika says, "My wristwatch stopped, too, on the fifteenth of August."

"Intreton does that." Leaning toward Emika, I ask, "In your memories, you never left the house, right?"

"Yes." She tilts her head and squints. "So?"

"Your desire to stay back wouldn't take a physical form, just memories or dreams. Just like your pasts can have alternative versions—the real one, the post-extraction, and the other one, which seems unreal but actually happened, though no one remembers."

Pressing her temples hard, her face scrunching in pain, Emika reveals, "I do have some conflicting memories."

"I am sorry," I say, reaching forward to touch her hand. "However, as a time corrector, Vincent can coexist in more than one reality. And he can

---

[13]   See.

see your physical state in all realities. But your memories were confined in that house because you're not reality-proof." Squeezing her hand, I explain, "Your desire to stay back and Vincent's desire to spend his life with you created that reality." Shaking my head, I cut a dry smile. "Vincent wanted that life so badly that he drove at one-hundred-fifty miles per hour from Seattle after his TV interview." My voice trembles slightly as I stare into Emika's eyes. "Just to meet you." I sigh. "But you were already gone."

Ravi takes the last sip of his tea. Placing the cup on the side table, he asks, "So, what did you do when you saw the intreton?"

I walk over to him to fill his cup. "I have an intreton absorption device, so I freed his house from the alternate reality where Vincent was dwelling with Emika. At that time, Vincent fainted, and Dr. Lee began to treat him."

Anna hammers her right knuckles into her left palm. "Why did he faint?"

"The intreton was concealing the memories of all past time correctors from entering Vincent's mind. Those memories broke free and caused an information overload."

"That's it?" Chris asks.

I smirk. "That's it? The recollections, the talents, the darkness, the pains, the joys of at least fifteen time correctors, and memories of everyone they cared about. Do you think that's a small feat?" Pointing at his head, I ask, "Can your mind conceive that the future can happen before the past, yet their outcomes can co-occur?" I lean toward Chris. "If one were to transform all the information inside Vincent's head into an electromagnetic pulse, it would cause a blackout to the entire US—for months." I narrow my eyes at Chris. "Can your mind take it, Dr. Washington?"

Chris bows his head. "I am sorry, sir."

Spinning the whiskey in my glass, I continue. "And, because that house was the epicenter of the alternate life with Emika, all the memories surrounding her were displaced." Lifting my finger, I stress, "Not lost." Then, I turn to Emika. "Vincent from the future concealed the door inside the core linking to Emika's life. He made sure that Vincent never nudges Emika from her newfound freedom." Trying to swallow my sorrow, I confess, "He blames himself for Akane entering Emika."

"How do the memories of other time correctors affect Vince?" Ravi asks, scratching his head.

I shrug. "Vincent can drive like Fangio. Each of Chopin's pieces is etched in his memories, and he can play them seamlessly. He can swing the *katana* like Miyamoto Mushasi. They were all time correctors, of varying degrees." I pause before divulging, "When a child is chosen as a time corrector, all the talents and struggles of the previous ones get absorbed into that child but remain dormant unless an activation occurs."

"Activation?"Asks Ravi.

I stretch my arms and back; this will be a long evening. "There are three stages—the first happened when he learned of Akane's disappearance on November 23, 1991." Pushing my glasses up my nose, I turn to Emika. "That was moments before you were born." Turning to the rest of the crew, I say, "Most time, correctors fail to get beyond this stage. But Vincent moved on to the second phase when he entered the core and freed Emika. Several correctors before him could not take the memory overload of stage two. So, Chronos was cautious with the last one." I punch my left palm with my right knuckles. "It had to be someone whose struggles are as staggering as his brilliance." Shaking my head sadly, I say, "After stage two, Vincent's memories can never be transferred into a machine. Even thousands of Quantum World's helmets couldn't handle it." I look down before mustering the courage to reveal the ultimate truth. "His consciousness will die with him."

Unless he resets everything and hands a key to someone else.

Breathing hard, Ravi asks, "And what about the third level?"

I don't look up from the floor. "Let's hope we don't come to that."

But we will, Vincent. After what you said in the core following Vandal's escape yesterday, you left me with no choice.

Chris squints at me and asks, "What is the core?"

Rolling my eyes, I quip, "How do we measure time?"

"Earth's rotation around its axis and its revolution around the sun," he says.

Smirking, I add, "The universe doesn't care for Earth's time, past or future." I exhale and explain, "The core is an extension of the universe's time on Earth. It's made of intreton and is the purest source of energy. It maintains parity with Earth's time and keeps all realities separate unless a time corrector invokes it. That results in a tear in the fabric of time and reality as mortals feel it." I stare at Emika. "Like the one that freed you."

Ravi leans forward. "Who invoked the turbulences you faced?"

He seems to have read Vincent's book about me. Tightening my grip on the whiskey glass, I say, "Those occurred due to an action that is yet to happen."

"What action?" asks Emika.

Shaking my head, I smile. "Revealing that will change our reality."

I will never change it. That made me who I am—Philip Nardin.

Anna stomps her feet impatiently. "But *how* did she come back?"

Emika turns to Anna and nudges her hand. "Who?"

"You will see," Anna says, smiling crookedly.

Ravi shakes his head, shutting his eyes while Chris takes out his handkerchief and wipes his forehead. He puffs, "Oh, boy!"

They'd concealed the single most significant development in Vincent's life from Emika. Why?

Turning to Anna, I explain, "The core has no past and no future. Everything is occurring in the present. Therefore, future actions can have consequences in the past. A time corrector either forms a logical link between them, or their actions create those links."

Emika's eyes are glowing in anticipation. "Umm . . . Okay?"

I lift my finger. "But Vincent's actions must make sense to our world, where things are linear." As their eyes stretch wide with curiosity, I lean back. "After the extraction, the core had to readjust the past to justify Vincent's action." Shaking my left fist, I say, "So, Emika's suffering becomes a reflection, justifying Vincent's action for the extraction." Then, I shake my right fist. "This resulted in Akane trying to escape Emika's shell since the late fall of 2023. Emika's confusion, anger at Vincent, and indiscretions resulted from this tussle." I turn to Emika. "I am sorry. You were at the crossroads of reality—living your current one and the one the core was forging for you to make sense of Vincent's extraction in the future."

I shake my head. "The core selects the path of least resistance with minimal impact to the outside world. Instead of being engulfed in the turbulence, the blast from the intreton left Akane comatose. Her parents were fine, but Akane's health took precedence over getting her stuff from school. So, Vincent kept some of her artifacts." Lifting a shoulder, I clarify, "You know, the photo frame, the scarf, and the violin."

"During his high school graduation, Vincent pleaded with Akane to return. With the altered reality, instead of entering Emika, Akane first gained consciousness, but a part of her remained inside Emika from the fragments of an alternate reality. She had no memories of her past until the late fall of 2023, when she started to get some of it back in pieces, which is when Emika was deeply conflicted. And, on August 14, 2024, Japan time, when Vincent extracted Emika, all of Akane's memories returned, and everything was readjusted as if she'd never entered Emika in the first place." I squint at Anna. "Does that answer your question?"

Shutting her eyes, trying to absorb all this, Anna nods. But Emika's eyes have not blinked.

I touch her hands. "You need to blink." She now knows the ultimate price for the clarity she experienced.

As she closes her eyes, her tears drop on her hands. She swallows hard and tries to gather herself. Managing a defeated smile, she asks, "Akane is back?"

Pointing at Emika, I glare at Anna. "Why didn't you tell her?"

Anna shrugs. "Escaped my mind."

"What?" I shake my head in disgust. "Anna, I have lived three lives. I have seen the future happen before the past. Your theatrics won't fly here." Apologetically, I turn to Emika. "I'm sorry. Akane came back on November 15, 2024—exactly thirty-three years since she was taken—to Vincent." I clear my throat. "And between the time Vincent freed Emika and the day Akane returned, Chronos hid the door marked 'Akane' so that Vincent couldn't access it and accidentally change her reality."

Emika wipes her eyes. Her voice trembles as she admits, "That's Nozo's birthday." Turning to her ex-colleagues, she asks, "Why? I would have gone home with my Nozo and never bothered you three or Vincent." Nudging Ravi's hands, she asks, "What did I do wrong?" She gets on her knees and pleads with her hands clasped. "Please leave Vincent be. Akane is all that he ever wanted . . . I have seen his notebooks. He doesn't need to know about Nozo or me." She begs, "Can someone please drop Nozo and me at the airport?" Then, she looks around at her ex-colleagues. "I will never show my face here again." She fetches her cell phone from her bag.

I signal Tabi to take Nozo to another room. The little one doesn't have to see this. And Tabi knows what's going to happen. Edward brings a bottle of water for Emika.

Pulling Chris's cuffs, Emika implores, "Can you take me to the airport?" She then touches Ravi's hand. "How could you? I called you *Oniisan*. Remember?" She looks at her cell phone, covering her mouth and weeping. "Uber can't locate this place."

Both Chris and Ravi are silent, their heads down with shame. Anna keeps staring at Emika, biting her lip.

I lift Emika from the floor while Edward hands her a glass of water. Glaring at the other three, I raise my voice. "Vincent is like my son. What does that make Emika?" Snapping at Anna, I accuse, "You are behind this, right? Do you want me as your enemy? The White House, the Senate, the Pentagon . . . they all tried." Narrowing my eyes, I ask, "Do you want to join them?"

"N–no, sir," she stutters.

Snapping my fingers at Chris and Ravi, I remark, "What are you two? Clowns? Do you even have minds of your own?" I lean closer to the three and grind my teeth. Keeping my eyes on them, I point at Emika. "Vince walked into the abyss for this girl. And this is how you treat her?" I then turn to Anna. "Explain yourself to Emika. Now!" I yell, my voice resonating across the fifty-foot-long hall.

A trembling Anna turns to Emika. "I . . . I wanted you to feel the pain Vince did on the seventh of January when he drove for hours to Seattle to get your favorite flowers. And when he came to your doorstep, he found you with Brad. Do you know how he felt when you took that circus clown to his house, though we were all gathered to celebrate him, his book, and his invention?" She pounds her chest. "I know . . . because he told me, privately, in his basement den, the evening you brought Brad." Pointing at Emika, Anna says, "You made him feel like trash . . ."[14] Her voice breaks.

I lean toward Anna. "You think Emika doesn't feel the pain?" Touching Emika's hand, I say, "She doesn't even realize what drove her to those actions." I put my face within an inch of Anna's. "Do you feel accomplished? Does Emika's sorrow make you feel powerful at this moment?"

She shakes her head. "No, sir."

I turn to the other two. "Do you feel powerful after the way you treated Emika?" They are dead silent. Grinding my teeth, I ask, "Do you know

---

[14]   Chapter 13 of *The Winding* (Book 1).

what power is? Vincent can alter reality to suit him best. But he doesn't—that's power."

I fold my hand into a fist and say, "Let me show you power." I lift one eyebrow and one side of my mouth in a smirk. Sparks generate through my fingertips, turning the room a blinding white. Emika, Edward, Anna, Ravi, and Chris cover their eyes as the sparks dance around my hand.

Slowly, as they open their eyes, I say, "I can change reality so that you three idiots never meet Vincent."

Thank you, Vincent, for granting me the power to generate sparks with a snap.

Anna panics. "Sir, then Vincent will never meet Emika. We hired her."

"I can change that reality, too," I respond, enlarging the sparks.

"Please don't do this," Emika pleads. "I'll have no place in Vince's life. I'll leave with Nozo."

Closing my fists, I dissolve the sparks. I look at Anna. "See the difference here? She is still pleading for you three."

Anna wipes her eyes, gets up, and touches Emika's face. "I'm so sorry."

"Well played," Emika scoffs. "You lied to me about the position at Quantum World, right?"

Ravi leaves his chair and takes Emika's hand. "No lies there. You are joining us."

Emika wipes her tears. "Why?"

"You're brilliant," Chris says, standing next to Ravi. "And we love you."

Anna takes Emika's other hand. "I know you're enough for Nozo. But shouldn't she at least know Vince?"

Emika swallows hard. "I don't know."

I text Tabi, and a few moments later, she returns to the room with Nozo. Turning to Emika, I ask, "Can I hold your daughter?"

"Sure."

I take her and look into her unmistakable eyes; Amara Idrissi, Iman Alami, Amara Abajian, and Vincent Abajian all had those eyes. Everyone in the room is gazing at Nozo. She reminds me of little Vincent when I first picked him.

As I kiss her forehead, Nozo pulls my beard and shouts, "White beard!"

Emika shakes her head at Nozo. "Leave the beard."

"No," Nozo protests, pouting her lips and furrowing her brows.

"Let her, I insist." I touch her little pink nose. "What's your name?"

She tilts her head. "Nozomi. You?"

"It's Philip, but you can call me Grandpa."

Nodding, she asks, "Like *Sofu*, Mama's papha?"

I blink. "Yes." I look into her curious eyes and hold her gaze. "Nozo? What do you want?"

She tilts her head and smiles. "You've candy?"

"What's your favorite?" I ask, touching her nose again.

She shuts her eyes, thinking. Then, she opens them wide. "Choco."

Edward presses the call button on my phone and holds it out to me. I lean toward it and say, "Gai, can you make a batch of chocolate candies that a two-year-old will find irresistible?"

"Certainly. It will take an hour or so."

I look at Nozomi's sparkling eyes and then at Emika's affectionate face before handing Nozo back to her. "Nozomi Amari is a beautiful name."

Emika rests Nozo's head on her shoulder. "Thanks." Rocking Nozo, she asks me, "Why didn't you bring his memories back?"

I stare into her kind brown eyes. "There was a lot on our plates." Stretching my arms, I continue, "Training him to be the next time corrector, dealing with Vandal. And we did not want to steer him from Akane, either."

And you moved on, too. Right?

Scanning the faces in the room curiously, Emika asks, "What about Dr. Kauffman?" While Anna, Ravi, and Chris squint, Emika exhales in exasperation, lifts her brows, and explains. "Rebecca . . . His shrink? Wouldn't Vince contact her if he realized he had lost his memory?"

"No idea," I say, trying not to let anything show on my face. Emika knows more about Vincent than I thought.

Emika confesses, "I tried to move on." Kissing Nozo's forehead, she says, "There's no substitute for Vincent, but I'm fine with just Nozo and me."

Anna turns to Emika and shakes her shoulder. "What about that guy— Markus? You trust him enough with Nozo."

Emika clicks her tongue and glares at Anna. "We had a past. Now, he is just a friend. At least from my side."

I can spot a lie from a mile away, and this "just a friend" comment does not seem right. Well, that's for Vincent to figure out.

"I'll do what I can to bring Vincent's memories back."

Leaning forward, Ravi asks, "I'm curious. What else can a time corrector do?"

"Who do you think created that airplane mess in Seattle?"

Ravi shrugs. "Vandal?"

"Right. And how do you think the plane disappeared and then appeared back in the hangar?"

All their jaws drop, except Tabi's and Edward's. Emika softly murmurs, "Vincent?"

Suddenly, Anna snaps her fingers and turns to Ravi. "Who guessed it at the dinner?"

"You did," Ravi says, rolling his eyes.

Clapping, Anna exclaims, "Do I know my boy, or do I know my—?" She joins her hands, staring into my glaring eyes. Crumpling her lips, she says, "Sorry, your boy."

Pressing her lips together, Tabi smiles. Chris crumples his brows and says to her, "I bet you knew this all along."

She grins. "What do you think?"

I lean back and smile. "After the incident, Vince went to Japan to spend a few hours with Akane."

Looking at her watch and raising her brows, Anna asks, "What? Isn't there an embargo on flights?"

"He doesn't need transportation to go anywhere," I declare, smirking.

Ravi leans forward. "How?"

"You will know."

"Are you interested in knowing more about the core and time correctors?" I ask everyone.

Anna's eyes gleam. "Yes."

"Splendid. I'll be right back." Before leaving the room, I turn back and state, "Ed, Tabi, come with me."

Taking my walking stick from beside the door, I hum, "The lunatic is on the grass . . ."[15] I enter the hallway. Standing below Van Gogh's *Café Terrace at Night*, I call Vincent.

Well, Vince, I wish yesterday's conversation about commercializing an alternate reality had taken a different direction. You leave me no choice.

---

[15] Pink Floyd's song "Brain Damage."

Vincent picks up after three rings. "What's up?"

"When you've time, take your old cell phone and head to the core. Try to find out why you learned to make omurice and visit your memories associated with the airport on February 15, 2024, Chez-Giraud in the fall of 2023, and August 3, 2023."

"Sure. But why?"

"You gotta trust me on this. Also, do these in your backyard. And try and take a break from the core. The suit can't protect you from these frequent trips between home and Japan."

"I miss her."

"I know. But you're damaging your health faster than intreton can regenerate. The suit is not designed for frequent trips. This will be the protocol till you become one with the core. Bye, Vincent."

I lift my shirt cuffs and show Tabi and Edward my bracelet. "This turns red when Vince goes unconscious. When it does, you two will head to Vincent's house, pick him up from the backyard, change his clothes, and set him down in one of the beds in his house."

Tabi shrugs. "Why can't we all go together and carry him?"

Edward touches Tabi's head. "That can't be Nozo's first memory of her father."

"You're right." Pointing at my walking stick, Tabi asks, "What's with that? You were fine yesterday."

I chuckle. "I am older than I was yesterday."

Humming the refrain of "the lunatic is in my head," I head back to the fifty feet long living room, where the others are. Tabi and Edward follow.

Returning to our seats, I say, "Let's start from Vincent's training—the fall of 2024."

CHAPTER 5

SHURIKEN

"My heart was too tiny to hold this love. But I wanted to squeeze them all in."
—*Vincent*

September–November 2024

(Philip's island)

<u>Vincent</u>

M Y UTILITY JACKET IS ZIPPED up to my neck, but the stubborn wind pulls in and puffs my coat. I squint to see beyond the thick air, whose moisture combines the North Sea, North Atlantic Ocean, and the Norwegian Sea. A gust of wind robs Philip's fedora hat from his head. Jumping, he stretches out his arm and yells, "Fuck!" The hat disappears into the dense mist.

My hair is at the mercy of the wind; the strands are flying or falling over my eyes. I hear all-terrain wheels cracking, smashing the rocks and pebbles. Piercing through the mist, the light from the circular LED head-lamps reveals the identity of the vehicle—a six-by-six G-Wagon. There is no rumbling from an engine, so it's electric. The struggling, dark-red light of the setting sun shines on Edward as he gets out of the car with an M16 hanging from his shoulder. Then, he aims the gun at us.

Raising my arms in shock, palms out, I turn to Philip, shouting over the wind, "What's wrong with Edward?"

Grabbing my collar, Philip drags me to the edge of the cliff. My toes are the only thing touching the ground. He brings his head close to mine and looks into my eyes. "Jump, or he will shoot."

Looking down, I see a hundred-meter drop to the meeting point of the three seas. Clutching Philip's hand, I feel my blood rush to my head. My heart thumps as I screech, "What?"

He reaches into his pocket, pulls out a two-inch-wide steel bracelet, and then clasps it onto my right wrist. "Press the green button before you snap your fingers to make sparks. And snap before you reach the ground. Else you will be ground meat."

Holding onto Philip's hand, I shriek, "Snap?"

Squinting, he tugs my collar. "That's how you create a spark."

"Can you?"

"Not unless you grant me. Now, fly." Then, he pushes me off the cliff.

I can't see anything as I free-fall, facing downward. The air is blasting on my face, each droplet hitting me like shards of glass. My eyes burn from the thick, misty, salty air and ocean water mix. I'll be dead in a second—two, if I am lucky.

Philip, you old fuck. Wait till I get my hands on you.

But I must live to avenge this. I fight the wind to pull my wrist to me. Ah, there is the green button. As soon as I press it, a deep-blue metallic mesh covers my jacket, trousers, and shoes. A helmet covers my face, and I can see everything clearly—even the tiny droplets of the mist. Awesome! I look down—just about one hundred feet to the ocean. I snap my fingers, and gravity becomes almost nonexistent. Then, I am floating. I can do this all my life.

(Core)

Everything becomes familiar in the core—the giant tourbillon, the changing seasons. But why was I here the last time? Floating through, I enter the door marked "Crossroads." It opens into a circular hall with equal-sized sections along its perimeter. Each unit is separated by sparks, just like those from my fingers. I walk into the first one and see a young Philip holding a baby Vincent.

Approaching Philip from 1984, I say, "Give me your hand."

With baby Vincent cradled in his left arm, he extends his right hand.

Snapping my fingers, I create a spark brighter than any lightning. I smile as I touch his hand. "Here. You can now make a spark with a snap. Every action you had to take by physically going to the core will be redone as if you always had this ability."

His eyes well up as he looks at me with gratitude. Sniffling, he asks, "Why?"

My voice cracks as I admit, "I owe my life to you." I leave the hall.

Outside the door, future Vincent is waiting for me. He sighs. "Did you give Philip the snapping ability?"

"Yes?" I squint. "Something wrong?"

He scoffs. "It was predestined." Placing his hand on my shoulder, he instructs, "Learn to forgive yourself."

"What?"

He lifts his hand from my shoulder and waves it in dismissal. "Did you read the journal I gave you?"[16] he asks.

I shrug. "Seriously? That fairy tale?"

He chuckles. "Let's meet some of the characters, then." Pointing at my fingers, he says, "Intreton from the sparks is more stable than the core. You can use it safely to create an intreton shell when in danger."

"Danger?"

---

[16] Chapter 17 of *The Winding* (Book 1).

Without answering, he pulls me to a door marked "Origins." I see a 3D projection of towers, cathedrals, courtyards surrounded by colonnades, and hypostyle halls. Vincent from the future points at the image. "This was the kingdom of Gaia, invisible to humans."

I walk around the projection. "Where was it located?"

"Underneath Philip's island."

A white-bearded man clothed in white robes, with a scythe sword in his left hand, comes forward. "I ruled this kingdom to bring prosperity to Gaia and exterior Earth by sharing our fortunes."

"So, you're Chronos or Cronus?" I ask.

He laughs. "You, indeed, come from a divided world. This is the core, Vincent. Let's not delve into pedantic differences."

"So, you're both."

Pointing at the projection, Chronos continues, "My children and I had the foresight, and we saw a future where the world's military and political heads unite against humanity. I didn't want to interfere." Chronos clenches his jaw. "But three of my stupid sons had different plans." Lifting his finger, he declares, "They thought conflict to be the best solution."

"Stupid?" a voice echoes. "I did nothing wrong by erupting Vesuvius. Humans are the root of corruption. They show their true colors in crisis." A long-bearded man appears and shakes my hand. He reveals, "I'm Zeus. Nice to meet you, Vincent."

Then, another man emerges, banging his spear on the floor. "I was more creative. I created turbulence, entered Gavrilo Princip's body, and killed Archduke Franz Ferdinand of Austria." Lifting his shoulder and delivering a crooked smile, he continues, "Gavrilo didn't die of tuberculosis. The intreton in his veins poisoned him."

My nostrils flare. Without even inquiring about his identity, I demand, "What else have you done?"

He shuts his eyes and spreads his arms, exhaling deeply. "I whispered into Hirohito's ears to bomb Pearl Harbor."

My eyes widen with shock. "The same way—by entering his body?" I inquire.

"No. I did something more primal." Hopscotching sideways, he grimaces. "I went to 1921 when the crown prince was in Europe. I created turbulence and showed him a lie about Japan's future as the most powerful

Axis power if he bombed Pearl Harbor." He squats and rubs his hands together, smiling crookedly. "Oh, Vincent, it was such a spicy lie." Standing straight again, he reveals, "Then, the whole thing appeared like a dream to Hirohito in 1941." He taps his chest. "I'm Hades." Running his fingers through his wavy hair, he smirks. "And the most handsome of my brothers."

I fold my hand into a fist and clench my jaw. "Instigating conflict was your idea of helping people?"

Hades pouts and looks down. "Sorry, dude." Tapping his temple, he reveals, "Someone whispered to me to do this . . ." He closes his eyes tight. "I don't remember who, though." Opening his eyes, he says, "He asked more . . . I did more . . ." The future Vincent glares at him, and Hades jerks back and turns to me. He shrugs. "I can't remember."

So, this is what Philip meant when he said world wars resulted from turbulence.[17] Why did the future Vincent glare at Hades?

A hoarse voice interrupts my thoughts. "I tried, too." As he appears, I see his hair tied into a bun. Smiling, he admits, "I sunk US vessels and made it look like the Soviets did it. I made them through the turbulence." Spreading his arms wide with pride, he confesses, "I had been doing it for hundreds of years. Katsushika Hokusai even painted my work. Those waves are not mere tides. They are intreton." Finally, he introduces himself. "Poseidon. Pleased to meet you."

I turn to Chronos. "What do you mean 'a future where the world's military and political heads unite against humanity?' Has that future happened?"

He points his scythe at the ground. "It has here. But in your world, it will happen much later."

"When?"

Rushing between Chronos and me, the future Vincent warns Chronos, "Not one more word." Turning to me, he smiles and says, "You just have to wait."

I sigh, exasperated. "So, what's next?"

Chronos walks up to a raised marble dais. "I sunk Gaia under the ocean, which became the core that produces intreton. And I let humans be humans. Then, one day, everything changed." He pauses.

---

[17]   Chapter 9 of *The Winding* (Book 1).

The surrounding 3D image changes to what looks like Philp's private island but with a palace built on top. A boy comes out of the palace, dressed in a medieval peasant's outfit, with chains around his neck.

"I'm Arne," he says as he approaches me.

I remember his name from the journal. Quickly freeing him from his shackles, I ask, "So, you're the first human time corrector?"

He shakes his head. "I wanted none of it." He points his finger back at the palace, saying, "All I ever wanted was to spend time with her."

A girl, about sixteen years old, emerges from a dark corridor. She is radiant, with silver hair. I've seen this glow before, back in second grade, when Akane first walked into my classroom. I close my eyes, trying to remember someone else who shimmers like her, but I can't. Why?

"I'm Estrid," she says, coming forward to touch my chest. "You have my Arne's soul."

"What?"

Touching my shoulder, the future Vincent explains, "She means you are a time corrector." He then points at Arne. "He was the son of a peasant who befriended the landlord's daughter, Estrid."

Arne smiles sadly. "I played chess with her and listened to her play the harp. That was my only fault."

Future Vincent interjects, "Nope. Your fault was you were poor and an orphan." Turning to me, he clarifies, "While Estrid's parents were okay with the innocent friendship, some local rich boys tricked Arne into a fishing trip out of jealousy. They tied him to stones and dropped him into the ocean—the same spot where Chronos hid Gaia."

Arne stares at his hands, his eyes wide. "My body began to glow blue, and the ropes fell away. I swam to shore. But when I got there, everything changed. The palace was in ruins. I realized that hundreds of years passed outside the core."

Coming forward, Chronos points at Arne and says to me, "With his power, he built roads and tunnels and helped develop ports."

Arne turns his head toward Chronos, saying, "I did none of it for humanity." Tears flood his eyes. "Could the roads, the bridges, the ports lead to Estrid . . . even if they are forged across time?"

Chronos furrows his brows. "After Arne's passing, I decided to pass the baton." He laments, "Yes, I have made mistakes in choosing the wrong ones. Some only lasted a few minutes." Pointing his finger at me and widening his eyes, he says, "You're different. I took a peek into your future and your past. Your struggles perfectly balance your talents—the resilience needed to be a time corrector. And I passed on Arne's soul and the intreton when you were born."

"What's my job as a time corrector?" I ask.

"Keep the core from getting into the wrong hands," Chronos confirms, swinging his scythe over his head. "Manage the discord between Earth time and universe time."

I squint at him. "Manage or stop?"

Coming between Chronos and me, future Vincent assures me, "There will be moments when you may need to invoke a discord."

Paying no attention to that statement, I turn to Estrid. "What happened to you?"

Tears roll from her eyes, and her lips tremble. "I killed myself by drowning in the same place where I thought Arne died. And from then on, my soul keeps looking for Arne."

I turn to Arne. "Couldn't you bring her back to life?"

Future Vincent touches my shoulder. "Death is permanent." Spreading his arms wide, he says, "Yes, Arne and Estrid exist here, in spirit." He points up. "On Earth's surface, the quest was on."

I squint. "Quest? Was?"

Wiping her eyes, Estrid reveals, "I was looking for you, but then . . ." She stops, placing her hand on her mouth.

"Then what?" I ask, touching her shoulder gently.

Estrid looks at the future Vincent helplessly while he removes my hand from her shoulder. Before Estrid can speak, future Vincent explains, "She can't risk revealing the future."

"I can't remember anything." I get on my knees. "How did I become this time corrector? I see a hazy face of a girl. Who is she?"

Estrid turns and walks away. Then, she stops, looks back, and winks. "Someone needs to grow up mentally. And someone needs to come back. You will have to make some tough choices."

Raising my voice, I demand, "What tough choices?"

"You just have to wait," future Vincent chimes in.

Is there anything they will tell me? I get up and touch future Vincent's shoulder. "How come you don't need a suit like me?"

He shakes his head. "I am not physically here. But to enter, I only needed the suit until April 13, 2027."

"What happens after that?" I ask, shaking his shoulder.

Pointing at my intreton-powered suit, he smiles. "You will become one with the core."

"How?"

"Take a deep breath, Vincent, and hold it in . . ." He snaps his fingers.

(Philip's boat)

Someone is sucking water from my mouth and giving me CPR. I'm on a boat. So, that's why future Vincent told me to hold my breath. A little clarification would have been excellent. I slowly open my eyes and see round glasses, chubby cheeks, and hair parted down the middle of a head. Dr. Lee slaps my face.

"Wake up, Vince." Then, he inserts a syringe with liquid intreton straight into my chest. I sit up, stretch my eyes wide, and puff for breath.

Then, Philip kneels down beside me, shaking my shoulder. "You okay?"

I nod. Edward stands a few feet away, Hulk in his arms. My dog leaps down from his hands and comes running at me, licking my face. My eyes still can't focus. I shake my head.

(Vincent's home)

Why did I get this enormous house? It's so far from downtown, where my penthouse was. Why was I drawn to it? The cherry trees? The mountain view? The addicting yet deafening silence?

The water is heating in my gooseneck kettle, fifteen feet away. I can hear every molecule of the gurgling water trying to get away from each other and pushing against the kettle walls. Looking at my watch, I smile.

Five seconds to reach ninety-five degrees Celsius—perfect for a pour-over. Today, I will use the Kalita Wave. I toss a coin and hear it whooshing through the air, finally dropping into my hand after precisely four seconds when my kettle goes off.

I take the first sip of light-roasted Sumatran Sulawesi, the unmistakably earthy notes dancing on my tongue. Outside, I can distinguish the sound of every single leaf dancing to the wind. I have memorized every dialogue in every movie I own. I can count the number of raindrops that fall every second and hear each coffee drop, agitated inside the paper filter. Sometimes, I can even hear the sound of sunlight touching dust. Do my heightened senses come from intreton or my loneliness? Yes, it's just Hulk and me. Either I have forced myself to seek inner joy in this seclusion, or the loneliness has found me. I guess that loneliness and I can be less lonely together. Wow! I need to write that down.

Why haven't I furnished the main bedroom? What was I waiting for? What *am* I waiting for? I can read and write *hiragana* and *katakana*. But I did not write the Post-its with the markings *migi doa* and *hidari doa*. I asked Anna once, and she said, "They were always there." How could that be? I'm the first owner of this house.

Who made me buy this place? It couldn't be Elise, as she was long gone. It's too big for one human and a dog. But I love it; it is like this house has always known me. It has its own music, which teases me of a life I could have had. The music sounds like Chopin's fourth ballade, but I can't connect the notes to my life.

Hulk scratches my slippers, wagging his tail. We leave for the backyard, and he runs around, the falling leaves crackling in the wind. I shut my eyes as some dry leaves circle around. How many? Twenty-three. No, twenty-five. Opening my eyes, I count twenty-four. Damn, I was close. Yes, it's just Hulk and me. Shutting my eyes and breathing deeply, I smell disappearing summer in the woods, the scent of looming Autumn colors, the imminence of snow on those mountains, the harmony of cold and warm breezes—I can feel them all. I can hear the leaves turn to autumn color. I can distinguish at least three types of cicadas—the Kanakana, the Minmin seminar, and the Abra. They're desperately screeching to hold the looming winter at bay.

I look up at the lonely sky, sprinkled with clouds reflecting the setting sun in orange, red, and yellow—all longing for some memories. I smirk at this tease. Panting, Hulk comes running back, three fall leaves stuck on his face. Taking them off, I ask, "Bug, wanna make some memories?"

We go inside. Wagging his tail, he sits next to the piano bench. Shutting the doors, I welcome the defeating silence—life.

Looking down at my perennially smiling pup, I ask, "You want me to play you something?"

He whimpers and wags his tail.

I pull the bench and sit at the mahogany Steinway gifted to me by Philip. I always wanted to play the piano as a child. I thought it would bring me closer to Akane. I'd be her accompanist as she played the violin. Closing my eyes, I start keying Chopin's Étude Op. 10, No. 12. Sparks emit from my fingertips, pulling my fingers to the correct keys. I never took a single lesson in my life, but Chopin enters my body when I touch the keys. And I can play anything by ear. I close my eyes, and my mind travels to 1991—the day she called me family.

* * *

(Spring of 1991—Montagnola, no dress code day)

I sat between Akane, on my right, and her mother, Theresa Jansen Egami, on the left. Akane's father sat next to Akane, clad in a bespoke tux. Theresa, like Akane, was wearing a satin kimono.

Mr. Masayoshi Egami stretched his arm to touch my shoulder and smiled. "Do you like the tux?"

I stood up and bowed. "Thank you so much, sir. I like it very much."

Theresa ruffled my hair. "You don't need to bow every time." Tapping on my chair, she insisted, "Sit, sit."

As they served our food, *Theresa-san* touched my hand. "Do you want me to cut your meat, sweetheart?"

No one had ever said that to me. I stared at my hands, watching my tears drip on them. *Theresa-san* kissed the top of my head. Confused, she put her fingers to her mouth. "Did I say something wrong?"

Akane took the napkin from her lap and wiped my tears. Turning to her father and pointing at me, she asked, *"Kare mo Kazoku desu ne?"*[18]

Mr. Egami kissed Akane's head. *"Mochiron. Kuraga san to ohanashi masu."*[19]

I didn't know what they were saying, but it had its own melody. Just like her violin. At that moment, I thought that no one called me sweetheart, and no one offered to cut my meat. I was not used to feeling loved by a parent and was puffing for breath. I was supposed to be worthless, an orphan, and a bastard; that's all I knew. The bruises on my chest and thighs from the school bullies were testimony to being poor and an outcast. I was just eight. My heart was too tiny to hold this love. But I wanted to squeeze them all in.

Standing up, I looked at Akane and her parents. "I'll wash my face and be back."

The exit door was thirty feet from our table. I covered my ears to block out the loud music—"Brother Louie" by Modern Talking. All the senior students were dancing, and I dodged them on my way to the exit.

I'd made it halfway before Rudy Von Stein pulled my lapel. "Nice tux, son of the help. Did you steal it?"

"Please don't hit me." I clasped my hands together.

Luther grabbed me from behind. "How'd you get it?"

"Akane."

Rudy pushed me to the floor. "Runt."

I got up and ran for the door as their voices echoed, ". . . terrorist . . . worthless . . . bastard."

Outside the hall, I sat on the floor with my back against the wall, covering my ears. After a few moments, I saw her navy satin kimono as she sat next to me. Akane took my hand, locked her fingers with mine, and rested her head on my shoulder.

"I'll be here as long as you need. Papha will talk to Mr. Kruger." She ruffled my hair and smiled with her apple-red lips, eyes shutting into two lines of lashes. "Maybe you will come and live with us in Japan."

"Huh?"

She stood up and offered me her hand. "Let's walk."

---

[18] He is family, too, right?

[19] Of course. I'll speak with Mr. Kruger.

As I grabbed her hand, our hands looked different. They became the hands of adults. And she was not in a kimono but a floral, chiffon top. I looked at her face. "You're not Akane."

She tilted her head. "Why would I be her?" Tears ran from her hazy face. "Couldn't you tell me you loved me at least once? Look at us now, separated by an ocean and by time." Then, she pointed at her pregnant belly and smiled sadly. "I have to do this all by myself now." She touched my face and said, "I'm so glad you moved on. You deserve better than me." She moved her hand to her belly. "A part of you will always be with me."

"Who are you?" I stretched my arms out to hold her, but she disappeared in the next moment.

(Back to the present)

I open my moist eyes, then look at my fingers and listen to the keys. When did I start playing Chopin's Ballade No. 4?[20] What does this song mean to me? Who was that pregnant woman? How could I do that to someone? That's not like me at all. Why is my memory around certain things so hazy?

I press my temples. Bingo! I used to go to this shrink, Dr. Kauffman. When was the last time I went there? Let's call her. I grab my phone and start scrolling through my call history. What happened to my call log before August 30? Scanning through my contacts instead, I call her.

Seconds later, I hear, "The number has been disconnected."

What? Bringing up Google, I type "Rebecca Kauffman + Psychiatrist + MIT." A chill runs down my spine as I read that Rebecca and her husband, Bernard, died in a head-on collision with an autonomous semi on I-10. My heart thumps at a picture of their golden doodle, Max, dead on the road. I drop the phone and pick up my Hulk.

Staring into his large, warm eyes, I assure him, "I won't let anything happen to you." He licks my nose, and I start to rock him. On the floor,

---

[20] It was played in the background when Vincent learned about Akane's disappearance (November 23, 1991). Akane came as Emika the first time (August 3, 2023). It was also Vincent's ringtone when Emika called him.

my phone vibrates, Tabi's profile picture on the screen. With Hulk on my lap, I pick up the phone and answer it. Sniffling once, I kill the tremble in my voice. "Hey."

Gasping, she says, "I resigned from the *Tribune*."

"Why?"

"I just couldn't. Revenge took everything from me. Revenge made me a journalist. I am empty, worthless without it." She breathes into the phone heavily. "What do I do now?"

"Can you make it to my office at ten o'clock tomorrow morning?"

"Why?" she asks, sniffling.

"Don't be late."

Did I ever mention Akane to Dr. Kauffman? There wouldn't have been any reason to; all she was helping me with was getting back on track after Elise's death. But why does it seem I spoke about Akane? What prompted me? Fuck it.

Touching Hulk's button nose, I ask, "Wanna go to the basement?"

We pass the home theater, library, study, and wine cellar before reaching a concealed door behind my bookshelves. I slide the books until a "poster" of *The Two Towers* is revealed. Leaning forward, I let the eye of Sauron scan my retina. The bookshelves slide, revealing a hall under my garage.

"Lights." The room lights up.

"System on."

"Welcome to the temple cave, Dr. Abajian," announces Athena[21] in her husky voice.

I have connected twenty-five computers to create a one-hundred-screen beast—ten rows wide and ten rows long. These computers also monitor every real-time communication to and from Quantum World. But I never look at them. Since last August, whenever I visit the core, I record all the movements in a GoPro. People I meet in the core never appear on the recordings. When I come back, I feed the data into my 3D hologram. The more I travel, the more precise the map becomes. Since it is outside the

---

[21] Athena was an intelligent agent, much like Ludwig. Vincent and Anna programmed her when they were professors at the university. Her demeanor is quirky like Anna's. Athena controlled the security to the AI lab in the university. She now controls the security of Vincent's house.

space-time continuum, it can also help me travel quickly. And it's almost impossible to know the directions. Getting lost in the core is easy and is terrible for my health.

Looking at my cell phone, I ask, "Ludwig, can you get into this 3D schema and create a routing protocol to quickly navigate important places—like Philip's island, Philip's home, or even major cities? I'll have to use small turbulences to make the journey."

"Ah. So, you want me to point to the exact pocket outside the space-time continuum that will help you get to a space in the real world."

I lean back in my chair and smile. "Exactly. But I want two options. I want to either view the place from the core or leave the core and immerse myself into the real world."

"Ah! A window *and* a portal. It might take me some time."

I look around. "Athena? You here?"

"I'm always listening. I could be your wife. Can I call you honey?"

I chuckle. "Whatever."

"As you wish, honey."

I shake my head and then rest it on my palms. "Can you help Ludwig with his navigation project? To make it hackproof."

"Nice to meet you, Athena. You have a beautiful voice," announces Ludwig.

"Ludwig—the name of a maestro and the voice of the thespian, Sir Patrick Stewart. I'm already falling in love with you."

"Hey, what about being my wife?" I snark.

"Oh! I am split between you and Ludwig."

"Ah! My luck." I take a deep breath. "Anyway, get this done in a week. Since the core is removed from the space-time continuum, this upgrade will transcend time and help Philip in his past travels."

"Certainly, Vincent," responds Ludwig.

"Also, I will create multiple copies of you and Athena into chips and insert them into my watches, the suit Philip built, and my eyeglasses. I may not have access to my phone all the time."

"Always happy to help, Vincent," confirms Ludwig.

"Of course, honey," says Athena impishly.

(Quantum World—Executive conference room)

I'm looking through the designs of the prototypes for the project we're working on. Anna, Chris, and Ravi are waiting for me to accept at least one. All three are sitting on my left in the conference room—a thirty-six-chair room overlooking the Cascades. Tabi occupies a chair on my right side. She doesn't know why she is here, nor do my colleagues.

Anna rolls her eyes. "Enough already. Just pick one."

I lift my shoulders and flip through all the designs again. "Why are they all helmets? What's a helmet got to do with memory transfer?"

Ravi points at a binder on my desk. "Research shows that prospective customers trust helmets."

I take the binder and flip through bar graphs and pie charts. Sighing, I hand the binder over to Tabi. "This garbage is research?"

Tabi shrugs. "It's called market research."

"And why do they like helmets?" I massage my temples.

Ravi leans forward. "They believe it will protect their head." Knocking on the table, he chuckles. "They don't understand that their head will interact with the inside of the helmet. So, there is no external trauma the helmet will protect their heads from."

"We're gonna have a lot of fun building gadgets for people whose consciousness is not worth transferring," I say, smirking.

Anna shrugs. "Pretty much."

I look at Tabi. "Why pick and commit to a design if we are not launching anything for two and a half years?"

"To create a buzz." Snapping her fingers, she explains, "BMW made a prototype as early as 2016 for a car they only released in 2022—the Vision." Moving her eyes from me to the rest of my crew, she describes, "Buzz is managed through the press, social media, and other channels. But the people will almost always need to know what the product may look like." Nudging my wrist, she smiles. "Cheer up. You can still change the design later on. How many real cars end up looking like the prototypes?"

Raising my brows, I sigh. "I wish they did." I spread all ten designs on the desk and turn to my colleagues and Tabi. Then, I wisecrack, "Since these drawings are a product of unimaginably painstaking research, I'm gonna use the most rigorous test known to humanity to pick one." They all lean toward me with eyes wide open in anticipation. And I start pointing. "Eeny, meeny, miny, moe . . ." My colleagues roll their eyes, and Tabi's voice shrills with laughter. As I reach "tiger," I pick the tenth design.

Anna waves her hand. "No, no, it has to be the next one."

I snap my fingers. "No. The 'moe' always landed on Akane, and she hid, and I sought." My breathing gets ragged. I press the cap of my Montblanc Meisterstück fountain pen and grind my teeth.

I know you cheated in hide-and-seek. And then, one day, you just left me and hid inside a time turbulence. The core has doors to everyone in my life except you. What happened to you?

Sensing my grief, Ravi turns to Anna and taps her wrist. "Vince is right. Wherever the final 'moe' lands, that's your pick."

Chris chimes in. "Yep." Then, he takes out his cell phone. "Let me check."

Anna stops him. "You guys always suck up to Vince." She squints at Tabi. "You're a journalist with integrity. Please look up the rules of eeny, meeny, miny, moe."

Tabi tilts her head. "Okay?"

Ravi puts designs one and ten in a folder and discards the other eight. Then, he looks at all of us. "What about colors?" He is still trying to keep me distracted.

"Yes, yes, colors," exclaims Anna, clapping and grinning ear to ear.

Furrowing my brows at Ravi, I ask, "Why do we need colors?"

Anna pouts her lips and bangs on the table. "I want colors."

"Color gives a sense of identity," Tabi says, pointing at the "research binder."

Chris looks at Tabi. Crossing his arms, he says, "I'm intrigued. You're a famous journalist. What brings you here?"

I take Tabi's hand and turn to my three musketeers. "Gang, meet Tabitha, our new Director of Media. She is our liaison with the press, social media, TV networks, and other crap we suck at."

Tabi squeezes my hand in surprise. "Huh?"

"Yeah, it's news to her." Raising my eyebrows, I ask my colleagues, "Are we supporting my decision?"

Ravi smiles. "Of course." Then, he squints. "But HR may object."

Pointing to myself, I smirk. "Object me? I'd like to see them try."

"Yes. Fuck HR," Chris says, standing up to shake Tabi's hand. "Welcome aboard."

"I'm fine with it because she loves colors." Anna smiles. Then, she squeals in excitement, looking around the room. "Let's call the product The Mind."

Tabi nods at Anna. "Sounds perfect."

Anna starts to count on her fingers, blinking with every color she lists. "I want this to come in pink, fuchsia, coral, turquoise. What else?" With lifted brows and wide eyes, she continues, "Rose gold, silver, pearl white with rose-gold trims . . ."

Tabi takes a sip from a bottle of water and looks at me. Then, she takes my hand in both of hers. "Thank you!" she says, her voice trembling.

I cover our joined hands with my other one. "There's one more job for you." I turn to my original gangsters. "You have time now?"

We get out of my car at a two-acre piece of land surrounded by mountains, facing a building that used to be a state-owned arts college, now shut down. I point at the facility. "I bought the land from the city to renovate the building and transform it into an orphanage and a boarding school."

Chris puts his hands on my shoulder. With gleaming eyes, he asks, "How can I help?"

"In whatever manner Tabi desires."

Tabi lifts her finger, signaling me to wait. Then, she takes out her inhaler and pumps it three times. Finally, when she processes my words, she shakes her head and asks, "What?"

I touch her shoulder. "I can't bring back Amina and Farid,"[22] I say, pointing at the building, "but with this, you can help hundreds of children like them to a better life." Squeezing her shoulder, I add, "Never say you are useless beyond being an investigative journalist."

---

[22] In Chapter 15 of *The Winding* (Book 1), Tabi's younger siblings, Amina and Farid, were killed in a drone attack orchestrated by the then Secretary of Defense, the late Dick Graham.

Her voice quavers. "Okay." Then, her eyes get teary as she says, "That can't be the only reason, though."

I wipe her tears with my thumb. "It's not." Taking a deep breath, I confess, "This is where little Vincents won't feel worthless because they are poor and orphans." I look into her eyes. "And there is no one better than you to oversee this."

Ravi touches my shoulder. "How will you pay for all the upkeep?"

I fake a smile, disregarding the vacuum in my life. "I'm rich, with no family besides Hulk."

Anna pulls my lapel. "Idiot. Where do I sign up to make regular contributions?"

"I'll match hers," Chris volunteers.

Tilting his head, Ravi smiles. "And you think I won't?"

I look at their smiling and kind faces. Blinking back tears, I state, "I'll ask Jean[23] to draw up paperwork to add you all to the trust."

Pulling on my sleeve, Tabi asks, "Can I have naming rights?"

"Sure."

Tabi walks a few steps toward the building, then turns back to us and spreads her arms. "Ladies and gentlemen, presenting 'Amara's Tree of Life.'"

A cold fall wind comes out of nowhere. I tighten my scarf and pull down my ivy cap. I haven't cried in front of humans since August 2001, and I don't want to change that. Ever. Looking away, I take out my pocket square and dab my eyes. Then, I turn back to look at Tabi's bright eyes and smiling lips. She now has a purpose. And if this name helps her, so be it. But I still need to know.

"Why?"

She holds her hair against the wind and smiles. "Look around you. Look at yourself. Nothing would have happened without Amara, right? Vince, all she ever cared about was you. It wasn't easy for her." Coming close, she kisses my cheek. "The name stays, or I go."

I give her a fractured smile. "Okay."

---

[23]   Jean was mentioned in Chapter 15 of *The Winding* (Book 1). He was Vincent's classmate who often accompanied the bullies. But now, he helps Vince with the legal paperwork—pro-bono as a repentance.

"Amara?" Ravi echoes, tilting his head. "Is she the one in your book about Philip?"

Anna, Chris, and Ravi wait for my response, their eyes wide.

"The same. She was an Armenian prostitute who died in Paris. But the book doesn't say everything." I clear my throat. "In her dying moments, she confessed to Philip that she had a child with one of her suitors. She made Philip promise to take care of that child." I pause, forcing the widest smile possible so my eyes shut and the others don't see the tears forming in them. "And he did by paying for that child's schooling." I gulp my tears. "Amara's last name was Abajian." I pound my chest. "Philip was my invisible guardian."

The wind stops. Anna, Chris, and Ravi stare at me, their mouths gaping.

Chris walks toward Tabi. "You knew all this?"

"Philip's butler and most trusted confidant adopted me as a daughter. I was practically raised in that mansion." She shrugs. "Vince is like an older brother I grew up only hearing about." Tabi takes my hand and wraps it around her shoulder. Looking up at me, she says, "He is so much more than I imagined."

We walk back to the car. Anna and I sit in front while Tabi is sandwiched between Chris and Ravi in the back. As we leave the property, Anna taps on my wrist. "If you ever say you have no family again, I will bust your balls." Curling her lips, she mutters, "Idiot." She gulps.

"Noted."

As I change gears with my hand pushers, Anna leans over and whispers, "Chris is trying to hit on Tabi. Did you see how he opened the door for her?"

"Allow me." I adjust the rearview mirror. "Hey, Tabi, you seeing anyone?"

She scrunches her face. "No."

"Hey, Chris, does that answer your question?"

"What?"

I look at Tabi in the mirror. "He wants to ask you out, but he is intimidated by you."

Staring at Chris now through the rearview mirror, I ask, "What're you waiting for? And if you ever hurt her, I'll make you play tennis against me, with Anna on your side."

Anna and Ravi burst into laughter. Anna looks over her shoulder at Tabi and points at Chris. "You should see this sloth on the tennis court."

Chris hits his knees with his knuckles. "You all suck." Then, he turns to Tabi on his right. "Tabitha, can I take you out to dinner?"

She shrugs. "I can try you out."

Through the rearview mirror, I see Tabi staring at me. Smiling, I say, "I'll get you two a table at the Chez-Giraud."

I press my temple with my right hand, keeping my left on the wheel. When was the last time I was there? With Elise? If so, why do I think I was there just a year back? With who? I see the hazy face of a woman with short hair. Is this a vision of an alternate life? Who is she? Where is she? Is she the same woman I saw while I was playing the piano? I should ask Anna when it's just the two of us.

(Quantum World—Executive conference room)

A week later, we are all sitting in the conference room again. Tabi pushes her glasses up her nose.

"Okay, last order of business. Your new phones are here. You guys need to unlink your social media from your old phone numbers. You're public figures, so your Facebook, Twitter, and Instagram must be professionally managed."

Leaning back, I smile. "I deactivated my accounts a long time back."

Tabi points her finger at me, saying, "You're the face of the firm, so you need them. And we will be professionally managed by a PR firm."

Anna leans toward the table. "What will it have?"

Tabi lists with her fingers, starting with her thumb. "News about product launches, some tech, and economy stuff." Then, she looks at me and taps on the conference table. "There will be nothing about your political views, hobbies, or anything. Let's keep you like a mystery, slowly revealing you along with the product." She packs her folders into her bag and scans our faces. "The PR firm will manage your social and professional media accounts." Pointing at my cell phone, Tabi says, "I haven't copied your contacts from your old phone. Can you do it? And inform your new number?"

Placing the two phones side by side, I say, "Should be easy. Everyone in this room, Fred, Krista, Sasha, Philip, Edward, our lawyers, Jean, Little Paw's." Knocking the table, I confirm, "And copy Ludwig and Athena. That's it." I begin to transfer the numbers.

Anna, Chris, and Ravi share glances with each other. Putting my elbow on the table, I lean forward. "Did I miss someone?"

Anna waves her hands. "No, no," she says. "We were just surprised how easily you remember all the names." Staring at Chris and Ravi, she adds, "Right, guys?"

"Absolutely," confirms Ravi, nodding quickly and glancing at Anna and Chris.

Chris rushes to stand up. Nudging Tabi's shoulder, he asks, "Let's go?"

One by one, the musketeers and Tabi leave my conference room. What are they hiding? Who did I miss? My new phone vibrates with a message from Philip. "Come here. Urgent."

(Philip's mansion)

Philip nudges my shoulder. "No car? How did you get here so quickly?"

I shrug. "I had Ludwig create a mapping schema inside the core. You can use it, too."

"What?" he asks, tilting his head.

I chuckle. "Leave the genius to me. Your resources and my abilities, remember?" I point at his TV in his study. "So, where is this footage from?"

Philip stares at the screen. "Underground hold in my island, where I keep my intreton." He turns to Edward. "I pay a fortune for the special forces there. How did someone get in?"

"Intreton? Didn't your rocket take everything?"

"I kept a bit for assurance—a bargaining chip against rogue governments."

I look straight into his eyes. They are the eyes of the person who raised me, so I must be careful. "Who would go up against you?"

He chuckles. "With that much intreton, no one." Then, putting his palm to my cheek, he says, "Plus, if you ever get injured, I need a good supply. I can't let anything happen to you." He pauses. "Also, I need it for travel inside the core."

"No, you don't. I have always transferred power."

Lifting his brows, he smiles. "What if you stop?"

"That'll never happen," I rebuff, waving my hand in dismissal. "Now, let's look at the footage frame by frame."

We import the CNN footage into Philip's computer, then look for some time stamps. There! A wall clock at 7:30 p.m. is in the background of a frame. I keep moving the frames to get a clue about the date.

Pointing at the screen, I turn to Philip. "So, the guy taking the footage wants to expose you?"

Philip frowns and slaps his hand on the agarwood desk. "Yes!"

Turning to Edward, I ask, "What's his name?"

"He calls himself Vandal."

Zooming in on the skylight in the frame, I see a full moon. Bingo! That'd be two days back.

"Gentlemen, I'll be back in an hour," I say to Philip and Edward before pressing the green button on my bracelet and snapping my fingers.

"Ludwig, show me the underground hold of Philip's island at GMT 7:30 p.m. two days ago."

A giant, hazy image appears. I focus through my intreton-powered lenses, and the view becomes clearer. It is 7:15 p.m., according to the watch Philip made for me. All the guards are in a deep sleep. Maybe Vandal used an anesthetic like methoxypropane.

"Let's get closer to Vandal."

We zoom in. Vandal is scanning the boxes for intreton. I can even see the scan result, which shows each carton holding about ten canisters of intreton. There are about a thousand such boxes. I form a fist and clench my jaw. There is enough intreton in that holding room to start an interplanetary war. What if this Vandal steals them?

"Let's zoom in a bit more."

What is he wearing? Is that an intreton-powered suit like mine? He is not in the core. So, why is he wearing it? Unless . . . he is expecting me.

Turning his head back, he looks over his shoulder, staring at me. Fuck! He can see me. How?

Vandal drops his scanner and points his hands at me. Then, he snaps his fingers, generating sparks! Not as powerful and gravity-breaking as mine, but enough to rupture the walls between the known world and the core.

So, that's what you want, motherfucker?

Shattering the wall, he sprints through with his raised fist, aiming it at my face. I barely dodge and manage to hit his head with my elbow. He falls but stands up quickly and runs away, back toward the wall. He crosses the border of the core, jumps over the intreton boxes, turns, and throws a *shuriken* at me. Then, he vanishes.

The metal star spins through the air, hurtling straight at my head. I can see it in slow motion—the blades flash in the lighting of the hold—and I can hear the whizzing sound as it cuts the air. I snatch the *shuriken* from midair with my thumb and index finger, an inch from my face. I can tell from the color and texture that it's an alloy made primarily from intreton. So, he is making weapons. Wait, there is something etched into the weapon's metal.

"We meet at last, Vincent. I'm Vandal—a word I learned from you. Remember?"

I raise my eyes.

No, I don't remember. Who are you? You knew I'd come. You came prepared two days past, waiting for me with this shuriken *and wearing that suit.*

Snapping, I exit Philip's hold.

(Philip's mansion)

"Please explain this." I hand over the *shuriken* to Philip. After closely inspecting it under his magnifying glass, he gives it to Edward.

Edward squints at the writing, then looks at me. "Someone from your past?"

I shake my head. "I can't recall. But he can break the walls between the core and reality." With my hands on my waist, I say, "And he can snap and make sparks. How does he have my powers or Philip's?"

Philip looks at Edward, then at me. He shrugs. "Have you transferred it to anyone?"

"Just you." I point at the *shuriken*. "The way he threw that shows he has been practicing for decades." Shaking my head, I murmur, "I don't know how I caught it."

Philip grins. "I know how you did." He goes to his display case and fetches a *katana*. "This is Musashi Miyamoto's *katana*. He became a time corrector for a brief period while fighting Kojirō Sasaki. His skills are in you. And when you take this *katana* out of this *saya*, they will be activated." He gives me a hard stare. "Time to up the game."

As soon as I hold the sword, the blood in my veins surges as it flows through my body, making my pulse race. As my bones crack and readjust their joints, I shut my eyes in pain, my muscles realigning to become one with the sword. The pain disappears.

Smirking, I look at Philip. "Thank you. I need to work on my fighting skills."

Philip points his finger at me. "I need your opinion on something."

I sit across from his desk while still admiring my new possession. "What?" I ask.

"Can we commercialize the sparks from the core?"

My jaw drops. "That's pure intreton—the stabler kind, right? But it can be weaponized."

Smiling, he explains, "Not weapons . . . but creating a market for an alternate reality for people."

"Like what?"

He leans back and closes his eyes for a moment. Then, snapping his fingers, he opens his eyes again. "People use VR or doping to escape the drudgery of their lives. But, eventually, they have to face reality—bad spouse, abusive family." Frowning, he poses, "What are their options? Lengthy divorce or living through the pain? We can save them by offering life in the same property but different realities."

"You want to take away the consequences of actions? You want to take away the beauty that comes from pain?" Standing up, I put my hands on his desk and lean forward. "No more art, literature, invention arising from pain?"

Philip waves his hand at me. "Relax, Vince. Sit." As I sit back down, he explains, "Not everyone could afford it. And those who could are rarely artists or scientists."

"Why haven't you done it already?" I ask, crossing my arms.

He cuts a wry smile. "Requires a different power level."

"But I transfer my power while I am in the core."

He admits, "You can commercialize it with your current power level." Sighing, he adds, "But if you want someone else to do it, you must transfer all your power. And to do that, you need a power level far beyond what you have now."

"When will I have it?"

"It will come to you."

Is this the same power the future Vincent was referring to—the level I will have on April 13, 2027?

(Dojo)

Three of Dojima's finest are down, writhing in pain—one holding his chest, another his shin bone, and the third gripping his wrist. My two *bokkens* have pierced their protective gear. They were down in a fraction of a second.

How did I do that?

Dojima inspects my *bokkens*—one the size of a *katana* and one that resembles the *wakizashi*. He states, "Only an expert in *Hyōhō Niten Ichi-ryū* can do this." Holding my hands, he asks, "Have you been practicing it? Did you read Musashi's *Book of Five Rings*?"

(Vincent's home)

As he rests on my lap, I run my fingers over Hulk's head. "I'm sorry, bud. I had to leave for a bit."

I switch on the TV. The news anchor from CNN narrates.

"Vandal's claim that Philip Nardin is sitting in a pile of weapon-grade intreton is a hoax. Those were intreton-C for energy and medical purposes. Mr. Nardin's lawyers and the directors of the CIA, Homeland Security, and Secretary of Defense confirmed the video was false. Those boxes had no intreton. We have a senior political analyst, a criminal psychologist, and the author of the book . . ."

I switch off the TV and take my cell phone out to call Philip.

"How did you manage that?" I say when he answers.

"I gave the Secretary of Defense a choice: conscience versus a retirement package containing a yacht, a private jet, and a mansion in the Hamptons. Politicians talk about doing the right thing till they see the green. Add an offshore account and house in Malibu. POTUS himself would polish my shoes with his tongue."

"I bet he already does," I joke. "What about the directors of Homeland Security and the CIA?"

"Even easier. One is closet gay, and the other has children with the nanny."

"How do you know all this?"

Philip chuckles. "I have eyes on everyone."

So, you're not the virtuous man I thought you were. But I'm on your side and will continue to be. Though, I am not sure about your proposal to commercialize the sparks.

Out loud, I say, "You've kept a lot of intreton."

"The core continuously produces intreton. And I need to collect it and store it before someone else does. Do you think the DoD, the Russians, or the Chinese are better suited for this?"

"No."

"Did you give my proposal a thought?"

"Not yet. Good night, Philip."

Mistakes make us who we are. Taking that away from us means no more suffering. We simply can't choose a reality that suits us, ignoring our faults. What's next—criminals choosing a different reality to avoid a penalty?

I nuzzle my nose against Hulk's. "Sleepytime?" I ask.

Hulk follows me to the unfurnished main bedroom. I have tried to sleep in some guest rooms, but I have weird dreams about the same woman. In those dreams, she is sleeping next to me.

I unfold my sleeping bag on the floor and crawl inside it. Hulk curls himself around my head. Lying there, I scan through Musashi's *The Book of Five Rings*. Why does it seem like I know the content before even reading it? Perhaps because Musashi's memories are in me. Setting the book aside, I press my temples hard.

Staring at the ceiling, I ask, "Ludwig, can you play Chopin's fourth?"

From my Bower & Wilkins surround speakers comes Ludwig's voice. "Certainly."

The notes flow through the bedroom. I have no idea why my eyes are flooded with tears each time I hear this. Yet, I'm so drawn to this opus. The music is trying to tell me something, but I can't decipher the memories hidden in the notes. Hulk puts his head on my forehead and licks away my tears. Why is the reset time in my wristwatches and clocks on August 3, 2023? Why was the call history on my old phone empty before August 30?

One day at a time, Vince.

Taking a deep breath, I say, "Lights off."

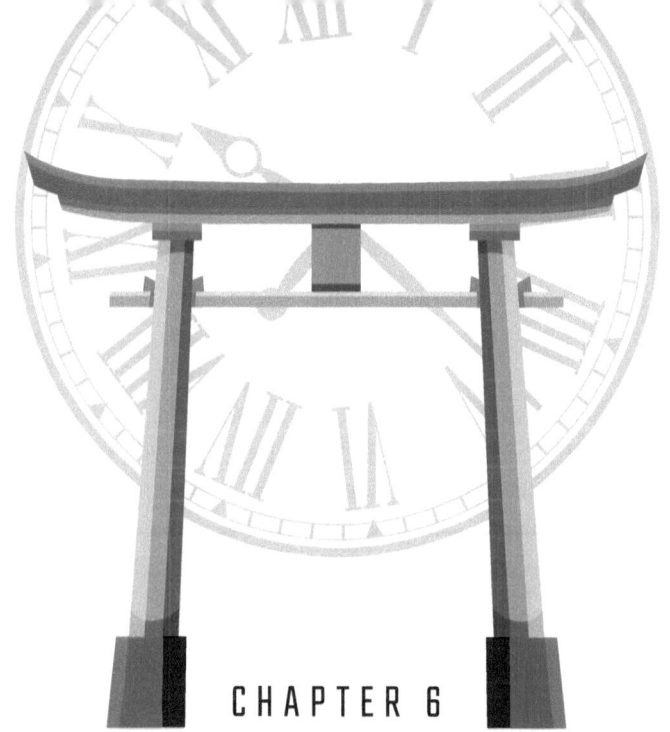

CHAPTER 6

FLURRIES

*It's possible because the girl on my right returned before the first
day of flurries, as she had promised thirty-three years ago*
—Vincent

November 15, 2024–August 2025

(November 15, 2024)

<u>Vincent</u>

APRIL 13, 1612. KOJIRŌ LEAPS toward me with an overhead strike, swinging with surgical precision. The blade of his *katana* swishes against the wind and cuts through strands of my hair. I see these in slow motion as the shrill of the blade piercing through the air rings in my ear. If I stood a little taller, then I'd be dead. I have less than a microsecond, but why am I not striking him? I shut my eyes as the afternoon sun pierces through them. I see a girl with silver hair telling me, "I'm trying to find you."

Why is my mind taking me to a composer in a world I don't know? It's 1842, and the floor is filled with hundreds of crumpled, torn pieces of paper. The music is simply not flowing through my fingers. How can I write it if I don't hear it? As I close my eyes, a girl with silver hair cries and tells me, "I'm trying to find you."

My mind takes me inside an Argentine race in something called an automobile. It's the 1957 German Grand Prix, and Hawthorn is catching up with me. Suddenly, a girl with silver hair appears in the seat next to me and says, "I'm trying to find you."

Is it 1989? I'm sitting in a classroom, solving a math problem. Abruptly, a ray of light pierces through the clouds outside and shines on a girl whose silky hair is held back by a pair of jade chopsticks. She shimmers brighter than the light that shines on her. She comes toward me, her apple-red lips smiling and her reddish-brown eyes glimmering.

"Found you."

Then, massive turbulence engulfs her as I fall to Kojirō's strike, and I tear another piece of paper and hit the piano keys with my knuckles. The sound pulsates through time and resonates in my ears in 1957 as Hawthorn wins the corner, and I cover my ear with one hand while keeping hold of the steering wheel with the other.

It's 2007, and I'm chasing a girl in a hoodie who has been stalking me for over a year. I yell, "Who are you?" She runs toward Harvard.

It's 2024, and I see a short-bob-haired woman getting inside a Toyota Camry outside my house. Tears flood her eyes as she waves her hand.

"See you later, Vincent."

I'm awake, and Hulk is panting on me. Akane is Estrid? Who was the girl heading toward Harvard and the woman outside my house?

Why can't I eat breakfast at home? I just prefer to kill my appetite with a doppio. But I don't feel this way elsewhere.

I'm sitting on the piano bench in front of the Steinway. I keep Akane's scarf, her violin, and our photograph on top of the piano.

It's been thirty-three years since you disappeared. I have combined two short pieces by Liszt—Liebestraum No. 3 and Consolation No. 3. I call it "Akane no uta."[24]

I pull the bench closer to the keys, and Hulk sits by my feet. As I start with Liebestrum, drops of tears form in my eyes.

(Mid-August 1991—Cafeteria lunch)

I took out the last rubber band from my hair. This one was pink. Sasha stretched her arms and batted her eyes.

"That is mine."

I handed it to her, along with Krista's white one and Akane's red one.

Akane lifted her shoulders, smiling. "It was my idea when you dozed off in history class." Fred, Krista, and Sasha pressed their lips together, trying not to laugh.

I scowled. "Now I know why everyone was laughing at me."

Rubbing my hair, Krista said, "None of us have your wavy and curly hair." She smiled mischievously. "You look like a girl."

While I gave her the stink eye, Akane touched my shoulder and apologized. "*Gomenasai.*" Her bright eyes stared into mine, then she nuzzled her nose against mine. "I'll make it up to you on your birthday." Pulling me by my cheeks, she kissed my forehead and declared, "*Watashi no,* Vince." Then, she tugged my sleeve and asked, "Will you miss me tying rubber bands if I get lost?"

I felt a cold breeze chill my bones. I took her by the arms and shook her. "Why would you say that? Why would you leave me?" My breathing got frenzied—almost hyperventilating.

"What's wrong, bud?" Fred demanded. His eyes look worried.

Moving her hand left to right, Akane instructed Fred, "Shh." She gently rubbed my hand. "We are all here. I am here as long as you want. Okay, silly?"

---

[24] Song of Akane.

Sniffling, I pleaded, "Please don't get lost." Turning to Fred, Krista, and Sasha, I said, "I have no one except you guys."

Wrapping her arms around my neck, Akane assured me, "I will never leave."

The others joined in, saying, "Promise."

(Back to the present)

I scoff. Some promise! I had no one except those four, and in a few months, it was just three. And then, I removed myself from those three. At least we still keep in touch via phone.

You were gone, and I kept moving from one place to another, hoping for a miracle. And then, after so many years, I just gave up. I will mend the bond I fractured with Fred, Krista, and Sasha when I visit Copenhagen. Although Fred, Krista, and Sasha never bring you up, you are always on my mind.

I switch my left and right wrists and conclude the Liebestrum.

I take a deep breath and begin playing Consolation No. 3 with my eyes shut tight, trying to hold back my tears.

Do you remember holding a blue tux inside a purple parcel the first time I heard this? I'd always hoped that when this music is in the background one day, there would be three consecutive knocks on the door, and I'd open it to see you. I have given up on that hope.

As I key the final note of Consolation No. 3, I hear a pecking on my glass windows. Opening my eyes, I turn, and there is the red robin. I wipe my eyes and inhale deeply.

Never thought I'd see you again. When was the last time?

Then, my doorbell rings three times in succession as it flies away. I roll my hand into a fist and clench my jaw. "It better not be the Jehovah's witness." Pushing back the piano bench, I stand up and turn to the door. Hulk remains lying by the piano bench.

Upon opening the door, I see the back of a petite woman whose long hair is held back in a bun by two jade chopsticks. I gulp. This can't be! She is dressed in a Burberry trench coat and bespoke six-inch-high heels. Is it her? How?

Not knowing the nature of this trick, I blurt out with a shaky voice, "Are you lost?"

My jaw drops as she turns around. Her smile is radiant, from her beaming lips to her glinting eyes flickering in restrained tears. She locks her gaze with mine, then brings her hands to her mouth and breathes deeply.

What trick is this? I look at my JLC Reverso. It's ticking—six ticks per second. So, we are not removed from reality. As I look back at her face, my tears gush as if they were waiting for this moment.

I know your face; it stands out among millions in Shibuya. It's deeply etched in my memory. I have sketched your face, imagining how you might look growing up. And boy, was I right. I don't cry before humans, but you are everything.

Her face gets all blurry as tears block my eyes.

But I can't rub my eyes; what if, at that moment, you disappear again?

I want to hold this image forever. If this is a dream, then I don't want to wake up. How did this happen? Is it linked to my first trip to the core, which I faintly remember? I don't care how or why. My nature to seek logic is diminished because of the miracle before my eyes.

Blinking back her tears, she comes closer and grabs the lapel of my robe. Smiling, she tilts her head and says, "Not anymore."

Flurries begin to drop—gently savoring every last second of the air before reaching the earth and disappearing. She drops her trench coat on the bluestone patio. I see her wristwatch—a platinum Philippe Dufour. Her skin glows against her short-sleeved, cobalt-blue, bell-bottomed jumpsuit. The belt, tied like a bow on the right side of her waist, is made from the same cloth. She shimmers, brighter than her platinum bracelet lined with an array of two-carat diamonds. She takes off her jade chopsticks, and her silky hair falls to her waist. Stepping back into the open, she twirls around and lets the flurries touch her slender arms. Each flurry sparkles and glints as they get close to her skin. Light shimmers more brightly around her.

She turns to me and smiles, squeezing her eyes into two lines of thick eyelashes. Opening her eyes wide, she says, "I told you I'd be back before the flurries, right?"

I fall to my knees. I shut my eyes as every moment without her reflects back at me. My voice trembles as I respond, "You left out the thirty-three years part." When I look up at her, she touches my head. "I told you not to go," I rasp. "How could you just leave me like that? I kept waiting and waiting. How could you be so cruel, Akane? Are you gonna disappear again?"

This is the first time the flurries are touching my skin since she left me. I forgot what they looked like, what they felt like. I open my palm to see the flurries drop, float on my tears, and dissolve.

She kneels before me and kisses my forehead, eyes, cheeks, and lips. Wrapping her arms around me, she rests my head against her shoulder. Her essence—black orchid, black truffle, and patchouli. She runs her fingers through my hair.

Whispering, she assures me, "I'll sit with you as long as you need." Pushing my head back, she looks into my eyes, then touches my cheek. "I'll never leave you again. *Watashi no ai. Watashi no amai*, Vincent."[25] Tugging my lapel, she says, "Found you, silly."

Resting my head on her petite shoulder, I close my eyes.

Miyamoto Musashi dodges a second blow as air displaced from Kojirō's *katana* whips his eyes. Musashi hits Kojirō Sasaki's head with lightning speed, breaking his skull. The tears on Chopin's piano begin to glow one by one, and his fingers follow them. He completes his Ballade No. 4, Op. 52. Juan Manuel Fangio steps on the accelerator of his Maserati, takes a risky corner, leaves Mike Hawthorn in his Ferrari seconds behind, and wins the German Grand Prix.

But the girl in the hoodie unveils her face before heading back to Harvard. Akane? Her clothes transform into a pink, floral kimono with a maroon obi. The scene changes from Cambridge, Massachusetts, to a shrine in Kyoto. She is standing with a *torii*-shaped wooden prayer plaque—*ema*. The *ema* has my name in katakana, and hers is in *kanji*.

Smiling, she asks, "Looking for this?"

A short-bob-haired, glowing woman is smiling at her newborn. As I walk closer, I see the baby has my eyes. The woman smiles through her tear-stained face. "I am sorry for breaking up with you and letting someone else take your place. I thought you moved on, so I didn't stay . . ."

---

25   My love. My sweet Vincent.

I touch her head and look into her eyes. "There's nothing to apologize for. Just hang in there. When the petals fall, I'll be back home—just a day for me but a little longer for you."

Why is Akane at Harvard? Who is the lady in the hospital? Who is that baby? Why does she have my eyes? Why can't I simply enjoy the miracle before me? Yes, I have everything I want right before me. I should live in the present and let the past figure out a way to match the future.

Standing up, I pull Akane with me. My tears are gone, and I can see the face I've searched for all my life—those large, burnt-sienna eyes, the beautiful mole above her lips, and those apple-red lips.

Smiling, she teases, "Won't you invite me in?"

"I'm so sorry. Please come in."

Picking up her trench coat from the patio, she waves behind her at a Maybach in the driveway. Two giants open the trunk and start to unload her luggage.

I ask, "Are they also coming in?"

Placing her hand on her mouth, she shakes her head. "No, silly. They'll be in a hotel nearby."

Upon entering the house, her eyes widen with joy. She turns to me. "You've done well."

Hulk tilts his head, then runs toward Akane as if he already knows her. Waving both her hands, Akane squeals, "*Kawaii.*" She gets down and picks him up, letting Hulk lick her face. Nuzzling her nose against Hulk's, she asks, "What's his name?"

"Hulk."

When she places him on the floor, Hulk licks her feet, then tilts his head contemplatively. He goes back to his bed and keeps looking at her. Then, he again runs toward her. She picks him up again, looking at me.

"Do I remind him of someone?"

"No idea. Are you hungry?"

"Not now. But I would like to cook with you. You remember the culinary club?"

I place my hand against her cheek and then hug her tight. "Yes."

Sitting barely an inch from me, with her legs folded on the sectional, Akane, dressed in an olive-green jumpsuit, meticulously picks strands of my hair, curls them with her thumb and index finger, and moves on to another strand.

Anna, Maddy, and Tabi have their lips pressed together, trying not to laugh at my predicament.

Ravi rests his chin on his hand and leans toward us. "So, ten years in a coma? And then twenty-three years with no memory of the past?"

Akane tucks her long hair behind her ears. "Yes, Ravi." She bites her trembling bottom lip, fishes my pocket square, and dabs the corner of her eyes. "Because of my mental collapse, I could not attend university. So, my parents brought the *daigaku* home."

She rests her head on her palms and keeps quiet. The pin drop silence is punctuated only by the cicadas, the ticking of the clocks, and Hulk's whimpering as he rests on Anna's lap.

Akane sniffles and rubs the bottom of her nose. "*Gomennasai.*[26] It's not easy to sit on the Egami board, being a woman and only half Japanese. Having no formal qualifications makes it harder. The board will pick one of my useless cousins to be the CEO when Papha retires." She scoffs. "They will run the firm to the ground." Then, she looks at Maddy, Ravi, Chris, Tabi, Anna, and me. "My Vince and you are all so accomplished. And I am so uneducated."

Tabi pumps her inhaler, then comes forward and holds Akane's hands, sitting next to her. "You're Vincent's Akane, and that is enough for us."

Akane lifts a finger to her cheek and swipes a tear. "Thank you."

"We are just dysfunctional people hiding behind some academic degrees," Chris chimes in.

Placing Hulk on the floor, Anna approaches Akane, touches her shoulder, and rolls her eyes. "Besides, your Vince thinks we are all uneducated, anyway."

"Huh?" Akane asks, squinting.

---

[26]   I'm sorry.

Anna furrows her brows at me. "According to Vince, you're uneducated if you don't go to Cambridge or MIT. Or if you can't recognize symphonies by the first one or two notes," Anna grumbles, pointing her finger at me while looking at Akane. "And listen to this. You're uneducated if you can't hear the sound of brushstrokes in a painting hanging at a gallery." Anna kisses Akane's head and hugs her, assuring her, "You're home, sister."

Glaring at Anna, I wag my finger. "I'm not like that."

Everyone except Akane and Maddy leans a little forward and speaks out. "Really?"

"Wow."

"Sure, Vincent."

"Next time, we'll record you."

Akane looks around and tilts her head. "When I'm in the US, can I shadow you guys to learn how your business works? Ours is too diversified and complicated for me now." She clasps her hands and bows her head. "It will be a great honor for me. I just need the experience."

Touching Akane's shoulders, Anna says, "Of course. Welcome aboard!"

As the clock strikes six, Chris pours another glass of Balvenie 26. Smacking his lips after his first sip, he turns to Akane. "So, when did you get your memories back?"

Akane's eyes light up. "August 14, afternoon, Japan time."

So, that would be the night of August 13, Seattle time. That was the day I became a time corrector. But I don't remember how. Do my actions that night have anything to do with her coming back? I take her hand and kiss it.

Akane smiles. "I remembered this guy as a child." Wrapping her arms around me, she continues, "Then, I saw him on TV and bought his book. Since that day, all I wanted was to meet him."

Maddy tilts her head. "You came alone?"

Pointing at the door, I turn to Maddy. "You haven't seen two tree-sized humans outside? Masato and Michisato—her bodyguards. They are bigger than my Yoshino cherry trees."

Leaning away from me, Akane glances at me from an angle. "You have cherry trees on your property?"

"I have fifteen."

She sighs happily. "I love sakura."

Smiling, I say, "Maybe that's why I bought this house."

Anna clears her throat and glances at Ravi and Chris. They, too, clear their throats.[27]

"What are you hiding?" I ask, glaring at them.

Anna bites her nails. "Nothing, Vince." Then, she bats her eyes. "What you said was so romantic."

"What's wrong with you?" Then, I point at my watch and ask, "Who's hungry?"

Everyone except Akane raises their hand.

"How about Sichuan Palace? We haven't been there since Elise."

Ravi clears his throat. "Ahem! Yep, that's right. Let's go there."[28]

I glare at Ravi. "Again?" I turn to everyone. "What's with the throat clearing?"

Anna quickly jumps in front of me. "No, no. No, no. It's just a little cold here, that's all." Rubbing her arms, she adds, "Brrr."

Rolling my eyes, I quip, "Truly Oscar-worthy."

They are hiding something. But, right now, I don't care.

Coming out of the bathroom in her bathrobe, Akane enters the main bedroom and sits beside my sleeping bag. Placing her hand over mine, she asks, "Why haven't you furnished this room?"

"The other rooms were furnished when I bought this place. I never got to this one."

Locking her eyes with mine, she asks, "In your TV interview on August 15, you said your love was unrequited." She squints at me. "Who is she?"

I look blankly at the floor. "I don't remember," I murmur, touching my head. "My memories around the last fifteen months are a bit hazy." Kissing her fingers, I say, "And, frankly, I don't care." She puts her hand under my chin and lifts my face. "You can tell me anything," she assures me.

---

27 In *The Winding* (Book 1), Vince bought the house with Emika, but he doesn't remember that.

28 In *The Winding* (Book 1), when Emika joined, they all celebrated her addition to the team at the Sichuan Palace. That was eight months after Elise passed away.

I breathe in deeply, staring at the Cascades glowing under the moonlight. "When you bought me my tux and called me family, I didn't know what to do. I didn't know what to do when you tied that scarf around me, and you stayed with me every day in the infirmary till I healed. I didn't know what to do when you played that violin on my eighth birthday." I pause, closing my eyes. "By the time I realized the true nature of my feelings . . ." I sniffle. "It was too late." I open my eyes to look into hers. "And now that you're here, I'm still that silly Vince, who doesn't know what to do."

She takes my hands. "My turn. There was something so different about you than all our classmates. You hid your sketchbook from others, but you showed it to me. You patiently listened to my violin practice, and I loved seeing you draw and study. I noted the names of the books you borrowed from the library. When I gave the list to Papha, he thought I'd be a mathematician or an artist." Shrugging, she smiles. "I just wanted to feel close to you during vacations. I couldn't be with you, but I could at least read what you were reading." She squeezes my hands. "Vacations were lonely! That's why I wanted you to sketch me for my birthday. I wanted to feel your presence through your pencil strokes." Then, she lifts her palm to my cheek. "Maybe we can do something to reduce your confusion."

"What?"

"To start, why don't we stop using different bedrooms? It's been five days already."

"I'd like that very much."

Running her fingers through my hair, she teases, "Silly."

(Akane's G700)

A stewardess leans over me. "Would you like some champagne, sir?"

I nod, pointing at Akane. "Only if she is."

Tilting her head, Akane asks, "Are you comfortable?"

"I'm glad you made me cancel my flight." Placing my hands behind my head, I survey the interior of her G700. Stretching my legs, I smile. "This is so much better than first class."

Once again, Akane is in a bespoke jumpsuit—a chartreuse yellow one this time. The stewardess places two champagne glasses on the table in front of us.

"Why did you leave the perimeter and walk close to the clock into the turbulence all those years ago?" I ask.

She smiles. "I thought I saw you inside the light."

"What?" How would my image appear? Does Philip know anything about it?

She points at my empty lap, saying, "We could have gotten Hulk."

"I don't want to take chances in a pressurized cabin. Besides, Anna loves him."

"*Sokka.*" Then, she leans back and squints at me. "Why were Ravi, Anna, and Chris staring at each other when I ordered mango and green tea mochi?"[29]

"I don't care." I lean forward and take her hands. Is she truly Estrid? Kissing her hand, I ask, "Did it ever occur to you that you may have known me before meeting me?"

She closes her eyes, takes a deep breath, and bites her trembling bottom lip. "The day I saw you for the first time in school, I felt I may have known you all along." Smiling, she points at my eyes. "Especially those large, green-blue eyes."

"What?"

"I don't want to talk about it right now. Let's do something else." Leaving her seat, she comes to mine, saying, "Scoot."

I move over a bit, and she sits on my lap, hugging me tightly. She nestles her head into my neck and whispers, "I won't move."

"I'd like to see you try."

(Thyme & Cumin, Copenhagen)

As my tongue touches the savory scallop ceviche, tempered with sweet and tart mangoes, Anika, our waitress at Thyme & Cumin, shows up. Bending

---

[29]   In Chapter 4 of *The Winding* (Book 1), Emika orders the same.

slightly, she asks, "Everything okay, Mr. Van Gogh?" That's my cover name—Pablo Van Gogh.

I take a bite and look up at the smiling blonde. "Can you ask your chef how the taste will change if she substitutes the black peppers with Sichuan peppercorn and the salt with aged soy sauce?"

"Absolutely, sir." She hastens back to the kitchen.

Across the table, Akane is covering her face and laughing. Her cover name—Hana Hokusai. She has concealed her looks with oversized sunglasses and a scarf.

Sasha Chen's voice can be heard over the pots, pans, and sizzling flambe. "What? Must be a reviewer. Let me check."

I move closer to the kitchen door, four feet from my table. Sasha comes out with a butcher's knife and places her chef's hat on a table. She smiles and walks toward me. When I step under the light, she stops. Her smile morphs into a frown, and her dark-brown iris hardens, turning to daggers. Baring her teeth while keeping her eyes on me, she shoves her knife into a log-style table.

This is the day Vincent dies.

Lifting her shoulder-length black hair, she ties it into a bun with a green hairband. She flares her nostrils as she starts walking toward me again. Sniffling, she says, "So, this is how you will play it. First, you disappear for twenty-three years. Now, you show up as someone else."

She comes close, stretches her arms, and pushes me. "What did we do wrong?"

My voice cracks. "Nothing." I try to touch her hands.

Tears form at the corner of her eyes. "Don't touch me." She pushes me again, and I step back. "You didn't come to my wedding."

I remain standing. "I'm sorry!"

Again, she pushes me. "You never showed up when we opened this place when we got our first Michelin star."

I bend my head down.

Anika comes running. Standing between Sasha and me, breathing quickly, she reminds Sasha, "We shouldn't hit customers."

Moving Anika aside with her right hand, Sasha says, "Customer, my ass; he is my brother." She grabs my ear, pulls my face down next to hers, and turns to Anika. "Don't you see the resemblance?"

Squinting, Anika desperately tries to find similarities between an Abajian and a Chen. Fuming at her ignorance, Sasha screeches, "Oh, for fuck's sake, get Krista now."

Panting, Anika runs toward the kitchen.

Pulling my lapel, Sasha shakes me as tears roll from her eyes and cover her cheeks. Sobbing, she asks, "Why did you disappear?" Then, she stands on her toes and pulls my head down. She stares at my face for a few moments, then kisses my forehead and cheeks before wrapping her arms around my neck. Her voice cracks as she whispers, "I missed you so much." I kiss the top of her head and shut my eyes tight, keeping my tears in.

"What's going on?"

I lift my head and see the other chef untying her long, platinum-blonde hair—the Galadriel of our school. She takes two steps and raises her eyebrows, and her blue eyes glow brighter. Her voice trembles as she utters, "Vin?"

She drops her chef's cap and runs toward me. Moving Sasha aside, she jumps, hanging from my neck. As she kisses my cheeks and forehead, I sigh with relief; Krista is far more composed than her wife. Then, she lets me go as her smiling lips crumple and her nostrils flare. Her pale face turns red as she glares at me. Before I even realize it, she slaps my right cheek.

As I touch my stinging cheek, Krista grumbles, "That was for not keeping in touch beyond texting." She tugs my lapel. "You couldn't drop in your sorry-ass face once?" Shaking me, she demands, "Even our wedding?" Another slap, this time on the left cheek. "I was there for you . . . we were there for you." She lines up for a third slap, but someone grabs her wrist, pleading for her to stop.

"Please don't hurt my Vincent," Akane says, removing her sunglasses and scarf.

Sasha and Krista let go of their prey and move toward Akane, their eyes wide in shock. Shaking, Krista mutters, "What? The. Fuck? How?"

Turning to me, Sasha asks, "How did this happen?"

I shake my head. "She found me. Like always."

(Krista's and Sasha's house, Copenhagen)

Krista's and Sasha's abode is a Bauhaus-inspired, minimalist duplex apartment. While Akane tells them her story, I walk around the duplex. The shelves are filled with Krista's and Sasha's wedding pictures. As I look across them, I see photos of our graduation and photos from our play where I played Gandalf and Fred was Saruman. My lips wobble, and my breathing quickens as my eyes fall on my school trophies, glistening in the light. Breathing hard, I run my fingers over them. The alloys are sparkling; Krista and Sasha kept them like new.

(August 2001, a day before graduation—Dorm room)

Fred stared outside the window, sniffling while denying it was the end of an era. I zipped my patched, secondhand duffel bag, which once belonged to David Kruger. Krista pointed at my karate, chess, art, culinary, and math trophies.

"Won't you pack them?" she asked.

I shrugged. "No space in the bag." Scoffing, I explained, "No home to keep them. No parents to cherish them."

Sasha lifts her finger. "Shut up!" Placing her hands on my cheeks, she asks, "Um, how about Krista and I take them to Le Cordon Bleu?"

"You will?" I asked, my voice cracking.

They both hugged me. Krista assured me, "We'll treat them as our own. We will cherish them." Her eyes welled up. "Promise me you will come and check on them."

"I will."

(Back to the present)

Lifting my left arm, Sasha tucks herself into my side and wraps her arm around my waist. She wipes my tears and says, "While you carried Akane's artifacts, we took care of yours." She points at the trophies and asks, "You wanna take them with you?"

My voice croaks. "This is their home."

Akane's and Krista's eyes are fixed on us. As soon as my eyes lock with Krista's, she turns toward the window. The setting sun glows on her blue eyes. She scoffs, her arms crossed.

"Come and check on them after another twenty-three years. We will have them shiny as new. What else are we good for?"

Sasha warns Krista, "Enough already."

I sit on the floor by Krista's chair and take her hand. "Please?"

She still doesn't look at me. "You're famous and brilliant. We are expendables, so you didn't keep in touch. Why would you beg for my forgiveness?"

While Akane shakes her head, Sasha yells from the kitchen, "Don't stretch it!"

I wrap Krista's hair around my face like a beard. "Hey, Galadriel, look. I'm Gandalf the White, begging for your forgiveness." Then, I point at my hair. "Tie as many rubber bands in it as you want. I will never complain."

Krista narrows her eyes at me. "Promise?"

"Promise."

Krista's lips break into a smile, contrasting her wet eyes. She squeezes both my cheeks, and my lips pucker like a goldfish. Smiling, she says, "You haven't grown one bit."

Sitting next to Akane, I say, "I'm tired of playing the grown-up for over two decades now."

I hear a thumping noise outside the door. Getting up, I declare, "Fred is here."

"Let him ring the doorbell," Sasha says with a smirk. "That'll be some workout for him."

Sasha gets up to answer the doorbell. Fred enters, thumping on the wooden floor. He then drops his luggage, and we all greet him. Akane remains back, as per our plan. He hugs Krista and Sasha and then glares at me.

I raise my hands, palms out. "My face is already sore from being slapped."

He smirks. Waving his hand in dismissal and faking a smile, he assures me, "Water under the bridge." He comes forward and hugs me with his massive arms. A little tighter, and my ribs will crack.

He lets me go, fetches a Heineken from the fridge, and sits in the living room. The chair screeches against his weight. Then, he looks at Akane and remarks nonchalantly, "Hey, what's up?" before taking a beer chug.

Tilting her head, Akane responds, "Nice to meet you, Fred."

Fred furrows his eyebrows and stops chugging. Eyes stretched wide, he turns to Akane again. Coughing, he spits out the beer. I laugh so hard I have to grab my belly.

While smiling mischievously, Sasha, patting Fred's back, inquires, "You okay?"

"The fuck!" Fred shouts, leaving his chair and approaching Akane. Pointing his index finger, he scolds, "Next time, give us a warning before we have to raise a needy, eight-year-old genius."

Akane bends her head. "I'm sorry."

Pointing at me, Fred says, "He never smiled. Sasha, Krista, and I became his clowns, parents, and siblings. Kruger's hairs became all gray by 1992."

Krista pulls down Fred's pointing arm and places it at his side. "That's enough."

Fred fetches a handkerchief from his pocket and wipes the residual beer from his face. Then, he looks at Akane again. "Give me a hug."

Akane gets lost in Fred's arms as he swings her. Kissing Akane's head, he admits, "I missed you, too. You were the sweetest in our group."

Lifting their arms in protest, Krista and Sasha shout, "Hey!"

(Bedroom)

I'm in my MIT sweats, and Akane is in her silver satin sleepwear. She ties her hair up, gets under the covers, and looks into my eyes. As I touch her neck, there is a knock on the door.

"Are you guys busy?"

Akane whispers to me, "Throw me your robe." Stretching my hand to reach the chair next to the bed, I hand Akane my robe. She wraps herself in my robe, then says, "Come in."

All three of them walk in. Smiling sheepishly, Sasha asks, "Um, could we chat till dawn? Like we did after sneaking into Vince and Fred's dorm room, you know?"

Akane and I fold our legs. "Sure," Akane says.

Sasha and Krista jump onto the bed, and Fred lounges on the chair, propping his feet on the bed.

(1990—Dorm room)

Akane, Krista, and Sasha hid under the beds when there was a knock on the door. Scooting down, I saw the first two puff their cheeks, waiting to exhale, while Sasha bit her nails, waiting to inhale. Fred opened the door, and the dorm room inspector walked in.

Squinting at Fred and me, he said, "I heard noises."

Clasping my hands in front of me, I said, "Sir, it was Fred and me rehearsing."

"Don't stay up too late." The inspector shut the door and left.

The girls began to breathe and crawled out from under the beds. Fred put his finger on his mouth as they were about to talk. "Shhh. No girl voices."

With my hands on my waist, I glared at Fred. "We are kids. We all sound like girls."

Fred looked up and snapped his fingers. "Okay, then. Not more than two voices at a time."

All four of us chorused, "Yes."

Fred shook his head in despair.

The doorknob began to turn again, and we brought our hands to our mouths. It was too late to hide. The inspector must have heard us. But when the door opened, we were relieved to see the headmaster, Kruger, not the inspector.

Pushing his black-rimmed glasses higher up his nose, he turned to the girls. "Ah! When the report came that you three were missing, I knew where to look." Wiggling his brows at the three girls, he inquired, "What are you ladies doing here?"

Akane moved forward and clasped her hands, looking up at the head-master with her large, pleading eyes. "My fault, sir. I asked them to come and see Vince and Fred rehearse." Pointing at Krista and Sasha, she implored, "Please don't punish them."

Placing his hand on Akane's tiny shoulder, Mr. Kruger chuckled. "On one condition. I get to watch the rehearsal as well."

I put on my gray beard and Fred his white beard, both of us taking up our staffs.

Glaring at me, Fred declared, "The halfling weed slowed your mind, Vincent." He shook his head, quickly correcting, "Sorry, Gandalf."

Pointing my staff at him, I retorted, "How can you elect madness over reason?"

We then pointed our staff at each other and made sound effects. Mr. Kruger, too, created sound effects.

I fell per the script, and Fred directed his staff at me for the final blow. Suddenly, Akane wrapped herself around me. "Don't hurt Vince."

Fred rolled his eyes. "I wouldn't have."

Mr. Kruger pulled Akane from me and touched her arms. "It's just a play."

Then, he turned his intelligent eyes at the prospective thespians. "You need more rehearsals." He looked at the three girls. "Make sure they call each other by the character names and sound convincing."

Sasha and Krista saluted. "Aye, aye, sir."

He took a deep breath. "You three must leave for your rooms before four o'clock in the morning when it's time for the second inspection."

(Back to the present)

As a child who lacked parental love, home, and warmth, I'd found some purpose that day. Perhaps I'd been born to rehearse with Fred while Akane, Krista, and Sasha watched us. A part of me never left that room and that memory. Sighing in bliss, I scan their faces. I see them as eight-year-olds, with large, wondrous eyes and chubby cheeks, pulling my hand.

"Come back to us. Come back to the room. We have been waiting, and you've gone too far."

As their faces blur behind the curtain of moisture in my eyes, Sasha tugs my hand and asks, "What?"

I wipe my eyes and see them all in their early forties. Krista locks her eyes on mine. "He is just happy, and we are all together."

Clearing his throat and glaring at me, Fred remarks, "Then he shouldn't have—"

Sasha puts her hand over Fred's mouth and says, "Let it go."

(The following day)

The early morning sun shines on Akane, who kicked the blanket away during the night. I run my finger across her face.

She opens her eyes. "What?"

"Just looking."

Pulling my sweatshirt, she tugs me closer. "Is that all you can do?"

Walking into the kitchen, I see the counter filled with potatoes, onions, garlic, seasonal vegetables, olive oil, balsamic vinegar, aged soy sauce, red snapper, flour, and chocolate. Sasha chops onions while wiping her eyes, and Krista mixes chocolate, eggs, and flour. Fred is sitting across the counter, checking his iPad through his reading glass.

The oven timer rings, and Krista takes out a fresh batch of her chocolate caramel cookies. Inhaling, I can see the memories of our baking class. Stretching my arm from the other side of the counter, I go for a cookie as Krista slaps my wrist, lifts her finger, and warns, "Later."

Counting to five, I ask, "How about now?" pouting my lips.

Krista lifts her brows and remarks, "Oh! God. You haven't changed at all." Smiling, she ruffles my hair. Her eyes twinkle in joy as she says, "Love it, though."

Pouring myself some Nordic-roasted brewed coffee from the Chemex, I point at the busy counter. "Need help?"

Sasha tilts her head. "Can you chop onions? Peel potatoes? Debone each snapper and assemble it back together?"

I pull her cheek. "Hey, who taught you all that?"

Grinning, she shows me her middle finger.

Krista looks at Fred, who is still glued to his iPad. "Thanks for all your help, Fatso."

Fred yawns and then peeps over his rimless reading glasses. "What can you guys teach me that three divorces could not?"

Crossing her arms, Sasha retorts, "So, your divorce rate has nothing to do with your zero help in the kitchen." Tapping her chin, she looks up. "Wonder what it is?" Tilting her head, she quips, "Um, is it your clandestine escapades with your secretaries?"

Fred sighs, glancing at his empty beer bottle. "I can't help it."

Krista points at Fred's bottle, rolling her eyes. "Get your fifth one. It's just eight in the morning."

As I start chopping onions, Krista comes to my left side. "So, you and Akane are together, right?"

"Seems that way. Why?"

Sasha comes to the right of me. "I remember how her eyes glowed when she said, 'Found you.'" Rubbing my back, she says, "I'm so glad she finally found you."

Fred places his elbows on the kitchen counter. "Everywhere you were, her eyes were glued to you, while yours were stuck to your books and drawings. Sasha, Krista, and I noticed."

Krista ruffles my hair. "You're incredibly fortunate."

"I know."

Akane shows up in my buffalo-plaid robe. I didn't know the well-lit room could grow any brighter. She hugs Fred, Krista, and Sasha and finally comes and kisses me. Then, she knots her hair into a bun with jade chopsticks. She opens the cabinet with the Lazy Susan, goes through the contents, and fetches a large *tamagoyaki* pan. Shrugging, she says, "I want to make us breakfast."

I stare at Akane and the rest of the gang. Smiling, I say, "This is all so perfect."

(Dinner)

Sitting down for dinner, we get a roasted red snapper with potatoes, onions, and tarragon butter. The starter is a ceviche with Sichuan pepper and aged soy sauce this time. Akane ensures everyone's plate is full before serving herself and then sits on my right. Today, she is wearing a burnt-orange jumpsuit.

On my left is Krista, with Sasha and Fred on the other side of the table. My heart is drumming with joy, and my lips are puzzled between trembling and smiling. Akane cuts a fish, adds some potatoes and a dash of lime to her spoon, and stares at it with a soft smile. She then turns to me.

"Eat, silly."

After a few bites, I look at everyone's smiling, content, happy faces. Sighing, I say, "This is my first Thanksgiving with you guys. You all went home, and I stayed back in school and ate with the custodians."

Stretching her arm across the table, Sasha touches my hand. "I'm so sorry," she says, biting her lip.

"Don't be." I wash my bite down with San Pellegrino sparkling water. "I learned about the other side of our academy. Honest laborers struggling to put food on the table for their families. They stayed back so their families could have a good meal and a better life." I pause for a moment and take another bite. "Being poor, I had more in common with them than my classmates."

Fred glares at me. "All these years as your roommate and not a single word."

"There's more," I sigh.

Krista touches my hand. "Go on."

I take four sips of Chateau Lafite 2001—our high school graduation year. Clearing my throat, I begin, "I helped them clean the library, clean the bedspreads before the school opened." I bite my trembling bottom lip and compose my thoughts. Holding Akane's hand, I stare into her eyes. "After you were gone, from the summer of 1992, I made your bed before the first day the students came back, following summer breaks. I put blue bellflowers in a glass of water by your bedside, hoping you would return and occupy that room." I remind her, "On August 28, 1991,[30] you told me not to forget that it was your favorite flower. Remember?"

Her lips quiver. *"Hai."*

Krista squints at me. "Jeez, Vin . . . Weren't we good enough to tell? Why did you keep all this to yourself?"

With a mouthful of food, Fred smirks. "Apparently not." Then, he chugs an entire bottle of Heineken, resting it next to his wine glass. He clenches his jaw.

What are you marinating, Fred?

"What's to share?" I turn to Akane. "The posters in your room showed the changing taste of time from Madonna to Michael Jackson, Bryan Adams to Backstreet Boys. The only thing that stood the test of time was a bunch of bellflowers in a half-filled water glass on the windowsill, waiting for you to come back."

Fred leans toward Akane. "Every year, when school reopened, he would sneak behind Mr. Kruger to see if you returned. And every year, Sasha, Krista, and I would observe him and escort him to our class. Then, one day, he passed out on his way to class."

Akane puts her silverware down and covers her mouth.

Fred lifts both his hands. "I carried him with my own two arms to the doctor. That day, he became my little brother. We stayed with him all day and all night."

"What did the doctor say?" Akane asks, tears welling in her eyes.

Fred picks up his napkin and confirms, "Starvation. He stopped eating because he knew you wouldn't show up. After that, we closely watched him every moment we were in school."

---

[30] This is mentioned in Chapter 8 of *The Winding* (Book 1).

Touching my left hand, Krista looks at Akane. "Vin never paid any attention to anyone's faces after that."

Holding Krista's hand, I rectify, "Not everyone. Not the ones I already knew." I turn to Akane. "At school, a new face meant nothing if it wasn't yours," I confess, my voice cracking. "Even Philip's face was fuzzy. That's why I could never recall him." I close my eyes. "I saw faces again when I went to Cambridge, but I kept looking for Akane." Pausing, I finish my last bite of the red snapper, then place the silverware on the plate. "Want to know why I distanced myself from you three?"

Krista places her hand over mine. "Only if you want to tell us."

I finish my glass of wine and pour another. "You three were the last to leave for vacations and the first to come back—not just once but from Christmas of 1991 through summer of 2001." Turning to Fred, I say, "You canceled your library date to be with a lonely loser like me. All because I was missing Akane on her birthday." Sasha leaves her seat across the table and sits on the floor beside my chair, touching my hand. Looking at Krista and Sasha, I comment, "Instead of going to a dance, you two decided to stay with me just to watch me play chess by myself."

Akane refills my water glass and offers it to me. "Drink."

I chug the whole glass. "On graduation day, I felt so ashamed when I took the train to Berlin before joining Cambridge. Being poor and worthless, I could not gift you anything for graduation. I had spent all my earnings from waiting tables to buy a book[31] for Mr. Kruger." Running my hands over my eyes, I confess, "I took you three for granted and never entertained the possibility that you may need me. I felt deficient. Maybe my absence could be the best gift for you." I gulp. "Away from me, you could lead a normal, Vince-free life."

Sasha rubs my hand. "Did we ever make you feel ashamed?"

"No," I whisper, bending my head.

Krista kisses my other hand, her tears falling on my skin. "Or deficient?"

My voice cracks as I repeat, "No."

Then, Krista drops my hand. "You ass. The three of us kept debating. Is it something we said? Something we did?" Shaking my shoulder, she

---

[31]   The book is *Watchmaking* by George Daniels, as referenced in Chapter 6 of *The Winding* (Book 1).

says, "We, too, were kids, Vin—trying to play grown-up." She points her finger at me. "Just for you."

I look at her face, blurred through a curtain of tears. "It was all me," I say, wiping my eyes.

We all jump as Fred bangs the table and stands up. His face is red, and his nostrils flare as he glares at me. "All these years, I thought I pushed you away."

"Fred, no," Sasha warns. "Let it go."

"Let him speak," I insist.

Gesticulating wildly with his hands, Fred begins, "Being his roommate, I got the motherload of Vincent. Midnight piano recital on CD, lights on all night, studying or playing chess. And the constant whining . . ." Mocking me, he pitches his voice higher. "'I don't like that music; I like this. That's not art; this is.'" Sitting back down, he finishes his wine and pours some more. "Every year, I thought of requesting a room change."

Staring into his eyes, I ask, "What stopped you?"

He narrows his eyes at me. "Because I love you, motherfucker." After taking a few deep breaths, he continues, "On graduation day, when Sasha and Krista were wasted, I dropped you at the train station. On our way, I thought I would sleep soundly in my dorm room for at least one night before heading to Manchester. Then, you hugged me, and you got on the train." Sniffling, he puts his hand on his shoulder. "I can still feel that hug." He swallows hard. "Then, the train whistled, and you leaned out and waved from the door. I'll never forget the smile on your lips, your tears, and how Akane's scarf was dancing against the wind." Fred wipes the corner of his eye with his napkin and continues, "The train disappeared, taking you with it. Right then, I realized what a stupid dick I was to even link your absence with joy. You were my brother. What if I didn't see you anymore? And boy, was I right. Back in the empty dorm, I couldn't sleep. I was up all night, hoping you'd come switch on the lights, play chess, or listen to some piano drivel and annoy me. What wouldn't I give for one more minute of annoyance? When the morning sun hit the horizon, I ran away. It wasn't the same without you."

Fred's breathing gets heavy as he stands back up. He bangs the dinner table again. "All these years, when I never saw you, I thought it was my fault. Were my thoughts evident in my words? Is that why he doesn't show up? I kept blaming myself." His eyes turn red as he says, "But it was you all along." He leans over the table, catches me by my collar, and pulls me forward. His voice quivers, and his eyes are bulging and wet. "If you ever think of another hiatus, let me know. Because I'll break your skull with my bare hands before you can try it."

Pulling me out of Fred's grip, Sasha shrieks, "Fred!"

Akane is silent, her tears leaving the confinement of her eyes and trickling down to her chin. She now sees the fractured life we lived without her for almost ten years.

Fred wipes his tears and turns to Akane. "Why did you leave us? What was so important about that clock? That turbulence didn't just break Vince. It smashed us all." He points at me. "And we had to grow up fast so that he didn't do anything stupid." Then, he comes around the table. His voice breaks as he hugs me tight. "I'm sorry." Krista and Sasha join in. Fred looks over his shoulder at Akane. "Waiting for a red carpet?"

It's our last evening together, and the five of us are sitting on the docks on the Nyhavn riverbank, with multicolored medieval houses in the background. I'm swinging my legs like a child. I've become one around Akane, Fred, Krista, and Sasha. The wavy locks of my hair are filled with rubber bands. But I don't care how ridiculous I look. Sitting on my right, Akane wraps both her arms around my neck and rests her head on my shoulder. Next to her is Krista, resting her head on Akane's shoulder. On my left is Fred, and on his left is Sasha.

We are quiet, listening to water splashing as it hits the docks, the flapping wings of the seagulls, and the boat horns getting farther away. The sky glows orange, yellow, purple, gray, and blue as we witness an early sunset and the beginning of winter. We wrap our arms around each other. We are not making any childish promises; we don't need to. We know we will always be there for each other. The five of us are now trying to pick up the shattered pieces of our broken childhood and plaster the cracks of fragmented adulthood made by time turbulence. It's possible because the girl on my right returned before the first day of flurries, as she had promised thirty-three years ago.

(Akane's G700)

The steward leaves the 2000 Moet & Chandon Dom Pérignon bottle on the table. I pour Akane and myself a glass. She takes off her Armani Couture overcoat and hands it to the steward.

Staring at her charcoal-gray jumpsuit, I ask, "Do you only wear jumpsuits?"

"When I travel, yes. It's easy to pack, put on, and take off." She winks at me. "Easy for you, too!"

I feel the blood tingling in my cheeks, and I smile involuntarily.

She stretches her hand out and wiggles her fingers, asking for mine. Then, she looks out the window, contemplating for a few moments, before looking back at me. "We were both kids in school. And we met as adults just two weeks back. It may be a little forward and awkward now that I shadow your colleagues—colleagues who report to you." She pauses.

I look into her eyes. "Say it."

"I'm falling in love with you."

So what if she is shadowing my colleagues? So what if it's just been fifteen days? I lean forward. "I don't care about social constraints and the length of knowing someone. And I have waited for you for three decades. That should count. We fought the constraints of time, space, and time turbulence. That must count." I bring her hand to my lips and kiss her every finger. "I love you."

Sensing waterworks, I hand over my pocket square. Akane grabs it and dabs her eyes.

"How do we make this work?" I ask. "With the Pacific Ocean between us?"

She takes my hand and brings it to her cheek. "I'll keep dropping by and stay for months. You can do the same. Maybe you can move operations to Japan."

I rub her soft face with my thumb. "Can you keep some of your clothes in the empty closet?"

She tilts her head and blinks. "*Naze?*"

"Then, I'll know you will come back."

She laughs. "You need proof, silly?"

"Yes."

She folds the pocket square back in my pocket and sits on my lap. Running her fingers through my hair, she says, "All right. And I won't take the violin, the scarf, or the photo frame. I'll keep coming back to look at them." She looks at me, and her eyes glow. "You need to tell me your favorite suits and watches."

"Why?"

She winks. "I'll keep them with me, and you can use them when you come to Japan. Deal?"

"Deal."

"We will make this work," she promises, bringing her lips to mine.

✲

(Nardin residence grounds)

A few months later, I'm standing on Philip's lawn. Twenty of Edward's finest men have surrounded me, and all I can do is smile. Not because I can take them out all at once but because of how wonderful the last seven months have been. Akane came three times and stayed with me for four months.

Edward's men are equipped with a wooden sword and a military knife, and they are circling me slowly. I just have a rope. Edward drops a cloth, and the men come at me. Once they get within a foot of me, I press the green button on my bracelet and snap my fingers.

This place is removed from time and space. I can see and touch them, but they can't see or touch me. I could take minutes, which would be just microseconds for them. Using the rope, I tie their hands and legs together.

I snap my fingers again. Edward's finest are on the floor, their hands and legs tied. With wide eyes, staring at their tied hands and legs, they all exclaim at once.

"How did you do this?"

"What the fuck, Dr. Abajian?"

"Colonel Tealeaf, can you free us?"

I take a knife from one of my victim's sheaths and cut the ropes.

Clapping, Philip comes forward. "Good job." Rubbing my hair, he looks into my eyes—almost apologetically. His eyes glinting, he says, "I like it when you smile."

I spread my arms. "I have everything. And I'm picking her up again today."

"I'm so glad she found you."

Touching Philip's shoulder, I ask, "You don't want to meet her?"

"I can't." His voice cracks with guilt.

"She doesn't blame you," I assure him. "And I never did, either."

Placing a hand against his chest, he reveals, "But I do. She was just a child." Then, pointing at his array of limited-edition vehicles, he changes the topic. "Choose whatever you want to pick her up."

Pointing at one, I ask, "How about that one?" I clasp my hands together. "I promise there will be no scratches, and I'll return it tonight."

He covers my joined hands with one of his. "I don't care if you scratch them or break them. And you don't have to return it." He winks. "It's all yours, anyway." Smiling, he asks, "Anything else?"

I take a folded paper from my jacket pocket and hand it to Philip. "I want to gift her something special for her birthday. Can Bernstein and the company get this? I'll pay you."

He looks at the paper and smiles. With a glint of pride in his eyes, he says, "Impeccable taste. I'll get it for you." Then, he lifts his finger and scowls. "Never offer to pay me again."

"Also, Philip. I need a retractable *katana* attached to my suit."

"Sure. Can you do me a favor?"

"Anything."

"Keep an open mind about commercializing alternate realities?"

I'm waiting by the hangar, about a hundred feet from her plane. She waves as the door opens and transforms into the airstair. She is wearing a bespoke linen jumpsuit, but the fit is baggy. On her head is a Hermes linen beret.

I open the car door for her as Michisato and Masato load her luggage into her Maybach, parked in the hangar. She picks up Hulk from the passenger seat and sits, kissing him on the head as I click her seat belt. She lifts her finger and turns to me as I reach for the ignition button.

"Not yet."

Taking off her beret, she pulls me by my collar, locks her lips with mine, and runs her fingers through my hair. After a few moments, she pulls away. Nuzzling Hulk's button nose, she says, "Now, we can go home." She points at the steering wheel. "What car is this?"

"Pagani Huayra."

(Quantum World—Executive conference room)

With Akane's insistence, the conference and office room now overlook a temperature-controlled *tsubo-niwa*. It has waterfalls, a koi pond, and Japanese maples. The garden is supposed to calm my nerves.

After mainly shadowing Anna, Akane has become our international adviser, sitting in on most of our meetings. Today, she is dressed in a charcoal, pin-striped skirt suit with a white shirt. I'm in the head seat, and she is on my right. Next to her is Ravi. On my left are Anna, Chris, and Tabi. We are waiting for the angel investors—Richard Nicklas and Patrick Kovac. They run Kirkland Investment, LLC.

Akane taps my wrist. "Why do you hate them?"

Anna rolls her eyes. "Frat boys with money, unwilling to release funds they owe us." Glaring at me, she adds, "And Vince won't take investments from Mr. Nardin."

I lift my brows. "I am not that desperate."

Akane takes the brochure of Kirkland, LLC. Looking at it, she covers her mouth and giggles. "*Kirkulando,* LLC."

I touch her hand. "You know them?"

She smiles, her eyes becoming two lines of lashes. "You will see."

Rick and Pat finally enter the conference room. Upon sitting down, they prop their feet up on the table. They unbutton their jacket sleeves and roll them up to reveal their trinkets—Rick's all gold Submariner, Pat's all gold Daytona, shining against their artificially tanned skin.

Scratching his bald head, Rick turns to me. Skipping the pleasantries, he says, "I read your proposal. Neurolink sounds more like a piece of shit."

Pat runs his fingers through his dyed blond hair. "It's undoable. And it's not science." Then, he laughs sarcastically, exposing his bleached teeth.

Leaning forward, I scoff and remark, "You two know about science?"

Rick takes his feet off the table and turns to me. "Look, your idea is shit. But we would like our money back if you want to go forward with it."

Tilting my head, I say, "Back? You haven't given us anything. According to our contract, we should have received a hundred and fifty million. So, technically, you're in a breach of contract. We are running operations with an endowment freed from the uni." I put my elbows on the table and lean forward. "You will hear from Bernstein, Ozawa, Toscanini, and Mehta."[32]

Pat now takes his feet off the table as well. "Son of a bitch."

Exhaling in disgust, Akane softly remarks, "*Baka.*"

Pushing her swivel chair back, she stands and turns to Rick and Pat, saying, "With all due respect, I think Vincent's request is reasonable and within the contract."

Rick snaps his fingers at Akane's face. "Who the fuck are you? Daddy gave you a pony, so you think you know what money is?"

Blood rushes to my head. Banging on the table, I snarl, "Don't take that tone with anyone in this room."

Touching my shoulder, Akane says, "I can fight my own battles."

Anna, Chris, Ravi, and Tabi are just silent observers now.

Akane smirks, and her eyes transform from warm to cruel as she crumples her brows. She sits opposite Pat and adjacent to Rick. "Niyamoto Holdings bought Kirkland, right?"

Pat shrugs. "So?"

Akane smiles, but it doesn't reach her eyes. "Except Niyamoto didn't have the money, so they took a loan from Egami Financials. If Niyamoto can't pay Egami, Kirkland will be Egami's."

Rick shrugs. "So?"

Petite, delicate Akane stands up, takes out her business card, and hands it to Rick. "I'm Akane Egami, vice president of the entire Egami Media."

The blood drains from Rick's and Pat's faces, and their eyes widen.

---

[32]   They are Philip's lawyers and now also the legal team of Quantum World.

Akane's voice turns hoarse. "In other words, I have you by your balls." She taps her chin and squints. "Let me speak in a tongue you two understand." She points her finger at Pat and Rick and clarifies, "You two are my bitches." She sits and crosses her arms. "How much money do I have, right?" Looking at the door, she yells, *Masato-san, Michisato-san, koko ni kite kudasai.*[33] Heavy, pounding footsteps sound and the ground seems to shake as the two giants rush in. Akane points at them. "They will chop off your balls and feed them to your wives and girlfriends with one signal from me." Clapping like a child while shooting daggers at them, she sneers, "I can make sure they eat them with a smile."

Tabi pinches her arm to check if this is a dream. Anna's mouth gapes. Ravi chugs a glass of water, and Chris swivels his head, looking between Akane and me as if watching a tennis match.

Coming back around the table, Akane sits by my side. She then turns to Rick and Pat. "If you don't like an idea, that's fine. But you don't need to be rude, sir. If you're rude again, I'll dismantle Niyamoto Holdings, buy Kirkland, and sell it for ten yen. The only assets you will have will be those cheap trinkets on your wrists." She knocks her knuckles against the table. "So, what will it be?"

A pale Rick stands up, his forehead beaded with sweat, and he stutters, "We—we will release the money as per contract, Vincent."

The two frat boys walk sideways with their backs plastered to the wall to avoid proximity to Michisato and Masato. Upon reaching the door, they fling it open and rush out.

Brushing invisible lint from her shoulders, she turns back to the sweet Akane I know. Squeezing her eyes into two curved lines of thick lashes, she smiles. "Negotiations—Akane style."

Anna, Chris, Ravi, and Tabi finally breathe and close their mouths. Anna places her hands on the table and bends her head, saying, "You are a goddess."

I place my hand over Akane's. "I don't think you have any risk of your useless cousins taking over."

Crossing her arms, she remarks, "I don't think Quantum World should depend on crooks like Pat and Rick." Smiling, she murmurs, "My birthday is coming."

---

[33] *Masato-san, Michisato-san*, please come here.

Understanding where she's going, I say, "I can't take money from you."

Shrugging, she looks at Tabi. "Not all of the Egami money is mine."

Moving her admiring eyes from Akane, Anna turns to me and asks, "How did you come up with the Neurolink?"

"I am a genius."

Flipping through the blueprint of Neurolink while scratching his head, Ravi poses, "Why do we need to code the skills? Why can't we transfer the consciousness of a pianist, an artist, or a violinist into our client's mind?"

Smiling, I explain, "Assuming he was alive, can we parse the skills of Władysław Szpilman from his memories of the Holocaust? How can we scrape out Picasso's skills from his misogyny?" Narrowing my eyes, I clarify, "Every artist and scientist have vices or demons, and we can't risk those entering our client's mind. We will use codes that create basic skills, not transfer maestro-level genius." Grabbing my shaking left hand with my right, I add, "Maestro-level genius should not be transferred." I massage my temples. The memories hurt.

Placing both her hands over mine, Akane lifts her brows. "You okay?"

I sigh. "*Daijoubu desu.*"[34]

(Summer 2025—Vincent's office)

The architect of my embarrassment, Akane, is nonchalantly flipping through swatches while sitting opposite the fireplace in my office. Clad in a peach-colored, knee-length dress with a blue belt, her sunglass on top of her head, she is shimmering brighter than the sunlight shining on her.

Me? Oh, don't worry. I am standing upright, no pants on, my dress shirt barely crossing the seam of my boxer shorts. I wish that were it. But three generations of well-suited tailors with the last name Anderson from Anderson Atelier of Saville Row are taking several measurements of my crotch area with surgical precision.

My door swings open, and the three musketeers and Tabi enter. Glaring, I ask, "How about knocking for a change?"

---

34   I am fine.

While pumping her inhaler, Tabi smirks. "Oh! My god." Then, she sits to the left of Akane.

Anna covers her face, desperately trying to contain her laughter. Chris's jaw is dropped, and Ravi simply manages, "Wow," with raised eyebrows.

Anna sits to the right of Akane and keeps staring at my boxers. She rests her chin on her palm and winks. "My, my." Then, she turns to my Akane. "How can I ever thank you for this spectacle?"

Smiling through her pressed lips, Akane keeps flipping through her book of swatches.

Ravi and Chris sit in the chairs opposite the couch the three ladies are occupying.

Squinting, Ravi asks, "What's going on?"

I point at Akane and frown. "Her Majesty thinks my existing suits are not good enough to meet her parents."

"Andersons have dressed every man in my family," Akane says, pointing the finger at me. "You're family." Looking at my crotch while biting her lower lip, she adds, "And a man."

The senior-most Anderson steps back and squints at me over his reading glasses. "Do you dress to left or right?"

"Pardon me?"

Akane presses her lips together mischievously but continues sifting through swatches.

Mr. Anderson coughs. "Ahem!" Narrowing his eyes, he rephrases, "On which side your penis naturally hangs?"

"My what?" I ask, furrowing my brows.

Chris holds his stomach and falls from the sofa, laughing, while Ravi slaps the coffee table, panting for breath. "Maddy should be here."

Rolling her eyes, Akane casually remarks, "It's left, *Anderson-san*."

I grit my teeth. "Awesome. Now, the world knows."

"Is it always left?" Anna asks Akane. "Like, when he gets excited?"

I shake my head, hoping Akane will end the matter there. Instead, she winks at me and smiles. She snaps her fingers. "Good question." Tapping her chin, she explains, "With pants on, yes, but then, it moves." She forms a fist and moves it from left to right. "Like this." Akane, Anna, and Tabi cover their mouths and giggle.

Holding his belly, Ravi leans toward Akane. His whole body shakes as he curls his thumb and index finger into the "okay" sign. Catching his breathing, he manages, "I haven't seen such an on-point demonstration of anything."

I feel the blood rush to my cheeks, and I exclaim with my hands on my waist, "Did they need to know that?"

"Why not?" Akane says, shrugging. "Fred, Sasha, Krista . . . they all know."

My jaw drops. "Since when?"

"Thanksgiving." Waving her hand, she dismisses my fuming face and turns to the three musketeers and Tabi. "Want to see the swatches I picked for my Vince?"

They all lean toward her as she shows them all the swatches. Tabi points at one. "Oh! I like that one." Glancing at me, she confirms, "He will look awesome."

Akane sighs. "Hmm. That's the problem." She winks at me. "The suit won't stay on him for long." Her own words make her flush.

I point at the swatch book. "Can I have a look?" Then, I proceed to fetch my trousers.

Shaking her head and tightly gripping the swatch book, she playfully says, "No." Then, she turns to the three Andersons. *"Anderson-san.* I'll need twenty dress shirts, four sports jackets, four linen suits, and ten woolen suits."

Everyone's jaws drop at the size of the order.

Scanning me from top to bottom, Akane continues, "I want the suits to have minimum padding to drape over Vince's natural slopes. We will do a trial fitting in Tokyo. Please add everything to my account." Bowing, she hands over the swatch book. "I have marked everything."

The three Andersons collect the swatch book and bow before her majesty. "Always a pleasure, Ms. Egami."

After they leave, I say, "I can pay for my suits," as I zip my trousers and fasten my belt.

Shutting her eyes into a double layer of lashes, she smiles. "It's my treat. I have wanted to do this since I called you family."

Lifting her head from her cell phone screen in a rush, Tabi shrieks, "Fuck!" She points at the TV in my office. "CNN, now."

I turn the TV on to see the CNN news anchor reading a threat letter posted next to him on the screen.

"I'm Vandal, and I have chosen Stellarcloud Web Services for my Denial service attack. You rebuffed my last claim as a hoax. And maybe you will do the same this time. But can you afford it? Stellarcloud Web Services provides cloud support to the CIA and FBI and digital infrastructure for banking and stock trading. Come Monday, your whole network will crumble. To prove my threat is not a hoax, I'll perform a minor attack on your DNS server that will last for one hour, starting at 1:00 p.m. today. There is no countermeasure, as I'll be attacking your IPs directly, and my attacks are potent, peaking at over two terabytes per second.

"I'll refrain from attacking your network for a small fee of 5,000 bitcoins. It's a small price for what will happen when your network goes down, and the stock market tumbles. Then, I'll hack into your system, CIA database, and the stock market and make some funny trades. How about that? If you don't pay before Sunday, 11:59 p.m. GMT, our fee to stop will increase to 10,000 bitcoins, and we will increase our demand by 5,000 bitcoins daily. Please send the bitcoins to the following:

Redacted."

The news anchor then interviews the CEO of Stellarcloud, Mr. Justin Benson. "Mr. Benson, what do you think of this threat?"

Clearing his throat, Benson loosens his tie. "We have an impenetrable network. This is someone sitting in his mother's basement looking for validation of their pathetic lives."

The news anchor takes out his cell phone and holds it to the camera. "Then, can you tell me what this is?"

We can see the website www.stellarcloud.com, which returns nothing but a yellow smiley face with a red blotch. The CNN feed abruptly cuts to commercials. They caught Justin off guard.

Anna, Chris, Ravi, and Tabi start arguing about the claim's authenticity. The banner at the bottom of the TV screen shows that the stock price of Stellarcloud is already down by twenty percent.

I press my temple, thinking of the words carved into the *shuriken*.

How do you know me? Who are you? You don't need the bitcoin if you can afford that intreton suit.

Akane comes over to me and touches my hands. "What's on your mind?"

Vandal wants to hurt me. This room is full of people I love. Why did he choose Stellarcloud?

Kissing Akane's hands, I look into her anxious eyes. "Does the Egami Group have stakes in Stellarcloud?"

"No."

"Ludwig, who owns the biggest stake in Stellarcloud?"

"Philip Nardin owns more than forty percent of Stellarcloud."

So, that's why Vandal chose Stellarcloud. He has some beef with Philip and me. Or maybe he thinks hurting Philip will hurt me?

"Ludwig, connect me to Philip."

"What's up?"

"I am with my team here. You heard the news about Stellarcloud?"

"Yes. What do you want me to do?"

I squeeze my eyes shut. "Can you move all of Stellarcloud's services to your infrastructure? Vandal will end up chasing a ghost."

Anna, Chris, and Ravi are looking at each other and murmuring.

"What's his plan?"

"What's he doing?"

Philip asks, "We have time?"

"It's Friday afternoon. The stock market will be closed for the next two days. Let the world think it's a hoax. Let's frustrate him."

"I'll talk to Justin Benson," Philip says. "Have fun in Japan."

"Thanks."

I take off my glasses and toss them on the desk, then lean my head forward and put it on my palms, elbows resting on my desk. Looking at my colleagues, I say, "For Neurolink, we need to move beyond a rudimentary multifactor authentication. Every human has unique brain waves, and we can deploy an electroencephalogram for biometric validation for the user of The Mind. We need to record that and connect it with a unique MAC address. And every helmet address with the unique MAC address will be mapped with the user's brain frequency and the network they use. We need to increase the security of our network."

Ravi peers into my eyes. "Vandal will try to hack us?"

"Yes," I say, gritting my teeth.

I will inform the world how secure our network is, enticing him to attack.

I scratch my head.

And then what?

I leave my seat and pace across my seven-hundred-square-foot office.

What else, what else? Who else is close to me?

I stop and stare at Akane. "Ludwig, make a four-way call with Fred, Krista, and Sasha." They all answer within a few minutes.

"What's up?" Sasha asks.

Fred says, "Hey, Vince."

Krista laughs into the phone. "Wow, Vinny remembers us!"

Ignoring Krista's joke, I lean into the phone. "Do not use the autonomous mode in your cars for the foreseeable future, and don't trust the navigation tech, either. These might be hacked soon. Do I have your word?"

"Is everything okay?" Sasha asks.

"It will be if you listen to me. Can I have your word?"

They all chorus, "Yes."

"Good." I hang up without further explanation. There'll be time for that later.

Grabbing my handkerchief, I wipe the sweat off my forehead. Pacing the room, I ask my team members, "You all heard that too, right?"

They all nod.

Walking up to Ravi, I put my hand on his shoulder. "Relay this to Maddy."

Touching my hand, he blinks. "Thanks for thinking of her."

"Sure." I sit next to Akane. "Look, guys, Vandal will now make his presence felt. He may resort to violence. And I can't let anything happen to you." I turn to Tabi. "Can you contact your press connections and inform them Vandal might target these technologies? Vandal might shift his focus elsewhere."

But he may not, so I must warn everyone I care about. I wish I knew his identity. Then, I could go to the core and fish him out.

(Country club)

<u>Ravi</u>

Sitting perpendicular to Chris and me, Anna fetches her daiquiri from the table. Chris chugs the remainder of his stout and touches his belly, burping silently. The Tiffany crystal light shines sparkling dimples on their faces.

Chris leans forward and signals us closer. "Wasn't it weird how Vincent subverted the Vandal attack?" he asks softly.

Anna clicks her tongue. "There is more to him than what we know." Frowning, she continues, "Like, why did he faint when he was at his house that day? Why was Philip there?" Snapping her fingers, she turns to Chris. "Tabi knows something. Ask her."

Scoffing, Chris lifts his brows. "You think I haven't tried?" He crosses his index and middle finger. "Vince and Tabi are tight. She won't reveal shit."

Putting her drink back on the table, Anna leans forward. "Will Akane invest? We can't rely on Pat and Rick."

Wagging his finger, Chris laments, "That's not the issue. Will Vincent allow it?"

"Akane is the only person Vincent cannot say no to," Anna argues.

I smirk. "There was someone else."

Anna glares at me. "Why did you have to bring her up?"

"What's on your mind?" Chris asks, putting his hand on my shoulder.

I drink half my Moscow Mule, gathering my thoughts. "I know Emika hurt Vince. But if you remember, right after that congressional hearing, Vince told us it was Akane inside Emika who initiated the relationship with him." I shrug. "What did he mean? And now that Akane is back, I wonder how Emika is." Meeting Chris's and Anna's gaze in turn, I say, "It's easy to forget her under the glitz and glamor of Akane"—I point at my Audemars Piguet Royal Oak, Chris's Patek Philippe Nautilus, and Anna's Blue Crocodile Hermes Birkin—"and the rare gifts she showers us with." I exhale in exasperation. "But I can't overlook that we once called Emika our little sister. How could we just forget her?" Chris and Anna bend their heads down. "She was the life of our lab, always playful. Remember how Hulk would sniff her out? And what about the smile she brought to Vincent's face?" Sullen, I admit, "But we have shut out Emika from our lives, too."

Anna scowls. "We shut *her* out?"

I lean toward her. "Do we have the same phone numbers? Even our social media is professionally managed." Tapping hard on the table, I say, "Every day, I feel like calling her to see if she is okay. If she needs something." I stare at Anna. "Yes, they may have rushed into things. But Vincent deeply loved her."

Anna lifts her brows. "Rushed? Deeply loved?" She sighs, stirring her drink. "You don't know the half of it."

"What do you mean?" Chris asks.

Anna signals the waiter for another drink. "Remember the Thanksgiving plus Emika's birthday party?"

Chris and I nod.

"I accompanied Vince when he picked out the watch for Emika. He didn't need my input for the wristwatch but desired it for our next stop— Tiffany's, for a ring."

Chris's eyes widen. "No way!" he exclaims.

I lift my brows in shock. I hadn't known Vincent had been committed to that extent. He'd been with Elise for years, and the subject of a ring never came up.

Anna takes a tissue out of her purse and dabs the corners of her eyes. Taking a deep breath, she continues, "I asked Vince if he was rushing, and he said there could be no substitute for Emika. He planned on giving her the ring on February 14, 2024. But he never got the chance." She exhales and touches her chest. "I had to get it off my chest. Fuck, that feels good."

The waiter gives a second beer to Chris and replaces my Moscow Mule and Anna's daiquiri. Chris rests his head on his hands and looks at Anna. "Before Vince gets serious with Akane, can you tell him about Emika?"

After stirring her drink for a few seconds, Anna says, "Sure."

"Sure what?"

I look over my shoulder and see Vincent, who then goes around the table and sits opposite Chris and me. He takes off his navy linen jacket and folds his sleeves, revealing the rarest of rare timepieces—Philip Nardin's masterpiece.

Biting her fingernails, Anna swings the conversation. "Sure, I'll talk to the product designers about the placement of the Wi-Fi status indicator."

Man, she is good at randomly making shit up.

A waiter rushes to Vincent. "What can I get you, sir?"

He looks up. "Double scotch, Macallan 30. No ice, please." Circling his index finger, he says, "Add my friends' orders to my tab."

Pointing at Vincent's left wrist, I ask, "Hey, can I look at your watch?"

"Sure." He takes it off and hands it to me. I look at the exquisite, hand-polished details. I know Philip Nardin is famous for his reset dates. "Why is the reset date August 3, 2023?" I ask, returning the timepiece.

"Beats me, but it's the same as the clocks I have from Philip."

Chris, Anna, and I exchange glances. That's the day Emika started as a postdoc in our center. And Mr. Nardin knows it? What else does he know?

Scanning our faces, Vincent says, "I want to change the reset date, but I need to ask her before that."

"Ask who?" Chris questions.

Anna rolls her eyes and punches Chris's shoulder. "Akane, you moron."

The waiter puts the glass of whiskey on the table. Vincent drinks the whole thing in one gulp and turns to the waiter. "Two more of these, please." Then, he leans forward. "This stays among us, the OG. Okay?"

We all nod as the waiter brings Vincent two more glasses of double scotch. He gulps one of them down before continuing. "In her culture, asking the parents before dating is customary." Chuckling, he confesses, "We were way past that after a week. But I must talk to Masayoshi and Theresa if I want to proceed further." He pauses and finishes his second glass. "And then ask Akane, too."

Then, Vincent looks at Anna helplessly. Anna stretches her hand out to take Vincent's. "When do you want to ask?" she asks, choking up a bit. I know she is now conflicted about whether to bring up Emika at all or not.

Gripping Anna's hands, Vincent says, "Her parents, after I fly to Japan tomorrow. Her? Sometime next year." Vincent takes a deep breath. "If she says yes, I will replace August 3 with that date."

Smiling, Anna raises her eyebrows. "*If* she says yes? Idiot." Her voice quivers with joy.

Placing the half-empty third glass on the table, Vincent wipes his mouth. Looking lost in his thoughts, he says, "It's all so surreal. What if I wake up one day to find that Akane coming back was a dream?" Staring at us vulnerably, he asks, "How could I piece my life back together?"

Gripping Vincent's hand, Anna assures him, "It isn't a dream. And you deserve every ounce of this joy." Chris and I nod.

Vincent confesses, "I don't remember feeling this weak." Vincent releases Anna's hand. He massages his temples while looking at his whiskey glass. "Hey, guys, I often dream of a girl who looks like Akane but with shorter hair. At times, she says goodbye. Other times, she has a child. Is she someone I forgot?"

The three of us exchange glances, realizing that bringing up Emika will only derail Vincent from a scarce resource—joy. Anna nods subtly, taking the entire load on her shoulders. She turns to Vincent.

"The perennial pessimist tells you that you shouldn't be happy." Then, she pokes Vincent's arm. "Fuck pessimist Vincent. Embrace your joy, idiot. You deserve every single drop of it." She gestures to the waiter. "I want one of those scotches."

Wiping her eyes, Anna looks at Chris and me. Nodding, she asks, "Let's be happy?"

Emika, wherever you are, I hope you have moved on. I wish you all the joy.

Vincent turns to me and squints at me in an introspective way. "How're things with Maddy?"

I smirk and shake my head. "We have run out of things to say. She doesn't understand my world, and I left academia. She also finds our camaraderie pretentious and silly."

"Why don't you do some activities together?" Vincent asks, tilting his head.

I scoff. "It's beyond pasta and pottery shit."

Shaking his head, he smiles. "Volunteer at the Humane Society. That's how Elise and I survived as long as we did. We helped several Hulks to find homes." Then, he snaps his fingers. "Why don't you two help Tabi at the orphanage? We already have over twenty refugee kids, mostly from Afghanistan and Iraq. Maybe you and Maddy can meet some little Vincents and Tabithas and make them feel at home."

Why didn't I think of that? It might work. My voice shakes as I say, "I will. I'll talk to her."

Vincent leaves his seat, offers me his handkerchief, and ruffles my hair. "If you need anything, I'm always a phone call away." Then, he turns to Chris and Anna. "I meant all three of you."

Anna pulls Vincent's sleeve. "Hulk stays with me. He doesn't need to deal with high-pressurized compartments."

CHAPTER 7

EMA

"Across time and reality, this is where we will find each other."
—*Vincent*

August 2025 to April 2026

(August 30, 2025)

<u>Vincent</u>

'M SITTING IN THE OWNERS' box at the Egami Hall. Masayoshi touches my right shoulder and smiles. "Anderson did well. You look like a billion dollars."

I smile in gratitude. "Thank you."

Akane is sparkling in her bespoke maroon dress. Sitting on my left, she first leans forward and looks across me, checking on her parents. Convinced they are lost in their conversation, she crookedly runs her tongue across her lips. Lifting her hand, she tickles my earlobes and neck. Not fair!

I turn to her and whisper, "Just wait till I get my hands on you."

She bites her lip, pinches my left arm, and whispers, "What will you do?"

"Ahem." Theresa, sitting to the right of Masayoshi, clears her throat. We may have crossed a line. At the age of forty-two, I feel like a teenager.

It's challenging to read if Masayoshi is awake or asleep as his eyelids squish his eyes. And his curled, thin lips always look like he is smiling. His face is like porcelain, without a single wrinkle, except when he lifts his eyebrows. His closely cropped hair shines like silver. Theresa's gray eyes are deeply sunk in her sockets—a feature more profound given her high cheekbones. Her wrinkles are more visible when she smiles.

The Egami Grammophon is signing a piano prodigy, a Tokyo University of Arts student who recently won the Chopin competition. Her performance is customary before she signs a contract with the Egamis. The entire Japanese media is here. I had no idea a debutant classical pianist could pull media attention that rivals pop stars. The pianist takes a final bow after keying the last note of Chopin's Concerto No. 1, Op.11. While the entire hall booms with thunderous applause, only a tiny fraction of photographers capture the moment. What are they waiting for? I flip through the program pages. All it says is "Surprise from the Egamis."

Leaning right, I ask, "*Masayoshi-san. Nan desu ka?*" pointing at the program.

Lifting his cuff, he checks the time on his Roger Smith Series 4 Triple Calendar wristwatch. Glancing at me through his reading glass, he smiles. "No idea."

Very convincing. I look to my left to see Akane is gone. My hands tremble each time she leaves unannounced. Nine months have passed since she came back. Yet, it hasn't fully sunk in. What if she disappears again? My life would spiral into a meaningless vacuum.

I lean around Masayoshi and tap *Theresa-san*'s wrist. "Where is Akane?"

She touches my shaky hand assuringly. "Close enough. She will be back."

The service brings us champagne, and I wait for Akane as the stage darkens. Then, the spotlight shines brightly on a solo violinist. And, like always, she is more luminous than the light that touches her. Her face is projected on the three-hundred-inch screen above the stage. Akane shuts her eyes, takes up her violin, and plays Massenet's Méditation.

Are you doing this for me?

The music takes me back to the moment she tied that scarf around my neck after the bullies beat me up. She wouldn't even leave my side at the infirmary. Thirty-four years later, the time has turned back to this moment. I want to meet little Vincent in the corridor after he discovers Akane was engulfed in the time turbulence. I want to tell him, "Just wait for thirty-three years." As her notes magically synchronize with my heartbeat, I take out my pocket square and dab my eyes. I look at the screen as she presses her trembling lips together and concludes the final notes of Méditation.

Wagging her fingers at the audience, she tells them not to applaud yet. After taking a few deep breaths, she smiles, connects the bow with the string, and begins her rendition of "Happy Birthday," as she did on August 30, 1991, mixing parts of Méditation and Zigeunerweisen.

Masayoshi touches my shoulder. "You should wipe your tears before the final act."

"There is more?" So he knew.

As Akane finishes the final few notes, the screen shows the photograph of us eating ice cream—a picture taken by Mr. Kruger on August 28, 1991.[35] Akane blinks back her tears and smiles. She points her bow at the projection.

"*Sore wa Vincent to watashi desu.*"[36] Then, she points her bow at us as a light shines on me. The audience turns to the reserved box, with Akane announcing, "*Asoko ni Vincent ga imasu.*"[37]

I cover my mouth with my hand as my heart flutters.

Then, she adjusts her microphone and smiles ear to ear, shutting her eyes. "*Tanjōbi omedetō, watashi no ai, watashi no inochi.*"[38]

The hall booms, "Happy Birthday, *Vu~insento.*" I bow to the crowd, and we all sit as Akane bows again and leaves the stage. Every single camera flashes on my face, and I shut my eyes.

---

[35] Chapter 8 of *The Winding* (Book 1).

[36] That is Vincent and me.

[37] Over there is Vincent.

[38] Happy Birthday, my love, my life.

Finally, when the sound of the shutters dies, Theresa says, "Every summer, every Christmas, she became miserable. Masa and I never understood the depth of her feelings . . ." Pausing, she catches her breath. "She said she always knew you. So, we decided to bring you with us after the Berlin trip." Her voice cracks. "But then, everything changed." She wipes her eyes.

Leaving my chair and crossing Masayoshi, I take Theresa's hands. "What do you mean? She always knew me."

Masayoshi touches my shoulder. "She never revealed." He wipes his eyes. "All we know is your memories brought her back, Vince. How can I ever thank you?" he asks, his voice cracking and clasping his hands together.

I envelop his beseeching hands with mine. "Please, sir . . . I don't know what I have done to deserve this love."

I feel a triple tap on my shoulder. I know who it is. Locking her eyes with mine, Akane lifts her shoulder. "Maybe it was just a simple act." Then, she looks at her parents, squishes her eyes, and holds my hand. "Can I kiss him a little bit?" She joins her thumb and index finger and asks her doting papha, *"Chotto, Kudasai?"*[39]

Masayoshi-san shrugs. "Go on. I am not looking."

Akane wraps her arms around me, locks her lips with mine, and then bites my lower lip. Then, she whispers. "I have lewd intentions. Can't wait to get to our penthouse."

We part ways with Akane's parents after dinner at Narisawa as we get into Akane's Maybach. I take her hand and kiss it. "Thanks for the wonderful evening." She brings her face close to mine, and suddenly, instead of kissing me, I sense she wants to yell at me. Involuntarily, I jerk my head back.

Akane covers her lips. "Did I do something wrong?"

Gently touching her neck, I assure her, "No." I stare into her eyes. "I just felt you would call me an apathetic, spoiled brat." Bending my head, I look at the car floor and confess, "I have these weird memories."

"I'll never say such a thing." She lifts my head and turns it toward her. "Anyone who conceives Amara's Tree of Life can't be any of those."

---

[39] A little, please.

Running her thumbs over my cheeks, she says, "If someone from your past is capable of such words, maybe you shouldn't remember her." She gazes deeply into my eyes. "But I don't care about your past. I just want a future with you. Okay?"

"Okay."

(Akane's penthouse)

We took a bath in her penthouse. Now, I am standing next to the ninety-two-key Bösendorfer, staring at the Tokyo skyline—the Tokyo tower, the rainbow bridge, and all the well-lit apartments taking away the spotlight from the galaxy up above. On the horizon, I see planes—incoming and outgoing. The dark, Prussian-blue sky slowly gives in to the orange light of the rising sun. I take my eyes from the skyline and look at my wrist—Roger Smith Series 5, 40mm Open Dial. The Tokyo skyline reflects on the sapphire crystal dial encrusted with 18-carat red gold bezel. It's a birthday gift from the Egamis, welcoming me to their family. Unlike in 1991, I don't need to squeeze the love into my tiny heart. Akane somehow expanded it.

Two petite hands grab me from behind. Her right hand sneaks through the folds of my monogrammed robe while her left hand unties the rope. I turn around and see my Akane dressed in navy satin sleepwear. She runs her fingers lightly over my face, stopping at my Adam's apple.

Pulling her by her waist, I ask, "What did you mean when you said that maybe it was just a simple act?"

"I don't wanna talk about it."

"Okay. How about telling me what was running through your mind when you played the violin tonight?"

She pulls me by the lapel. "Let's take you on tour, then." She winks. "Mind and body."

(August 31, 2025—London)

Markus

I brought her favorite pizza and a bottle of wine. Will my luck turn today? We will watch the Premier League in her apartment. Emika warms up the pizza, pours the wine into two mismatched glasses, and sits on my left. Then, she feels my fingers running over her shoulders. Smiling, she takes my hand and kisses my fingers. She stares into my eyes and swallows.

I could drown in your chocolate-brown eyes.

Holding my hand tightly, she admits, "I am still at a crossroads. Vincent is still in my heart. I know it's unfair to you. I want to be free from him, but I can't when I look into Nozo's eyes." Placing my hand on my knee, she bites her lower lip. "I am so sorry."

How long will it be like this? I helped you move on. Have you entirely forgotten our dates, our nights at your place, my place? I took you to the doctors during all the checkups and to the hospital for labor. I brought you home. When you run out of Nozo's food, who restocks it? I have changed Nozo's diapers and powdered her rashes. I even know your cycles. Who waters your plants when you work late? Who installed your stupid mason jar lights? How many more months of patience?

I sigh. "Sorry. Take all the time you need. I will always be here."

That's who I am—a fucking doormat?

I switch on the telly, and Emika scrolls through her cell phone. She elbows me. "Look at this headline. How is this news? *Mainichi Shimbun* is now a tabloid."

I glance at the headline—"Childhood Love Rekindled at Concert." Nozo cries, and Emika rushes toward the crib, leaving her cell phone on the coffee table. As she consoles her nine-month-old daughter, I quickly snoop through the news app on her cell. Oh, yes! I breathe in deeply. Thankfully, she only read the headline. If she finds out Vincent is with the Japanese heiress, his childhood flame, she will lose hope of getting him back. But then, she would find a way to get in touch with him. Which means she would tell him about Nozo. If he ever says yes, then my dreams are over. Yes, she must be kept in the dark. *Tell me, Emi would you consider them a tabloid if you knew they covered Vincent?* I change her preferences—not interested in this story, not interested in *Mainichi Shimbun*, not interested in Egami, not interested in Vincent Abajian. Then, I put the phone back on the table and cheer for Manchester City.

Emika comes back into the room, bringing Nozo with her and sitting her on her lap. The baby is laughing, shaking her arms, and staring at her captivating mom. Nozo has the sweetest baby teeth—tiny white tips from her pink gums.

Smilingly, she opens her mouth and utters, "Mam-ma," while drooling onto her chin.

Emika's eyes well up. Her lips tremble with joy as she locks her eyes with Nozo's. "*Hai Nozo-chan, boku wa kimi no mamma desu.*"

I can't speak that language, but I will learn it if it makes you happy.

Elbowing my arm, Emika almost cries. "Her first words." Then, she hugs her daughter and rocks her.

What can I do to capture this moment? I can't even touch you.

I take out my phone and turn to Emika. "Can we pose for a photo, please?"

With her eyes shut, holding her tears back, she says, "Yes."

I move close to Emika without making her uncomfortable while she places Nozo between us, and I snap a picture on my cell phone. Turning to her, I ask, "Do you want a copy?"

"Yes, please." Her voice quavers.

After sending the picture to her through WhatsApp, I rename the image on my phone "My small family."

Maybe I can have a perfect life one day—a small house in the suburbs, a hatchback, with Emika by my side and Nozomi in the back. Then, I clench my jaw.

Who am I kidding?

(Backstage of Egami Studios, Tokyo)

Vincent

"No, that's too much makeup," Akane instructs Naomi, pointing at my face. Then, she squints. "It dulls his natural glow."

Naomi bows. Breathing heavily, she wipes her forehead. "*Gomennasai, Akane-san.*"

As Naomi nervously restarts, Akane inspects my wardrobe alternatives—Tom Ford, Armani, Brioni, and others. Repeating, "*Warui, warui, warui,*" she shifts the suits from left to right. Then, she stops at one charcoal suit and squints at me. She shakes her head, returns to the rack, and repeats, "*Warui.*" Then, she stops again, pulls out a blue Brunello Cucinelli glen plaid suit, and holds the suit up to me from a distance. Tapping her chin, she remarks, "That's my Vincent." She then repeats the process with shoes, neckties, and pocket squares. She sifts through fifty near-identical white shirts before picking one.

"Is she like this with every guest?" I ask Naomi, pointing at Akane.

Going over my face with a brush, Naomi explains, "This is the first time she, or any Egami, has entered the dressing room." Taking a deep breath, she admits, "That's why I am so nervous."

Smiling, I assure her, "She won't bite you."

That's only for me.

(Egami Studios)

"Quantum World has had a meteoric rise. Do you think it's overvalued?" asks Kaori Dupont of *Egami News.*

Leaning forward, I explain, "We are pioneering a trillion-dollar sector that will disrupt robotics, computer science, education, the neural network, and healthcare. I'd say we are undervalued."

Picking up a blush-colored model of The Mind, she looks at it, smiles, and puts it on over her short hair. Pointing at it, she asks, "This will transfer consciousness?"

I nod. "Yes, once it's developed."

She takes it off and examines the helmet some more. "I like the color." Then, she asks me, "Does it come in many colors?"

Right now, I can picture Anna's grin. Struggling not to laugh, I give in. "You will have a whole palette to choose from, or even your favorite anime characters—Naruto, Levi, Mikasa, Kiki, Totoro. Whatever you want." In the background, I see Akane lifting her thumb and smiling.

Clapping and nodding like a middle schooler, Kaori says, "*Sugoi.*" Then, she transforms her expression into a serious one. "Dr. Abajian, your company's valuation will rise if you attract more investors, right?"

"That's one way to compute valuation."

"Are you seeking investments outside the US?" Kaori asks, leaning toward me.

I look at the camera. "Our product has no geographic limitations. So, why not?"

(September 18, 2025—Akane's penthouse)

There is not enough room to walk straight; Akane's penthouse is bursting with people. If I'd worn a crumpled tux, it would get ironed in this crowd. The deputy prime minister, the minister of internal affairs and communications, the minister of justice, TV personalities, producers, actors, directors, models, and musicians are all here to wish Akane a long and prosperous life. I'm jumping through the crowd to see where she is.

A green-haired Japanese man dressed in a bespoke golden suit introduces himself. "*Egami Takashi Desu.*"

So, you're one of her useless cousins.

Smiling and shaking his hand, I say, "Vincent Abajian."

Lifting my hand, he inspects my tanned skin. Raising his gaze, he stares into my eyes. He squints at me and asks, "*Doko kara kimashita ka?*"

This is the hundredth time someone has inquired about my origins. The word "US" doesn't seem to quench their thirst as they usually mean, "Where are you originally from?" If Akane were not an Egami, her halfwhite and half-Japanese looks would elicit the same inquiries. But it is in their mind. Always. They lack the audacity to voice it.

Gritting my teeth, I respond, "Earth."

"Bhery phunny."

Suddenly, Akane pulls me out of this crowded maze. She then kisses my lips. "I know you hate crowds. This is the last one." Smiling, she says,

"Promise." She pulls me next to her Bösendorfer, the skyline just beyond it. Theresa pulls Masayoshi toward her, and Akane stands next to her father and me. Masayoshi taps his champagne glass three times, and the crowd quiets. I can hear the sound of the central AC and the traffic about a hundred stories down. Taking a deep breath, Masayoshi kisses his daughter's cheek.

Turning to the crowd, he says, "No matter her age, *Aka-chan* will remain the stubborn child who has to get what she wants." Pointing his thumb at me, Masayoshi winks. "And her eyes have been on this gentleman since he was a little boy." He then turns to his right and hugs his beloved treasure. "*Tanjōbi omedetō, Aka-chan.*"

The crowd cheers, "*Tanjōbi omedetō, Akane-san.*"

Masayoshi teases, "I was not through." In a fraction of a second, the room becomes pin-drop silent. He then leaves his station and stands beside me, touching my shoulder. "Vincent, whose hand my daughter can't let go of, is building a future." He pauses, looks around the room, and continues, "I commit to investing ten billion US dollars in Quantum World." Lifting his finger, he clarifies, "I'm not doing this because my daughter loves Vincent but because every analyst in my firm tells me to do so. Vincent will also get stock options in Egami Enterprises." He smiles and winks at me. "Although you never asked, you can date my daughter."

The roaring burst of laughter of the crowd echoes through the wooden floor, walls, and the *shōjis* as Akane touches her lips to mine.

Akane's parents have just left for their mansion, and she is staring at the skyline while sipping her 1982 Chateau Lafite Rothschild—the year of her birth. I don't think the wine could make her lips any redder. This is my chance, so I sneak into the bedroom. Upon returning, I take the gift box from behind my back and bring it in front of her.

After placing her wine glass on the counter, she opens the case, and her eyes glow. She looks at me and tugs my sleeve. "Stradivarius?"

I bring her close. "Yes. It's the 1713 Schreiber—unclaimed. I'd been looking to get you one from the golden period, and this was up for auction, so I asked Philip to get it for you."

She wraps her arms around me and kisses my lips. "Thank you."

"Let's play something now."

I sit on the piano, pull my cuffs, and play the first three notes of Zigeunerweisen. Just as she is about to play her first note, she notices my wrist and points her bow at it. "What's that bracelet?

I take a deep breath before getting up from the bench to gently take the violin from her and place it on the piano. Then, I make her sit on the bench while I take her hands and kneel in front of her on the floor.

Looking into her eyes, I say, "It's time I tell you who I am beyond your silly and the CEO of Quantum World. What you will know soon is only known to Philip, Edward, and Tabi." I pause and then admit, "And Vandal."

(Time cave in Vincent's home)

"Welcome to the time cave, Dr. Abajian," welcomes Athena.

Now that Akane knows about me, I can use the core to come here and return to her quickly. This saves me time at the cost of a bit of exertion. For my travels, I create turbulence inside the core. As long as I keep it under a few minutes, there is no risk of the turbulence leaking into the external world. This is my life until I find common ground, where the words "Akane" and "home" would point to the same geographic spot. Akane wasn't even a bit surprised by my ability.

She said, "I sensed you had your way with time. That's how I perhaps knew you before I knew you." She did not explain any further.

I sit before one hundred monitors and rest my forehead against my palm. This system can monitor everything connected to the Quantum World network, but I can only see the global network address to the outside world. This system can't pinpoint individual computers. What if I use The Mind to monitor the activity? Every copy of The Mind will have a unique MAC address and brain frequency.

I close my eyes and press my temples. When we beta test Neurolink, will Vandal hack our network to steal the MAC address and know the beta users' identities? He could then hack into their digital infrastructure. Should I stop it? I can't catch him if I do. How could I figure out exactly which machine performed the hack?

I open my eyes and snap my fingers. Bingo! Yes, The Mind has to become a virus. The software of The Mind will embed a code that will monitor activities in and out of every connected infrastructure of our beta users. It has to surpass the security protocol of firewalls. I rub my hands. This is exciting.

Bring it on, Vandal.

Now, I just need to write microcodes and inscribe them into The Mind.

"Ludwig, open PL/I[40] and Prose."[41] I put on my headpiece and think the code, and it writes automatically. "Ludwig, create a protocol to bypass everything and inscribe this code into every copy and version of The Mind's software."

"Is this ethical, Vincent?"

"In the strictest sense, no." I don't have time to debate the ethical repercussions with my team. "But this will catch Vandal unless law enforcement gets to him first." Is Vandal one person or a group?

"Ah! Well, in that case, utility supersedes ethics."

"Um, let's call this code The Enigma."

"Perfect! And who knows? Maybe law enforcement will catch him before you deploy the code."

"Yes, I will delete The Enigma if Vandal gets caught."

I'll entice some beta users—billionaires and celebrities—to test the Neurolink before the official launch. I smirk and rub my palms. Vandal will try to hack us to get into the system of one of the beta users. He will try to bring me down for whatever reason. Then, The Enigma will record every transaction, and we will find him. Philip's cloud is too complicated and riddled with queries to pinpoint one discrepancy. It has to be my network. I have to be the vulnerable one. I won't share this with Philip; he won't get my contempt for commercializing alternate realities yet having no qualms about using The Mind like a virus. I hope Tabi and Akane never have to find out about this.

---

[40] PL/I (Programming Language One) is developed by IBM. Vince uses that to inscribe codes.

[41] Prose is a software that students in Vincent's university created using funds from the Center of Inventive Studies. Later on, those funds were stripped from the university and used to fund Quantum World.

"Right, Hulk?" I look down at my feet, searching for him. He is always near my feet. But today, he is with Anna. I feel his fur, his warmth on my feet, even when he is not here. I sniffle. Boy, I miss him—his furry coat, the smell of butterscotch in his ears, his licks.

Let's get back to Akane. I snap my fingers.

(Back to Akane's bedroom a few minutes later)

I change into my monogrammed pajamas and slip under her covers. She turns to me and opens her luminous eyes. "Will you reduce your trips through this core?"

"Why?" I ask, gently running my finger across her face, neck, shoulder, and arms.

She crumples my shirt in her fist. "It's not healthy. Use my plane; you are worth the wait." Sinking her lips into mine, she whispers, "Let's go to Kiyomizu-dera in spring!"

"What's there?"

She puts her finger on my lips. "Shhh! Silly. We will be." Wrapping her arms around my neck, she winks. "Forever."

(Quantum World—Executive conference room)

Anna grins at me and says, "A few days in Japan, our boy moves from opposing colors to offering an entire palette. And now, anime!"

"Yeah, yeah. Whatever."

Winking, Anna teases me, "So, are you dressed to your left or right today?"

Gritting my teeth to hide my smile, I blurt, "Shut up." Looking around, I see the rest of my crew struggling not to laugh at Anna's remarks and my reaction.

Tabi puts an *Ebi nigiri* in her mouth and shuts her eyes in pleasure. Still chewing, she turns to me. "Let's keep your relationship with Akane private for a few more days."

"Why?" I bang on the desk.

Shaking his head, Ravi chuckles. "Look at Vince, defiant like a teenager."

Tabi pumps her inhaler and looks at me. "The press will spin the story differently. They will say you're with Akane because the Egamis are funding us ten billion. We need to control the story."

Anna puts a piece of *maguro sashimi* in her mouth. "Fuck. This chef is a genius." She squints at me. "We are not paying him, right?"

"Nope. The ramen stall, the sushi bar, and the organic grocery are all part of the Egami deal. Akane comes with the deal, too, as a board member."

Tabi then takes the remote, switches on the TV, and turns to me. "Let me know what you think?"

A woman with tightly curled white hair and a reading glass appears on the screen. On her desk is the nonworking prototype of The Mind.

The woman leans forward. "Hello, I'm Dr. Laura Feldman, a neuroscientist with Johns Hopkins University. We have spent decades trying to solve the memory loss problem, especially related to Alzheimer's and dementia." Then, she picks up The Mind prototype. "I'm proud to say that the talented scientists at Quantum World have developed a system of storing your memory in this device and transferring it back while restoring the neurons that decrease with age." She leans closer to the camera, removes her glasses, and puts the helmet on. "This is the future. Are you ready?" The infomercial ends with a disclaimer: "Neither Dr. Laura Feldman nor Johns Hopkins is affiliated with Quantum World."

I nod. "Okay, run it."

"Thanks." Tabi gathers her folders and puts them under her arm.

Chris glances at me with glinting eyes. "Thanks for sharing the Egami stocks, by the way. I know they were only meant for you."

"I shouldn't be the only billionaire in this room."

Tugging my hand, Anna bats her eyes. "So, how are things? And why is Akane not here?"

Biting into a *maguro nigiri*, I explain, "She is getting roped into her business. It gives her a sense of identity, power, and purpose against a deeply entrenched patriarchal, monoethnic culture."

"What do you mean?" Ravi asks, squinting.

Exasperated, I exhale, "It's not easy being half-Japanese, a woman, and in a relationship with someone of mixed race. The rules of men and women are different. If the men board members have undergraduate degrees from Tokyo University, the women need MBAs. Being half-Japanese, she might need one from Harvard or Wharton." Staring at the table pensively, I scoff. "For all its rich culture, Japan is still reluctant regarding acceptance." Looking at my colleagues, I add, "Especially in politics, corporations, and administrative positions in academia. Music and art are the only exceptions, at least on the surface."

"Half? I have heard her mention that before . . . But she is Japanese?" Anna asks, scrunching her face.

"Doesn't matter—the passport or the land of birth. Ethnicity trumps everything there." As the faces around me grow somber, I wave my hand. "Let's change focus." Scanning their faces, I say, "Something's bothering me."

"Go on." Anna squints at me.

Looking up, I sigh. "Even with technological maturity, the cost of The Mind will still be steep for regular people. I'm sure medical insurance companies will deem it unnecessary."

Tabi leans forward and touches my hand. "It can be solved. You just have to put on an act."

"An act?" I ask, tilting my head at her.

"Come back from Japan in May. I have a plan," she explains, grinning from ear to ear.

(April 14, 2026—Twilight Express Mizukaze)

We are in our private suite on the overnight train, heading to Kyoto to see the cherry blossoms. I pictured it from her stories and through her violin as a child. When I finally came to Japan in 2014 with Elise, witnessing the cherry blossoms had no meaning because Akane was lost in turbulence. And the cherry trees at home only teased a strange void.

Akane snaps her fingers an inch from my face. "What's up?"

Locking our eyes, I explain, "You and me exploring the world I witnessed decades back through your words, and your eyes seem surreal." My heart flutters as I close my eyes and smile. "I want to capture this and relive it across lives, space, and time—"

The train screeches, almost rupturing our eardrums. We both cover our ears.

With her ears covered, she breathes anxiously. "This had never happened before."

The train stops. I move Akane's hands from her ears. "He is here."

"*Dare?*" she asks, eyes wide.

"Vandal." I touch her arms. "Stay put, don't panic. I'll resolve this."

I know what future Vincent meant when he said, "You can use it safely when needed."

I snap my fingers and create a spark. Akane's jaw drops as she points at the spark. "This is what appeared in Berlin."

Gritting my teeth, I say, "Now, it bends to my will." Then, I look at her. "This will form an impenetrable crystal shield, and I'll cover you. You will be fine, removed from this reality and invisible to the outside world. And no one can hurt you."

I cover my Akane like a cocoon. She and the shell are now only visible to me. Touching the outer wall, I tell her, "I'll be back. I love you." She touches the inner wall. Snapping my fingers, I enter the core.

"Ludwig, prepare a path to the control room of this train."

The path lights up, and I snap my fingers to create another turbulence, leave the core, and enter the control room. In the center is a concave desk with endless monitors showing routes to each train station. Several ones are blinking. The operators, four of them, are incapacitated. I de-suit myself. Where is the fuckface?

I shriek in pain as I feel a sharp object cut my neck. Even before I touch my neck, I can feel the blood squirting. I reach over my shoulder and pull out a *shuriken*. It sunk deep to penetrate the intreton in my body, missing my medulla by a hairline. Was that intended?

Quickly turning around, I see Vandal all suited up. I don't need to suit up. He knows who I am. He is taller—much taller than me. Bending his knees, he throws five *shurikens* before retrieving a dagger from his belt. Taking out my retractable *katana*, I slice through the *shurikens* one by one, each shattering to pieces from the ground, scratching the control chairs, tables, and lampshades before taking out one of the monitors.

I slant my head, breathing hard. "You can't fight me," I snarl at him.

He jumps at me with his dagger. As he pounces near, I make four precise cuts on his suit and rip it open; he can't enter the core anymore, despite his snapping ability. He falls, rolls, and retakes a fighting position while ensuring his suit's face covering is intact. He retracts, builds momentum, and leaps at me. I kneel down, catch him by his suit, and use his momentum to toss him against the wall. As his back smashes into it, the thud is followed by a crack in the wall. He groans and falls flat on the floor. He grunts, holding his chest. Pressing his back against the wall for leverage, he stands up. Then, shattering the glass window with the handle of his dagger, he jumps out. Should I chase after him? He can't use the core with his suit ripped, and he can't get far with his wounds.

I form a fist and clench my jaw. Yes, let's do this. Then, I hesitate. What about these people? If I chase Vandal without waking them, the delay will get longer, and authorities will inspect the Twilight Express. They will check the roster and won't find Akane. Then, they will alert authorities about her missing, making Masayoshi and Theresa panic. They have had enough of that. What if I wake these people, start the train before it is too late, and chase after Vandal? But that would mean Akane has to spend longer in the intreton casing. And she would be terrified if I'm not there when the train starts to move. She shouldn't spend that long inside that shell.

I grit my teeth. Dammit! Even in his loss, Vandal wins.

I press the green button on my bracelet and suit up before shaking one of the operators. He slowly opens his drugged, heavy eyes. I ask, "Can you operate the control room?"

"*Hai.*"

"Great. Wake the others, and put an APB on a person with four cuts. Two on the shoulders and two on the thighs."

Though confused, he says, "Thank you, sir," and proceeds to wake everyone up.

I snap my fingers.

Back in our suite, I tap on the intreton casing, which dissolves. Akane bursts out of it and grabs my shoulders, shaking me. "What if something happened to you?"

Kissing her forehead, I assure her, "I heal quickly."

(April 15, 2026—Kiyomizu-dera)

The afternoon sun shines on the roof of Kiyomizu-dera and the surrounding sakura, making everything glitter. For each step I take, Akane, in her pink, floral kimono and burgundy obi, is leapfrogging past me, turning around, and smiling at my bewilderment.

Springing toward me, she tugs my gray and navy kimono. "What's on your mind?"

Sighing in delight, I admit, "For the hundredth time—you." She is not surprised by my response. The surrounding beauty holds no value without her in my life. Yes, I'm a foreigner, and people are squinting at me, some even laughing. I don't care. With her by my side, I am always home.

We walk down to the Otowa-no-Taki waterfall, known for its wish-granting powers. She points to the long-handled ladle underneath the water and then brings it to me. "Drink."

Closing my eyes, I oblige. Then, Akane does the same. As we continue on our way, she nudges my arm. "What did you wish?"

I hold her hand and keep walking. "The same wish I made the day I turned eight; please let me be close to you all my life." Akane runs her fingers under her eyes to catch her tears. I put my arm around her shoulder. "Your turn."

She tilts her head. "I want to find you in every life, every reality."

We are now standing next to what is known as the love stone in the Jishu Shrine. Akane points me to the second stone about thirty feet away. "Stand there. And don't guide me." She then covers her eyes and begins her thirty-foot journey. About a minute later, she grabs my kimono, opens her eyes, and laughs.

"What?" I ask, looking into her eyes.

"Let's walk. I'll tell you as we go." She points her finger at me and says, "Promise me you won't laugh."

"I won't."

She holds my right hand, and we begin to walk while she swings our hands between us like children. We did that in school. She smiles and begins, "I was seven years old the first time I was here. I told Mamma and Papha very decisively that I wanted to marry you." Then, she glowers, grits her teeth, and forms a fist with her right hand like a child whose candy is denied. "They burst into laughter at my resolve."

Trying not to smile at her plight, I remark, "Aww. I'm sorry they didn't take your marriage plans seriously when you were seven."

She stops to examine my face, narrowing her eyes when she sees me pressing my lips together to hide my grin. Crossing her arms, she looks away. She says, "I won't say anymore."

I stop and touch her shoulder. "I'm sorry." We begin to walk and swing our hands again.

"Papha laughed and told me we needed to grow up first. And Mamma said that if I ever cross the distance between the two stones and open my eyes and see you, my wish will be granted. I did that every year till November 15, 1991, hoping you would be there on the other side when I opened my eyes."

She stops swinging our hands but keeps walking. "After I woke up from my coma in 2001, with no memories of my past, my parents brought me here. They were sure you were the key to my memories. 'Close your eyes, and when you reach the other end, open them and see what you remember,' said Papha each time. But something was blocking my memories." She pulls my sleeve and wipes her eyes with it. Her voice quavers. "I couldn't remember a damn thing." Then, she stops walking and looks into my eyes. "When I got my memories back, I thought that if you were unattached, I wanted to bring you here and make you wait for me on the other side." She rests her head against my chest. Her shoulders shake as she cries. "I'm glad you were unattached when I found you."

I kiss the top of her head. "Attached, unattached, this silly is always yours." There's no one and nothing more important.

(Late fall 1991—Library, Montagnola)

Although fully healed, my ribs were still sore. As I pressed them, Akane pulled the chair next to me. Leaning on the table, touching my hand, she asked, "Still hurts?"

"A little." I touched the scarf she'd wrapped around me a week back. I was unsure how I felt but could not move my eyes away from her. Like an idiot, I asked, "You want the scarf back?"

Smiling, she said, "Keep it with you . . . till I return from Berlin."

I grabbed her hand and asked, "Do you have to go?"

"Just two days." Then, she opened her geometry book. Pointing at the chapter on congruent triangles, she nudged my sleeve. Handing me her yellow highlighter, she asked, "Can you highlight the most important part?"

I took the highlighter from her and thought for a bit. At eight, I was still lost when it came to the nature of my feelings. I did not want her to go to Berlin. But I knew she had made up her mind. Uncapping the highlighter, I ran it across her left cheek. "There," I said.

The afternoon sun shone on her wide-open eyes. Startled, she asked, "What?"

Looking down at the desk, mustering all my courage, I confessed, "I highlighted the most important part."

(Back to the present)

I move her head from my shoulder and wipe her tears with my thumbs. I kiss her left cheek—the same spot I once highlighted. A puff of wind pastes her kimono to her skin. She closes her eyes as I bring her face against my shoulder.

I can feel her heartbeat and mine as I whisper into her ears, "Do you feel the same way you felt when you were seven?"

She looks down as her face flushes. "*Hai*." Using my body as a shield against the wind, she looks up and smiles. "How about we work on it after you're done with your product announcement?" The wind passes. We enter the shrine. Smiling, she says, "Follow my lead."

Before entering the red *torii*, she bows, and I repeat. She then washes her hands with water—first left, then right. Then, she pours water into her mouth and signals me to repeat the actions.

We now walk into the *saisenbako*, and each of us offers *goen*.[42] Then, she pulls a rope attached to a large bell, pulling it once to expel the demons. I like this step. After ringing the bell once myself, I want to repeat the process. But she takes my hand and shakes her head. I pout. In return, she kisses my hand. We enter the worshipping area. She bows twice and claps twice. I follow her lead. Then, she sits on the floor with folded knees, keeping her hands on her chest, and closes her eyes. What is she praying for? Do I have to pray for anything? Yes. I follow her stance and close my eyes. If I'm reborn, then I want her in every life.

After a few moments, Akane stands up, and I follow her to the *ema* display—wooden prayer plaques. She buys a vermilion, *torii*-shaped *ema* that's seventeen by fourteen inches. On the left *hashira*, she writes my name in *katakana*—*Vu~insento*. She writes her own in *kanji* on the right—*Hashira*. On the *nuki*, she writes the date, April 15, 2026. She hands me the *ema* and points at the *shimaki*.

"Write something here. It must have words from both of us."

With the plaque in my left hand and brush pen in my right, I ask, "For?"

She tilts her head and squeezes her eyes into two lines of lashes. Then, she whispers into my ear, "To stand the test of time and reality." She steps back, crosses her arms, and looks away. "Unless you don't want to."

I know this is just a superstition. But I want to believe in it. Badly. Shaking my head and smiling, I write, *Across time and reality, this is where we will find each other—Vince.*

She takes the plaque and examines it. With her smiling lips opposing her moist eyes, she looks at me. Wiping away her tears, she says, *"Arigatō."* Then, she hangs the plaque on the *ema* stand next to a row of cherry trees. The red *ema* stands out, shimmering in the setting sun.

The lanterns come alive against the setting sun and slowly turn red, orange, and yellow. The golden hue from the sky touching Mount Otowa's peak is flawlessly balanced by the dimly glowing lights on the streets and inside the *machiyas*—which all seem painted by an artist whose sorrow could

---

[42]   Five yen.

only translate to love. Time may have ceased in this corner of the world. The artificiality of metropolis, and the triviality of humans, have been exorcised here. And in this city where profound art and culture hide behind effortless simplicity, I feel reborn. Every single drop of grief and pain that I've felt since November 15, 1991, is gently washing away in the evening scent of the incense, the spectacle of the lanterns, the echo of the toll bells augmented by the symphony of evening cicadas, the taste of exhilarating fresh air soaked in sakura blooms, and the touch of her hand, entwined with mine.

(Same time, April 15, 2026—Amari residence, Kyoto)

Emika

Mum lights up the lantern outside the *machiya*. Little Nozo looks like a doll in her floral kimono. She is standing and staring at the fully bloomed sakura in the *tsubo-niwa* of my parents' *machiya*. Next to her is a bookshelf filled with Papha's accolades—Order of Chrysanthemum, a knighthood from the UK, Jules Léger Prize, and five Grammys for best classical instrumental solo. He is softly keying Chopin's Andante spianato et grande polonaise brillante on his custom ninety-two-key Shigeru Kawai. His keying is magical. Wish I had that. Next to the piano are at least a dozen pictures of me since I was one year old. My favorites are the ones with Haru. As the water reaches its boiling point, Mum rushes into the kitchen for our customary *genmaicha* time.

I wrap my hands around her shoulders and sit beside my standing Nozo on the tatami mat. The wind shifts outside the glass window, and the petals fall like pink snowflakes.

Nozo's eyes expand as she brings her hands to her chubby cheeks and remarks, "Huh!"

Kissing her cheek, I ask, "Pretty?"

She nods her head with her eyes fixed on the sakura.

Papha stops playing and scoffs. "Doesn't her father have fifteen of those in his backyard?" Then, he gets up, pushing the piano bench back.

While bringing the tea set and placing herself between Papha and us, Mum quickly remarks, "Not the time, Hiroshi."

Sitting on the floor for his tea, he sneers, "Right! She is just thirty-five." His eyes are fixed on me as he grimaces and remarks, "Too young to know the difference between the good and the useless. Give up on the piano, give up on the violin." He shakes his head. "Give up Vincent for a blonde clown . . ." Squinting, he inquires, "What's his name?"

I kiss Nozo's cheek. "Why don't you play with the toys in the next room?" As she runs toward the room, I sit across from Papha. "Markus. And that clown was there for all my visits to the doctor. He took me to the delivery room." Gritting my teeth, breathing hard, I admit, "And we are just friends now."

Papha snarks, "*Sugoi!*[43] Making way for the next one?" Turning to Mum, he asks, "*Ocha o Kudasai.*"[44] While Mum pours us tea, Papha looks back at me through his reading glasses. "How about you try a substance abuser next time?"

I swallow back my tears. Banging on the table, Mum shrieks, "Hiroshi!" Placing her shaky hand tenderly over my wrist, she says, "She is all we have."

Gasping for breath, avoiding eye contact, I say, "All I wanted was for Nozo to see her *soba* and *sofu.*" Staring straight into my papha's piercing eyes, I fight back. "Not for you to pass judgment on my life."

I know I made blunders, Papha. But can't you just be my papha for a change? A shoulder where I can hide from this world?

Standing up, he clears his throat. He croaks down at me, "Your life isn't worth judging." He then walks into the room where Nozo is playing. His voice is gentle as I overhear, "What do we have here? Wow, you finished the puzzle? You are just as bright as your mom."

As tears roll down my cheeks, Mum brings my head to her shoulder, assuring me, "*Chichi* loves you."

Pulling my head away and wiping my eyes, I ask, "Then what would he sound like if he hated me?"

In Chez-Giraud, you asked me to be kind, patient, and tolerant of my parents, Vince. Would you tell me the same if you ever met them—especially Chichi?[45]

---

[43]   Awesome!

[44]   Tea, please.

[45]   Chapter 11 of *The Winding* (Book 1).

CHAPTER 8

GRENADE

"I'm sorry if I've ever hurt you or if I do in the future"
—Philip

May 2026–September 2026

Vincent

THE EGAMIS HAVE FILLED TIMES Square, the Shibuya, Ginza, Hong Kong, Shanghai, Central London, Paris, San Francisco, Sydney, and Los Angeles with prime-time digital billboard ads featuring The Mind, my headshot with a thinking pose, and moving texts with the words: "What is Neurolink?" Tabi has unlisted our numbers and addresses from directory services.

(Set of What's Tonight? Los Angeles)

"Please welcome our third guest for tonight—Dr. Vincent Abajian," announces Maurice Johnson as he stretches out his hand. He leans over and whispers into my ear, "Tabi is a friend."

I am sitting closest to Maurice's desk, followed by the CEO of Health-Net, Beth Poirot, on my right and the Secretary of Health and Human Services, Greg Walter, on her right. On top of the coffee table in front of us are three water bottles and a nonworking model of The Mind, in yellow.

Pointing at the helmet, Maurice asks, "So, how does it work?"

Leaning down, I pick up the yellow helmet and point at the interior. "The intreton-c will connect with your neurons through small electric signals and form a link." Pointing at the Wi-Fi signal, I say, "The Wi-Fi will link up with our labs and store our consciousness."

"What if someone steals the gadget?" Greg asks. "Won't they access the owner's conscience?"

I chuckle. "This is 2025. Can you drive my car by simply stealing my key?" Then, I smirk at Greg. "I am part of the key." Tapping on The Mind, I explain, "This forms part of the key, the other being the biometric cocktail of brain waves, retina, and fingerprints." I look at the camera in the hope of enticing Vandal. "I don't think a hacker can hack The Mind or the cloud we are building."

Take the bait, Vandal, because I will keep a door open for you in April.

Maurice takes a sip from his coffee mug. "About this Neurolink . . . What is it?"

"I'll reveal it during Seattle's Annual Global AI conference this September," I say, adjusting my tie.

Beth takes The Mind and playfully puts it on her head. She teasingly comments, "Oh! I love it," poking my arm. After taking it off, she smiles at me. "$100,000 . . . that's steep."

Turning to Beth, I click my tongue. "Shouldn't you cover it?"

"Is it necessary?" Smirking, she turns to the audience. "At Health-Net, customer health is a priority." She points at me and adds, "Against your claims, this might do more harm."

The audience cheers, "Uuuuh."

In about a minute, the audience will change their tone. Idiots. I clear my throat. Sneering at Beth, I ask, "So, the EpiPen was unsafe? Or unnecessary? How many cancer treatments have you denied? Before you moved to insurance, weren't you a board member who decided to lift the price of Daraprim from $13.50 to $750?"

She leans across me and glares at Maurice, her face all red and eyes bulging out. "You need to vet your guests."

The audience changes its tune. "Booo." So predictable.

Maurice winks at her. "Maybe you need to answer my guest and the American people."

(Five days before the show—Vincent's home)

As I'm two sips into my double espresso, my home security in Athena's voice informs me, "Tabitha Bishara is in."

I wrap my robe around me and head toward the living room to see Hulk lying on his back, getting belly scratches from Tabi. She is in her UC Berkeley sweats and has a canvas tote.

Sitting on the sofa, I ask, "How is everything with the orphanage?"

"You should come more often. The kids idolize you," she says, then pumps her inhaler.

Yawning, I retort, "They have you."

She rolls her eyes. "Modesty doesn't suit you." Taking out a thick red folder from her tote, she says, "Details of your co-guests—Beth Poirot and Senator Greg Walter. Beth bribes Greg, and in return, Greg lets Beth deny insurance claims and keep premiums high." She opens the folder. "His properties cannot come from an annual salary of $174,000, and neither Greg nor his wife comes from wealth."

I snoop through the folder. "Is it conclusive that he received all these from Beth?" Grinding my teeth, I say, "Greg and Beth were involved with Dick Graham and . . . Elise?"

Tabi squeezes my hand. "Yes. According to my sources."

"From the *Tribune*?"

"Yep," she says. "They helped kill the photographs of you and Akane all over Tokyo and Kyoto from reaching the hands of tabloids. The Egamis are powerful enough to stop most, but here and in Europe, I have set up an alert to anything with your name and Akane's together after news of your birthday celebration leaked."

I place my hand over hers. "Thanks. I'm starting to see your plan in making the insurance firm cover The Mind." Looking through the evidence, I chuckle.

"What's the grin?"

I smile. "Might add Philip to our plan."

"How?" she asks, squinting at me.

I wink at her. "Watch the interview."

✺

(Back to the set of What's Tonight?)

Greg wrinkles his brows. The veins in his forehead pop as he argues, "Beth did nothing wrong." He grabs my arm and stresses, "You are an arrogant bastard."

Quickly removing his shaking grip from my arm, I smile. "Of course not, since you're the lawmaker." I scratch my head and look straight into Greg's gray eyes. "Weren't you Dick Graham's chief of staff when he pushed Alleren's allergy drug, Clear-day?"[46] Greg flares his nostrils as droplets of sweat form on his forehead. "In fact, you wrote the brief in which it was deemed safe. You got a cut, too." Turning to my left, I ask, "Maurice, how many people did Clear-day kill?"

"Two hundred and fifty thousand reported deaths."

I pull my cuffs and adjust my pocket square, clearing my throat. "You know what's more interesting? The lady to my right was the head of marketing at Alleren when Clear-day was launched." I point my thumb at Beth and stare into the camera. "None of the insurance denials would be possible

---

[46] The conspiracy surrounding Alleren's Clear-day, and the involvement of Dick Graham and Elise Graham (Vincent's deceased ex), is sprinkled throughout *The Winding* (Book 1).

without the blessing from our beloved Greg Walter." Taking a few folded papers from my bespoke gray and maroon plaid suit jacket, I drive it home. "I have some evidence, which will be published in the *Tribune* tomorrow."

Greg's face turns red. Fuming, he tries to grab the pages from me.

Holding them out of reach, I wave my finger at Greg. "Now, now. Don't get all greedy." I face the camera. "Did you know he has a mansion in Beverley Hills in his wife's maiden name?"

The studio booms with booing from the crowd. I can't help but smile at what's coming.

"My wife is independently rich," Greg argues, grinding his teeth at the camera.

I jeer, "Wow! Paralegals make more than football coaches?"

Breathing quickly in panic, Greg points his finger at me. "You son of a . . ."

Moving on to another page, I continue, "A yacht in his daughter's name, using her mother's maiden name. And a beach house in Maui, in his son's name." I flip to another page and look at the camera. "Aren't taxpayers entitled to know who pays for Mr. Walter's lifestyle? The evidence will unequivocally show it's the lady to my right, Ms. Poirot."

Greg pulls out his pocket square and wipes his forehead, puffing.

I angle my body to my right, looking at Beth now. "Your denials have killed more people than most pandemics."

Leaning forward, Beth turns to Maurice and spits, "How can you let this motherfucker talk to a woman like that?"

Maurice sneers. "Wow! Where was your empathy for women when you denied medically required abortions?"

Beth grabs a bottle of water and gulps down half of it. I can see the veins on her forehead throb.

My phone vibrates in my pocket with an alert, but I ignore it. Picking up The Mind and tapping on the helmet, I declare, "I will not release this unless the product and the network are safe." Then, I put the helmet back on the table and stare directly into the camera. "No politicians will ever fight for coverage of Alzheimer's." Pointing my finger between Beth and Greg, I stress, "What you see here is not unique. Every politician is Greg, who is on the payroll of the likes of Beth." Shifting my finger to the camera, I ask, "Is there someone who can disrupt the medical insurance industry and care for the people they insure? Do you want Health-Net to keep robbing you? Do the shareholders and board of Health-Net care for the people they are legally bound to protect?"

My cell phone vibrates with alerts, and I ignore them with a grin. I need a few more.

(Two days before the talk show—Philip's house)

Moving the bishop, I look straight into Philip's piercing eyes. "Checkmate."

"Astonishing! Dave taught you well." His eyes glint with pride. Then, he asks, "Thoughts of commercializing the core?"

"Still on the fence." I am not on the fence; I am dead set against it. But I just can't bring myself to say that to Philip.

I am indebted to you. Maybe I can do something else for you.

I take a deep breath before sipping the finest Jamaican Blue Mountain coffee in my cup.

Noting my discomfort, Philip changes the topic. "If you want a more significant market for your product, the price must be far less than $100,000."

"Why is the onus on me to bring costs down?" I place the cup on the saucer. "If this solves problems associated with Alzheimer's, shouldn't insurance firms bear most of the cost? Patients will save a lot on medicine and years of therapy with The Mind."

Philip leans back and smiles. "They train agents to deny claims as unnecessary. They have a strong lobby, and politicians are in their pocket."

"If you were to run Health-Net, would you deny the claims?"

"No, I would run it differently." He exhales deeply in despair. "But I won't buy the firm."

"Why?"

He smiles wryly. "It's overvalued. Perhaps I would buy it if the market cap goes down by fifty percent."

Smiling back at him, I remark, "Look for a thumbs-up sign from me when I'm the guest on *What's Tonight?* Then, my friend, you can buy the firm." Taking out my phone, I set up an alert for stock quotes from Health-Net.

"Why?" Philip asks, taking off his glasses and leaning forward. "A penance for keeping you on the fence."

✦

(Back to the set of What's Tonight?)

As the faces of Beth and Greg change from angry red to fearful white, I deliver my final blow. "The two of you look pale. You could use a pint of blood." I take a second's pause and smile at what I'll say next. "Shouldn't be a problem with all the blood of the American people on your hands."

My phone vibrates again, and now I take it out of my pocket. Stocks of Health-Net are down from $750 to $110. Wow. I am currently a stock market manipulator. I face the main camera and raise my thumb.

Do it, Philip.

Maurice narrows his eyes at me. "What was that?"

I shrug. "Me picturing tomorrow's headline." Then, moving my right hand from left to right, I say, "'CEO of Health-Net Fired for Corruption' and 'Internal Affairs Begins Investigation Against Secretary of Health and Human Services.'" I rub my hands together and grin.

✦

(Backstage of What's Tonight?)

I'm heading out of the dressing room when someone taps my shoulder. Turning, I see only a silhouette of a man's face against the blinding lights from the ceiling.

"You left The Mind in the dressing room." He pauses and continues, "Sir."

"It's just a shell. But thanks, though." Without taking the helmet from him, I turn around and begin to walk away. Stopping, I lift my finger and turn back. "You witnessed history today. Maybe you can auction it on eBay," I say, winking.

What accent was that? It's LA, so maybe he was just rehearsing a character.

(Vincent's home)

My phone rings as I'm about to feed Hulk. It's Akane.

"Hey."

"That was hot. Can you come over?"

"I'll be there after feeding Hulk."

"I'm sorry to deprive him of his daddy."

"Why can't we move in together? That way, he will know his mum better."

"I love you."

"I love you, too."

Hanging up, I press my temples and shut my eyes. Was there someone other than Elise who referred to herself as Hulk's mum?

(Entertainment room in Vincent's house)

Anna has drawn two things on my floor-standing whiteboard. The sketch on the left looks like Mickey Mouse, and something circular on the right. Tabi and I are supposed to guess. Our opponents, Chris, Maddy, and Ravi, are trying not to laugh.

I'm yet to take charge of drawing, and we are losing one-zero. Earlier, Tabi drew two identical tic-tac-toes to denote *The Imitation Game*. I'm not sure what's worse—this game or their drawing skills. I exhale in hopelessness. Ravi's hand is interlocked with Maddy's—the volunteering helped. Shrugging, Chris points at the hourglass. Time's up, and we are now losing two-zero.

Gritting her teeth, Anna looks at me. "It was supposed to be *Batman Begins*." She points to what looks like Mickey Mouse. "That's Batman." She moves her finger over the circle she drew. "That's a sun denoting *begins*."

Scratching my head, I ask Anna, "Don't tell me you took drawing lessons?"

"I did." She puts one hand on her waist and holds up four fingers with the other. "For four years."

I point at her artwork. "That would kill your art teacher." Then, I look at everyone and frown. "This game is stupid."

Maddy winks at me mischievously. "You are a sore loser."

Tabi crosses her arms. "And mean. I'll tell Akane." She scowls at me. "She will spank you."

Rolling my eyes, I quip, "Yeah, that'll teach me." I get up from the chair and stretch my arms. Turning to Tabi, I ask, "Is my speech ready?"

Collecting the magic markers, she says, "Almost." Then, she looks at her watch. "How about we come back for round two after pizza?"

As we move upstairs, the house smells of molten mozzarella, sizzling pepperoni, roasted peppers, and mushrooms. I yawn and stretch my back. "I haven't had pizza for so long."

While Tabi turns on the oven warmer, I assist Maddy and Ravi with the plates and wine. Chris fetches the glasses while Anna taps her chin and mutters, "Whose slice besides mine should I try?"

My phone rings. Glancing at it, I see Akane's face on the screen. With my hands full of plates, I ask Tabi, "Can you please answer it?"

"Hey, Akane." Tabi puts it on speakerphone.

"Hi, Tabi." Akane responds in her musical voice.

Tabi leans over the phone, crosses her arms, and whines, "Vince is being mean."

"Where is he?"

"Right next to me."

"Vince?"

"Yes?"

"Don't be mean."

"I wasn't," I argue, shaking my head.

Breathing into the phone, Akane says, "I have a question for Tabi."

"Yes?" Tabi asks.

"Can I be by Vincent's side when we enter the venue?"

Clapping, Tabi lifts her voice in jubilance. "That'll be perfect. A year would have passed since the funding, and now, no one will question conflicts of interest." Snapping her fingers, she winks at me. "Let me see if we can book you two on the morning show the next day."

"*Sugoi*. Vince?"

"Yes?"

"I have a board meeting coming up in three weeks. I want to show them the possibilities of growth with AI. Can you help me?"

"Sure. You want to do it over Zoom, or do you need me there?"

"What do you think?" she asks sternly.

Chris and Ravi lift their brows while Anna wiggles hers.

Smiling, I say, "I'll be there."

"You better be."

"Yes, ma'am." I indulge.

"Have fun, and don't be mean. *Oyasumi nasai*." She hangs up.

Pointing at my face, Anna giggles, then addresses everyone, "Just look at him, all blushing."

Suddenly, Anna snatches my phone. Hitting my knuckles on the kitchen counter, I demand, "Hey, give it back."

She smiles mischievously and starts running around the dining table. Wiggling her eyebrows, she says, "I wanna see the dirty texts between you and Akane."

Chasing her, I shout, "There aren't any!"

"Catch." Anna tosses the phone to Ravi as I am about to catch her.

After catching it, Ravi hands the phone to me. Anna fumes at him, giving him the stink eye. "Sucker."

Stretching my arms, I say, "How about some pizza for Vince?" Then, I open the pizza box marked "Idiot" by Anna. Covering the pizza are only onions, mushrooms, artichokes, garlic, and spinach. Turning to Anna, I ask, "The fuck? When did I change my pizza order?"[47]

They all shrug and look at each other.

I close my eyes and sniff the pizza. "I love the smell, though, and it looks healthy."

As I take the first bite, I see a hazy image. I share a pizza box with a girl with short, bobbed hair. Hulk is begging for a piece. Touching his head, she lovingly gives him some breakfast cereal. Around the kitchen counter, I see moving boxes. Who is she? I squeeze my eyes to get a closer look, but

---

[47] In *The Winding* (Book 1), Emika changed Vincent's pizza order to a healthy, vegetarian option.

everything disappears. Did I move into this house with someone? I rest my elbows on the kitchen counter and my head in my palms.

Tabi touches my shoulder and asks, "You okay?"

"Yes," I say, massaging my temples.

(Nardin residence)

After taking a sip of my Jamaican Blue Mountain, I say, "Never thought you would work with the DoD."

Leaning back, Philip looks out the window. "NASA was interested in my intreton-powered spaceship to see the feasibility of commercial space travel. The DoD wants to test the practicality of such an aircraft for long-distance flights." Lifting his finger, he asserts, "My only condition was that it should not be weaponized." Then, he smiles with pride. "The X60 will revolutionize air and space travel. The working prototype will be ready next month."

"But what made you agree to this?"

Smiling deviously, locking his eyes with mine, he reveals, "That event will happen in the future. You will find out soon."

So, I am involved in this decision? Revealing it to me now may change the future. I sigh.

Detecting my discontent with this, Philip stands up and pulls my cuff. "Let me show you something." Leaving his fifty-foot-long office, study, and studio, we go to stand in front of his painting *Gnossienne 1, 2, and 3*. The piano in the picture has ten white keys and seven black keys.

Smiling, Philip looks at me. "Can you extrapolate AABCCB on these?"

"The first six notes of Gnossienne 1? Of course." I touch the canvas on those painted keys in sequence. Turning my head to Philip, I say, "The mystery is killing—"

Before I finish my sentence, the floor starts to retract, save the tiles on which Philip and I are standing. The retracted tiles transform into stand-alone steps, supported by carbon fiber rods. The steps light up, illuminating a path downstairs. My eyes widen. I am at a loss for words.

Grinning, Philip says, "Let's go down."

After stepping down fifty more steps, we reach a kitchen large enough to serve dinner to about a hundred people. Twenty robots are busy chopping, baking, roasting, frying, and making broth.

"Who are they cooking for?" I ask.

"You will meet my staff soon."

I touch Philip's shoulder and whisper, "Which one is Gai?"

The sound of knives chopping vegetables and cleavers cutting through meat stops as the robots turn to me. "We are all Gai! Pleased to meet you, Master Vincent."

Philip nods at them and starts walking, and I follow him. He snaps his fingers, and an entire stone wall retracts like a Japanese door. After we pass through the opening, the wall conceals the kitchen again. As Philip claps thrice, the display podiums rise from the ground—layouts of the pyramids' interiors, photographs of the interiors of forbidden rooms in the Taj Mahal, the first automobile from 1885 made by Carl Benz. Next to the car is a thirty-foot-long case displaying every unowned Stradivarius violin.

Philip spreads his arms as we walk past the violins. "It was easier buying all these than bidding on just the 1713 Schreiber." He looks at me and smiles. "You can now gift these to an aspiring prodigy. Everything is yours and Tabi's."

I don't want any of these; I don't wish my childhood poverty to be balanced in this manner. A little further down the display room is the first tourbillon made by Abraham-Louis Breguet. Philip's tourbillon encasing the core is just a massive replica of this. My jaw drops as I see the *Mona Lisa*, Dali's *Persistence of Memory*, and Van Gogh's *The Starry Night* side by side. Unable to express my thoughts in words, I stare at Philip. He ruffles my hair.

"Leo made more than one." Then, he adds, "Do you think *The Starry Night* and *Persistence of Memory* in MoMA are the originals?" He scrunches his lips. "How many people sneeze and cough on them?"

As we cross the room, the floor descends into a seeming abyss. "Where does it go?" I ask.

"It's the most secured vault in the world. It only reveals itself if I want it to. The vault is connected to my brain waves—the same tech used in The Mind."

We enter a room with thirty-seven clocks aligning with the Coordinated Universal Time. Philip goes to the center of the room and opens the back of the clock displaying the Greenwich Mean Time. He presses a green button, and the floor on which we are standing starts to descend rapidly, my jacket and hair flapping upward around me. The buoyancy makes me feel light, and I place my hand on my chest to steady myself.

We reach a two-story, rectangular hallway about a hundred meters long and fifty meters wide. There is a capsule elevator in the middle of the hall. At least a hundred people in black suits are working on screens or paper in the room. So, the Gais are cooking for these people. There are 3D holograms of the terrain of his private island. About fifteen people are moving the holograms back and forth between computer screens. Seven people analyze all the traffic in and out of the White House and the Capitol. Philip claps once, loudly, and everyone stops what they are doing.

Then, he puts his hand on my shoulder. "Everyone, this is Vincent Abajian."

The people give a chorus of hellos and then return to their work.

I ask Philip, "What are all these?"

He waves his hand in a gesture that encompasses the hall. "This room has thirty supercomputers analyzing data from all my satellites." Pointing at the monitors, he says, "Each of them has a fifty-monitor system, analyzing data from the healthcare sector to the stock market for any irregularities." He pauses. "We are on high alert since Vandal broke into my facility." Then, he touches my shoulder. "I'm sorry we were not fully operational when he attacked the train in Japan."

I sigh. "I almost had him."

"Now, I'm always on alert. I'll know as soon as he makes his next attack." Philip lowers his head. "But I won't be able to flush him out."

"I know. He could be anywhere, doing damage remotely."

That's why we will use Neurolink. Let him hack us, and we will know his location and identity. But we aren't ready yet.

But I don't tell Philip my plan.

"Listen carefully," Philip says, shaking my shoulder. "You must sit out some of the attacks."

"Why?"

"He wants our attention. Sitting out will make him do something rash. He doesn't know you were behind stopping the cloud infrastructure attack, so he became hasty and made the train attack, nearly exposing his identity." Lifting his finger, he explains, "Tactful retaliation is the key."

"Okay."

Walking around the hall, I see a team of researchers interacting with a 3D hologram of an aircraft and a tank. Approaching them, I ask, "Can I see those?"

"Sure," one researcher says, handing me a pair of gloves and a 50,000 pressure-sensitive digital pen.[48]

I take the 3D hologram[49] of the plane—if I can call it that. The aircraft's wings can be flapped and even move back to make it look like an eagle diving into the water.

Looking at the researchers, I ask, "For diving?"

The researcher who handed me the pen and gloves says, "Yes. We call it the 'Falco plane.' It's an X60 with flappable wings."

I flip the model but see no wheels. Instead, the aircraft has extensions that look like the legs of eagles.

Squinting at them, I ask, "Excavation of intreton?"

"Yes."

I point to the hologram of the tank. "What do you call that?"

"An Amphi tank."

Touching the model, I see it has four barrels and propellers. From the hologram, I gather it can swim—hence the name. Philip's use of his intreton to wage war makes my heart race.

Taking off my gloves, I lean toward the analysts. Lifting my voice, I ask, "What are these for? How many have you guys made?"

Their faces turn white, and they look beyond me at Philip.

He touches my shoulder. "Follow me." As we leave the holograms behind, Philip tells me, "I don't think Vandal is a lone wolf."

---

[48]   This was one of Vincent's inventions when he was a professor. The funding was done through the Nardin Group. In *The Winding* (Book 1), Vincent uses it to analyze and interact with a 3D computer simulation of the time turbulence.

[49]   As mentioned in *The Winding* (Book 1), the interactive 3D hologram than can be taken out of a computer screen is also Vincent's invention.

I detect just a hint of fear in the tone of his voice.

Are you scared of Vandal, or are you hiding something from me?

He continues, "He may have the backing of a hostile government—maybe even domestic." As we reach the capsule elevator, he puts his hands on my shoulders, meeting my gaze. "I don't want war. But I want to be ready for those running him."

I stare into his eyes.

Why are you pressing my shoulders so hard?

"If we catch him, where will you keep him?" I ask.

The door to the capsule elevator opens, and we both enter.

"What happens if those hostiles take control of your Falco plane and Amphi tanks?"

He grins. "They are invisible to radar and every satellite, barring the couple I used to autopilot the ship out of the solar system in late 2023."

As the elevator descends, I feel nauseated, not just because of the downward buoyancy. I hold my chest, trying to even out my quick breathing. Is this all for Vandal? Will my inventions be used to wage catastrophe? What does Philip know that I don't?

The elevator stops at an oval-shaped room with walls filled with 3D holograms of intreton-powered suits. In front of each suit is a bracelet, like mine, which can conceal the suit. At the center of the room is a crystal cage, intreton rays crisscrossing around it like lasers. A wall projection screen shows Philip's island on the other side of the cell.

Philip points at the cell. "That's where we will keep Vandal." Then, he gestures at all the suits. "They are all made of intreton-c but reinforced with carbon fiber for strength and lightness." Turning to me, he says, "Pick a color."

I point to one that looks like a blend of Prussian blue and viridian green. "That's the one—the color of my eyes."

Philip grabs my wrist, removes my bracelet, and replaces it with the one corresponding to the suit I picked. "This one will glow green and blue when there is an emergency. Be ready to suit up then."

"Right."

He puts another bracelet on his own wrist and smiles at me. "Mine will turn red if you're in any distress."

"What if you are in danger?" I ask. "How can I know?"

His voice cracking a bit, touching my shoulder, he says, "Your life is far more precious than mine." After pausing, he asks, "Still on the fence about commercializing an alternate reality?"

Lowering my head, I say, "Afraid so."

How can you be so selfless to think my life is more precious than yours? I don't want to give you hope about commercializing an alternate reality, but I don't know how to tell you.

❋

(Vincent's office)

I take a small sip of my double ristretto and taste the subtle hints of blueberry and citrus—quintessentially Ethiopian. This perfectly balances Rachmaninov's No. 3, playing through my Bang and Olufsen Beolab 20. Hiroshi Amari, my favorite pianist and conductor, orchestrated this one. The name Amari seems way more familiar than just an idol. Why? Isn't that name listed on a couple of our patents?

Tabi knocks once and enters, holding a four-inch binder and some stapled papers. Then, she places the binder on my desk. Pushing her eyeglasses up her nose, she points at the bunder. "This is the conference program. Look over it, and let me know if you have any questions." She lifts her finger and instructs, "The reporters will pore over you when you enter, holding Akane's hand. Direct all of their questions to the next day's morning show."

I nod. "Noted."

Tabi hands over the stapled pages. "This is your script for the showcasing. Akane planned the stage, the music, everything." She smiles. "I think you will like the surprise."

Placing the pages next to my keyboard, I smile back. Time for the world to know about Akane and me. My phone vibrates with a call from Philip.

"What's up?" I ask.

"There is a problem with JPX. It's not on the news yet. Our satellite has picked up an abnormal level of offshore digital traffic, trying to dump Egami stocks and buy firms Egami is eyeing to acquire. Vandal may have hacked Egami servers."

"Fuck!"

"I'm trying to get them to halt all tradings until we isolate all unauthorized trade requests. It might take days."

"How can I help?"

"Be with Akane. Help her through this. She is new to this world."

"Sure." I hang up.

I'm so sorry to have doubted you when I saw your arsenal of weapons.

I rest my head on my hands and try to slow my breathing. Tabi locks the door, sits by me, and rubs my back. "Go."

"What?"

"Go to her." Tapping on her Omega De Ville, she confirms, "We have three weeks to prep. She needs you now."

(Akane's penthouse)

Akane is not in the living room. Opening the main door, I see Michisato and Masato laughing at some video on one of their cell phones. I walk into her study, attached to our bedroom. There's a nonresponsive JPX website on the computer and a PowerPoint slide with the projections I helped her calculate last week. I flip through some finance and management books in Japanese, sitting on the desk. My heart drums faster. Where is she? No. I won't lose her again. I open her closet, and everything is in place. I walk into my closet—all fine. I grit my teeth.

Where are you?

The water is turned off in the bathroom. I check the bathtub—empty. When I slide back the shower door, I find her dripping wet and lying on the floor in a fetal position. I take off my suit jacket, fold up my sleeves, wrap her in her white towel, and carry her to the bed. I return to the bathroom to bring two more towels and her monogrammed bathrobe. I touch her forehead. I jolt my hand back. She is burning up! I begin to dry her from her head to her feet. I wrap her in her bathrobe and dry her hair using her blow dryer. Her tears drip as I get done drying her hair.

Bringing her head to my chest, I say, "I'm here as long as you need."

Her lips quiver. "So many people depend on our stable stocks for retirement, emergencies . . ." She pauses as I wipe her tears with my pocket square. "I join, and this happens. They are right. I am just a *half*—"

Shaking her shoulder, I interrupt, "Shhh. Never say that. Every trade has stopped, and JPX will remain closed till every server and computer is isolated and secured."

"How do you know this?" she asks, pulling my sleeve.

"Philip is heavily invested in JPX, and I believe he owns most of Egami's stocks outside your family."

She kisses my hands and corrects me. "*Our* family." Then, she stands up and sneezes. "*Sumimasen*. Maybe we will take the hit and trade at a lower price."

I pull her back to the bed, against the backrest. "Won't happen. Philip will deploy buy and sell orders for Egami securities using different brokers as soon as trading resumes. This will push prices higher."

"That's manipulation," she says, eyes wide.

Staring into her innocent eyes, I smile. "That's finance. Anyone with a conscience wouldn't like it. Conscience won't make you the CEO."

She purses her lips. "Okay."

"Stay there," I say, pressing her shoulder as I stand up. "You're burning up. I'll get you some meds and make you some fish soup."

Thank you, Philip, for helping her.

I bring her a rich dashi cod soup. "*Tabete o kudasai.*"

She swallows the broth, bites into the fish, and smiles. Crumpling her brows, she asks, "Where is yours?"

"I made only one bowl."

Blowing on a spoonful of soup, she brings it to my mouth. Smiling, she says, "We'll share." Crossing her arms, she looks away, "Else, I won't have it."

There's no arguing with her. After sipping the rich soy and ginger dashi, I say, "Take a nap, and then we can go over your presentation."

Pulling my shirt, she asks, "Can you nap with me?"

"Yep."

"Did you like the tux I got you for your showcasing?"

"Of course. It looks like the first one you got me in 1991." I take a deep breath. "The day you called me family."

She kisses my lips. "My dress will be the same color as the kimono I wore that day." Her eyes light up as she looks at me. "I can't wait to wear it and announce what you are to me to the world."

(Five days before the Annual Global AI Conference—Vincent's office)

Hulk keenly observes me as I pace around my office, memorizing my script. This will be my third rehearsal before my team. They will be in any minute now. Vandal has made US news outlets concentrate more on what's happening outside the country's borders. There's a world outside the US? Wow. Who would have thought? The stock exchange in Japan was closed for a week. And last night was Akane's first presentation before the board. I'm waiting to hear from her.

My cell phone vibrates.

"Hi, Philip."

"Are you alone?"

"I'm expecting my team in five minutes."

"Vandal has hacked into air traffic services in Japan, Singapore, and Hong Kong."

My voice trembles. "What?"

"Several planes have been rerouted from their destination for no reason. Vandal may have altered the navigation systems. And unlike the train episode, he is doing it remotely. My satellites can't pick up a source."

"What can I do?" The guy I fought didn't seem bright enough to hack the stock market or do this. I grind my teeth. It has to be a team.

"It's not safe for Akane to travel."

"Can't I transfer some power to her so she can use the core to come here?"

"You want to burden her with that for just an evening? Anyway, she is encumbered running her firm."

"You're right. My head is not in the right place."

"Your focus right now should be Quantum World and Neurolink."

"Thanks for thinking of Akane."

"Of course. Talk later."

You saved Akane from Vandal's onslaught of JPX. And now this. You shouldn't feel like you have to; I don't blame you for November 15, 1991. I don't know what I have ever done to earn your help. Maybe after the conference, I will give in to your proposal of creating a market for an alternate reality. Let them all dwell in alternate realities and fucking die. Well, maybe not.

Just then, my team enters my office. I immediately turn on the TV, sighing heavily in exasperation.

"Breaking news from CNN. We've just received reports of a head-on collision between Flight 667, leaving Haneda for Seattle, and Flight 3078, landing in Haneda from LA. Flight 3078 was not even supposed to land at Haneda; its destination was Hong Kong. There are no survivors." Pressing his earpiece, the anchor continues, "Japan, Hong Kong, China, and Singapore will close their international air traffic until they secure their traffic controls. This shockwave is catastrophic for international trade. This incident has Vandal written all over it. This is his fifth attack, starting with Mr. Nardin's facility, the attack on Stellarcloud's servers, the Japanese train system, JPX, and now this."

I bite my fingernail.

So, you have resorted to killing. How long before you get to those I love? Akane, Anna, Chris, Fred, Hulk, Krista, Maddy, Philip, Ravi, Sasha, Tabi? Have I left out anyone?

Anna rushes to the small fridge in my office and fetches me a bottle of water. "Drink," she says.

Chris comes over and holds my trembling hand as I gulp the water. Then, he loosens my necktie and top button. "Thanks." Helplessly, with trembling lips, I state, "Someone, please call Akane."

Tabi calls her, putting the phone on speaker. Akane answers after three rings. "*Konnichiwa*, Tabi."

"Can you talk to Vince?" Tabi brings the phone close to me.

"Vince?"

My voice cracks. "Listen to me carefully."

"No, you listen. I can get a flight permit. If not, I'll sail to Taiwan and then fly to you. I planned the stage—"

"I am not going to spend another thirty-three years without you. Please, stay back for me."

"But Vince—"

I grind my teeth. "For once, listen to me. You didn't in November 1991. I can't lose you again."

She coughs into the phone and then hangs up without a word. I feel the wetness on my cheeks and realize all my resolve to hold my tears back before my team has failed. Anna touches my wrist while covering her mouth in disbelief. Chris and Ravi lean toward me.

Then, Tabi's phone rings, and she picks up. She nods. "Yes. You got it." After hanging up, she comes forward and rubs my back. "We will be here as long as you need."

"It was Akane, right?" I ask, glancing at her phone.

"Yes."

I look at my colleagues with teary eyes. "I can't lose any of you."

Pressing my shoulder, Ravi assures me, "You won't."

"I want Hulk on my lap."

(Four days before the Annual Global AI Conference)

It's 4:00 a.m., and I've already downed a double shot. I have to make it up to Akane. A smile forms on my lips when I think precisely what to do. I walk into my closet and put on my blue tux.

Kissing Hulk, I tell him, "I'll be back soon. But you'll be at Little Paws for two days. Auntie Anna will also be traveling. Okay, bug?" He whimpers and lies down.

I press the green button on my bracelet and snap my fingers.

(Akane's penthouse)

She is taking a late-night bath—which means I have forty minutes. Let's check the fridge. There is some salmon and shrimp. Hmm. Can I make risotto with Japanese rice? Why not?

I put on my apron and get the rice boiling. What about wine? I need something from 1982—her year of birth. Ah! There it is—the Lafite Rothschild 1982. My eyes fall on a different bottle—Screaming Eagle Cabernet 1991. Wow! What's that for?

I place the pan-seared salmon on the bed of risotto and arrange the shrimp around the perimeter of the rice, topping it off with grated truffle. I hear her footsteps as she follows the aroma and reaches the dining area. I quickly hide behind the pantry, observing her through the ajar door.

She looks around. "Silly." She places her hands on her waist and orders, "Come out now."

Showing up, I clasp my hands together. "I'm sorry for yelling and ruining your plan."

She comes over to me, kissing my lips. "Why are you wearing the tux?"

"For you. I'll also give my presentation to you. It will be like those dorm room rehearsals."

Wiping the corner of her eyes, she says, "Can you keep the food warm? I'll be back in fifteen minutes."

"Of course."

As she leaves for the bedroom, she turns back and points her finger at me. "No peeking."

"Promise," I say. Then, I put the food into the oven warmer.

Precisely fifteen minutes later, she emerges in a navy satin dress with a waist bow—red and white polka dots, the color of the obi she wore in 1991. She sits on the dining chair, touches her hair, and looks up at me.

"How do I look?" she asks, just like she did in 1991.[50]

I take a large sip of water. "You just unclogged all my blocked arteries." Going over to her and touching her dress, I ask, "This is the same fabric?"

---

[50] This scene is from Chapter 2 of *The Winding* (Book 1).

"Yes. I had to locate the mill where it was made." She kisses my hand. "It was worth it, right?"

"Yes. Every bit of it," I say, my voice shaking.

"That's why I was so hell-bent on attending the conference."

I sit next to her and bring her hand against my cheek, staring into her large eyes. "Can we not have an ocean between us? I know you can't move, but I can."

She wraps her arms around me. "Okay, let's do this."

❋

(Two days before the Annual Global AI Conference)

Another TV interview. Tabi promised this one would be shorter than the last one. The tanned interviewer with bleached teeth runs her fingers through her blonde hair.

"Is it wise to launch Neurolink in two days amid a crisis? Wouldn't your customers want assurance of security?"

So, Tabi was right; Trisha is an idiot whose parents bought her a degree from Brown. I take off my glasses and wipe them with my pocket square before putting them back on.

"How fluent is your English?"

She shrugs. "I'm a native speaker."

I'm glad you're not a surgeon or an engineer.

I scoff. "So, you should know the difference between showcasing and launching." I lean forward and tap on the desk. "We will be showcasing the product in a couple of days. We will beta test in early April 2027 and launch it in late April next year." Okay, let's build some trust and generate some positive feedback. I look at the camera and smile. "Our customers and their information security are our top priority."

Trisha leans closer. "What about Vandal?" she asks.

If it weren't for that fucker, I wouldn't be alone in the presidential suite at Four Seasons. Why did he only attack the Southeast Asia airline grid? Why is he trying to block Akane from coming here? I can't let my expression reveal my thoughts on TV. I can't let him suspect that The Mind and the Neurolink will catch him. Let's throw him a challenge.

Looking at the camera again, I smirk. "He can't hack our network." Under the desk, my hands are shaking. What if he takes the bait and I fail?

(Day of the Annual Global AI Conference—Presidential suite at Four Seasons)

The shit they serve as coffee is revolting. I requested an Origami Dripper and Ethiopian beans in my suite at Four Seasons. I wanted a palatable cup before the circus. Instead, I'm lying on the floor with spilled coffee on my robe and carpet. My fingers could barely lift the cup when I felt my heart going slow and my head becoming light.

My frequent trips to Japan and back, through the core, have pushed the limits of my suit and my body. But I want to spend all my waking and sleeping hours with her. I wish Hulk were here to lick me back to health. Grabbing onto the carpet fabric, I crawl toward the armchair. Using the armrests for support, I stand up. My head is spinning as I sit in the chair. The emergency case with intreton-filled syringes is just four feet away, on the other side of the coffee table.

Take only a tiny dose. Else the damage will be irreversible, Dr. Lee had warned.

I grab the case, take out one of the four syringes, and push a little of the intreton into my veins. Instantly, everything changes; I can see the minute dust on the carpets and the furniture and the crumples in my perfectly ironed shirt. Oxygen forces into my nostrils without me trying to breathe it in.

I can make out every word my neighbors say as if the walls are made of paper. "I want full custody of Adam. You get that, Susan?" The jarring sound of cars honking on the streets, every "Fuck you, I'm walking, here" and "Watch your step, motherfucker" is on a mission to pierce a hole through my eardrums. I put my hands over my ears and rush to the bathroom, dunking my head into the bathtub I'd already filled in preparation for a bath.

The deep, melodious rumbling of the six-liter V12 inside my Pagani Huayra is too dull to distract me from the empty passenger seat. I wanted to shout that the girl who called me family in 1991 is with me. Finally, she and I will be family. Tonight was supposed to be Vincent: 1, Turbulence: 0.

My phone vibrates with a notification from Tabi. They are in. Time for me to arrive.

※

As I walk through the door, I shut my eyes against the constant flashing of cell phones and cameras. A stampede of reporters is standing between my team and me. The clicks of the shutters and the flashing lights make me look for her familiar face. I know it's in vain, but I open and close my right hand, hoping to find Akane's hand.

Please, take my hand and rescue me from this crowd.

A reporter wearing a corduroy sports jacket comes out of nowhere and stands right before me. "How about a pose, Dr. Abajian?"

I wave my hand and walk toward the rescuing arms of my team. Anna comes forward and hugs me.

I whisper, "You look so lovely. Let's run away."

Punching my chest, she frowns. "Idiot."

I shake hands with Ravi, then with Chris. Hugging Maddy, I acknowledge, "Thanks for being here."

When Tabi comes over, I kiss her forehead. Then, I survey the room. It's hard to see since all the lights are shining on my team and me. But my eyes stop on a woman in a silky gray suit and pink blouse. She shimmers in the darkness, and her resemblance to Akane is uncanny. She is Akane with shorter hair. Wait, isn't she the one who comes into my dreams, with the child, who tells me I have moved on?

Who are you?

The blond guy standing close to her is whispering something into her ear. Maybe they are a couple.

Focus, Vince. Focus. You have Akane.

Shaking my head, I turn toward the media as someone asks, "What can you tell us about Neurolink?"

Can't they just wait? I tilt my head and smile. "You'll just have to wait half an hour. Else I have to say the same thing twice. I hate that."

Another reporter pushes through the others and comes in front. Panting, she asks, "Will you delay your launch because of Vandal? Do you have any message for him?"

As I approach the reporter and her camera crew, Tabi whispers, "You don't have to answer this."

Gently pushing past her, I whisper back, "Fuck, I do." I take the mic from the reporter and look around. "I won't delay anything." I can't get out of my head that Akane is not here because of Vandal. "And I have one message for Vandal: why don't you drop your mask and face me?"

I hand over the mic and walk toward my team as some reporter yells, "Is there a Mrs. Abajian on the horizon?"

Shutting my eyes, I clench my jaw.

Yes, you would have all met her if it weren't for Vandal.

Taking a deep breath, I plaster a smile on my face. "It's not a mathematical improbability." I turn in the general direction of the question. "But more importantly, it's none of your fucking business."

Anna pulls my hand. "Let's get backstage."

"Ready?" Tabi asks, ruffling my hair.

"No."

Ravi nudges my shoulder. "You'll do just fine."

As we walk, I turn to Anna. "What about those who can't get a seat at the gallery?"

"I have it covered. Frida will take care of streaming it on a projector."

"Who's Frida? Anyone helping her?"

(Stage)

A young man clad in an unbuttoned denim shirt over a black T-shirt, wearing a single-ear headset, points at a marked area. "Please step onto this, sir, and you will be pulled up."

When I'm ready to go up, my colleagues lift their thumbs. Tabi launches Akane on a video chat, who blows me a kiss from the screen. Then, I'm raised to the stage to the notes of Nocturne, Op. 9, No. 2. The ceiling is plastered with constellations. My eyes almost well up; Akane planned this whole thing. Have I ever told her all that she means to me? I need to plan something.

I walk past a barstool with a bottle of water on it. As I get to the center of the stage, almost every audience member takes their cell phone out. I bow to the fake Van Gogh and the pianist, whose only skill is to run his fingers convincingly over a piano to simulated music. They bow back and leave the stage.

Adjusting my mouthpiece, I point at the crowd. "Have you ever wished you could play or paint like that?"

Every corner of the hall booms as the audience shouts, "Yes!"

Like you care. I would bet all my money that half of you can't tell Chopin from Cher. A four-inch floppy disk is sufficient to store all your collective consciousness.

A lot rides on my Oscar-winning performance today. I tilt my head, pretending to show concern. "But you feel discouraged when you realize how difficult it is to master the fundamentals." I widen my eyes and snap my fingers. "It doesn't have to be like that." Another light from the ceiling shines on a woman holding a red model of The Mind.

As she comes close to me, I turn off my mic. She brings her lips close to my ear. "We need a pretend kiss."

Bringing my face about a millimeter from hers, I say, "What an unimaginable travesty."

She giggles, hands The Mind model to me and leaves the stage.

I hold the helmet with my left hand, switch my microphone back on, and then point at the helmet. "This is our signature memory transfer helmet." Spreading my arms, I ask, "What do you call this?"

The crowd roars, "The Mind!"

Holding The Mind with both hands, I nod and say, "You're a beautiful crowd." I move forward a step, almost to the edge of the stage. "When you buy this, you can choose an array of talents and skills as an upgrade. You don't have to send it back to us. It will all be done remotely using what we call the Neurolink. Does that answer your questions?"

The entire stage shakes as thousands of people sing, "Neurolink, Neurolink . . ." while clapping and whistling. Setting The Mind on the floor, I throw my hands in the air and slowly push them down, quieting the crowd immediately. Wow, I didn't know if that would work.

"I'm not telling you that you will wake up and magically play the piano like Lang Lang or paint like Dali. But the fundamentals can be codified into your brains."

What if we fail? My throat feels dry, and my breath quickens. I walk back to the barstool and take a large sip from the water bottle.

I force a smile. "Ladies and gentlemen, we at Quantum World are building a more humane AI, where humans and robots complement rather than compete. Imagine the billions you can save on training new employees." Holding up my hand and lowering my voice, I warn, "There are some risks involved. Someone can hack into the system and upload programs like mind control for our customers. Firms, nations, and governments can use this to create compliance, thereby taking away our free will." I reassure them, "That's why we are working on an encryption system that utilizes your biometrics to confirm any uploads. And unless we are ready with that, we won't release this product. Because we cannot build a better world without you."

I squat and spread my arms wide. Then, I stand and ask, "Are you with me?"

The crowd cheers, "Yes!"

Let's play with you a bit.

Placing my hands behind my ears, I say, "I can't hear you! Are you with me?"

They stomp, clap, and roar. The whole auditorium shakes as they scream, "Yes!"

Bowing, I conclude. "Thank you so much, ladies and gentlemen. You're awesome. Those registered for the event will get a sign-up sheet for our newsletter. You can even place your order and receive a developer discount."

As I walk backstage, someone from the crowd shouts, "How much do we pay now?"

Adjusting my mic, I say, "You pay nothing till we ship, sir. We are not Tesla."

Then, I leave the stage, take The Mind model with me, and am escorted to the dressing room.

(Backstage)

Even before my eyes can adjust to the change in light, Anna rushes toward me out of nowhere and tugs my lapel.

"You. Are. Awesome. I love you."

Placing The Mind on the floor, I sit on a chair and take deep breaths, loosening my collar. How did this place get so crowded?

The crowd in the dressing room bifurcates and makes way for Tabi. She opens her clutch, removes a few tissues, and wipes my forehead, and Ravi points the Dyson air fan in my direction.

Waving his hand at the crowd, he says, "Please give us some room."

Tapping his Patek Philippe Nautilus, Chris reminds us, "The journalists and media whores are gathering in the dining hall." He snaps his fingers. "Chop chop, guys."

Getting up, I stretch my back. As we all walk to the dining room, Tabi grabs my hand. "Most of those you will meet are shallow and stupid. But keep smiling."

I scrunch my face at Tabi's remark while a bespectacled girl comes and shakes Anna's shoulder. She points at her tablet, saying, "Here is a list of people who watched the livestream." Swiping the screen, she adds, "And these are people who signed up, Dr. Calimaris."

Touching the girl's shoulder, Anna smiles. "Thanks, Frida. See you at dinner. And for the hundredth time, it's Anna."

Frida glances at me, and she pales. Turning to Anna, she mutters, "Thank you, Dr. Calimaris—I mean, Dr. Anna. Sorry, only Anna. Just Anna." Puffing, she hurries out the door.

Pointing at the floor, Anna asks, "Where's the helmet?"

"Who cares? It's just a shell." I shrug. "Maybe someone took it as a souvenir."

(Exclusive dinner)

A random guy with a mismatched suit and hat comes toward me and wraps his arm around my shoulders, telling me, "I have five million Instagram followers." Pouting, he says, "Smile." Then, while typing on his cell phone, he asks, "How do you spell 'neuro' and 'quantum'?"

Oh, you ignorant fuck.

Someone whose botoxed lips are thicker than the Gutenberg Bible steps forward. Poking my chest with her two-inch fake nails, she announces, "That bit with Mozart and Picasso was totally awesome."

That was Chopin and Van Gogh, you moron. Who gets to be influenced by you?

I nod and smile. "I'm glad you liked it."

As more samples from the clown shop of the social media circus line up, Anna comes to rescue me. Glaring at the crowd, she says, "How about we do this after dinner?" She pulls out a chair at a table section marked "Vincent Abajian." Turning to Tabi, she asks, "How the fuck can you tolerate these shameless social media people?"

"I don't," Tabi says, puffing her inhaler into her mouth.

I see Ravi, Maddy, and Chris chatting with a woman in a gray suit and pink blouse on the other side of the table. Wait, isn't she the one I saw before the presentation? As our eyes meet, her face turns pink, and she smiles. That smile is concealing something.

Who are you? You have no name tag on the table.

I take my seat. Pointing at the stranger, I ask, "Who do we have here?" Her jaw drops at my question, and then she covers her mouth.

Why? Am I supposed to know you?

Anna grabs my right arm. "That's Emika. She was a postdoc researcher at the uni. She was also on two patents we cited."

Then why is she not a founding member of Quantum World? Or on the final patent? Why is everyone staring at me? Why are they so pale?

I smile and lean toward Emika. "Ah! Forgive me. You must be brilliant. Why didn't you work for us? We can exceed any salary and stock options." Pointing at Anna, I smirk. "Did she scare you?"

Rolling her eyes, Anna quips, "Idiot."

My eyes are fixed on Emika. Why does she seem important?

I bring my lips close to Anna's ear. "Remember, I spoke about a girl in the country club?"

She nods. "Aha."

"Emika looks like her." Then, I get even closer to Anna's ears. "Do I have a child with her?"

She covers her mouth and giggles. "Fuck no. If you did, you'd remember. You're not that kinda guy."

The servers bring food, and everyone digs in. Showing my steak to Anna, I ask, "They call this Wagyu?"

She rubs my shoulder. "Don't be obnoxious. You had a long day."

I drape my arm over her chair. "Okay, Mom."

My phone vibrates in my pocket as I'm cutting the steak. It's Akane.

Akane: Why were you flirting with that model on stage? Bad Vincent.

I can feel the blood rush to my face, and a smile forms on my lips.

Me: I'm a bad boy.

Shaking my hand, Anna asks, "What's going on?"

I show her the text, and she grabs my phone and changes the text to: Punish this bad boy. I roll my eyes as Tabi takes a look. Covering her mouth, her shoulders shake as she laughs. She takes the phone from me and adds: This bad boy needs a spanking. I glance at Emika, whose eyes are fixed on me. But her gaze doesn't seem creepy at all. She wipes her eyes with her napkin as Ravi touches her hand reassuringly. Maddy doesn't seem to mind that at all. What's going on?

My bracelet suddenly turns Turkish blue. I can't catch a break! I shake my head and click my tongue. Turning to Anna, I say, "Be right back."

"What? You need food."

I leave the table and rush out of the hall, calling Philp on my cell.

"Talk to me."

"Get to the rooftop. I'm in a chopper with Ed. You baited Vandal, and now, he's here."

Locking the stall in the restroom, I snap my fingers. The dose of intreton I had earlier makes my transition from the stall to the core to the roof almost instantaneous. I am on the rooftop even before my body can register the shift. Breathing deeply, I feel exhilarated; I could do this all my life.

Philip waves his hand at me, his lower body tethered to his seat belt in his Eurocopter EC120 Colibri. He pulls me in, and I shut the door behind me. The earsplitting whir of the rotor blades transforms into a high-pitched beep. I cover my ears.

Edward is piloting the helicopter. "We don't have much time," he yells as he lifts the chopper off.

Philip hands me a headset and a pair of binoculars, then points at the Seattle Needle. "Look at the FedEx plane heading toward the Needle."

"Fuck."

Touching my shoulder, Philip says, "That plane has no pilot. We must get there before the Air Force does to avoid collateral damage."

"What's the plan?"

Philip and I suit up as our chopper ascends over the FedEx plane, strapping parachutes on our suits. I snap my fingers, and we both enter the core.

"Ludwig, guide Philip to the cockpit and me to the control towers."

"Very well."

Snapping my fingers, I create another turbulence and enter the control tower. Five people are incapacitated—two on the floor and three in their chairs. Cups of Seattle's Best are knocked over on the control panels, with coffee dripping onto the floor. The place smells of stale coffee and burnt plastic and paper.

I jerk my head as I hear a dagger swooshing through the air, straight at me, missing my nose by a hair. Five *shurikens* follow the blade. I note the direction they are coming from, though I can't see who is throwing them. Before the *shurikens* can pierce me, I snap my fingers, enter the core, and land right in front of Vandal. Before he can react, I kick his face, cracking his mask, though it remains on his face. He grunts as he falls, blood gushing out from his mouth through the cracked mask.

His shoulders shake as he laughs. "You will lose. I will not stop until you cry tears of blood."

Then, he takes out a hand grenade, and my heart beats frantically.

Haven't you killed enough?

Wheezing, spitting blood, he says, "You will have to choose: catch me or save these five worthless fucks."

Despite it being muffled from his mask, I can detect a hint of a Bavarian accent in his voice. His laugh slowly becomes high-pitched, almost like he is crying. While blood continues to dribble down his chin, he says, "I know all about you, Vincent."

He pulls the pin from the grenade, then rolls the weapon at the injured officers. Lunging at him, I kick him in the chest. His ribs crack, and the force puts him through the window of the control tower, shattering the glass to bits. The shards rain down, and I cover my head but remain standing.

I just have four seconds; that's not enough time to create a spark and take the grenade into the core. Intreton may leak out from the core, too. Using both hands, I snap my fingers and join those sparks together. Then, expanding my hands, I make the sparks big enough to reach every corner of the room. The grenade detonates but reacts with the core to create an electromagnetic pulse, which throws me against the wall. I feel my back crack, and the intreton is healing it. From the tower, I can see the pulse reverberate through two or three city blocks, taking out the power. I cover my ears against the deep base of the EMP, followed by cars honking and tires screeching for the next minute. My heart is smashing against my chest as if trying to come out of my rib cage to tell me, "I have had enough."

My lungs constrict, and I'm puffing for breath. What will it take to catch this fucker? How is it that he wins every time? He can't organize and carry out all these attacks by himself.

I sigh, exhausted. But I need to get back to dinner.

As I pull my chair out, Anna nudges my sleeve. "Where were you? Did you see what happened?"

If only you knew.

I feel my eyes getting heavier. "Yes, I sensed it," I say, glancing at Tabi.

Touching my hand, Tabi says, "Let's get you a fresh plate, and then you should get back to your suite. You must be tired." Tabi knows.

Squinting at me, Ravi observes, "You need rest."

"I'm fine." I look around the table. "Where's Emika?"

Everyone looks at me with wide eyes.

"Don't you have a girlfriend?" Anna asks, tilting her head.

I frown at her. "What's that supposed to mean?" Though, she may have a point. Why would I worry about someone I don't even remember?

Anna quickly retracts. "Nothing, Vince. Sorry."

"I'm not hungry," I say, standing up and buttoning my tux jacket. "See you guys later."

(Presidential suite)

I'm too tired to sleep. Vandal's savage laughter is ringing in my ears nonstop.

What do you want from me? What did I ever do to you?

I take my cell phone out and see fifteen missed calls from Akane. Poor thing; she must be worried sick. I call her.

"Was that Vandal and you?"

"Yes."

"Are you okay?"

"Can I come over?"

"Can your body take it? I want you here, but—"

"It can."

"Hulk?"

"He's at Little Paws for the weekend. I was supposed to be here for the whole program."

"And?"

"I wanna be with you now."

(Core)

I enter the door marked "Crossroads."

Touching Philip's shoulder, I assure him, "My life is not more precious than yours." My voice cracks. "Thank you for your help with JPX and for convincing me to keep Akane away." Then, I admit, "I was starting to lean toward commercializing alternate realities, but . . ."

Philip frowns.

My heart gets heavy at the thought of the rift my following words may open between us. "But today, I saw what a maniac could do with little access to intreton. It is dangerous in the wrong hands. Even in the right hands, it can be perilous." I pause as I gather my thoughts. "As long as I am the time corrector, I can't let alternate reality arising from the core be a market. I am sorry."

Philip's eyes flood with tears, and he falls to his knees.

"What's wrong?" I ask, putting my hand on his shoulder.

I have never seen you like this.

He places his hand over mine and whispers, "I'm sorry if I've ever hurt you or if I do in the future."

(A day later—Akane's penthouse)

Akane removes a piece of rice from my lips with her tongue and smiles. Then, she forks a bit of grilled salmon and brings it to my mouth. "Eat, silly."

Biting into the salmon's crispy skin and soft flesh, I smile at the blissful experience of cooking with Akane. "What do you think Philip meant about hurting me?" I ask.

Like a child, she lifts her shoulders and pouts. "*Shirimasen.*"

I pick a *tamagoyaki* and bring it in front of her lips. "Eat."

"Open your mouth," she says, selecting the *nattō.*

I shake my head and crumple my nose. "It stinks."

"Someone needs a spanking."

"I'm ready when you are."

My phone vibrates with a call from Philip. Ruffling my hair, Akane says, "It's okay. Take it."

I put the phone on speaker. "What's up?"

"When you've time, take your old cell phone and head to the core. Try to find out why you learned to make omurice, and visit your memories associated with the airport on February 15, 2024, Chez-Giraud in the fall of 2023, and August 3, 2023."

"Sure. But why?"

"You gotta trust me on this. Also, do these in your backyard. And try and take a break from the core. The suit can't protect you from these frequent trips between home and Japan."

Holding Akane's hand, I lean toward the phone. "I miss her."

"I know. But you're damaging your health faster than intreton can regenerate. The suit is not designed for frequent trips. This will be the protocol till you become one with the core. Bye, Vincent."

Akane squeezes my hand. "Limit your trips till flights are resumed, please."

Looking at her face, I can sense there's more. "But?"

She smiles. "We will move in together, either in the US or Japan, after launching your product. Promise."

I kiss her bare ring finger. "*Kimi o aishiteimasu.*"

"*Watashi mo desu.*"

(Vincent's home)

"The requested conference call is ready in your time cave," Ludwig informs me.

Looking down at Hulk, I say, "Hey, let's plan something extraordinary. Wanna come?"

He wags his tail and jumps into my lap. I kiss his button nose.

Getting on the call, I can tell that Sasha and Krista are in their bedroom, and Fred is in a hotel.

"Guys, I need a big favor," I start.

Krista squints into the screen. "What?"

"Can I book your entire restaurant for April 15 next year? I will be bringing my friends from the US."

"Have you picked out a ring?" Sasha asks, giggling.

"How did you guess that?"

"We raised you," Fred says, rolling his eyes. "Aren't you supposed to wait till your product launch?"

"I'm done waiting," I say. "About the ring, it's a Kashmir sapphire; it matches the color of her cobalt-blue jumpsuit. Philip acquired it for me."

Krista squeals. "Awesome."

"Not a word to Akane, though," I say, holding up a finger.

"This will be amazing!" Sasha claps her hands together.

"So, we are all set?" I ask. "And Fred . . . You'll be there?"

"Wouldn't miss it for the world."

I smile. "Thanks, guys. I love you."

After that, if she says yes, I will change the reset dates on all my watches and clocks to April 15, 2026. Now, where is my old phone?

CHAPTER 9

CYANIDE

"Please don't hurt her. Kill me instead"
—Vandal

September 2026—Seattle Hyatt

<u>Vandal</u>

I CAN'T EVEN STAND STRAIGHT WITHOUT pressing my hand against my broken ribs. The intreton injection is taking too long to heal my wounds. Every breath is a grunt, and every grunt leads to coughing up blood. I look down on the floor at the trail of red blood and green intreton I've left. The intreton-powered suit is shredded to bits. I've covered my jaws and nose with intreton patches.

My scars don't disappear as swiftly as yours, Vincent.

Breathing hard, I form two fists. I wipe the steam from the bathroom mirror and look into my eyes—red with blood and tears.

Remember 1999, Vincent? That locker room?

(1999—Karate championship, Montagnola)[51]

My eyes were wide in horror. You kicked Rudy's neck after spinning three hundred and sixty degrees in the air. I stood silent as I heard my brother's bones crack, and he fell. I kept looking between the referee, the doctor, and the headmaster, Kruger. No one rushed to Rudy as he lay there, motionless.

I shouted from the gallery. "Someone help him!"

Then, you leaned over and whispered something to Rudy. Soon after, the cheering began. First, it came from a girl, then a boy, and then the hall was roaring with the thunderous cheer of, "Vincent, Vincent, Vincent." Not a soul cried for Rudy.

My twin sister, Dina, nudged my sleeve. Her eyes filled with tears, and she covered her mouth with her hand. "Hank, Hank, why isn't Rudy getting up?"

I rubbed her tears with my thumbs and then grabbed her hand. "Come with me."

We followed you to the locker room. Placing my hand on my sister's shoulder, I said, "Wait here." I found you weeping into the mustard and red scarf you always wore. Mustering the courage to go near you, I poked your toned arm. "Why did you hurt Rudy like that?"

You wiped your eyes and turned to me. At that moment, I saw the devil in your green and blue eyes. There was no sorrow in them when you asked, "What's your name, brat?"

I stepped back and wiped my tears. "Why do you care?"

Cruelty still in your eyes, you smiled. "I don't." Then, you stood up and poked my shoulder. "After all, you're the brother of a vandal."

"What's vandal?"

---

[51] Chapter 11 of *The Winding* (Book 1).

"Look it up." Then, you sneered. "Because from now on, the vandal will exist on paper." Rubbing my head, you winked. "Rudy is history. Will you take his place?" you asked, snapping your fingers. "Will you become a bully?"

Tears filled my eyes as I whispered, "History? That will break my mom. She only loves Rudy."

"Like I give a fuck."

That's when I realized that maybe I wouldn't see my brother anymore. I punched on the metal lockers with my right hand and then shut my eyes in pain, holding my right knuckles with my left hand. As I dropped to my knees, I looked at you. You wore your Gi and wrapped the scarf around your neck.

Before leaving the locker room, you turned back. "Good luck with your life." On your way out, you spoke to Dina. "You with that brat?"

She came rushing over to me. "What happened?"

(Back to the present)

We were kids, Vincent. Just eight.

Leaving the bathroom, I open the freezer to fetch the ice tray. I cover my face with it; I need to heal quickly.

(1999—Vienna)

A week after the match, the doctors took Rudy off life support. It was hopeless, they said. A few days after that, we buried him. It was my parents, my sister, the priest, and me. My father sat on the grass, drinking from his Johnnie Walker Black Label, while my mom hurled curses. I could not hear a single word the priest said.

Pointing her finger at my dad, Mom kept yelling, "He is dead because of you, because of your casino." Tears poured from her eyes with every word, snot ran from her nose, and spit flew from her mouth. "You brought misfortune to others, and God took my firstborn—my beautiful Rudy." Pointing at my dad, my mom looked up at the sky. "Why couldn't you take him?" Then, she pointed at Dina and me. "Or these two? I never wanted them."

Frightened, I wrapped my arms around my five-minute-younger sister, sweet Dina. She was shivering in her black dress with puffed sleeves and a white collar.

Hearing Mom's last sentence, Dad yelled, "Shut up, whore!"

We turned to him. He was staring at Mom with swollen, red eyes, clenched jaws, and every vein bulging out. Then, he hurled the half-empty bottle at my mother. She didn't even flinch. The bottle narrowly missed her and shattered against the gravestone, spilling whiskey on the engraved name: Rudolph Von Stein—1982-1999.

✲

(1999—Montagnola)

Back at school, Rudy wasn't even mentioned at the school assembly. Vincent killed him, and he was freely running around with his friends Fred, Sasha, and Krista. Rudy's friends, Jean and Luther, simply forgot about the fight.

One day, I approached Jean and told him, "Vincent killed Rudy."

Rubbing my hair, he said, "No way. He got injured later. That's what the doctor's report says."

A few days later, the school captain and Vincent's roommate, Fred, came to my third-grade class and talked to the teacher. "Headmaster wants to see Hank and Dina—the Von Stein twins."

Holding our hands, Fred escorted us to Mr. Kruger's office. As we sat outside his office bench, Fred assured us, "You will be fine, kids." Then, he left.

A man wearing a fedora rushed out of Mr. Kruger's office. As he walked past us, he looked at us and tipped his hat. When we entered Mr. Kruger's office, we saw him moving a heavy duffel bag.

"Do you need help, sir?" I offered.

He shook his head and returned to his chair. Looking through his black-rimmed glasses, he stated in his deep, melancholy voice, "There has been an incident in Vienna. Someone will escort both of you home."

(Back to the present)

The police arrested my father for keeping narcotics in his casino.

He did that to pay for our school fee, Vincent. He wanted us to have a better future. Rudy's death made him careless, and he was caught. The police seized our homes, our cars, and our lives. It all started with you.

He hanged himself in prison, and his body was kept in the morgue for a postmortem. Following that, our bank accounts and assets were sealed. My mom, Dina, and I moved into a distant relative's house.

(1999—Vienna)

My mom never shed a tear for him. She never left the bedroom, her rosary beads, or her Bible. My sister and I lived on dry bread and stale cheese that the local grocery store owner gave us instead of throwing away. I would scrape the mold from the cheese before feeding my sister and me. We were waiting for someone from the school to come and rescue us.

And then, one day, someone knocked on our door. My sister smiled for the first time in a long time, and her blue eyes brightened. But it was just the priest, and her eyes returned to being heavy. Still, we felt safer with a proper adult in the house, so we hugged him.

He took out his handkerchief and wiped our tears. "The police have released your father's body. Can I speak to your mom?"

I ran upstairs and found my mom's hand hanging from the bed and a small bottle on the nightstand. I rushed toward the bed and saw her motionless, eyes wide open, mouth foaming.

Shaking her, I cried, "Mom, Mom!" My heart leaped to my throat. I screamed at the tops of my lungs, "Help!"

My sister rushed to me, the priest right behind her. He looked at the bottle. "Cyanide."

This time, there were no curses to drown out the priest's sermon as my sister and I buried our parents. But we still couldn't hear him over the rain and the thunder. We were soaked, water dripping from my hair. Dina was shivering, her dress stuck to her skin, her teeth chattering. About twenty feet away, I saw two men waiting for their spoils. They were supposedly from protective services, but I didn't believe that for a second. One guy twirled his torn color-wheel umbrella as he slowly approached us, smiling with his brown teeth. The other guy wore a hoodie, a cigarette dangling from his hand as he came close to separate me from my sister.

I held her hand tightly as tears trickled from her eyes. I shrieked, "Please don't take Dina! Take me instead."

Then, tires screeched as two cars came speeding toward us. Four men with guns rushed out of the first car and surrounded Dina and me. Her eyes wide with fear, Dina looked at me and asked, "Are they going to kill us?"

My heart was thumping with panic as I put my sister behind me. I knew I couldn't fight these men. Feeling helpless, I clasped my hands together. "Please don't hurt her. Kill me instead."

A man got out of the second car and walked toward us. He had a limp and carried a suitcase in one hand and a handgun in another. As he came near us, the other men made their way. He leaned down to examine our faces. He was wearing a white half-mask that covered his nose, one eye, and one cheek. The portion of his face that was visible was burned.

Smiling at us, he said, "No one's gonna hurt you. Not anymore." He turned to the two men from the protective services and threw the briefcase at them. "Divide it or fight for who gets to take all of it. Now, scram!"

The guy in the hoodie caught the briefcase and ran. The guy with the umbrella ran after him, and both vanished in the heavy rain. From a distance, we heard a man howl in pain.

Turning to one of his men, the masked man ordered, "Find the alive one and kill him. Divide the money among yourselves." Touching Dina's right shoulder and my left, he said gently, "Call me Mr. J." Then, he stared into my eyes. "I'll make you very strong, so you can hurt the one who did this to you."

"Who?" Dina asked.

He snapped his fingers, and a man brought an umbrella over to us. The masked man smiled at us. "Vincent Abajian. None of this would have happened if he hadn't killed Rudy." He tightened his mask. "But we need to make some adjustments. First, we need to move to the US."

(Back to the present)

Mr. J became our parent. Sort of. Touching my jaw and nose, I feel the pain sliding away, my breathing getting normal.

It wasn't easy, Vincent. Chronos didn't pick me. Mr. J injected intreton into my bloodstream, and my body rejected it like a virus. I become the petri dish of a biological experiment. Every day for ten years, I coughed up blood. Every day, Dina begged him to stop. But I had to become you—a better you. After years of trial and error, my body succumbed to the intreton. Vandal—created by you, perfected by intreton. Though, I can't spend more than a few seconds in the core to avoid suspicion from Chronos. Dina and I had to change our names and our backstories. An immigrant family adopted her, but we kept in touch. We mastered many accents, and we kept our eyes on you. I noted the crucial people in your life—Frederique, Sasha, Krista, and Kruger. Then came Elise, Anna, Ravi, Chris, and Emika. And now, Akane.

I drop the ice pack and laugh, my shoulders shaking.

Yes, Vince, Dick Graham bribed authorities to let the intreton through the scanners. But intreton did not leak out of the Lombard canisters. Following Mr. J's orders, I bribed the airport authorities in Bangalore to loosen one jar.

I grin. "I killed your Elise and two hundred other people with her."

Dina broke into Elise's office and put the drives in your house so you could see what Elise had been up to for yourself. How did that make you feel, Vincent? The woman you slept with, maybe loved, laundered money?

Lousy cancer got to Kruger before I could. I wanted to see the life slowly leave his eyes. He took money from the guy in the fedora and had all of Rudy's medical reports altered. Mr. J ordered Dina to remotely hack into the autonomous semi and make it collide with Dr. Kauffman's car.

I grind my teeth. "You forced us to kill a dog, Vince." I make a call. "Hank?"

"Mr. J, I have done everything you asked. All my work kept Akane from the AI conference, and Emika remained unaware of her. When do I strike?"

"You are a dumbfuck."

"What?"

"Did I tell you to do this Seattle drama?"

"No, sir. I am sorry."

"I have to go to plan B now. If you protest, I will hurt Dina."

My voice trembles as I say, "You have my word, sir."

"Good. Now, heal your wounds! Three more strikes. The final one will be her. You will not kill her, though; she must live. The manned Jaeger will be ready in early April."

Yes, I'll wait.

But Mr. J doesn't know I'll hack into your Neurolink and ruin Quantum World. I will end your legacy.

I lie down, placing my palm under my head. Grinning ear to ear, I turn sideways and face the yellow helmet from *What's Tonight?* and the red one I snatched tonight.

These shells will mark the beginning of your end.

Tears well in my eyes as I gently kiss the helmets, running my hands over them. "I never wanted you two. So, you must die."

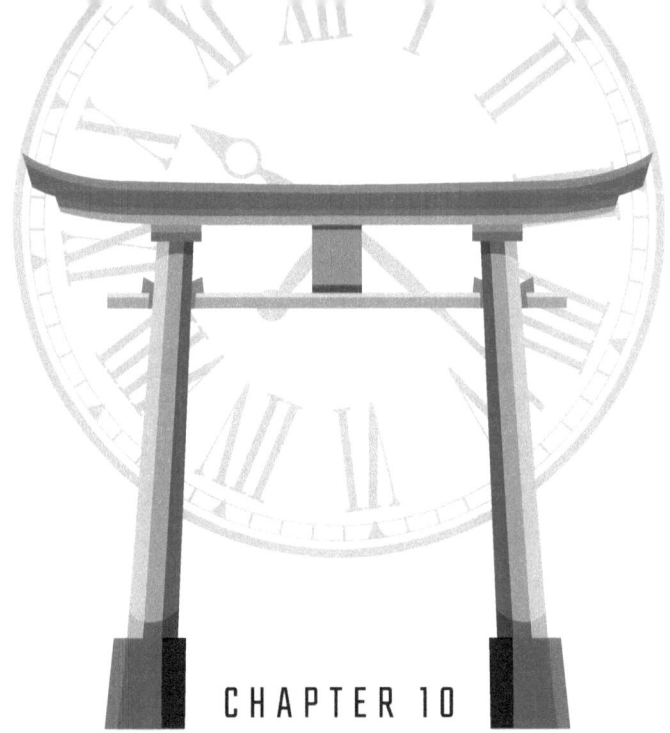

CHAPTER 10

MEMORIES—EPISODE 2

"You my papha?"
—Nozo

September 2026

Emika

PHILIP'S ROLLS-ROYCE TAKES THE FINAL left, and I see what was once home—just for a couple of months but with memories lasting a lifetime. My pulse races. All the outdoor and most of the interior lights are turned on. The house shines through the evergreens and the manicured front yard. A chill runs over my skin, and I rub my arms.

Touching my hand, Anna asks, "You okay?"

"Yep," I lie.

I can't say how I feel. I can't voice what I want. Vincent has been through so much. He deserves all the joy Akane brings him. I run my finger over Nozo's head and smile, though my lips quiver with the effort. My mind races through all the time I spent in this house—the first time Vincent and I visited, the day we moved in, the days I worked from home and played with Hulk, the day I brought Brad, the day I left town for London, and finally, the day I came back for a short visit after my interview with Nardin Robotics. I sigh. Across three continents, this is the only place I ever called home.

As Nozo and I step out of the car, I see Ravi and Chris getting out of Chris's car. Tabi opens the door from inside, and we all walk in. Before entering, I run my fingers over the bed of bellflowers on the front porch. They remain my favorite, even post-extraction from Akane.

With Nozo holding my hand, we enter the house. There is an addition—the mahogany Steinway with the seat and the keys facing the main entrance. My breathing quickens, and my eyes well up as I see who's resting beside the piano bench. My little boy—my Hulk. How could I have left this life? Hulk is unfazed by all the familiar people. But as soon as he hears the unusual footsteps of Nozo and perhaps the scent of someone he knew as "Mum," he wiggles his ears. He crawls forward, staring straight into my eyes. Constantly wagging his tail, he barks twice. Then, he takes two steps forward, and the barking changes to a shrill whine. I sit on the floor, and Nozo follows. The others, including Philip, stand still, observing.

Saying, "I can't watch this," Anna takes a few tissues from her purse and sits on the sectional.

I stretch my arms toward Hulk. "It's me, baby." Wiping my tears, I smile. "Remember your old mum?"

He tilts his head to the left and right before running and pouncing into my lap. As he licks my face, my tears, I run my fingers across his silky white and champagne fur. I nuzzle my nose against his. He then lies on his back, exposing his belly.

Smiling, I scratch his belly. Turning to Nozo, I tell her, "*Nozo-chan,* you can pet him gently."

Sensing an unfamiliar touch, Hulk sniffs Nozo.

Running my left hand over Hulk's head, I whisper, "That's your little sister, Nozo." I touch Nozo's head with my right hand. "*Nozo-chan*, this is your older brother, Hulky."

Nozo wraps her little, chubby hands around Hulk and says, "*Onii-chan*[52] Hulky." Hulk licks her face and neck, making Nozo giggle.

Ravi joins us, sitting on the floor next to me. He then wipes my tears with his handkerchief and hugs me. "Everything will be fine," he whispers.

How? I know I'm back with my old team. But the one I really came back for is not mine anymore. Maybe staying in London, dreaming about the perfect life, was better than a fragmented reality of perfection. Everything here is pristine. Everything fits perfectly, except for Nozo and me.

Standing up, Nozo looks around the house. Pulling my burgundy knit dress, she asks, "Is this your house?"

How can you be so perceptive?

I don't know what to tell her. I picked it for us but walked away, only to regret it. Yes, it was mine, but she must not get her hopes up, as it is not ours anymore.

Pulling her toward me, my voice trembles as I say, "*Shiranai*."[53] Standing up, I look at everyone's faces. Sniffling, I ask, "Can I walk around? I won't move anything, I promise."

Coming forward, Chris puts his hand on my shoulder. "I don't think Vince would mind at all." Then, he picks up Nozo and tickles her neck. "Who is Chris's favorite?" he asks.

She tilts her head at him. "Nozo?"

Walking away with Nozo, Chris lets me be with my memories. I move toward the kitchen counter and sit on the barstool where I had my last omurice before leaving for London. Hulk follows me and licks my ankles. I know that day, I broke Vincent's heart. But not once did he ask me to stay. He knew I was confused, living two realities. Not once was he selfish. But I'd gotten that all wrong.

Leaving the barstool, I approach his coffee corner, near a glass wall overlooking rolling hills, evergreens, and the Cascades. I gently touch his

---

[52] An endearing way of referring to an older brother. The more formal one is *Ani* or *Onii-san*.

[53] I don't know.

custom, wood-finish Lelit Bianca dual boiler. He has every brewing gadget known to humanity—the Chemex, the Kalita Wave, the Origami, the V60, the Hario Siphon. He spent countless hours showing me how to properly use them. The spouted and bottomless portafilters are placed next to the Lelit, right on top of the refractometer.

✳

(November 2023)

It was drizzling outside, and water formed gentle droplets on the glass walls before dripping down. But I was looking at something else—Vincent pulling shots, backdropped against the rain. I couldn't look past his wavy locks, how they moved up and down, ranging from chestnut brown to black, to see his effort at weighing the beans, grinding, and tamping. Anna was right about those wavy locks. I bit my lips; they were delish.

Putting two shot glasses side by side, he turned to me. "Let's do a test," he announced. When I stood next to him, Vincent pointed at the shot glasses. "One is from a bottomless portafilter, the other from a spouted one."

I took a sip from the first one and scrunched my lips at the bitterness washing through my mouth. Then, I tasted the second one. Blinking rapidly, I said, "So bitter."

"Both?"

"Yes, equally bitter."

Lifting his brows, he smirked. "Ah! Equally?" He then took out a refractometer. "Let's see what science says."

Placing my hand on the refractometer, I smiled. "Instead, why don't you simply drink your . . . sweet espresso?" I quipped.

Locking his eyes with mine, he chuckled playfully. "Hmm. Sweet espresso."

Then, he grabbed me by the waist and plonked me on the counter. Instinctively, my hands tangled in his beautiful hair. Leaning in, he licked the crema off my upper lip.

Pulling me close, he smiled. "I just tasted the sweetest espresso."

I was speechless. The drizzle transformed into heavy rain splashing on the glass wall, tempered with rolling thunder. Pushing my hair behind my ears, he asked, "Can we furnish the main bedroom?"

"Yes, when I move in for good."

(Back to the present)

I should have moved in for good that same day. Sighing, I open the top drawer next to the stove. It has all the recipes alphabetized by country of origin, neatly written in his cursive handwriting. My eyes fall on the fridge. I bring my hand up to cover my trembling lips as I see the two Post-its I had written three years back.

Could you not throw them away, Vince?

I cross the living room and look outside to the well-lit backyard—home to the fifteen cherry trees, whose blooming I only witnessed through a video. Beyond them is the lake, twinkling with reflections from the houses on the foothills and Chez-Giraud. And past the lake are hills and snowcapped mountains. This view was our favorite corner. Hulk jumps on a chair and wags his tail, locking his eyes with mine while sticking his tongue out and panting.

Kissing his head, I tell him, "I love you, baby. But if I sing to you, I won't be able to leave." I give him a smile. "Your dad and your new mum wouldn't like that."

What would Vincent have done if we'd been together when Akane returned? What would I have done if he had entered the conference center with Akane yesterday?

In the living room, Nozo is surrounded by four admirers—Tabi, Chris, Anna, and Ravi. She teaches them the Japanese words for dog, cat, bird, and cow. I walk up to the next floor. Is Vincent in the main bedroom? As I push open the door, my eyes widen; it's still unfurnished, with just a sleeping bag in the center of the room. I walk into Vincent's closet—shirts, sports jackets, and suits are perfectly arranged by color and pattern. My heart flutters at the sight of the charcoal plaid Zegna suit I got him. Did I pick it out, or was it the Akane in me who did? I kneel on the floor, and my tears drip onto the wood.

Why is it so difficult? I had my chance. Maybe he was always Akane's, and I was just a transfer station. Even though he never treated me like one.

I leave this room and enter the hallway to find Philip, Edward, and another man leaving the guestroom where Nozo was conceived. Smiling, Edward introduces the gentleman. "Emika, this is Dr. Andy Lee, the only leading expert in intreton medicine."

The short man, with chubby cheeks, round glasses, and hair parted in the middle, extends his arm. "Pleased to meet you, Dr. Amari."

"Lovely meeting you, Dr. Lee."

"You can go in," Philip says, pointing at the door." Then, he looks at his watch. "He will be awake in ten minutes."

I shake my head. "It's not appropriate—especially when Akane is not here."

Philip puts his hands on my shoulders. "The last face Vincent saw before losing consciousness was yours. So, it makes perfect sense for him to see your face when he wakes up."

I tiptoe into the room where Vincent is sleeping, just like I did on February 14, 2024, about an hour before Nozo was conceived. His left hand is on his stomach, and his right hand is on the bed. Following me to the room, Hulk jumps onto the bed, rests his head on Vincent's left ankle, and then stares at me. For the past two years, I had not thought I'd be this close to Vincent again—although I wanted to. He hasn't aged a day, except for a bit of gray in his hair. His breathing is even, and his lips flutter with every breath.

Can I touch his hand? Will I regret it if I don't? Yes. Gently, I slide my right hand under his and fold my thumb over it.

I'm holding you, Vince. Is it the last time? Is it wrong to say I love you?

As I lift his hand and kiss his fingers, my heart pounds. I place my left cheek against his hand, looking away from his face and staring out the floor-to-ceiling glass window overlooking the snowcapped mountains. My tears drip onto his hand as my shoulders shake. I run my fingers across his hand to wipe my tears from his skin.

I'm so sorry for everything.

What will he say? What if he doesn't want me at Quantum World? I feel goosebumps on my skin as I realize I must prepare for the worst—to pack and return to London. His breathing changes slightly, but I continue to look away.

Then, I hear him exhale, "You smell different."

Turning back, I ask, "Huh?"

Vincent

Taking a deep breath and clenching my jaw, I grab the branch and create a hinge with my right leg against the tree trunk.

I won't stop pulling till you come out.

With one mighty yank, I find myself on the ground five feet away from the tree, holding the severed stem. Did I get all of it? I get up and walk toward the tree. Yes! The space transforms into green meadows, rolling hills, and snow-capped mountains. The tree breaks into fifteen cherry trees, each blooming pink. Emika's violin disappears. I look at my hand. The branch has transformed into a luminous orb the size of a tennis ball.

I place the orb again on my chest. It illuminates my chest as my skin absorbs it. I can't keep my eyes open. As I shut them, an image of my Emika appears. She is smiling, but her eyes are wet. Waving her hand, she says, "See you later, Vince." She gets in her Uber and leaves me.

With no regrets or tears, I turn the doorknob and enter my house, my life of solitude. What happened to my home? This is a hospital room with a single bed. I check the date—it's November 15, 2024. Wasn't it August 13, 2023, when I performed the extraction? As I walk to the bed, I see Emi holding a baby. She forces a smile, trying to hide her tears. Giving her my pocket square, I take the baby. Those eyes . . . they are Amara's, and they are mine. The baby grabs my index finger, puts it in her mouth, and falls asleep. Lifting my brows, I turn to Emi.

She blinks. "Nozomi . . . it means . . ."

Handing little Nozo over to her loving mother, I kiss her forehead. "I know. Hope."

That's Hulk by my feet, but who is holding my hand, and why is it wet? That girl . . . I know her. She is wearing the same dress she wore the morning after my fortieth birthday in 2023. She wanted me to take her to Chez-Giraud. She is the girl who haunts me in my dreams, the one I saw at the conference. She was my Emi for a little while. Why is she crying? I freed her from Akane and me. There is something different about her. I inhale deeply—I know what it is. It's a weird way to start a conversation. Whatever.

Taking a deep breath, I say, "You smell different."

She looks at me. Her voice trembles as she asks, "Huh?"

Yes, you're free. The beautiful mole is gone. But why are tears still clouding your eyes?

I smile. "It used to be amber, sandalwood, vanilla, and vetiver. Now, it's lavender . . ." Shutting my eyes, inhaling deeply, I ask, "Umm . . . and tonka beans?"

She smiles. "I don't know."

"Suits you, though."

Her cheeks turn pink. "Thanks." She blinks, trying to hold her tears in.

I sit up and lean against the backrest as she slowly lets go of my hand.

What's with the reluctance? You must have moved on; you were pretty chummy with that blond guy at the conference.

I see marks of lipstick, tears, and eyeliner on my hand.

She sees me looking at them. "I'm sorry. I can remove them."

I smile at her, and our eyes lock. "It's okay. It happened several times when you stayed here, right?" She looks down as she nods, and her cheek turns pink again. Nudging her hand, I say, "Sorry for not recognizing you at the dinner."

She wipes her eyes. "I know what you did. Philip told us everything."

"Us?" I ask, squinting at her.

"Ravi, Chris, Anna, and me. I guess Tabi knew."

"I need to undo some wrongs."

"Like what?"

"It's about you and your status at Quantum World."

"Anna wants me to work under Ravi." She nudges my sleeve. "If you don't want me here, I can leave with . . ."

I touch her hand. "How can I undo the wrongs if you are not here?" Hesitantly, I say, "You said, 'With . . .'" Clearing my throat, I ask, "Can I meet her?"

She looks at me silently, her lips trembling.

I take her hand in both of mine. "I don't wanna steal her from you. I just wanna see her." My voice cracks. "Or maybe hold her?"

Using my robe's sleeve, she dabs the corners of her eyes. "That's not it. I just never thought this day would come."

Getting up from my bed, I kiss her head. Was that inappropriate? She didn't resist. We leave the room and stand at the staircase landing. Below, Anna, Chris, Ravi, and Tabi sit around a tiny girl who radiates as brightly as her mother.

Pointing at her, Emika says, "That's her—Nozomi. It means—"

I touch her hand. "Hope. I know."

Hulk runs down the stairs and sits next to Nozo, who gently rubs Hulk's head and says in the sweetest voice, "Hello, Hulky."

Philip and Edward are tinkering with my suit bracelet. "What are you two working on?" I ask as Emika and I walk down the stairs.

Without lifting his eyes from the bracelet, Philip answers, "You will know."

"What's with that?" I ask, pointing at his walking stick.

Philip rolls his eyes. "Age."

Your aging is irregular.

I sit on one corner of the sectional as Emika turns to Nozo. "I want you to meet someone." Everyone goes silent.

Spreading her arms, indicating she wants to be picked up, Nozo asks, "*Dare?*"[54]

With Nozo on her lap, Emika sits next to me. Pointing at me, she tells her, "*Kare wa.*"

Nozo leaves her mom's lap and looks straight into my eyes. She grips my lapels with her tiny hands, and I hold her by her waist. She tilts her head and widens her large eyes.

---

[54]   Who?

"You, my papha?" she asks with a London accent.

While Anna pretends to fix her eyeliner, Tabi looks away, fisting her hand in Chris's shirt.

I can feel every pump of my blood through my heart. What can I say? I was an absent father. As I turn to Emika, she points at my eyes and nods. I turn back to my daughter, and her face gets hazy behind the curtain of my tears.

"Yes." I bring her head to my shoulder. "I'm so sorry."

She lifts her head. "You good boy?"

"Mostly."

She smiles at me, squeezing her eyes into two thick lines of eyelashes. Running her tiny, chubby hands over my wet cheeks, she says, "Papha *o nakanaide*."[55]

Being a father to a human never crossed my mind. But when this little one calls me "Papha," I feel like my life just got split into two halves—the one before this moment and the one from this moment onward.

I kiss her forehead and her soft, pink cheeks. *"Mochiron."* Turning to Emika, I ask, "Can I hold her a bit longer?"

She looks down and runs her fingers under her eyes. "Yes."

"Since you will be working here, would you mind if I see her from time to time?"

"Sure!" she says, hugging a decorative pillow to her chest.

Where will they stay when they move to town? Should I buy them a house? I know Emika loves this one, so I could move to another one if she wanted to stay here. If I move to Japan, then I won't be able to see Nozo as often. I can't keep shuttling between Japan and the US through the core. Can't Akane move to the US? She can pick any property she likes. Emika and Nozo can stay here until we figure this out. I'll visit Akane and tell her everything.

I touch Emika's hand. "You and Nozo will stay here till we figure out logistics." Then, I turn to Anna and Tabi. "That's okay, right?"

The two women exchange glances before looking back at me. Smiling, Anna assures me, "I guess it's fine."

Tabi says, "You should tell Akane."

---

[55] Don't cry, Papha.

"Everything?" I ask.

"Just the lodging part for now. We will help you. Everything else, you need to tell her in person, as soon as you can get to the core."

Leaning forward, Philip tells me, "It will take you a week to heal."

Nozo falls asleep with her arms wrapped around my neck. I kiss her tiny shoulder. Hulk jumps onto Emika's lap and licks her chin. She, in turn, scratches his ears and belly. I should not feel content. My love is in Japan. If I reach for my phone, then little Nozo will wake up.

I turn to Anna. "Please call Akane. Just audio."

"Hi, Anna," greets Akane in her musical voice.

"We are all here at Vincent's house. We also have our old colleague Emika Amari and her little daughter, Nozomi."

"Beautiful names. What can I do?"

Anna shrugs at me, and I take over. "Akane?"

"Vince?"

Breathing anxiously, I blurt, "Emika used to work with us at the uni and was a co-inventor to some of our original works that made The Mind. We have decided to hire her."

"Okay?"

I'm terrible at lying. I look at everyone for help—everyone but Emika.

Tabi comes to rescue me after pumping her inhaler thrice. "Hi, Akane. It's Tabi."

"Hi, Tabi."

"Our guest house is occupied, and I moved in with Chris, so there is no space. Same with Ravi and Maddy. And Anna is still in her studio penthouse. And Emika has a child."

"That's it? Of course, they can stay at Vince's house."

"Our house," I correct her.

While Emika sniffles, Akane says, "Okay, silly. Can I speak with Emika?"

Inching toward the phone, Emika says, *"Arigatō gozaimasu, Akane-san."*

"Doitashimashite, Emika-san. Hmm, do I detect a *Kansai* accent?"

Smiling, Emika responds. *"Hai! Kyōto shusshin desu*[56]*"*

"Vince and I have so many memories there." States Akane. "Right, Vince?" She asks.

---

[56] I am from Kyoto

Lowering my eyes, I softly state, "Yep." Lifting my eyes, I see Emika scrunching a decorative pillow.

Akane continues lowering her voice, "Emika, just so you know, Vince has weird habits. He wakes up early and keeps making espresso till he is delighted with the outcome. The noise can be distracting, but he is my silly Vince. *Soshite, kare wa watashi no jinsei desu.* So, if you don't like something, just tell him nicely." Akane laughs into the phone.

Sniffing back her tears, Emika says, "I know his hab—" Quickly realizing her blunder, she scrunches her face. "Sorry, I meant sure. *Wakarimashita.*" She takes a deep breath. "Thank you so much for allowing me to stay here. Nozo and I won't burden you for too long."

Leaning toward the phone, I say, "Hey. They all know about me, the spark, and the core."

"Oh, good. No more secrets, then. Meet me when you feel better, silly." We hang up.

Emika used to call me "silly." Does she remember any of it? Why is she so weird? Who is rushing her to leave? Does she want to stay here for good? Wait, do I want her to stay here for good?

Leaving his chair, Philip comes over to me and ties the bracelet around my right wrist. Pointing at the small LCD screen, he says, "Press the red button next to the green one."

Upon pressing, it says, "Intreton absorption: 10%."

"It needs to be at least fifty percent before you can head to the core," Philip says. "The more trips you make, the more rapidly you lose absorption."

"Okay." Holding my Nozo, I stand up. Then, I hand her over to her loving mother. I touch Emika's hand. "Is it okay if I call you Emi?"

"*Hai,*" she says, her lips trembling.

I turn to Philip. "Can we airlift Emi's and Nozo's stuff from London?"

"Already on it."

"Perfect." Looking at everyone, I say, "At this time, I have four million Quantum World stocks." Turning to Anna, Chris, and Ravi, I ask, "Each of you has two million, right?"

Anna rolls her eyes. "Such a subtle way of saying you are wealthier."

I wave my hand dismissively. "I'll transfer one million of my stocks and one million unissued stocks to Emi. Any objections?"

They all shake their heads.

Securing Nozo in her left arm, Emika lifts her right. "I don't deserve it." "It's decided." I look around at everyone's silent faces and smile. "The motion carries. I'll ask Bernstein and colleagues to get on it first thing tomorrow." Smiling, I turn to Emika. "You are now a board member." I touch Emika's hand. "None of these would have happened without your work on our two foundational patents."

And, of course, there was January 7, the day I found out you were cheating on me, and I invented the third one.

I look at Nozo, who is drooling on her mom's hand. "I'll create a trust fund for Nozo with a portion of my Egami stocks. She will get the funds on her eighteenth birthday." I take a deep breath, reflecting on my struggle with poverty. "Nozo will have everything her father didn't." Touching Emika's shoulder, I declare, "Welcome to the co-founder's club." I smile and squint at her. "I hope you don't leave us this time."

CHAPTER 11

KOGARASHI

"I heard passes are limited to a tiny circle. Can you let me in?"
—*Emika*

October 2026—Vincent's Office

Vincent

CAN HEAR THE WIND HOWLING, despite the tightly shut windows. Each tree desperately tries to keep the winter at bay, preserving the red, yellow, and orange leaves for a few more days before they all fall, turn brown, and disappear.

Sitting in my usual chair, I have my head resting on my palm and my elbows on my knees. Sitting kitty-corner on a sofa, with her legs folded, Anna yawns while Chris walks to my polygonal Brewista coffee server and refills his mug and Ravi's. Stretching across Anna, he nudges Ravi to wake him up.

Yawning and saying, "Sorry," Ravi takes his cup. Chris occupies the other perpendicular sofa, leaving the seat closest to me empty. It's not yet 7:00 a.m.

Pointing at the empty seat, I look at Chris. "Where is Tabi?"

"Showing the newbie his office."

"Now?" I ask, tapping my Roger Smith.

Anna shakes her head in disapproval and says, "He is on London time."

As I scoff, Chris crosses his legs and leans forward. "Tabi needs all the help she can get with the press and media. And the guy is good. Plus, I gather Nozo is somewhat fond of him."

Why stop at Nozo? But why do I care? I have everything. My heart rate increases a bit as I tap on the desk.

"Was it spur of the moment that I asked them to stay at my place?" Grinding my teeth, I stress, "It's not fair to Akane; she doesn't know the past." Yawning, I stress, "I couldn't sleep." Staring into my coffee, I add, "I made breakfast for Emi and Nozo and left." I scan their faces. "Sorry for calling you guys this early."

Touching my hand, Anna assures me, "It's okay." Then, she looks at everyone and adds, "It wasn't spur of the moment." She squeezes my wrist. "It's your daughter, Vince. And it's Emika."

Clearing my throat, I ask, "All these months . . . Why didn't you guys jog my memory?"

Nodding at Chris and Ravi before speaking for them, Anna says, "We wanted to. But on that day in the country club, when you revealed your intentions about Akane, we decided not to. We did not want to distract you from your joy by bringing up something that was nothing but rocky." Wiping her eyes, she adds, "We didn't know you two had a child."

There's a knock on the door, and Tabi peeps her head. Then, she calls over her shoulder to the newbie, "Come in."

A six-foot-two blond guy reeking of Jovan Musk follows her. He has a small bandage on his nose. Jerking his head, he moves the portion of his hair covering his left eye and walks toward me with an extended arm.

"Markus Becker." He fakes a smile that doesn't carry to his eyes. Locking his gaze with mine, he asserts, "I have heard so much about you."

I don't think he has ever steamed his corduroy sports jacket or ironed his camel khakis. The hemline of his khakis touches the bottom of his scuffed suede chukkas. Is he always on the road? What accent is that? British—but not completely. Oh, fuck it.

Shaking his hand, I ask, "Really?"

So, what did Emika tell you? You are Brad in a sports jacket. Did Emika pick you up before the extraction?

Pointing at his bandaged nose, I smirk. "I hope the other guy is in worse shape."

Smiling, he brushes my question aside. "Just the aftermath of a stampede."

The stampede Vandal and I were responsible for. "I see. Let the doctor on staff have a look. It won't cost you anything."

"You are very kind."

Pointing at the three musketeers, Tabi looks at Markus and says, "You've already met the rest of the founding crew at the café in Seattle."

Anna waves reluctantly. Ravi delivers a nonchalant "Hey," followed by a dry "Wassup?" from Chris.

Tabi pokes her head outside my office door. "Linda, this is Mr. Becker. He should be in the system. Can you show him his workstation and ensure HR gives him his credentials? Also, take him to the doctor." Then, she turns to Markus. "Follow Linda, please."

After he leaves, Tabi pumps her inhaler, kisses Chris's forehead, and sits next to him. Rolling her eyes, Tabi begins, "He understands blogging and shit, but he has a single-track mind."

Shaking his head in despair, Chris admits, "I know, right?"

Anna nods, and Ravi scrunches his lips in disgust.

"Single-track?" I ask.

Tabi mocks Markus's accent and says, "'How far is Emika's office from my cubicle? Can I visit Nozo in daycare?' Emika, Nozo, Emika, Nozo—that's all he cares about."

Cracking my knuckles, I form fists and clench my jaw.

Moving to the edge of his seat, Ravi touches my hand. "Say something."

My hands are shaking. Holding my left hand with my right, staring down at the carpet, I mutter, "So, if I move out, this hair-flipping, Jovan Musk-reeking, budget J. Crew model will take my place—stare at the sakura, sleep in my bedroom, sleep with my Emi—" I quickly shut my lips tight. "Fuck!" Scanning everyone's faces, I plead, "Can you disregard the last part?"

"What's on your mind? Tell us. We won't judge," says Anna, rubbing my right hand.

I place my left hand over Anna's. "Thanks." Looking around the room, I say, "My mind is cross-fucking-wired since I woke the evening before last and found her holding my hands and weeping." Swallowing hard, I confess, "I love my Akane, but I can't stop thinking about Emi. When Emi and I were together, I transferred every ounce of my love and longing for Akane between 1991 and August 3, 2023, to her. But it was selfish of me . . . I had to free her." I take a deep breath. "This might be a residual feeling trapped in my memory loss." I glance at everyone helplessly. "This feeling will go away, right?"

Anna squeezes my hand. "These things don't follow any logical parameters."

Breathing quickly, I ask, "Am I cheating on Akane?"

"No," Tabi responds decisively.

Chris leaves his seat and fetches a bottle of water. Nudging my shoulder, he says, "Drink." Shutting my eyes, I take a large gulp of water and then wipe my mouth with my cuff. "I should be able to control what I feel."

Clearing his throat, Ravi leans forward. "You can't close your heart to escape what you feel." Then, after looking at everyone, he adds, "Umm . . . we all have a question, though."

"What?"

"Why does Nozo look like Akane in that ice cream picture?"

I scoff. "Emi and Akane were the same when Nozo was conceived."

Anna lifts her eyebrows and catches the hint. "You still love Emi, right?"

"Yes," I admit, sighing. "Akane and I would have remained just friends if Emika had stayed with me after August 15, 2024. But Akane and I have reached a point now Emika and I couldn't. Although, I don't know if Akane will still want me after I tell her everything."

Anna squeezes my hand again. "You didn't cheat on her. It was the past—something you forgot."

"I hope she sees it that way." I gulp. "I have this strange feeling when little Nozo grabs my finger with her tiny soft hands and calls me papha." Scanning everyones' faces, I confess, "I don't wanna let go of that..."

Pressing the button on my bracelet, I see the display read, "Intreton absorption, 25%." A few more days until I tell her everything. Turning to Ravi, I ask, "When does Emika start?"

"I asked her to settle in first. She is no regular employee." Leaning forward, he touches my shoulder and assures me. "No one can change the truth that you are Nozo's dad...your being with Akane won't change that." Pressing my shoulder, he adds, "everything will be fine."

Placing my hand over his, I blink. "Thanks." I look around at everyone and smile. "I don't say this enough, but I love you all." I close my eyes and inhale deeply to stop the waterworks.

(Garage)

"You needn't have," Emika says while helping me put Nozo in the car seat behind the passenger's seat. Then, she sits in the driver's seat, and I take the passenger's.

"Neither my Taycan nor my BMW i7 is child friendly. I want you and Nozo safe all the time. Nothing comes close to this electric G-Wagon. I hope you like the black exterior and beige interior."

Emika struggles to reach the steering wheel, then searches for the seat adjuster. I lean across her body and press the seat adjuster button on the car door. As her body moves toward the steering wheel, her breasts push against my arm.

Quickly removing my arm, I say, "Oops! Sorry."

Putting her hand over her mouth, she looks at me. "It's me. You don't need to apologize."

The diffused sunlight coming in through the window reflects on her. As I am about to get lost in her eyes, Nozo yells from the back, "Big car!"

Looking over my shoulder, I ask her, "Do you like it?"

"I guess," she says, shrugging.

Turning to her mother, I smile. "Tough to please."

"Takes after her papha."

I try to gather my thoughts. "Press the power button."

When Emika does, the car welcomes her with Debussy's "Clair de Lune." Her lips quiver. "Why?" she asks.

"It's your favorite," I say, smiling. "Also, the car has an autonomous drive mode."

Pressing her lips together, she nods. She grips the steering wheel tightly and mutters, "*Sokka.*"

Yawning, I navigate the ambient light settings, select the seasonal mode, and press enter. The color of the interior changes to orange, red, and yellow leaves falling from the ceiling.

Looking up with her bright eyes, Nozo spreads her arms. "Wow!"

I turn to Emika. "I worked on this customization. It has four weather patterns."

"Thank you," she whispers.

Going back to the screen, I select another option: "Emika's Spring." The ceiling turns cobalt blue and the walls into pink sakura, slowly dripping leaves like tiny pink snowflakes.

From the back, Nozo squeals, "Mum, just like *Soba* and *Sofu*'s house!"

Wiping the corners of her eyes, her mother nods. "Prettier, *Nozo-chan.*" Looking into my eyes, she asks, "How did you do this?"

"I combined all the videos of *hanafubuki* from the backyard and copied them to the system. It took me the whole night and part of the morning." Yawning again, I ask, "You like it?"

She tears up, and I hand her my pocket square. Dabbing her eyes, she says, "I have no words."

"Do you like staying in this house?"

"*Hai.*"

"I'll move, then. The house is yours, Nozo's, and whoever you want to share with." Our eyes lock as I say, "I know how much you love the bellflowers and the sakura." Lifting my index finger, I fake a smile. "Don't forget to furnish the main bedroom."

She then folds the pocket square and hands it back to me. Tapping my chest, she gives me a broken smile. "It was never about the sakura or the bellflowers. I would have furnished the bedroom if I'd listened to your voicemail in time." She runs her fingers under her eyes. "Or if I'd stayed back on August 15, 2024."

I know that. I can read your eyes, your lips. Do you know how fast I drove on August 15? All because I had a dream that morning.[57] *I'm torn. And if you think I'm oblivious, it might be easier for you.*

She leans toward me, lifts my right cuff, presses the red button, and reads the display. "Intreton absorption: 52%." Though her eyes are still moist, she smiles. "All the best. Akane will understand. She knows you only love her and no one else." She clasps her hands together. "Thank you for the car. Thank you for Nozo and Quantum World. You gave me everything, and you get what you want the most."

Forming a fist, I dig my nails into my palm.

Fuck, why is this so hard?

(Akane's penthouse)

I lean closer to Akane. Shaking her by the shoulder of her perfectly fitted maroon suit, I plead, "Say something." Her face is buried in my pocket square, and she is sitting on the sofa with her legs crossed. On her left is the Tokyo skyline.

She lifts her tears-soaked face from my pocket square. "How could I say those terrible things to you?"

"It wasn't you."

"She is the one who appears in your mind?" she asks. "The one with short hair who looks like me?"

"*Ee.*"

She dabs the corners of her eyes. "You looked for her when you stared into my eyes?"

"No. I never cheated." I stress, gripping her arms.

She touches my face. "I never said you cheated, silly." Running her fingers through my hair, she smiles, her eyes glowing in the morning sunlight. She closes her eyes, and the morning light touches her lashes, revealing droplets of tears. Opening her eyes, she tilts her head and asks, "Do you have a picture of Nozo?"

---

[57] The very first scene of *The Winding* (Book 1).

I hand her my cell phone, bringing up the picture folder titled "Emi & Nozo." She swipes through about fifty pictures, covering her mouth with her hand as tears flow down her cheeks. I know she realizes how much Nozo looks like her.

Lifting her eyes from the phone, she looks at me. "Nozo looks like you and me." Sniffling, she admits, "She could be my daughter."

"In a way, she is."

She hands my phone back and runs my pocket square across her eyes. Giving me half a smile, she says, "More people will ask her, 'Where are you from?'"

"I'd like to see them try," I say, my voice cracking.

Digging her nails into my hand, she asks, "Would you be there with her to ensure that?" She then scoffs and asks, "How could you be when you are with another woman?"

"So, now, you are another woman?" I retort.

She forces a fake smile. "We must do the right thing."

Looking away, she stares at the Tokyo skyline, reflecting orange in the rising sun. Turning her head, she presses her trembling lips together and looks deep into my eyes. Letting go of my hand, she digs her nails into the sofa cushion to the point of scratching.

No, Akane. Don't say that.

Breathing frantically, she murmurs, "You should be with them."

My heart wants to punch out my rib cage as I leave my seat to sit on the floor near her knees. "What?" My voice trembles. "I've waited thirty-three years for you."

She sniffles. "You loved her, and you still do. She still loves you, too. I can see it in the pictures. The way she looks at you . . ." She looks away from me. "I can't be the one to break a family—my Vince's family, at that."

Cupping her cheek. I turn her face toward me. "Yes, I loved her. And I searched for you in her."

"*Uso desu.*"[58]

Frowning, I stand up and lean over her. "Lie?" I growl. Placing my hands on her shoulders, I shake her. "I lied when you came back? I lied in

---

[58] It's a lie.

Copenhagen? Did I lie in Kyoto? That *ema* you hung in Kyoto, was that a lie? What part was a lie?"

She looks up, stares into my eyes, and whispers, "None of it. But you must do the honorable thing. Like my papha."

"What?"

She takes a deep breath. "In 1981, Papha was engaged to *Midori-san*. He visited the Netherlands for a business trip and created a music label—Egami Grammophon. He met a violinist with the Amsterdam Philharmonic Orchestra. They had an affair. They had a love child."

I walk into the kitchen and bring her a bottle of water. She takes a few sips as I sit by her, rubbing her back. Resuming her normal breathing, she continues, "But the woman never asked for anything from my father. She knew the Egamis and our society would never accept an outsider—a *gaijin*. But Papha was different. He confessed everything to Midori. And *Midori-san* asked my father to bring that woman to Japan."

Akane bursts into tears. "That woman was Theresa, and I was the child." She tugs my lapel. "Your Akane. I would be called a bastard on top of being a *hafu* if it weren't for Papha and *Midori-san*." She moves her hand to my face. "Do you want that to happen to your little Nozo?" Furrowing her brows, she adds, "I wouldn't want that for my daughter."

"The world has changed in four decades."

"Only on the surface." She clenches her jaw and rolls her fingers into fists. "I woke up from my coma to see the world unchanged." She scoffs. "In their mind, I'm always a *hafu*—despite the Egami name. They just don't have the balls to say it." Her voice softens as she looks at me. "You can't control what's in people's minds. But with you as her father, by her side all the time, no one will ever call her names. No one will dare to, even behind her back. She needs you."

I put my hand on my chest. "I am not evading my responsibilities."

"You have more to give her. Like Papha did for me." She puts her hand over mine. "In the years to come, the Abajian will carry a bigger weight than Egami . . ." Sobbing, she says, "Give it to our Nozo." Taking a deep breath, she adds firmly, "I can't love you if I can't respect you. You must do the right thing."

I can't lose you again.

Grasping for straws, I argue, "Who will call her names? Nozo will not be raised in Japan."

She scoffs, tilting her head. "And your beloved US is so different?" Frowning, she asks, "What's on everyone's mind when you walk into a room? Your accomplishments? Your brilliance?" She touches my face and says sarcastically, "How did that tanned skin get those eyes? Wow! So exotic. How did your parents meet?" Lifting her finger, she stresses, "And deep down, they pass judgment when you tell them you are an orphan. That's why you need to work harder than everyone else." She holds my hands. "Can you deny that?"

"No." Grinding my teeth, I clarify, "That made me resilient."

"Do you want your little Nozo to have to build your level of resilience to live a normal life?" She looks deeply into my eyes. "Do you understand?" Poking my chest, she stresses, "She is Vincent Abajian's daughter. Seeing you next to her will silence everyone, no matter what's in their minds. Do you understand?"

"Yes."

I get it all. But why are you putting yourself in Midori's shoes? Is this your maternal instinct for Nozo?

"What happened to *Midori-san*?" I ask.

Touching my hand, she smiles unconvincingly. "She is happy." Then, she clears her throat. "Your Nozo needs you more than anyone. And Emika has suffered more than anyone."

I realize the time I have with Akane is quickly eroding. Grabbing her hands, I ask, "What about us?"

She looks away. "I don't know."

"You still love me?"

"Don't be silly."

What? You always call me silly. What do you mean—my question was silly, or should I quit being your silly?

She tries to sniffle back her tears, but they break loose. "When flights resume, I'll have Michisato and Masato take your clothes and watches and collect mine from your house." Wiping her eyes, she asks, "Can I have Emika's number?"

"Sure."

"Now, go to your family."

I keep sitting as tears drop down my cheeks. I'm losing her again.

Touching my hands, she says, "Take your time. I'm not going anywhere."

As I lift my head, she gives me the half-finished water bottle. I gulp the water, and I swallow my tears. I'm staring at her face, absorbing every minute detail.

Pulling me by my collar, she locks her lips with mine. After a second's hesitation, I take her waist and bring her close. I feel her eyelashes against my cheeks and her tears mixing with mine. Moving her face away slightly, she kisses my forehead, nose, lips, chin, and cheeks. Then, she smiles—just with her lips, as her eyes are in disagreement.

"Now, go to your family. Go on. Snap."

"Are you not my family?"

She pushes her tears back. "Don't make me weak." Looking away, she adds, "And Vince, don't use the core to come here again."

With eyes wide open, I stand up. "You don't mean that."

"That would be unfair to your Emi and Nozo."

"What if I want to talk?"

"Cell phone, texts—everything regular humans use. I will still come to board meetings."

"Promise you will come to the meetings?" My voice shakes as I ask, "And you will respond to my texts?"

She nods. "Uh-huh." Still looking away, she sobs, "Now, please leave."

"You won't look at me?"

She doesn't turn her head. "I can't."

I touch my thumb to my middle finger.

I'm gonna snap. Look at me. It's me, your silly. Can't you turn your head once? I promise I'll go. Don't be so cruel.

I sigh.

Very well. Have it your way. Goodbye, Akane.

I snap my fingers.

(Akane's penthouse)

<u>Akane</u>

With my eyes filled with tears, turning back, I screech, "Vince, *ikanaide kudasai*."[59]

Couldn't you fight a little harder for me, for us?

I fall to my knees as my shoulders begin to shake.

I wanted to meet you from the moment I got my memories back. I wouldn't have barged in if I'd known you were attached. But you weren't. I lied; Midori-san *killed herself. But look at Papha; he is happy with Mum and me.*

If Emika and I were the same, Nozo would be my daughter. I can't take her father away.

I get up and walk to the *Butsudan*. I kneel before it. My throat feels dry, but I don't care.

Leaning toward the shelf, I ask, "Tell me, what did I do so wrong? Why did you play this game with me? Tell me I did the right thing." My lips quiver. "Because this hurts. Do you know what it means to hurt?"

I take out my cell phone and fetch the shared cloud photo drive titled "AV," short for Akane and Vincent. Was it the same reality where I walked into his house and found him? Was it the same reality where we took over a thousand pictures of us? Was it the same reality where I relearned the violin from Mum, just for him? I look at my hands. Will I ever get to touch his face again, run my fingers through his hair? Will there ever be a life where I can have him all to myself? Is that too much to ask?

I walk to my bar and take out the Screaming Eagle Cabernet 1991. The year I disappeared.

I didn't want to wait till your product launch. I planned to surprise you and propose to you with this bottle on April 15, 2027—a year after writing that ema.

With trembling hands, I start to uncork the bottle. The corkscrew misses the cork and cuts my hand.

Couldn't you make a deeper cut?

---

[59] Vince, please don't go.

I sit on the floor and raise the bottle. "I have waited so long and can't wait any longer. We will have a house in the US and one in Japan. Will you marry me, Vincent?" I put my palm behind my ear. "I'm sorry, what?" Shaking my head, I ask, "You can't? Why? You knocked up a girl?" I jeer, "Wow! And you thought she was me?" My tears reach my chin. "*Omoshiroi.*" As my shoulders shake, I look up. "Look what you've done to me, Vince." Then, I hear footsteps. "Is that you, Vince? Where are you? Please come to me," I say, peeking around all the corners of my penthouse. I sit on the floor. "So, it's not you."

Putting my mouth on the bottle, I take a long drink. Then, I spit it out on my wooden floor. "*Nigai*—like everything without you." I spill the whole bottle into the sink. "*Sayonara watashi no ai. Sayonara watashi no amai,* Vincent." Shoving the neck of the bottle into the garbage disposer, I grind my teeth. "Die, die, die, dreams die!"

I pick up my phone and call Emika.

"Hello?"

"Akane *desu.*"

"So lovely to hear your voice. Please understand that none of what happened is Vince's fault. There is no one he'd rather be with. I wish you and him a wonderful life. I'll move from this house at the soonest."

Why do you have to be so nice? Why do you make it so hard?

Taking a deep breath, I say, "Look, Vincent is all yours. He left thirty minutes ago. I'll not explain myself. But in the past, you or through me, you've hurt him a lot. Don't do it again." Clearing my voice of all my feelings, I say, "Don't leave him this time."

"I won't. I didn't want to create a barrier between you two."

"I know that."

"He will never forgive me, *Akane-san.*"

"Then you know nothing about him."

"Then, please, tell me."

Why am I telling you all this? Because I want my Vince happy, even if it shatters me. I want to help you, even though you stole my life and dreams.

I sigh. "You will see him in distress when he comes home. He won't be rational. Just hold his hands and say, 'I'll be here as long as you need.'" My voice trembles. "Let him be the one to speak." Taking a deep breath, I add, "In days to come, he will be very unreasonable."

"What?"

I don't need to explain everything. I did my job, and that's all I'll do. My voice cracks. "Enjoy my Vince." Blinking back my tears, I say, "Don't hurt him. Please." Then, I hang up.

I call another number.

"Everything all right, Akane?"

"Sasha, is Krista close by? Can you put the phone on speaker?"

"Krista here. What's wrong?"

"I'll tell if you promise not to blame Vincent. He needs your support. Fred's, too, okay?"

"Okay."

"I might do a few things to steer him to do the right thing. But it will be hurtful." Breathing hard, I request, "There is someone in Vincent's life . . . treat her like you treat me."

(Core)

Vincent

I never bothered with my past. I never cared what was behind this door. Why would I? But today, I need to know something. Why does everyone leave me?

It all started with you.

Turning the door, I enter a room lit with candles all over. The walls reflect images of a carousel, yet there is none in the vicinity. Amara sings Kreisler's Liebesleid to her six-month-old child, rocking the broken bassinet in the center of the room. That child is me. As I walk over to her, she looks up.

She comes close, putting her hands on her cheeks and widening her eyes. "Vincent? I never thought you'd come."

I lift my finger. "You thought right."

Wiping her eyes with one hand and grabbing my hand with the other, she says, "Sit by me."

I sit next to my mother on the sofa in the room. Then, she touches my chin and looks at me with the same luminous eyes that Nozo has. "How have you been?"

"It's a little too late to play mother," I scoff.

Blinking back tears, she admits, "I know." Suddenly, the baby cries, and she picks up the six-month-old Vincent.

"Can I hold him?" I ask, pointing at the baby me. He peeps his head from the torn blanket and smiles. I smile back. "You're me. I wish I could tell you everything will be fine." He holds my index finger and keeps smiling. Turning to Amara, I ask, "Isn't the basic instinct of a parent to protect their child?"

Running her fingers under her eyes, she lets me speak.

"Do you know what it is like for a child to be bullied every day because their name sounds different but not have a parent to talk to about it? I had to figure out everything myself." Tears well in my eyes, but I continue, "What to say? What to feel? How to eat? No one wiped my face when I made a mess. Then, a light comes along, and she gets taken away as soon as you start believing in some hope. Do you know what it is for a child to deal with sorrow from the tender age of eight? What does it do to a child?"

Touching my hands, she says, "I'm so sorry. Philip came here often and told me your headmaster loved you like his own child."

"I was not his only responsibility." Shaking her by her arms, I demand, "Why did you dump me? Was I so repuls—?"

She covers my mouth with her hand. "Don't say that. How could I raise you when I was a dying prostitute?" She takes a deep breath. "The orphanage was your fighting chance. And when you were born, a bearded old man told me that you're destined for great things."

I shake my head. "Chronos."

With little Vincent in my left arm, I wrap my right around Amara. In here, she is thirty-four, and I am forty-three.

Weeping, she admits, "I have only one wish. To have a life where I raise you in our own house. To give you everything, I couldn't."

"Why?"

She takes little Vincent from my arms. Then, she looks at him and me. "Why? Just look at his innocence, his sparkly eyes. His smile." Her voice shakes. "Why?" She pounds her chest. "Because he is mine."

Touching little Vincent's head, I smile. "They are your eyes. My daughter has the same eyes."

"You're married?" Amara's eyes brighten as she turns to me. "I'm so happy."

I rest my forehead on my hand. "I'm not." Breathing hard, I confess, "It's complicated."

"You can tell me," she says, touching my shoulder.

I lift my head. "Not in this life. Maybe in the life where your dream comes true, I will share all my joys and sorrows . . ." I pause as my eyes flood and my lips quiver. Against all my strength, I say, "Mum."

She places little Vincent back in the bassinet. Then, she touches my face and moves my head toward her shoulder. "Never thought I'd hear it."

My voice cracks. "Never thought I'd say it."

(Vincent's home)

Lifting my cuff, I see it's 11:00 p.m. Little Nozo must be asleep. There is no need to startle Emika with my appearance out of thin air. The front door it is, then. Whose Kia Soul is parked outside? A rental?

I tap on my wristwatch. "Athena, disable alarms."

Two steps into my house, I see Markus holding Emika's hands and nodding. Wow! Already marking his territory? Emika must have told him I would leave this house. But with Akane ending us, why would I move from this house? They are so engrossed in their chitchat that my presence is unnoticed.

Come on, kiss that fuckface, Emika. You've done it before. It won't even matter to me. Nothing will matter after what happened today. At least back then, you had the decency to keep Brad away from my house.

I don't see Hulk. Where is he? Has this fuckface been here long enough that Hulk's gotten used to him?

"Ahem. Where is Hulk?"

Emika quickly removes her hands from Markus's grip. Tucking her hair behind her ears, she says, "He is guarding Nozo."

Markus jerks his head, flipping his blond hair away from his eyes. The smell of his Jovan Musk reeks as he approaches me. He extends his arm. "Dr. Abajian, we met. I'm Mar—"

"I know who you are."

Pointing his thumb over his shoulder at Emika, he says, "I was just—"

"Leaving?"

He turns to Emika. "See you in the office when you start." Before passing by me, he says, "Pleased to meet you, Dr. Abajian."

What's wrong with me? He took care of my family. Maybe he thought it was his own. And can I blame him for having a thing for Emika? Who wouldn't?

Turning to Markus, I try to restore my shattered politeness. "Please, call me Vincent."

"Sure, Vincent." He closes the front door behind him.

Loosening my necktie and dropping my jacket on the floor, I sit on my favorite spot on the couch, under my mother's portrait. I place my head in my palms and take a deep breath.

Emika picks up my jacket and places it on the sectional. Sitting on my left, she unbuttons my cuffs and folds my sleeves. Then, she holds my right hand with both her hands and looks into my eyes.

"I'm ready when you are."

"For?"

"Anything," she says, lifting her shoulder.

Looking away, I say, "You can have the house to yourself and Markus after I move."

"Where will you move?"

"I don't know."

"Will that make you happy?"

"No."

"Then why do it?"

I clear my throat. "Someone should be happy. And it can't be Akane or me. It has to be you, Nozo . . ." I sigh. "And Markus."

Running her finger over my MIT class ring, she asks, "How do you know Markus and I will be happy?"

"I don't."

She squeezes my hand tightly. "Mark and I were a couple in the past. But for the last two years, we have been nothing more than friends—at least from my side. I can't stop him from working at Quantum World." Taking a breath, she says, "But you can. Am I clear?"

"Crystal."

It never is with you.

I stare into her eyes. "I don't want to fire him." After all, it's beneath my pay grade.

She kisses my hand. "Akane called me. I won't insult your feelings by saying I know what you feel." Running her fingers through my hair, she says, "We rushed last time. Can we start by being friends and see where it takes us?" She gives me a gentle smile. "I heard passes are limited to"—she presses her thumb and index finger together—"a tiny circle." Poking my heart, she locks her eyes with mine. "Can you let me in?"

Biting my trembling lips, I manage, "Yes."

Where was this Emika before? Is this what Estrid meant when she said, *"Someone needs to grow up mentally"*?

She kisses my forehead. "What's on your mind?"

My eyes fall on her untied sakura-print converse. Picking up her foot, I tie the laces into a Berluti knot. Her lips quiver. I look at her slender wrist and that Cartier Tank wristwatch I gifted her. Instinctively, I take her left wrist and wind the blue sapphire crystal crown. She sniffles and wipes the corners of her eyes with her right hand. Then, she just runs her fingers over my thumb and index finger. Slowly, tears start to drip from my eyes onto her wrist. I take out my pocket square, soaked with Akane's tears, to wipe mine off Emika's skin.

Pin-drop silence; I can hear the dry fall leaves, Philip's clocks, and Emika's heartbeat. I wait. I wait for fifty turns of her blue sapphire-encrusted watch crown.

Then, I clear my throat and stare at the floor, taking long breaths. "Akane did not even turn to look at me when I snapped my fingers." Turning my head toward Emika, I ask, "Would you be so cruel to someone who waited for you for over three decades?"

She wipes my tears with her thumbs. "Probably the hardest thing she did. Not looking at you and asking you not to visit her is her coping way.

She, too, was losing everything, right?" She closes her eyes and bites her wobbling lips. "Please don't blame her."

"No one asked her to lose everything."

She shakes her head and smiles. "No one asked you to free me, either, right? But you did it, risking me forgetting you. You did love me then, right?"

Looking down at the floor, sniffling, I confess, "I still do. Maybe that's why I didn't fight Akane harder." I look into Emika's eyes. "I can't flush Akane out, the way she rinsed me. I need time. I lived a fuller life in the last two years than I did in my previous forty-one." Clasping my hands, I beg, "Would you mind staying here with Nozo? I just need a bit of time to open up."

Unjoining my hands, she says, "Never beg before me." Then, she wraps her slender arms around my neck. "Nozo and I will be right here. Take all the time you need."

I scrunch her Caltech sweatshirt as she did to my sweats three years back. I rest my forehead on her petite shoulder as she grips my hair at the back of my head.

She whispers, "None of this is your fault."

Emika and Nozo are sleeping in the guest room where Nozo was conceived. I'm sitting on the floor of Akane's soon-to-be former walk-in closet. Flights have resumed, and our last time together will fade away as if nothing happened. Our previous two years will be just a memory. All I will have of her is the scarf, the photo frame, the violin, and the tux from 1991. The trinkets from 2024 onward would only tease me of a life that could have been.

I take two of her jumpsuits out of the closet—the cobalt blue one in which she returned and the burnt-orange one she wore for Thanksgiving.

Why did you come back if you had to go? What was so wrong with me?

I hang the jumpsuits up and kiss them goodnight. Then, I unfold my sleeping bag and get inside it. Hulk curls himself around my head. Now, I know what was so enticing about Chopin's fourth. "Ludwig, play Liszt's Liebestraum No. 3 and Consolation No. 3. All night long. Only in this room."

"Certainly."

"Lights off."

The resumption of flights was supposed to bring Akane here. Instead, I see my little daughter playing with my furry boy, and Emika is holding my hands, helping me as I confront the reality that Akane's clothes, shoes, and jewels are being removed. And half of my bespoke attire is being put back in my closet.

I hear the heavy footsteps of the twin giants, Masato and Michisato. My brain tells me those two giants are just redistributing clothes and accessories. But deep down, I feel like a watch movement, shattered before assembly. The escape wheel is so far removed from the balance spring that they might as well be from two different watches. Three years back, I'd do anything for Emika to stay and put her clothes in the closet. And when that reality is here, all I want is to get back to my last two years. How is this fair to anyone? Is that why Philip wanted to commercialize an alternate reality—so we could concurrently exist in our bubbles? Grinding my teeth, I form a fist. No, I can't let that happen.

My little Nozo asks Hulk, "*Onii-chan*, do you want a little treat?"

Emika pouts and then covers her mouth as Hulk barks.

Nozo whispers, "Can you roll over, *Onii-chan*?"

Hulk rolls over and sits. Then, he wags his tail, tilts his head, and asks, "Woof?"

Nozo leans down and runs her hand over Hulk. "Good boy, *Onii-chan*." Then, she hands him a tuna treat Emika made from scratch.

Turning to Emi, I say, "You've raised her so well."

"She can be stubborn," she warns, lifting her brows.

She gets it from Akane.

Masato and Michisato come down the stairs with two trunks of Akane's stuff. I walk toward them and lift my head almost ninety degrees to see their chins.

"*Mata ne, Vu~insento-san,*" informs Michisato.

Extending my hand and sighing, I say, "*Boku o wasurenaide kudasai.*"

Nudging my shoulder, Masato stresses, "N-e-v-e-r."

I look up with flooded eyes. Clearing my voice, I clasp my hands together. "Please protect Akane."

Masato's voice breaks. "*Mochiron*."

Before getting into their Maybach, they turn back, wipe their eyes, and wave. And in a few seconds, the Maybach that came here on November 15, 2024, with a promise of life, disappears. I touch the front door of my house.

Goodbye, Akane. Goodbye, love. Goodbye, li—

I feel a little tug on my sleeve and look down at a face radiating light, one that has my eyes. She was born on the same day Akane came back. I kneel and wrap my arms around my little Nozo, kissing her chubby shoulders.

If you are not life, then I don't know what is.

I pick her up and sit on the sectional, where Emika scratches Hulk's belly.

Lifting her head, Emika looks at me and smiles. "Masato and Michisato are so huge." Chuckling mischievously, she adds, "I almost thought the car wouldn't start."

This is her first unmitigated laughter since she came back. I want her to smile all the time. Leaning closer to her, I say, "If David fought those two, the Old Testament would have changed."

Laughing, she leans on me and falls on my lap. The next moment, she gets up and says, "Sorry for that."

I cup her cheek. "It's me. Please don't apologize." Stretching my arms, I remind her, "You're starting tomorrow, so it'll be a long day." I get up from the sectional. "I will make us dinner. What do you want?"

With glinting eyes, she requests, "Omurice?"

"Perfect. I haven't had it since February 15, 2024."

"Me, neither."

Emika did not offer food from her plate even once during dinner. There is no Akane in her. Nozo is sleeping in her room. Emika is sitting on the piano bench with her feet folded. On the piano is a Rubik's Cube, and next to it is a red origami folded into a robin.

After loading the dishwasher, I walk over to her. Sitting on the floor, I say, "Play something. You're Hiroshi Amari's daughter."

Droplets of tears appear in the corner of her eyes. Wiping them with my thumbs, I ask, "What's wrong?"

"I don't want to blame you for anything, but . . ."

I hold both her hands. "Go on."

"Your wish for Akane to return in August 2001 made me leave the piano for the violin. In one reality, I could play the violin before extraction, except for the four opuses." Staring at our clasped hands, she continues, "And in another reality, I still picked the violin and mastered all the major opuses. But when you combine the two realities, I struggle with both instruments. I'm sitting here, Vince, but the paths that led me here are fractured." Sobbing, she points at the Steinway. "My first love was always the piano. And all I can play are some jingles." She pauses and takes five deep breaths. "When you launch the Neurolink, can I be a user so I can play again?"

Staring into her eyes, I say, "I can do better."

"Huh?"

I sit on her right. "Do you have a Chopin prelude in mind?"

She lifts one shoulder. "Raindrop?"

"Come closer." She moves in closer. I say, "A little more." Her petite frame meshes with mine. "Place your left hand on my left hand, right on my right." As she stretches her hands and touches mine, I warn, "In a few seconds, you will see a little spark and feel a little sting, but don't open your eyes until the end. Okay?"

"Okay."

Closing my eyes, I focus on the only musician who was a time corrector—Frédéric Chopin.

Please, Chronos, I beg you. Just the skill, not the pain. She has been through a lot—and all of it was my fault. Please don't hurt her with Chopin's memories. All she needs is a little jolt. She will carry the rest.

I bring my hands and hers to the keys and begin to play the prelude to Raindrop. I open my eyes and see sparks from my fingers circle hers, enveloping our fingers as one as I keep playing. She starts pushing my fingers down two minutes in; the transfer is done. The sparks disappear. Very slowly, I retract my hands as she continues to play. I get up, stand beside the piano, and watch the daughter of Hiroshi Amari surpass his skills. She starts hitting the keys harder at around four and a half minutes.

What are you doing? What gates of alternate realities are you trying to open? What are you searching for?

Her pauses and keying are identical to mine. My Steinway never looked this beautiful; the keys shimmer with each touch of her fingers.

Concluding the opus, she looks to the right for me. Looking at the front of the piano, she sees me. Then, she stares at her hands in disbelief, not blinking even once. Her mouth gapes as she moves her eyes from her hands to the keys and back to her hands.

Panting, she locks her wet, wide eyes with mine. She blinks. Her voice trembles as she asks, "I did this? How?"

Sitting next to her, wiping her eyes, I clarify, "Yes, you played the whole opus." I take both her hands in mine. "Everything Chopin wrote is in your mind for eternity. And now, you can also play pieces by any other composer by the ear. You don't need sheet music."

"What did you do?"

I wink. "Gave you a bit of Vincent."

As blood rushes to her cheeks, she asks, "Isn't that Nozo?"

"Well, I'm a gift that keeps on giving." I point at her wristwatch. "You're starting tomorrow, so you should go to bed."

She ruffles my hair as she stands up from the bench. While taking the stairs, she looks back. "I missed you, and I missed us. And I will wait as long as it takes."

The lights are off. I couldn't sleep in my room. What used to be Akane's walk-in closet was a hope I could get back to my two-year-old life. But it's all gone. So, instead, I'm sitting in my living room, watching the giant evergreens dancing to the receding fall winds and the howling of winter. The cherry trees are grasping onto the last few leaves they have.

Let them go, Sakura. Your life will be whole again come next spring.

The wind stops, and flakes of snow start descending. Early winter; it's not even November. I take out my cell phone and record this first snow for a minute.

Inserting Liszt's Consolation No. 3, I send the file to Akane. I write, "*Kogarashi.* Funny, I kept hoping you'd appear before the first snow when you were engulfed. And now that you exist in the same reality as I do, I can't even fathom this little fantasy that you would show up. I hope you reply. You haven't returned any of my texts."

I pick up Hulk and kiss his button nose. "Your mum is here. Happy?"

(Vincent's office—Emika's first day)

Looking out my floor-to-ceiling office windows, I see all the fall foliage is gone. All the leaves are on the ground, and the trees are bare. Autumn was short-lived. This will be a long winter. The clocks are slowly winding down to get to the 8:00 a.m. meeting between Anna, Chris, Ravi, Tabi, me, and Emika. I take out my cell phone and scowl at it. Why is it so difficult to accept that Akane will never respond to my texts? She doesn't want me in her life.

Double ristretto time. Looking down at Hulk, I ask, "How about Kona?"

He looks up and then goes back to sleep. Measure, grind, Weiss distribution, tamp, puck screen, lock, and extract. Sipping my double ristretto, I look outside again. A solitary red leaf spins out of its pack, leaving its companions on the ground and flying away. Weaving through the air, it gets stuck on my glass wall. It screams that beauty and joy are transient.

Staring at the leaf, I chug the rest of my ristretto. I scoff. "Thanks, Estrid, for warning me about the tough choice. I couldn't have guessed it. Tell me, was it so easy for Akane?"

As the leaf flies away, I jerk at the sound of Linda's screech. "Dr. Amari. Oh my God! Of course, he is in. You don't have to ask." Three consecutive knocks follow. Some things don't change; they survive extractions and realities.

"Come in."

Glancing around the room, Emika observes, "The layout is the same as your last office but bigger and very posh."

I smile. "Do you like your office?"

She smiles back and acknowledges, "It's posh, too."

Walking around, she runs her hands over the familiar Lelit Bianca, the espresso cups with Van Gogh's painting *Wheatfield with Crows*,[60] and the Beolab 20 speakers. She sighs, "Memories," and sits on the sofa by the fireplace. I sit in the chair kitty-corner from here.

She points at her navy suit and asks, "Is this appropriate?"

"Of course." Taking her hand, I wind her Cartier. I chuckle. "You are a founding member. You can come in sweats and pajamas if you want." Pointing at the Lelit Bianca, I ask her, "Coffee?"

Touching her tummy, she says, "I am too full." She tucks her hair behind her ears. "Thank you for breakfast—mine and Nozo's. It saved so much time." She briefly closes her eyes and then opens them. "Not just today but every day."

"Sure."

Tilting her head, she asks, "I never see any plates in the sink. You don't eat?"

I look into her eyes. "I haven't had breakfast in that house since you walked out on me."

"What will make you break this oath?"

"When I see some proof that you won't leave."

She squints at me. "What proof?"

Linda knocks and comes in. "Dr. A, they are waiting in your conference room."

(Quantum World—Executive conference room)

Emika and I enter the room through my office. The sunlight hits the heated *tsubo-niwa*—reflecting the waterfalls, the koi pond, and the wilted Japanese maple. It's not calming my nerves; it's making me search for someone in a jumpsuit.

Snap out of it, Vincent. She made her choice.

---

[60] On August 3, 2023, Emika had her first taste of Vincent-made espresso from one of those cups, delivered from the same Lelit Bianca. She also admired those speakers. The scene is from Chapter 4 of *The Winding* (Book 1).

I clear my throat. "Ladies and gentlemen, we have a new board member—Dr. Emika Amari."

Anna, Chris, Ravi, and Tabi clap. Lifting her right hand, Anna says, "Woohoo."

Anna's mild-tempered jubilation fails to strike a chord. We all sit. I take out a leather-bound notebook and unscrew my Montblanc Meisterstück fountain pen. There is an awkward silence—no teasing me about Akane, no jokes whether I am dressed to my left or right.

You said you would come to the board meetings. How about calling us over my phone or the conference phone?

I keep counting the seconds until we hit 8:15 a.m. on my JLC Reverso, hoping for her appearance or a ring on any phone. I take out my cell phone, but there are no messages from her.

You said cell phones, texts, conferences, board meetings, and everything regular humans use.

I tear a page from the notebook and crumple it into a ball. Gritting my teeth, I mumble, "You are a magnificent liar, Akane."

While Anna, Chris, Ravi, and Tabi stare at each other, Emika lifts my cuff and feels my pulse with two fingers. She gets up, walks to the refrigerator, and gets me a water bottle.

Rubbing my back, she says, "Take deep breaths and drink the whole bottle." Lifting her finger, she emphasizes, "Slowly." Continuing to rub my back, she turns to the other members. "Please note, we have an absentee board member—Akane Egami."

Anna, Chris, and Ravi stare at Emika with open jaws and wide eyes. Yes, she is a different Emika.

As I finish my water, Emika takes her seat. Sniffling, she composes her voice. "I'm privileged to be a part of your team."

I look at each board member. Then, I lean back in my chair, shut my eyes, and take a deep breath. When I open my eyes again, with half a smile, I announce, "Let's get started."

CHAPTER 12

MEDIA WHORE

"Yes, he is sort of a media whore"
—Akane

November–December 2026

(December 15, 2026)

Vincent

I **MUST CLEAR MY NAME AND** that of Quantum World from the recent heinous murders. The demonstration should do it. What if I fail? My hands on the steering wheel tremble as we reach within a mile of the press conference at the Marriott. My breathing gets quicker. Gently pushing the brakes, I stop my 750-horsepower Taycan after moving to the right-most side of the road, next to the shoveled snow. I need to breathe.

Emika rubs my back. "You will do great," she assures me. Her eyes and hair catch the golden tinge from the setting sun piercing through the cascading, giant evergreens. Even the dust around her face is sparkling. "Come closer."

As she leans toward me, I lock my lips with hers. After a second's hesitation, she runs her fingers through my wavy locks. Then, she pulls my head away, breathing heavily. Squinting, she says, "You said you needed time."

Kissing the fingers of her left hand and the skin around her 34mm Patek Philippe, I say, "It's been two months."

Blushing, she asks, "When did you realize it?"

"Over the last few weeks. It became all too clear; the only truth I care about is my life with you." Holding the wheel with my left hand and Emika's fingers with my right, I begin to drive, accelerating slowly on the icy roads. "Defending Akane while supporting me couldn't be easy, yet you—"

"Vince?" she interrupts.

"Yes?"

"*Anata o aishiteimasu.*"

"I love you, too."

"Vince?"

"Yes?"

"You never shared what demonstration you will carry out today." Lifting her right index finger, she asserts, "No more secrets."

"Noted."

I park the car between Philip's Rolls-Royce Phantom and Kenji Ozawa's[61] black Bentley Mulsanne. Next to the Bentley are the cars of Anna, Ravi, Chris, and Tabi. Lifting my overcoat lapel and fastening my gloves, I leave the car. Walking to the passenger side, I help Emika out. She is attired in a tweed newsboy hat, a turtleneck cable-knit olive sweater, a faux-leather skirt, and suede boots. I tighten the top two buttons of her alpaca maroon overcoat, and she pulls my vicuña glen plaid scarf as the reporters circle around us. She wraps her hands around my arm as we head toward the entrance.

"Who is the beautiful lady?" asks a reporter.

---

[61] Founding partner of Bernstein, Ozawa, Toscanini, and Mehta.

I turn in the direction of the question. "Ask me after the end of the conference." Snapping my fingers, I lift my brows. "But do ask."

As security clears the way for us to enter the conference hall, Emika pulls me by my lapel and whispers, "We are all with you—whether you tell the truth or lie."

Seeing us, every reporter stands up with their cameras and cell phones, pointing at us, constantly clicking and flashing. Emika buries her face in my shoulder. There is a podium at the left of the hall with microphones from CNN, BBC, MSNBC, CNBC, and FOX, along with a water bottle. Next to the bottle is a portable headset with a microphone and an amplifier.

A table covered with a fitted cloth bearing the Quantum World logo is on the right of the podium. Behind the table, from left to right, are Anna, Chris, an empty chair, Ravi, Maddy, Tabi, another empty chair, Philip, Kenji, and Edward. Next to Edward is an apparatus, three feet tall, covered with black cloth, with a blue model of The Mind on top of it. Next to the device is a wooden chair. An intern comes and collects our overcoats as I escort my Emi between Philip and Tabi. Philip wraps his arm around Emi and kisses her head as she giggles, covering her mouth.

Standing behind the podium, I lift my cuff. It's 4:30 p.m., as per the black dial of my JLC Reverso. I turn the dial to reveal Japan time—9:30 a.m.

I hope you're watching this live. This is Vincent, the one you called a media whore.

I take a folded paper from my jacket pocket and lean toward the array of microphones. Pointing at my colleagues and lawyer, I address the reporters. "They expect me to read this." Squinting, I ask, "Should I?" Then, I walk to my left and stand in front of my colleagues. Adjusting my headset microphone while staring at Emika, I ask, "Do you have a spare coin?"

She fishes her wallet from her trusted Ghurka shopper and hands me a quarter. Kissing her hand, I say, "I love you," wanting the whole hall to hear it. I walk back to the podium as the reporters topple over each other to snap Emika's picture while she covers her irresistible face.

I toss the coin. Heads, I tell the truth. Tails—who knows? I look at the coin as it ascends to its maximum height and starts falling. I close my eyes for a second and rewind in my mind every moment since November.

Nozo is sleeping while drooling onto Maddy's lap. Ravi gently places his index finger in Nozo's palm, and she grabs it. Ravi and Maddy smile at each other. Maddy navigates her index finger across Nozo's nose, drool-filled chin, and chubby cheeks. I have the most beautiful family. Nozo is now a trophy everyone wants to hold. Tabi is next in line, waiting like a kid before a candy store. I don't think Maddy will give her up so easily. Hulk doesn't mind the shared attention as long as Emika keeps scratching his belly. We have a half dozen boxes of pizza, and Anna is lurking around them, tapping her chin with her right hand and rubbing her belly with her left.

Smacking her lips, she mumbles, "Umm . . . Am I hungry? It's 5:00 p.m."

Frustrated, Chris shouts, "Get a slice and come back."

Covering Nozo's ears, Maddy warns Chris, "Shh. She is sleeping."

"It's okay," Emika assures Chris.

Folding a Brooklyn-style pepperoni slice, Anna comes back and turns to Emika. "Are you suggesting we don't need the helmet?" she asks.

Lifting her finger, Emika reveals, "We just don't need a one-to-one connection between neurons and intreton that Vince invented. For most humans, a few electrodes of intreton-c can capture all the brain frequencies—beta, alpha, delta, theta, and gamma."

Ravi turns to me. "What do you say?"

She is right. Actually, for most humans, a corrupt floppy disk is sufficient. But we can't do that. I stand up, sit next to Emika, and take her hand.

"I know you're trying to save resources. But would Porsche tell its customers, 'Hey, since you will only be taking your kids to school, why don't we give you a three-cylinder engine with 50-brake horsepower?" Rubbing her hands, I continue, "Our first batch of users will be multibillionaires, and they want the full spectrum of connections for the $100,000 they spend. Okay?"

Emika frowns but nods, indicating that she understands.

You don't seem happy. Let's try this.

Smiling, I snap my fingers. "But . . ."

Her eyes sparkle with anticipation.

"After the first rounds, when we release the product for the everyday Joe, we can collaborate with doctors to determine what level of nuances we need. That way, the doctors will make the order, and we can evade the blame of calling anyone mediocre or stupid." Kissing her hand, I ask, "Does that satisfy you? How about you and Ravi make a presentation on this new product? It must have a new name . . . How about Echo?"

Looking at her new boss, Emika asks, "Ravi . . . Ravi, can we do that?"

Chuckling at her enthusiasm, Ravi assures her, "You decide. You are a founding member now."

She nods. "Right. I keep forgetting."

Chris chuckles at her innocence while Anna smiles and blinks at me. I nod, acknowledging that she has accepted Emika's place on the board.

Tabi, scrolling through her cell phone, mumbles, "Crap." Then, she looks up at me sympathetically. "Do you have NHK with English dubbing?" she asks.

"Yes."

As Emika navigates the TV, Tabi comes to me and puts her palm against my cheek. "People lie all the time." Turning to her cell phone, she mutters, "I have to inform Philip."

When Emika finds the channel, we all stare at the TV.

On the screen, Akane is sitting on a couch, glued to a Japanese guy with glasses and cropped purple hair. He is wearing a snug chambray suit over a T-shirt. He has his hand on her thigh. Akane has on a beige mid-length dress, and she is holding his arm with both her hands.

The talk show hostess turns to the couple and asks, "So, how long have you known each other?"

Akane and the guy nuzzle their noses at each other, and then, Akane says, "Kohta Sawano and I met on November 15, 2024."

I feel my heart in my throat.

How could you?

My throat feels dry as I try to absorb the lie.

Akane continues, "We traveled together to Denmark, where we visited our friends. And in April 2026, in Kyoto under the sakura, we professed our love. He has now moved into my penthouse."

While Kohta nods, the show hostess asks, "Can we show your photo from Kyoto?"

A photo of Akane in her floral kimono appears on the screen. In the picture, she blushes as the guy kisses her.

Pointing at the photograph, Anna looks at me. Her eyes widen with shock. "They have cropped out your face and replaced it with this idiot's?"

I clear my throat. "Not just the face—the stories, too." Emika entangles her fingers with mine as I'm about to form a fist.

If you needed a Japanese boyfriend for your fucked-up society, you just had to say it. I wish I never lost my memory and that you never returned, Akane.

"Tell us about your violin performance on August 30, 2025. It was your childhood friend's birthday, whom you referred to as your love," says the host.

Akane's face turns red as she leans toward the host. "How did you get that footage?"

"That's immaterial, *Akane-san*. Does *Sawano-can* know about this Vincent? Didn't you invest ten billion dollars in Quantum World?"

Akane kisses her Kohta Sawano on his lips before turning back toward the host. Squeezing her eyes into two lines of lashes, she smiles. "Kohta knows everything. Vincent is someone from my past who wanted a bit of media attention and begged for a little investment." She shrugs. "Calling him my love helped. And besides, ten billion is nothing for me. But for Quantum World, it's a lot." Then, she kisses Kohta's hand. "If my Sawano doesn't like it, I can withdraw our investment anytime."

Lifting her brows, the host asks, "So, your friend Vincent is a struggling businessman and media whore?"

Akane swallows, turning away from the camera. She breathes anxiously, and it's clear she's vulnerably staring at something.

I thought she only stared at me like that.

Who are you looking at? Come on, answer the fucking question.

Sawano wraps his arms around Akane and says, *"Hanashite o kudasai,"* pointing at the camera.

Running her finger under her eyes, Akane pushes her tears in. She gives the camera a broken smile. "Yes, he is sort of a media whore."

Emika touches my wrist to feel my raised pulse. She tells Tabi, "Please turn off the TV."

Anna comes over and tugs my sweatshirt. "Begged for investments?" Grinding her teeth, she says, "Call her now."

I gently remove her hands from my sweatshirt. Trying to control my breathing, I turn to everyone. "From this moment on, no one will call Akane." I lift my finger. "Am I clear?"

Everyone except Emika nods. She rubs my back and tries to assure me by saying, "Her expression . . . Akane is lying."

I stand up and put my hands on my hips. "Let's help turn her lies into truth, then." Clearing my throat, I turn to Chris and Ravi. "Could you get the cardboard boxes from my garage?"

"How many?" asks Chris.

"All of them," I confirm as I head upstairs.

Emika's hands cover her mouth in disbelief, Anna's eyes are wide, and Tabi is pumping her inhaler. Chris's eyes are glued to me, while Ravi gently shakes his head, trying to explain my actions to Maddy. They are mostly silent, observing me as I meticulously pack all twenty dress shirts, four bespoke sports jackets, four linen suits, ten woolen suits, and the ten monogrammed robes Akane gifted me. Next, I bubble wrap the Roger Smith box.

You said, Kimi wa kazuko desu. *Liar. Everything is a lie. All these trinkets are witnesses to a lie. Get out of my house.*

Nozo leaves Maddy's lap, comes to me, and nudges my sleeve. I know that nudge, and I know that face. I wish I didn't. I pick her up.

She places her chubby arms around my neck and asks, "*Nani o shimasu ka?*"

"Cleaning trash."

Bending her head and widening her eyes, she asks, "You need help?"

I pull her toward me and kiss her cheeks and her nose. "No, *Nozo-chan.* You're such a good girl."

Tilting her head, she asks with pleading, large eyes, "Then gimme candy?"

Tabi points at her bag. "Here, Nozo. I have candy."

As soon as I put her on the floor, Nozo runs toward Tabi, singing, "Candy, candy, candy." Tabi now gets her turn with Nozo.

I take out my cell phone. "Ludwig, delete the folder titled AV from my cloud photo drives."

"Ah. You want me to delete over a thousand pictures from all the connected devices across all owners?"

With trembling lips, I order, "Yes."

Tapping my chin, I mutter, "Umm . . . What else? I still have an empty box." I turn to the mantel over the fireplace. "Bingo."

Emika sprints at me as soon as she sees me going for the violin and the photo frame. Blocking me from the trinkets, she lifts her finger and asserts, "These stay here."

"Why?"

She squints at me. "Why? What have these got to do with the last two years?" Touching my chest, she asks, "Are they just Akane's artifacts? No. They made you the man you are—the Vince I love." She points at everyone in the room. "The Vince they *all* love." Lastly, she points at Nozo. "Her papha."

My voice cracks as I ask, "Those?" I point at the packed boxes.

"I will ensure FedEx picks them up tomorrow and Akane gets them. Okay?" Putting her hand on her hips, she asks, "Are you done?"

Lifting my finger, I smile. "Not quite. Let's call Philip." I put the phone on speakerphone.

"Vince, what's up?"

"Quantum World cannot depend on the whims of a moron *Sawano-san*. Right?"

"You're bright enough to know she was lying."

"I have the entire board minus Akane here. Do you still want to invest in us?"

Anna, Chris, and Ravi exchange glances.

"Yes, thirty billion, plus stock options for initial founders, including Emika. And also options for Tabi."

As everyone's jaws drop and their eyes widen, I ask my colleagues, "We are okay with Nardin in and Egami out?"

Ravi and Chris nod.

Wiping the corners of her eyes, Anna says, "She left us with no option." Then, she tilts her head. "Are we keeping our Egami stakes?"

"They are stable . . . I will keep mine for Nozo's trust fund." Shaking my head, I stress, "If we sell in bulk, only innocent stockholders will suffer. And it's not their fault."

Yes, Akane, if we sell them all, your dream of being the CEO will be over. But I would never do that to you, no matter what you call me in public.

"Things take time in Japan. By Christmas, we will be all set. Is that okay?" asks Philip.

"Yep." I hang up.

Thank you, Philip. Thank you for raising me and lifting me from this shit. And I am sorry for not allowing alternate realities to be commercialized.

Stretching my hands, I fake a smile. "Who's hungry? Let's reheat the pizzas." I walk toward the pizza stack.

Emika stops me midway. Wrapping her arms around me, she whispers, "None of this is your fault. And I am with you." Then, she adds, "Please, don't rush to conclusions about Akane."

(November 15, 2026—Vincent's home)

It's 2007. "You know what's better than a Reuben?" asks Dr. Bovet, smiling through his coffee-stained teeth.

"Nope."

Pointing at the girl assembling our sandwich, he says, "Watching her make it. Just look at how her hazel eyes and golden hair catch the deflected sunlight."

You're old enough to be her grandfather.

Touching my shoulder, Dr. Bovet asks, "Seeing someone?"

"Not at the moment."

Nothing lasts beyond a week. How can it, when I search for Akane in every girl?

Squinting, I inquire, "Why?"

Pointing at the door to the cafeteria, he says, "That girl in the hoodie keeps following you—across seminars, this café, the Sichuan Gourmet Brookline the other day. Why don't you ask her out?"

"That'd be like stalking the stalker."

"C'mon, don't be a sourpuss. Don't be that guy on his deathbed wishing, 'Oh, I should've asked the stalker out.'" He chuckles before adding, "I'll get a table and wait after collecting our sandwiches. You get her number." He lifts his finger and winks. "Then, we shall strategize."

What a stupid assignment. The stalker leaves the cafeteria after zipping her Burberry parka over her crimson Harvard hoodie. I lift my lapel of the thrift store overcoat, tighten my scarf, and follow her while fastening my gloves.

"Wait!" I shout.

My voice reaches her, cutting through the autumn winds, the crackling leaves, and the leaf blowers. She turns, but her face is hidden beneath the hoodie. She runs across the crosswalk, weaving through the honking cars. The road signs are all blurry.

As a Honda Accord brakes, almost hitting her, I yell, "Hey, watch out!"

We are now on two separate sides of the road. The wind removes her hoodie, and her long, silky hair dances to the breeze. She turns to me and smiles. If all the 1.2 billion people who use the Shinjuku Station were to gather together, I would still spot that face—in an instant.

Akane? In Cambridge, MA? During my PhD years?

The honking of the cars gives 0way to the melodious notes of "Clair de Lune," and I open my eyes to find Hulk licking away my tears. I shake my head. How was that possible? Akane at Harvard? Why were the road signs so blurry? Was that a different reality? Fuck it. I get up.

(November 15, 2026—Vincent's home)

Almost everyone is here for little Nozo's second birthday. Markus follows Tabi around like a puppy, and his eyes are fixed on my Emika. Chez-Giraud caters the dinner, and I'm finding it impossible to let go of Nozo. She looks radiant in the butterfly-printed, dark-red kimono that Hiroshi and Siri sent. The ribbons on her two-inch wooden slippers match her kimono. She is holding my tie while standing on my lap. I never thought my eyes were beautiful until I saw them on her face. I touch her tiny nose as she squishes her eyes into two lines of thick eyelashes.

She says, "Papha."

I kiss her forehead and her cheeks. "Yes?"

She kisses me back, a buttery lip and a soft cheek pressed against my skin. Stretching her eyes wide, she asks, "Am I old?"

Placing her head on my shoulder, I rock her and say, "Yes, granny. Very old—all of two years old."

Emika nudges my shoulder. I look up, and my jaw drops when I see her in the dress she wore for our first dinner together. My stare turns her face pink.

Shaking her head, she says, "I almost forgot." She gestures for a woman wearing glasses to come over. "This is Frida Chaturvedi."

Frida is wearing a flannel shirt, jeans, and Gucci loafers. Strange attire. I recognize her as the woman I met backstage at the AI conference.

With Nozo in my left arm, I extend my right hand. "Nice to see you again."

Frida grabs my hand with her sweaty palm and smiles ear to ear, her blue eyes gleaming through her glasses. A little sweat breaks out on her forehead.

"Oh my gosh! Pleased to see *you*." Raising her brows, she says, "I attended your Stanford lecture on singularity. I was the girl in the fifth row? Do you remember? Of course, you don't. It's been five years." Letting go of my hand, she snaps her fingers. "That day, you asked me a question, and I was so scared."

Her breath reeks of cinnamon candy. Squinting, I ask, "Scared of?"

"You."

Placing her hand on Frida's shoulder, Emika assures her, "There's nothing to be terrified of; he's just like us."

Frida nods. "Yes, yes . . . just like us." Speaking softly, almost inaudibly, she asks, "But how?" Quickly, she forces a smile. Looking around the house, she brings her hands to her mouth. "Your house is so wonderful. And Hulk is super cute. And so is Nozo." Then, she looks up, thinks, and locks her eyes with mine. Breathing anxiously, she says, "I didn't mean to say that Nozo looks like a dog. She is human cute. And Hulk is puppy cute." She slaps her head and curses, "Little shit, Frida . . . think, think." Staring at me, her hands clasped, Frida implores, "I am not crazy. Please don't fire me. I work very hard, and I volunteer at your orphanage."

"Hey, it's okay," Emika assures Frida.

I stretch out my right hand again. "Come here."

What made you like this? Why are you so nervous?

"What?" Frida asks.

"You heard me."

I place my hand on her shoulder. "I'm glad you're here. Now, relax. Make yourself at home. Get something to drink. Okay?"

Nodding, Frida murmurs, "I will drink. But I am not a drunk." Then, she walks away.

"What's with her?" I ask, looking at Emika.

She shrugs and pulls my hand. "Let's go."

Touching Nozo's back, I say, "Poor thing has fallen asleep. I don't wanna wake her for cutting the cake."

"She'll live," Emika quips, rolling her eyes.

The half-asleep Nozo holds a plastic knife as Emika, Anna, Chris, Ravi, Tabi, Maddy, Markus, Frida, and I sing, "Happy Birthday to you!" Markus's eyes are fixed on my Emika. Will he ever be subtle?

I take a deep breath and look around at my family.

See, Akane, you are out of my mind. From now on, November 15 is just Nozo's birthday. Not the day you disappeared—and not the day you came back.

(November 23, 2026—Vincent's home)

I'm sitting by the piano with my earphones connected to my portable hi-fi. As I replicate bits of what I'm hearing, I observe Emika reading from *Japanese Children's Favorite Stories* and convincing Nozo to eat *nattō*, steamed rice, fried salmon, and *tamagoyaki*. Hulk is gently snoring by my feet in his buffalo plaid sweater. Isn't this the perfect life?

As Emika high-fives our Nozo for finishing the *natto*, the morning light catches both their faces. Nozo's eyes glow like emeralds with a touch of blue, and Emika's eyes dazzle like a fireplace's warmth when it snows outside. That's it.

Pushing the piano bench back, I stand up. I pick up the Tourneau bag next to the piano paddle and walk to the kitchen. Putting the bag on the breakfast island, I stand beside Emika and shut off her faucet.

"Plates can wait." Then, I pull her and make her sit next to Nozo's high chair.

Nozo lifts both her hands and calls out, "Papha." I pick her up, and she wraps her tiny chubby arms around my head and says, "*Watashi no*, Papha."

Kissing her head, I assure her, "Only yours."

Emika's eyes twinkle at my response. Recovering from Nozo's possessiveness of her father, she points at the bag. "What's this?"

"Open it."

"I said no parties and gifts, remember? I just want a day with my little family before Thanksgiving."

"This won't interfere, trust me."

She rolls her eyes and opens a wooden box encased in a suede covering. Upon opening the box, she finds the 34mm Patek Philippe 18-karat rose gold Calatrava 7200R-001 inside.

Placing the watch on her wrist, she asks, "How does it look?"

"Breathtaking. This one is automatic, so it doesn't need winding as long as you wear it or keep it in a winder."

Tucking her hair behind her ears, she frowns. "I thought you liked winding my watch."

Chuckling, I set Nozo back down in her high chair. Then, taking Emika's wrist, I start to wind her new acquisition.

Our eyes lock as I say, "Automatic watches can be wound, too. Also, it was never about winding. I just wanted to hold your hand." I pause, breathe deeply, and say, "Happy Birthday!"

She blushes, smiles, stops, and then smiles again. Unable to construct a response, she takes a deep breath and points at the piano. "What were you playing?"

"Um, nothing."

"I want to know." Then, she tilts her head like Nozo. "You won't tell me on my birthday?" she asks, pouting her lips.

"Okay, I will play it for you. I'm not a composer, so I'm simply mixing bits."

Emika picks Nozo up and then places her on the floor by the piano before sitting in the chair closest to the piano.

I close my eyes. With no metronome to guide me, I begin keying the Raindrop prelude.

Hey, in a different reality, will you be able to find me? Will our paths converge? How hard will you strike the keys to bend time so we can meet at least once? Will this music be your North Star?

My keying becomes deafening, as if I am showing her how to knock on the doors that separate realities. About five minutes into the Raindrop prelude, I jump into Chopin's Ballade No. 4, eliminating the first forty seconds.

And if you ever find me by a miracle, what will you ask? Will you blame me for not looking for you? What if, in this reality, right before the end of my days, you told me not to look for you? So, I did not.

As my pulse rises, I continue Chopin's fourth for eleven minutes and then move on to his Nocturne, Op. 9, No. 2.

If we meet for a little bit, will you let me dive into your warm eyes and witness the setting sun? Even for a minute?

As I key the final note, I open my teary eyes.

With her hand covering her mouth, Emika remarks, "*Subarashi desu.*"[62] She comes and sits next to me.

Looking down at the keys, I realize that, among all possible realities, I'm living in one where Emika and I are in the same house, sharing a life. How is that not a miracle? The sun continues its course, glowing red, and shines on my hands and the piano keys.

She rests her head on my shoulder and asks, "What do you call it?"

"*Emika no uta*[63]—your second birthday gift."

Her voice cracks. "It far exceeds the first one." Lifting her head from my shoulder with sparkly eyes, she asks, "Can we play it together?"

"Four hands on a piano?"

"Nope, my hands under yours, then yours under mine. We'll do it twice."

If we do this, the sparks from my hands will connect with yours, and then our pauses and keying will be identical. And this will remain constant across realities. Do you want that?

Kissing her cheek, I say, "Okay."

As she places her hands over mine, I murmur, "Happy Birthday."

"Thank you. There is no place I'd rather be."

"Me, neither."

---

[62] This is so wonderful.

[63] Song of Emika.

(November 26, 2026, Thanksgiving—Vincent's home)

Looking around the table, I take a head count—Emika, Anna, Ravi, Maddy, Tabi, Chris, Sasha, Krista, and Fred. Nozo is fast asleep in her crib while Hulk naps on the sofa. The last bit of setting sun and the industrial lights over the dinner table reflect on our almost finished dinner. The menu was identical to the dinner at Sasha's and Krista's house two years back. Krista, Sasha, Emika, and I cooked while Fred played with his favorite niece—Nozo.

I put the orange napkin on the table. "Perfect," I declare. "Every single soul I care about, under one roof." Wish Philip and Edward were here, too.

Ravi nods, and Krista stretches her hand beyond Fred to touch mine.

Fred lifts his brows and scoffs. "Every soul? If you say so." Then, he washes his bite down with Chateau Lafite 1991 and finishes with half a bottle of stout.

I narrow my eyes at him. "Something on your mind?"

"How easy it was for you and her." He leans forward and gestures at Krista, Sasha, and himself. "While we three are caught in the crossfire."

"I never fired a shot," I say, pointing at myself. "Easy for me? Hey, I watched that segment."

Placing the dinner napkin on the table, Fred crumples his brows. "So, she lied about loving a B-grade producer. Wonder why?"

I grit my teeth. "Didn't seem like a lie to me." I tap on the dinner table. "You think I'm jealous of who she"—I sit up and verify my Nozo is still sleeping. Fisting and clenching my jaws, I continue—"fucks?" I am, but they don't have to know that.

Emika glares at me and then checks that Nozo is still sleeping, shaking her head.

I knock on the table. "Putting that shithead's face over my body is the lie. Replacing me in her stories is the lie." Fuming, I ask, "Who was in Copenhagen, mending our bond? Sawano?"

Fred's face turns red. "Why do you think she did that?"

"I don't give a fuck."

Turning to me, Krista shrugs. "I'm with Vince. I would never say what Akane said." She takes a sip of her wine before adding, "Or do what she did."

Narrowing her eyes in betrayal, Sasha turns to her wife. "Kris? We agreed to be on the same page . . . on Thanksgiving!"

I lean toward Sasha and ask, "Whose side are you on?"

"There is no side," Fred hisses at me. "Akane never left your side." Lifting his hands, Fred says, "Unbelievable. How can someone be so bright and yet so daft?"

Emika turns to Fred and says, "This is how your brother chooses to cope." Keeping her eyes on Fred, she touches my hand. "One day, he will understand what's happening inside Akane's head and heart. Maybe he already knows, but he just denies it. Maybe he needs to talk to her in person." Pressing my hand tightly, she pleads with Fred, "Until then, let him be."

Anna shakes her head and tells Fred, "Vince is the world's most brilliant idiot."

"Thanks. That really helps," I say, glaring at Anna.

Fred leans toward Anna. "You've read my mind, Anna. Maybe we should talk outside the confinement of this Vince Villa."

Shaking my head in dismay, I say, "She's gay, you moron."

Sasha lifts her hand, thinks for a second, then scowls and slaps Fred in the back of the head.

"Ouch! Didn't come with a label," Fred grumbles.

Pointing at Fred, Krista declares, "Ladies and gentlemen, presenting Frederique Deschamps—the man who converts secretaries to brides to millionaire-divorcées."

"Mum, what is gay?" asks Nozo, standing up in her crib and rubbing her eyes.

All our eyes turn to little Nozo. Leaving her chair, Anna picks up my Nozo. Kissing her cheek, she winks and says, "In this context, it means the perfect woman."

Emika, Maddy, and Tabi raise their hands in protest. "Hey!"

Anna turns to Sasha and Krista. "We need to show them, sisters."

Standing up, Fred turns to Emika and points at me. "If he gives you any trouble, just call me." Then, he looks at me. "I have heard the tales of this Yamazaki 55. Will it leave the folklore and be in a glass that I can hold?"

I pinch his belly. "Yes, that's what this needs more of."

Fred wraps his left arm around my shoulders and rubs my hair with his right hand. "Fuck you, brother," he whispers.

"Love you, too."

(December 1–December 14, 2026)
(Vincent's office)

Before entering my office suite, I grab Emika's hand. "Hey, that was a good presentation. You and Ravi did well." I whisper into her ears, "Especially you."

Her face flushes as she tucks her hair behind her ears. Softly, she acknowledges, "Thanks." Squinting, she asks, "Tabi wasn't in the gallery?"

Turning the knob, I say, "Yep. Wonder why?"

Inside my suite, right outside my office, I see Anna, Chris, and Ravi standing around Tabi, whose hands shake while tightly gripping a DVD sleeve. Her lips quiver.

Anna is shaking her shoulder. "What is it? Tell us." Linda is standing nearby with a bottle of water.

"She will only talk to Vince," says Chris.

"I'm here," I announce, opening the door to my office. The room greets us with the immersive sound of Bach's preludes from my Beolab 20 speakers. Lifting his head, Hulk sniffs Emika out.

The whole team files in as I turn the music off. Emika guides Tabi to the couch in front of the fireplace and then sits beside her, comforting her. Hulk leaves his bed and jumps onto Emika's lap. Anna, Chris, and Ravi make way for me as I bring a water bottle and pull a chair right in front of Tabi and Emika.

Rubbing her hands, I assure her, "We are with you." She swallows hard, and sweat forms on her forehead. "Turn down the thermostat," I instruct Chris. Taking out my pocket square, I wipe her forehead. Then, I point at the DVD sleeve and ask, "What's in there?" Looking at Emika, I gesture to Tabi's handbag. Emika fishes out Tabi's inhaler and hands it to her.

Tabi pumps it thrice and then takes a moment to resume her regular breathing. She clasps her hands together and says, "I'm sorry, I have not checked our media mailbox since Thanksgiving. And now, it's too late."

Taking the DVD sleeve from her hands, I hand it to Anna. "Play it." On the top of the disk, written in a red sharpie, is "Season's greetings from Vandal." Anna, Chris, Ravi, and I circle around the TV. Emika keeps herself stationed next to Tabi, offering her shoulder for Tabi's head while squeezing her hand.

The DVD recording opens with shaky camera work and a warning written in sharpie on a flattened cardboard box: "Inappropriate for children or those with a faint heart." The cardboard box is taken away from the camera, revealing two men dressed in boxer shorts and tank tops. Their heads are covered with two nonfunctional versions of The Mind—one yellow and one red. The helmets are tied to a DC power unit. Their hands and ankles are connected with zip ties to the chairs they are sitting on, and their mouths are duct-taped. They are grunting while trying to free themselves from the restraints. Their wrists and ankles have blood stains from the struggle.

My heart tries to beat out of my rib cage, and I can taste all the food I had last night, burning my throat as I recognize the two helmets.

Pausing the video, I turn to my colleagues. "Those helmets—one from the *What's Tonight?* Segment, and the other from the AI conference. Right?"

Wiping his forehead, Ravi says, "Looks like it?"

So, other than fighting him, I'd also been only a few inches from him outside the dressing room of *What's Tonight?* Clenching my jaw, I form a fist. I almost had him.

I turn to Anna. "So, either Vandal or someone working with him was in that backroom of the conference. Do we have a roster?"

Pointing at the screen, she shrieks, "Roster? Who could have predicted this?"

"Right."

As I press play, I can hear Tabi weeping. Chris sits next to her, joining Emika in comforting her.

The cameraman, presumably Vandal, speaks in a modulated and forced American accent as he says, laughing, "What do you we have here?"

Wait, the one I fought had a Bavarian accent. Although, this one has the same sinister laugh.

Vandal then points at the victims. "I'm sorry, ladies and gentlemen, they won't be able to sing for you. Umm . . . in the strictest sense. But allow me to introduce them. On my left is Miguel Fernandez, and on my right is Altaf Ali. Am I right?" he asks his victims. They are puffing, gasping to say something against the duct tape. Taking a more menacing tone, Vandal shouts, "Nod, you punks."

Continuing in his sadistic tone, he says, "And I'm playing Vincent Abajian, who is playing God. You want your consciousness transferred?" Approaching his victims, he taps the helmets. "What do we call these?" he asks, imitating my accent and voice. He laughs and answers, with a vibrato, "The Mind." Then, he lowers his voice. "You may think I'm the villain, and you're right. But my villainy is nothing compared to the devil that sleeps inside the sleek exterior of Vincent Abajian. You wanna see what he will do to you?"

He then sets his camera on a stand and pulls the cable from the DC generator.

Anna covers her mouth. Tears fall down her cheeks as she cries, "No."

I wrap my arm around Anna.   Chris's eyes widen, and Ravi bites his lips, his hands trembling.

"Shut it off," Emika pleads. She hides her face behind Tabi's shaking shoulders.

But my eyes are glued to the screen.

You killed hundreds when you made the planes crash in September. But somehow, this looks more heinous. You sick fuck. What have I ever done to you? Who do you report to?

First, Vandal turns the knob slightly, and his victims start to shake. "But that's just blue. Let's make it rare." He turns the knob right, and foam spits out around the victims' duct-taped mouths. "Medium rare is the best way to eat, right?" He moves the knob to the right some more. Miguel and Altaf jolt, trying to break themselves from the ties. The helmets start to smoke. Their boxer shorts get wet, and urine slowly drips onto the floor.

Vandal points at their wet crotches. "Bad children. That's why I always loved your older brother." Lifting his voice, he shrieks, "I never wanted you two. Burn in hell." Then, he turns the knobs all the way to the right. The helmets first catch fire, and the victims' bodies jerk rapidly for what seems like minutes on end until they finally stop rattling. The plastic helmets melt into their heads. The men are at peace—whatever that means.

Vandal concludes, "Ladies and gentlemen, presenting the pinnacle of Neurolink and Quantum World, conceptualized by Vincent Abajian, a.k.a. Victor Fucking Frankenstein.'"

I eject the DVD from the player and put it back in the sleeve. Anna, pulling my lapel, screeches, "You psycho! Why did you make us watch the whole thing?"

I point at the door. "You could have left." Grabbing my shuddering left hand with my right, I explain, "I had to watch it. I now know Vandal can master several accents and has one sibling alive and one dead. He is close to the one who is alive." Breathing hard, I continue, "They were abused by their parents—or just one parent who did not want more than one child."

That won't absolve your sins, you son of a bitch.

I kiss Emika's forehead, then sit in the chair in front of Tabi again. Holding Tabi's hands, I ask, "What's on your mind?"

"I should have checked my mailbox earlier." She closes her eyes and whispers, "I should have taken Amina and Farid to the well. I was the oldest. I was supposed to protect them."

Squeezing Tabi's hands, I assure her, "You were twelve—a child." I point at the TV. "This is not your fault." I give her a moment before adding, "But we need your help. Are you up for it?"

"Yes." Her voice trembles.

Picking up my phone, I call Linda. "Get Markus in here."

"Sure, Dr. A."

Holding Tabi's hands, I direct, "Have Markus make a soft copy of the video. Then, send it to Bernstein and colleagues and Philip. Only the lawyers will talk to the police. Vandal will get it out to the media in a day or two." Lifting my finger, I declare, "No one from this firm will speak to the press." I point at my watch. "Let's have a press conference on December 15."

Markus enters through the ajar door. After glancing at Emika and flipping his hair, he asks me, "Yes, Vincent?" Then, he peeks at Emika again.

Pointing at Emika, I stare straight into Markus's eyes. "Isn't she irresistible?"

He wipes his forehead. "I'm s-s-sorry?"

"Are you done ogling?" All eyes in the room are on me now. I snap my fingers. "If you are, we have work to do."

He stammers, "Y-y-yes . . . I am s-sorry." Sweat trickles down his forehead as he glances at the DVD sleeve Tabi is holding.

"We have an emergency, and Tabi will fill you in." I give him a stern look. "Can you help her?"

"Of course," he replies.

"You can leave now."

He leaves without looking at Emika.

Chris exhales a deep breath. "You gave the guy a heart attack."

Frowning, Ravi says, "December 15 is weeks from now. The press will be pouring all over well before then."

"Philip and I will need time to prep for a demonstration."

"What demo?" asks Chris.

"You will know."

Nudging my shoulder, Anna shrieks, "Tell me. Are we fucked?"

"No," I say, pressing the bridge of my nose and shaking my head.

Emika stands. "What about the victims? Do they have families? We must do something."

I nod. "You're right. We must do the right thing."

Turning to Anna, Chris, Ravi, and Tabi, I clasp my hands. "Guys, I need some time alone." As they all begin to leave my suit, I grab Emika's hand. "Not from you."

She tilts her head but doesn't say anything.

"I need to confess something." I walk back to my desk, take out the *shuriken*, and bring it to her. "From Vandal. Be careful. The edges are sharp."

Taking it, she flips it over. Her eyes widen as she reads the words inscribed on it. With her hand over her mouth, she asks, "You know him?" She puts the *shuriken* on the coffee table.

"I have no memory of him. But someone could have doctored his memory, which means Vandal reports to someone."

Pointing at the *shuriken*, she asks, "Who else knows about this?"

"Philip, Edward, and Akane."

"Can't you use the core to get to him?"

"I need to know where to look. I need an identity. Else I'd be lost among infinite doors." Swallowing hard, staring into my hands, I confess, "I can't go to the core."

She puts her warm hands on my face, tilting it up. "Why?" she asks.

I take a few long breaths before saying, "Akane told me to never use the core to visit her. And I had no plans to do otherwise." I grit my teeth. "But I am tempted to confront her after she lied like that." Taking Emika's right hand and placing it on my chest, I confess, "The temptation? The conflict? It hurts here."

Placing her other hand over mine, she smiles and looks straight into my eyes. "You know what?"

"What?"

"You don't have to do a thing. It's not your job to catch Vandal. You just be the genius. Be Quantum World's CEO, Nozo's dad." She pauses, taking a deep breath before adding, "And if the time ever comes, be my Vince." She lifts her hands from my chest to place them on my cheeks. "At the right moment, you will just open the doors to the core, with nothing dragging you behind. Just like the first time . . . remember?"

"Yep, when I freed you." Taking her hands from my face, I kiss her fingers.

She blinks, then smiles. "Thank you for handling the Markus situation."

"Am I gonna have trouble with him?" I ask, staring into her eyes.

"No." Biting her lip, she continues, "I know my words don't have much value, given my past . . ."

"I don't care about your past with Markus. But what was he doing at the house the day I returned after Akane ended things with me?"

She squeezes my hands and explains, "He came unannounced to see Nozo. He didn't know you wouldn't be there. When you came in, I was just telling him not to drop by without asking first. But he can't accept the reality that we broke up. Staring at me like that, especially in your office, is . . ." She pauses and tucks her hair behind her ears before revealing, "He did mean a lot to me, Vince. I won't lie. But . . ." Then, she blankly stares into my eyes.

Cutting a dry smile, I help her out. "If it weren't for Nozo or the color of her eyes, you'd be with him, right?"

She lifts her brows, surprised by my bluntness. Placing her right hand on my left cheek, she smiles. "It's not just Nozo." Then, she taps on my belly and changes the subject. "You skipped breakfast again. Let's put some *katsudon* in it."

So, you want to bottle things up.

❅

(Quantum World—Executive conference room)

Sliding the lawyer's statement back into the envelope, I turn to Tabi. "I won't lie." Ravi swings his head as if Tabi and I are playing tennis, and Emika leans forward to get a better look at my expression. Anna and Chris exchange glances, and they both shake their heads.

"It's not a lie." Exasperated, Tabi bangs on the table. "Those helmets are just shells."

Standing up, I lean toward her. "I won't deny they were the ones from *What's Tonight?* And the AI conference."

Tabi wags her finger and points out, "You lied in the Senate, on . . ."

I slap the table. "I speculated. And that saved you, Edward, and Philip. It revealed a greater truth, and things were at stake then."

Anna leans toward me, waving her hands. "Um, hello? The fuck? Are things not at stake now? Everything we worked on is at risk." Pointing at the TV, which is on mute, she says, "Every news channel is mudslinging Quantum World and you. Are you deaf?" In desperation, she turns to Emika. "Can you put some sense into him?"

"You guys don't get it," I say softly, sitting down again. "I will demonstrate the truth."

Squeezing my hand, Emika asks, "How?"

"You will see." Scanning everyone's faces, I touch my chest. "Please trust me." Turning to Ravi, I ask, "You have the papers?"

"What papers?" Emika asks.

Fishing out his tablet, Ravi confirms, "Yes, it's all digital now. Bernstein and company are thorough. After signatures, they will put an addendum with USPTO." He slides the tablet and the attached stylus over the near-frictionless conference table.

I glance at the editable PDF and smile. Then, turning to Emika, I point at her name on the tablet. "Please sign?"

"What is it?" she asks, tucking her hair behind her ears.

Smiling, Chris turns to Emika. "We are adding you as the fourth co-inventor to the two-way transfer of consciousness patent." He touches her shoulder. "Please sign it."

Emika looks around the table. "But I was not in the lab that day." She bites her lower lip. "I was with . . ."

I hand her my pocket square. "But that is not how we want to remember things. I want to change the truth." While she dabs her eyes, I continue, "I could have made alterations in the core. But even the slightest change could wipe out our Nozo. So, this is the way. Please sign it."

Taking up the stylus, she signs. "When did you decide?" she asks me.

"When I woke up and saw you crying, holding my hand. When I told you that, I needed to undo some wrongs."

She looks around the room and sniffles. "I don't know what to say. I love you all."

"Equally?" Tabi asks, winking.

Pointing at me, Emika chuckles and says, "Maybe him a little more."

(Vincent's home)

We have switched off the news and are about to start *Kiki's Delivery Service*. The shutters are down, and it has been ten days since an array of news and media vans were parked outside our home. Ten days since Nozo played outside, ten days since sunlight entered our house, and ten days since we peeked outside the curtains without the fear of losing our privacy. My leg is stretched over the ottoman, and Nozo is on my lap. Next to me, Emika is scratching Hulk's belly while resting her head on my shoulder.

Gripping my robe lapel to pull herself up to my face, Nozo locks her eyes with mine and tilts her head. "Tell me a story?"

"What story?" Emika asks, pausing the TV.

"Hulky story."

I kiss Nozo's cheeks. "I will tell you my version."

"Okay." She squeezes her eyes into two layers of eyelashes.

Clearing my throat, I begin, "There was a lonely pup—Hulk. And there was a lonely man—Vincent. One day, they met, and together, they were less lonely. They went everywhere together, did everything together." I pout my lips and lower my voice. "But it was always cloudy."

Nozo pulls my robe. "Then, then?"

I hold her hands, and she grips my thumb with her tiny, chubby hands. "One day, the sun pierced through the clouds, and with the light came a girl. Her name was Emika. Then, Emika, Hulk, and Vincent moved into a large house with fifteen cherry trees."

Waving her arms, she asks, "Like this house?"

"Exactly," Emika whispers.

"But then, on a cold winter evening, a demon came and took away Emika. The demon also made Vincent forget Emika. Vincent and Hulk went out to look for her. And it kept snowing and raining, and everything kept getting darker and darker. Vincent and Hulk were lost."

Frowning, Nozo wiggles her tiny finger. "Bad demon."

Both Emi and I press our lips together to hide our laughter. My voice gets somber. "Poor Vincent didn't remember anything. The house, Emika—all forgotten. And, in the darkness, Hulk could not guide him. Then, one day, the sun shone again, the clouds disappeared, and the grass became green again. The cherry trees turned pink, and Vincent could hear someone singing and playing the piano in the distance. Vincent and Hulk followed the voice and the piano, finding their old house and remembering it." Clearing my throat and swallowing, I continue, "Vince opened the door to see Emika singing '*Haru no Kaze*' and a beautiful child crawling on the carpet. The yellow sunlight and the pink cherry trees reflected on Emika and the child. And the prolonged winter, the demon . . . it was all just a long nightmare that occurred when Vincent traveled far and wide to fetch some bluebell flowers for Emika."

Nodding, my daughter approves. "Good story."

Emika wipes the corners of her eyes with my robe. Wrapping my arm around her shoulder and kissing her head, I ask, "Everything okay?"

"It is now," she whispers, crying softly.

Bringing Nozo closer, I ask her, "Who is the child?"

Nozo shrugs and pouts her lips.

I rub my face into her belly and tickle her. "*Nozo-chan.*"

Sitting up straight, Emika looks at me. "I had a similar dream—of playing the piano and you arriving. How?"

"The core connects us both. So, we can share the same dreams." And some of them, in turn, become a reality.

Tugging my lapel Nozo asks, "Papha?"

"Yes?"

"I want to go out and play."

"You will when those people outside our house leave."

She crawls over my body and lands on her mom, next to Hulk. "What do they want?"

"The truth."

Curling herself in her mommy's lap, she says, "So, tell them."

(December 15, 2026—Back to the Marriott conference room)

The coin lands—heads. After folding the paper, I put it back in my jacket. I would have done the same if it were tails.

Thank you, Nozo. This is for you.

Someone shouts, "Will your invention kill people?"

"Who is the real Vincent Abajian?" another person yells.

"A killer or a scientist?"

"Are you Frankenstein?"

My hands tremble, but I fake a smile and wink. "You forgot media whore."

Some journalists smile, and others start to click more pictures in anticipation.

I close my eyes and take a deep breath. Then, I open them again and take a large sip of water. Leaning toward the mic and tapping on the podium, I begin with, "I will not answer your questions. Instead, I will demonstrate something that might either exculpate or indict us." Turning to the left, I announce, "Philip, Edward—showtime."

Emika, Anna, Chris, and Tabi start murmuring. Philip leaves his station, touching Emika's and Tabi's heads as he passes them. Edward removes the black cloth from the apparatus. Every press member starts clicking pictures of what Edward revealed—an electricity generator with electrodes attached. The device can generate electricity with a potential difference of 440V, the same model Vandal used. As Anna and Emika stand up, covering their mouths with their hands in disbelief, the crowd buzzes.

What, you don't believe I will go to any extent to defend my name and my firm's? Have you any idea how hard I worked to build them? Vandal called me Frankenstein. Akane called me a media whore. Who knew that Akane and Vandal would be in the same context?

Chris and Ravi look at Tabi to see if she knows anything, but she keeps shaking her head.

Pointing at the apparatus, I bow before the audience. "Ladies and gentlemen, presenting a similar device to the one Vandal used." Then, I pick up The Mind. "This blue one is a working prototype—unlike what Vandal used. We call it The Mind-01. Nardin Robotics built it to our exact specifications." Knocking on the helmet, I stress, "The shell is made of reinforced carbon fiber." I flip it in my hands and display the interior. "Inside, you will see millions of intreton-c strands connecting to the electrical signals from your brain's neurons."

Even though one strand of intreton-c would be sufficient for all your brains put together.

Pointing at the generator, I continue, "Electricity from the generator attached to the electrodes should not pass through The Mind. But who knows what will happen?"

Everyone in the room is silent. I can even hear the blood pumping through my heart.

Turning to Philip, I ask, "Who will be the cook, and who will be the food?"

Philip snaps his fingers and says, "How about a coin toss? Heads, you will be the victim. Tails, I will."

I throw the coin, and it lands on my palm. Tails. While I show the coin to the crowd, Philip unbuttons his sharply cut, bespoke navy suit jacket and leaves it on the panel table, along with his Moritz Grossmann Backpage platinum wristwatch. After sitting in the chair, he starts folding his sleeves. Edward places The Mind on top of his head and attaches the electrodes over it.

The faces of my colleagues, Emika and Maddy, have all gone pale. Anna is biting her nails, her eyes wide.

Holding the knob, I turn to the silent crowd. I have done this experiment several times in Philip's house, but what if something goes wrong? I grab my water bottle and drink the remaining liquid. My pulse is racing. I take a few deep breaths.

Vince, the electrons will always behave predictably. They are not humans. They will never call you a media whore.

I hide the quiver in my voice by clearing my throat. "Ahem. I will now pass the electricity and try to fry the world's richest and most powerful man. Will he meet his end, like Vandal's victims, Miguel and Altaf? Is The Mind safe?" Pointing at the knob, I say, "No theatrics. Straight to 440 volts." As I turn the knob, the apparatus lights up, sparks generate from the helmet, and then the electrodes fall off.

I wipe the sweat from my forehead. Lifting my shoulders, I turn to the crowd. "Oopsies. Can anyone tell me what happened?"

The audience is quiet.

I lift my brows. "No triple-digit IQs in the audience? The intreton magnetizes the copper and repels the electricity from reaching its surface. And even if it comes to the surface, the intreton-c underneath will protect the head and the body."

Philip leaves the seat and comes forward. He places his hand on my shoulder and announces, "Vincent Abajian is creating the future. I trust in his invention and invest thirty billion in his firm." The flashes from the photojournalists light up, and I shut my eyes.

Walking to the podium, Philip continues, "We have seen what Vandal did. He infiltrated my facilities and accused me of holding intreton, wreaked havoc on the Japanese railway system, hacked into JPX, caused airline accidents, and was about to crash a plane in Seattle. But when he shared the video of him murdering two more people, you started to see his logic and questioned Vincent Abajian." He narrows his eyes at the crowd. "Why? What credibility does Vandal have?" He bangs on the podium, and the sound resonates across the hall. "To question the integrity of Vincent is to question me." He runs his finger across the room, then points it at himself. "Does anybody dare to question me?"

With his hands on his waist, he leans forward. "You spent two weeks defaming Vincent and Quantum World. In the next two weeks, you will sing praises." Furrowing his brows, he glares at the crowd. "You are pathetic." Then, he returns to his seat, retrieving his suit jacket and putting it back on.

I take out another folded paper with my handwriting on it as I return to the podium. Clearing my throat, I start, "The helmets used by Vandal were mere models. But we will pay our debt because our names were used. Miguel Fernandez was a short-order cook and a part-time lawnmower. He was single but had a younger sister and parents. Quantum World and Nardin Robotics will pay five million to each survivor. Altaf Ali recently immigrated from Afghanistan after the Taliban killed his wife. He was a father to a three-year-old son—Wasim."

Wasim is an orphan now.

I pause as my throat dries up. I lift the empty water bottle for any last drop.

And then, someone holds a bottle out to me. Uncapping the bottle, I smell the lipstick I tasted when I stopped the car on our way here.

Emika lifts my pocket square, hands it to me, and whispers while rubbing my arms, "We will take care of little Wasim." She puts the pocket square back in my pocket, kisses the edge of my lips, and then walks back to her seat.

After gulping the water, I wipe my eyes with my cuffs. "Wasim is Quantum World's responsibility. He will be raised in Amara's Tree of Life." Knocking on the wood of the podium, I stress, "We are his family." Pointing at my chest, I proclaim, "Vincent Abajian is his family." Tightening my tie, I ask, "Any other questions?"

A male voice speaks up from the audience. "The beautiful lady who got you the water . . . Who is she?"

I look to my left at Emika, smile, and lean toward the mic. "Everything. Her name is Dr. Emika Amari, and she is a founding member of Quantum World. We have a child together—Nozomi Amari Abajian. I urge you all to respect our personal lives and remove your media vehicles from our property. Thank you."

As I walk toward my team and family, the hall echoes with thunderous applause. Why? Is it because we are taking care of the victims or because I have shown some signs of being a weak, pathetic human? Or is it Emika?

(December 15, 2026—Vincent's home)

After putting Nozo to sleep, Emika comes into my study. She swivels my office chair toward her, pulls me by my necktie, and unbuttons my collar. "I hated you and loved you for that stunt." Then, she takes off my tie and shirt, saying, "I'm done waiting."

"Me, too."

(December 16, 2026—Vincent's office)

The sunlight hits my polygonal Brewista coffee server and refracts onto my bookshelves in all seven colors of the rainbow. Slowly, the spectrum drowns under the amber color of the brewed Jamaican Blue Mountain coffee.

On my desk are two stacks of papers—one finalizing the dissolution with the Egamis and one for the initiation with Nardin. This morning, Masayoshi called to thank me for the Yamazaki 55. He also apologized profusely for his daughter's conduct and called me honorable.

"This is not the Akane we raised," he said several times.

I keep signing the documents under the yellow highlights made by Bernstein and associates.

What would you ever be, Akane, without the support of your family's wealth? Maybe you would have ended up like Rudy or his twin siblings.

(1991—Montagnola)

I felt the touch of a small hand as I hid my head in Akane's scarf. Lifting my head, I saw a little boy standing before me, his blue eyes filled with tears. His face was all blurred from my own tears.

"Why did you hurt my brother like that?" he asked.

Kneeling, I put my hands on his shoulders. "Hey, I'm so sorry. Trust me, I did not hit him that hard. He will be back on his feet in no time. What's your name?" I tried to wipe his tears, but he jerked back from me.

"Why do you care?"

I got up, still wearing my Gi, and rubbed his head. "Don't be so hard on yourself."

"If something happens to Rudy, what will Mom do?" he asked, looking up at me. "She only loves him."

"I'm sure she loves you, too. And nothing will happen to your brother."

While leaving the locker room, I saw his twin sister. I knelt down to her height and touched her tiny shoulders. "Your brother is all alone. He needs you."

Then, one day, a few weeks later, I heard they left the school, unable to pay the hefty fees. I even asked Headmaster Kruger if they could get a scholarship if my unknown benefactor could also take care of them.

His hands trembled as he tossed his glasses on the desk. His voice croaked as he said, "No."

(Back to the present)

I can't picture that boy's face or his sister's—after Akane was taken, I made no attempts to remember any faces except those I already knew. Oh, fuck it. Closing my eyes, I fill my lungs with the aroma of freshly ground and brewed coffee.

My entire life changed during the AI conference. If Emika had seen Akane and me together, would I have ever known my little Nozo existed? Was this Vandal's intention—to keep me away from Akane and get me to reunite with Emika and Nozo? Why?

Who are you?

There are three knocks on the door, and Emika reveals herself in a multicolored woolen dress, knee-high boots, and a matching belt. Tucking her hair behind her ears, she declares, "We need to talk." She sits on the sofa by the floor-to-ceiling glass wall adjacent to the fireplace.

Light—be it the sun or the dullest bulb—must enjoy shining on her. I leave my desk and sit in the chair kitty-corner from her. Holding her left hand, I ask, "What?"

She exhales in exasperation. "Nozo keeps asking why her papha doesn't eat breakfast with us. Why can't you share a morning meal instead of just cooking and leaving?" She pauses and bites her red lips, gathering her thoughts. "Yesterday, you said it was time on our way to the Marriott." Looking down, blushing, she adds, "And that amazing night . . ." Her voice quavers. "What proof do you need that we are not leaving you?"

Kissing her hand, I ask, "Why is the main bedroom unfurnished? You said in 2023 that once you moved in, you would do it. Why does the walk-in closet adjacent to mine have no clothes of yours? You said you would fill it once you moved in for good. What's stopping you? Tell me, why are the stickers on the fridge still there?"

She frowns. "Sorry. I was waiting for you to bring those up. Also, the fridge door Post-its stay."

"Why?"

Squeezing my hand, she explains, "It is a placeholder for a beautiful memory." Then, she furrows her brows and confesses, "Also, I haven't shopped much since Nozo."

I take my cell phone out and place a call.

"What's up, idiot?" Anna answers.

"What are you doing?"

"Chitchatting with Tabi."

"Can you continue that while taking Emika on a shopping spree—clothes, furniture, whatever she wants?"

"On our way."

Running her fingers through my hair, Emika locks her lips with mine. Straightening her dress, fixing her lipstick, and getting ready to leave, she asks, "What's your plan for the rest of the day?"

"I have a date," I say, stretching my arms and walking back to my desk.

She narrows her eyes. "Huh?"

"I need to acquaint myself with this beautiful young woman. A date should do it." Shaking my head at Emika's wide, confused eyes, I continue, "She is hard to please, but she can't resist choco candy."

Emika rolls her eyes and smiles. Opening the door, she says, "She asks many questions."

"I am ready."

"Have fun spoiling her," she says as she leaves.

My phone rings. My heart skips a beat when I see Akane's name on the screen. I groan.

What do you want? How could you slander my name in public? I was not privileged like you. I had to build my name with hard work, sweat, publications, and inventions. When you tell a lie to the media, it becomes the truth—a recorded history. So, now it's true that I'm someone from your past who sought media attention. You snubbed thirty-three years of longing, sorrow, hope, and pain with your lies.

I form a fist and grit my teeth as tears drip down my cheeks.

Akane, if I'm ever in Kyoto, I will remove that ema *and burn it. You said we would stand the test of time. Liar.*

Swiping my finger down on the screen, I reject the call.

Goodbye. I wish you never returned.

(Night of December 16, 2026—Akane's penthouse)

Akane

I switch off my TV. Vincent cleared his name and his firm's. He professed his love for Emika. I stare at my shaking hands. Everything is happening the way I intended. Only Sasha, Krista, and Fred understood. Everyone else misread me—Vincent, Mum, Papha. I pat my shoulder.

Daijōbu desu.

In front of me on the floor are two duffel bags and one bento box with my dinner resting on the coffee table. By the bento is a tissue box surrounded by crumpled tissues.

I can't even eat rice with soy without hearing your voice. How could you remove me from your board? How could you dissolve the investment? Do you hate me that much?

Fresh tears fill my eyes.

Those were just words, silly. Do you think Sawano can take your place? No one can. Krista, Sasha, and Fred all said not to do it. Fred said you're daft, and you hate liars. I had to ignore your messages. But I had to lie before everyone. I thought that was the only way. Because in Kyoto, you said, Attached, unattached, this silly is always yours. *That little Nozo deserves every bit of her papha. And Emika, she did nothing wrong. Do you think I meant it when I said not to use the sparks to meet me? Just words, Vince, nothing else. Since when do you listen to what others say? Why would you make this exception for me?*

I fetch another batch of tissues and cover my face.

Couldn't you come even once—to check on your Akane?

A long and wide shadow blocks the light. Wiping my eyes, I look up. "*Nandeska, Masato-san?*"[64]

"*Sawano-san wa kochira.*"[65]

I tighten my satin robe. "Bring him in."

Sawano sits in the chair opposite my sofa, bending his head and clasping his hands together between his knees.

I remind him, "You will only come here if I call."

"*Mochiron,*" he mumbles.

Pointing at the two duffel bags, I say, "That's your payment. Never mention to anyone that I funded your B-grade grindhouse movie." Tapping on the coffee table, I stress, "Never mention the Egami name in connection with your work."

He collects the bags. But instead of leaving, he retakes his seat and looks down, staring at my legs. Perv.

Clicking my tongue, I ask, "*Ima nani?*"[66]

"*Sumimasen,*"[67] he mumbles. Fisting his hand, he gathers strength. Then, breathing hard, he says, "*Demo daisuki desu.*"[68]

My nostrils flare up as blood reaches my head.

Can you replace my Vincent, you lowlife, porn-making motherfucker?

---

[64]   What is it, *Masato-san*?

[65]   *Sawano-san* is here.

[66]   What now?

[67]   Excuse me?

[68]   But I really like you.

I grit my teeth. "*Omae wa bakadeska?*"[69] As I stand up, the cord to my satin robe comes loose, and Sawano tries to take a peek inside. Holding my robe closed with my right hand, I point toward the door with my left. "Get out!" I scream. "Before I chop you to pieces."

He wipes his forehead and collects the duffel bag. He trips over nothing and mutters, "*Sumimasen.*" He stumbles again and stammers, "*Gomennasai.*" Finally, he reaches the door.

What a klutz. How did he even trip? Good riddance.

I look at my cell phone screen saver and run a shaking finger over the photo—Vincent and me in Kyoto.

Watashi no ai. Watashi no amai, Vincent. I found you, but I had to free you, silly. I will love you forever, and you can't be split between your family and me. Go on, hate me and live your life. Forget me.

All I have are memories. My memories of that *ema* in Kyoto and our pictures are all that I have. But, if the legends are true, that *ema* must stand the test of time.

I haven't looked at our pictures in a while, so I go to our cloud drive. My jaw drops, and my heart starts thumping. Where is the picture folder? My eyes flood, and everything around me gets blurry.

How could you do that? Those were all I had. How could you be so brutal?

Tears drop on my cell phone.

Naze, Vince? I have to call you.

I dial your number.

C'mon, pick up. It's your Akane, Vince. Remember her? The one who tied the scarf around you? I won't take a lot of your time. I know you hate me. Just tell me why you took everything away. Just once, let me hear your voice.

"Hi, you've reached Vince. You can try leaving a voicemail, and who knows, I might just get back to you. Bye."

Can't you even talk to me? All I'm asking for is a minute. I would give everything up for just a minute.

---

[69] Are you a dumbfuck?

CHAPTER 13

RHYTHM

"That's the beauty of this reality, Professor. I can still play and be with you."
—*Emika*

December 2026–March 2027

Vincent

NOZO IS SITTING ON MY shoulders, holding onto my wavy locks, as we walk to a shop in Bravern Mall. Her chubby legs, with argyle woolen leggings and brown Gucci sneakers, hang from the side of my neck. I have a chocolate ice cream cone in my left hand and Hulk's leash in my right.

Pulling my hair, she asks, "I-kim, Papha?" I lift the cone up, and she takes a big lick. Then, she kisses my head, smearing it with ice cream from her lips and chin. "You the best, Papha."

I smile. "I love you, too."

The Taycan's trunk is packed with Nozo's new stuff—Lego sets, Kiki costumes, stuffed animals, outfits. Basically, everything she wanted. Should've brought the G-Wagon. After securing Hulk's harness and Nozo's car seat, we drive off.

In my rearview mirror, I see Nozo gently rubbing Hulk's head while whispering, "*Onii-chan* Hulky."

"Hey, Nozo, want to meet some friends?"

Throwing her arms in the air, she giggles. "*Hai.*" As we reach the highway in the mountains, she asks, "Papha?"

"Yes."

Through the rearview mirror, I see her tapping on her chin. "Ummm . . . Who sees the sun at night?"

Smiling, I respond, "Ah! When it's morning in China, India, Japan."

"Papha?"

I don't think I've ever heard a sweeter, calming word in my life. My heart beats a little slower each time she calls me that. "Yes?"

"Can you call China, Japan, or India?" she asks.

"Umm, why?" I look at her in the rearview mirror.

She shrugs like an adult and pouts her lips. Then, she clarifies, "Tell them to take care of the sun. How else can we wake up?" She crosses her arms, shakes her head, and mutters, "Silly papha."

My heart flutters at the word *silly.*

Even your mannerisms are like Akane's.

"Papha?"

"Yes?"

"How many stars are there?"

"Billions."

Trying to lean forward against her tight seat belt, she asks, "Is that many?"

"Yes." I smile. "Lots."

Her eyes widen. "Oh!" Then, she says, "Papha?"

"Yes?"

"I like calling you Papha."

"How much?"

She spreads her tiny arms wide. "Billions."

Parking between Chris's Jaguar I-PACE and Ravi's Mercedes EQC, I put my little one in the stroller and Hulk back on the leash.

Removing strands of hair from her face with her tiny fingers, Nozo asks, "Where are we?"

"This is called Amara's Tree of Life. You will meet some friends here." I check my watch—5:00 p.m.—almost dinner time for the kids.

"Amara?" she asks.

Pushing her stroller through the door, I say, "Your other *sobo*."

Lifting her finger, she deduces, "Your mama?"

"Yes."

Tapping her chin, she deduces, "Hmm . . . your mum, Amara, my mum, Amari." Her eyes brighten as she smiles. She lifts her voice to a shrill and infers, "*Watashi mo* Amari *desu*, Papha."[70]

I stop pushing the stroller and get on my knees before Nozo. Running my fingers across her buttery cheek, I say, "*Kimi wa* Amari *to* Abajian *desu*.[71] Your name is Nozomi Amari Abajian." The sizzling sound of stir-fry and the aroma of shrimp and andouille sausage conquer my senses. I snap my fingers. "Jambalaya! Chris is cooking. Let's go, *Nozo-chan*."

Anna, Chris, Ravi, and Tabi are all wearing chef's hats and aprons. Chris is tossing the food in a stir-fry wok, and Ravi is simmering the sauce. Anna and Tabi are on assembly duty, and the staff will carry the plates to the dining hall. Quantum World volunteers chop green chilies, tomatoes, cilantro, and green onions for garnish.

"Ahem! Can I sample?" I ask.

Everything in the kitchen stops, and for a second, all I hear is the sizzle of the fire and the flapping of the exhaust fan. All eyes are on Nozo.

Then, Tabi squints at Anna before dropping her hat on the counter and sprinting toward Nozo, declaring, "My turn."

"No way," Anna says, running behind Tabi.

---

[70] I am also Amari, Papha.

[71] You are Amari and Abajian both.

Lifting her from the stroller, Tabi peppers Nozo's chubby cheeks with kisses. Nozo giggles with her eyes shut. Scanning Nozo's outfit, Tabi smiles.

"Wow! You look like a million bucks." She touches Nozo's woolen gray alpaca overcoat, tightens Nozo's maroon vicuña scarf, and then rolls her eyes. Turning to me, she pouts, "So cute! But she'll outgrow them in a month."

Taking her from Tabi and kissing Nozo's forehead, I explain, "That's why I bought the outfit in bigger sizes every winter till she turns five."

Anna shifts her role from COO to drama queen, clasping her hands together. "Oh! Vincent, be my papha, too."

Nozo squints at her. Scrunching my turtleneck in her fists, she proclaims, "Only my papha."

Leaving their stations, Chris and Ravi join the gang. Taking Nozo from my arms, Chris asks her, "Who is my favorite?"

Tilting her head and squeezing her large eyes into lines of eyelashes, she smiles. "Nozo."

Ravi turns to me. "I am glad you brought her here." He pauses and smiles. "She will see her true dad."

Taking Nozo from Chris, I turn to Ravi. "She has to understand there isn't any difference between her and them."

"Enough with the serious stuff," announces Anna, elbowing me. "The bed I chose for you two is"—she folds her right arm and touches her nonexistent biceps with her left hand—"strong." She winks. "You should think of me and thank me every time you two are at it."

Chris rolls his eyes, Ravi shakes his head, and Tabi covers her face and laughs. My mouth gapes as I stare at Anna.

How can I unhear what you just said?

Seeing my bafflement, she nudges my arm and asks, "What? Are you picturing me—?"

"Oh, shut up!" Shaking my head and curling my lips, I declare, "Just shut up. Thanks for the image. Thanks for ruining 'it' for me." Taking out my car keys, I address everyone in the room. "I need three volunteers."

Frida, another woman, and a man step forward.

"Hi, Frida," I greet, handing my car keys to her.

She wipes her forehead with her sleeves. "Dr. Abajian. Hello." Once again, her breath reeks of cinnamon candy.

"It's Vincent," I correct. Pointing outside, I ask, "The Taycan . . . there are five green parcels and three red ones in the trunk. Can you and the others get them, please?"

"Of course. Of course," Frida stammers. Then, she leaves with the other two volunteers.

Turning to Anna, I ask, "What's with Frida?"

"No idea," Anna says, shrugging. "She is always nervous around us."

My heart suddenly pounds at someone's absence. I ask Ana, "Where's—?"

Before Anna responds, Debussy's "Clair de Lune" notes float in. I smile. "That answers the question, I guess."

Tabi's eyes brighten with pride as she says, "Yep. She bought clothes for every child today." She rubs my arm. "You're lucky."

The music room is still under renovation, but the carpenters, decorators, contractors, and handymen have all stopped their work to listen to Emika's divine interpretation of "Clair de Lune" on the Shigeru Kawai SK-EX— Emika's choice of piano. All fifty children, ages five to nine, are mesmerized from their respective places around the room, eyes wide and jaws dropped, consuming every note played by Emika's delicate fingers. Her magic has transported them to a world far removed from the pains of orphanhood, war, and misery. If I had known a pianist of this talent slept inside her, I would have never invoked Akane in August 2001.

I robbed you of your true calling. And yet, you show no remorse.

From the side, her face is hidden in her reverse-bob haircut. Her camel hair overcoat is on her lap, and her Ghurka bag is on the floor. She is wearing a Prussian-blue short-sleeved dress with a pleated bottom and a red belt. She has tucked away her sakura-printed converse on the floor and paddles the piano with her bare feet, adorned with vermilion-red nail polish with white polka dots. There is a solved Rubik's Cube on the edge of the piano. Her eyes are closed, with tiny droplets at the corners.

What are you thinking?

Maddy is sitting with a younger kid on her lap in the far corner of the room. He is the youngest of them—just three—and is our newest member.

Keying her final note, Emika opens her eyes, wipes them with her hands, turns to her right, and beams at Nozo and me. Her smile is tempered with a fluttery voice from the melancholy of "Clair de Lune" and her thoughts.

"Guys?" Pushing back the bench and keeping her camel coat on it, she stands up and asks, "When did you come?" while putting her shoes back on.

Before I can respond, the fifty kids facing Emika turn to me. Smiling ear to ear, arms in the air, they shout in chorus, "Vincent is here. Yay!"

They all run toward me, Hulk, and Nozo. Sitting on the floor, I surrender as some take refuge on my lap. A few decide to hang from my neck, grab my hair, and climb on my chest and shoulders. They all have to show me their new possessions.

Six-year-old Ayesha points at her new dress and nudges my hand. "Look, Vince. Miss Emika gave me this."

Touching her shoulders, I say, "Wow! You look so pretty."

Bowing her head down, she smiles through the corners of her lips. She turns her teary right eye up and asks, "True?"

Touching the burn scars on her face that consumed her left eye and wiping the tears from her right eye, I assure her, "Of course. Bring me anyone who says otherwise."

Five-year-old Farouq, pulling his new sweater while revealing his intreton-c-powered prosthetic left hand, tells me, "Emika gave me this sweater."

Six-year-old Mariya shows her new puffed-sleeve dress. "Do I also look pretty, Vince?"

"Of course," I say, setting her on my lap while inspecting her prosthetic right leg.

After every child gets my attention, Emika weaves her way through the kids and kisses Hulk and Nozo. "Vince, can I—?"

Lifting my finger, I say, "Just a minute." I bend down and tie her shoelaces.

She touches my shoulder. "What's in your hair?" she asks.

"Choco i-kim," I say, imitating Nozo.

She grips my shoulder tighter and laughs, covering her lips. "I will wash your hair."

"Okay." I make the final tether of the Berluti knot. "All secured."

"Can you teach me that knot?"

"We'll see." Standing up, I ask, "What was your other question?"

She stretches her slender arms over the heads of the kids. "Can I teach them music?"

The entire hall echoes with the shrill pleading of over fifty children. "Please, Vince, please," they say.

I scan their faces—pleading innocence that has remained unanswered throughout their short lives.

No one can hurt you here. If you want something, then I will get it. You're not orphans here. You're Vincent, and you're Tabi.

I look into Emika's eyes, which are gleaming with the anticipation of playing more of her piano—a life I robbed her of. Clearing my voice, I say, "Yes."

"Yay, thank you, Vincent," the children cheer, high-fiving Emika.

Lifting Nozo from the stroller, she calls out to the children, "Everyone, I want you to meet someone." Kneeling, she places Nozo on the floor like a doll. Touching Nozo's chest with her hand while holding my hand with her other, she says, "This is Nozo—our daughter." She smiles. "And, far more important, your sister."

Bako, the seven-year-old Nigerian, approaches Nozo. Looking at Emika, he says, "Nozo is so pretty."

Emika pinches Bako's cheeks. "That's because she is your sister. She is one of you. There is no difference between you two," she emphasizes, lifting her finger.

Seven-year-old Aissatou approaches with her hands on her hips. Frowning, she looks up at me. "Did you forget our drawing book?"

Getting on my knees and placing one hand on Aissatou's tiny shoulder, I point at Frida and the volunteers from the kitchen and say, "The green packets have your sketchbooks, the red ones have your pencils—color and black—and erasers."

She wraps her tiny arms around my neck. "Thank you."

Kissing Aissatou's head, I stand up. "Let's form a line, kids. And let's do it fast. We don't wanna be late for"—I clap—"jambalaya."

They all shout, "Jambalaya!"

Emika steps forward, tucks her hair behind her ears, and asks, "Can Nozo hand out the gifts?"

"Of course."

Emika whispers something to our Nozo and starts handing her the green and red bags for each child. Each time Nozo gives the gifts to the children, she hugs them and says, "I'm your sister, Nozo. Merry Christmas."

As the volunteers and Emika guide Nozo in her task, I walk past them with Hulk and sit next to Maddy. Touching the hand of the child she is holding, I ask Maddy, "Is he—?"

Kissing his forehead, she confirms, "Yes . . . Wasim. Wanna hold him?"

Setting him on my lap, I look at his hazel eyes, wavy hair, and pink lips. Running my hands over his cheek and his multicolored striped sweater, I say, "You're in good hands." I raise my voice. "Emi, when Nozo is done, can you guys come here?"

Nozo, holding her mother's hand, walks and stands before us. Putting Wasim on the floor, I tell Nozo, "This is Wasim. Can you give him the last drawing set?"

Nozo hands the set to Wasim. Smiling, she hugs him and says, "Hello, Oo-sim. I'm Nozo, your sister. Merry Christmas."

⁕

I gently place a sleepy Nozo into the car seat and harness Hulk. As we begin our drive to Summit Drive, Emika touches my hand.

"You've been very quiet during dinner." She points toward the back seat. "Did her questions tire you?"

"It's something else," I explain, kissing her hand.

"What?"

Taking a gentle right, I say, "You couldn't become a pianist because of me."

"That's fine." She squeezes my hand. "The joy I derived from playing for those kids is far greater than what my father did at Royal Concertgebouw, Staatsoper Unter den Linden, Carnegie Hall, or Takemitsu Memorial."

"You deserve to play there," I say, turning left.

"Then I wouldn't have met you. Is that what you want?"

I kiss Emika's hand again. "Of course not. I want you and Nozo. But your keying is celestial, and I robbed you of it."

She stares at our entwined hands. "Maybe in a different reality, I'm a pianist, wondering who comes to me in my dreams, how I can play tunes by ear, and how I can memorize every Chopin piece without reading or listening to them." Taking my pocket square out and wiping her eyes, she continues, "That's the beauty of this reality, Professor. I can still play and be with you. The kids are a better audience than the rich snobs *Chichi* entertained."

(Furnished main bedroom)

As I tighten my robe, Emika, dressed in her sleepwear, asks, "Where do you think you're going?"

"Study."

Raising her eyebrows, she bites her lips.

Squinting at her, I ask, "What?"

"Can't that wait?"

"It can."

Tapping on the mattress while scanning me from head to toe, she says, "I can't test the strength of this bed all by myself."

(January 2027)

Fuck, it's 7:00 a.m. already? Emika must have switched off my alarm. But I did wake up to a different tune. I can still hear it. Emika singing Aoi Teshima's "Breakfast Song" while keying the Steinway downstairs. She is stopping intermittently and continuing again. What's going on?

Shaking my head, I get up and wash my face. When I go down to the main floor, I see Emika leaving the piano bench after every verse, feeding Nozo a spoonful of her breakfast, then returning to the bench for another verse. One spoonful of *nattō* for every verse of the song. Then, Emika blunders by offering Nozo a second spoon before completing another verse.

Banging on the high chair, Nozo protests, "No." Crossing her arms, she moves her mouth away. "Song first."

Upon noticing me, Emika looks at me helplessly. "I was never like this . . . Can you help?"

You were not, but Akane was. Still is.

Now I know what Masayoshi meant when he called Akane a stubborn child. Sitting on the piano bench, I smile. "Me on piano, you on vocals and feeding duty."

If someone sang this to me, I'd eat the stinkiest of *nattō*. Hulk sits by his finished food bowl and whimpers. While playing my piano, I say, "Good boy, Hulky." He lies down by my feet as Nozo imitates me with a mouthful of food.

"Good boy, *Onii-chan* Hulky."

Coming out of the shower, I see Emika has replaced my outfit on the suit valet, accompanied by a Post-it note that reads, "This is better." I take the note and carefully place it in my closet's cufflink drawer—inside a box marked "things to take to the grave," housing handwritten letters by Akane, Fred, Krista, Sasha, and the last note by Mr. Kruger.

(Nozo's room)

I have covered Emika's eyes with a thick ribbon and am walking her toward Nozo's room. "Are we there yet?" she asks, exasperated.

After I remove the ribbon, she stares at what used to be a monochrome wall. Her eyes glimmer as she witnesses a nine-by-eight-foot rendition of *The Starry Night*. She turns to me, her eyes wide and her hands covering her mouth.

"You know I paint, right?" I tease.

"Yes, but . . . this well? The strokes are exactly like the original one." She starts to blink, and after a bit, she covers her cheeks with her hands. "It moves, Vincent." Tugging my shirt, she demands, "How?"

I spread my arms and say, "I am, after all, Vincent."

Squeezing her eyes shut, she whispers, "I never thought these days would come when I was in London or when I came to the conference and heard that Akane was back."

(February 2027—Quantum World Lab)

Chris and Anna are wearing The Mind and sitting in our AI lab. They are the first alpha testers. His is ultramarine blue, and hers is pearl white with rose-gold accents. The helmets monitor their pulse rate, blood pressure, blood sugar level, and breathing and are programmed to stop at any signs of stress. So far, both are doing great. The doctors on the staff are swiveling their heads between the two subjects, and the monitors display all of Chris's and Anna's vitals.

Seeing Tabi biting her nails, Emika leaves her seat to my right and sits beside her. Rubbing her arms, she assures her, "Chris will be fine."

The computers in my time cave will monitor all their activities once they use any data from The Mind. But none of my colleagues know that. If anyone hacks into Anna's and Chris's systems, I will know without stepping into Quantum World. Those data ethically belong to Anna and Chris, but ethics won't catch Vandal. Clenching my jaw, I grip the armrest.

Are you coming for me? I'm ready. Enigma will get you.

Suddenly, the armrest breaks, leaving splintered wood. The cracking sound startles everyone.

Emika nudges my arm. "You okay?" Her eyes are wide with concern.

Staring into the broken armrest, I say, "Yep."

"He's fine," she broadcasts to everyone.

The voice-activated response of The Mind states, "Transfer complete," first for Chris and then for Anna.

Ravi and Emika remove The Mind from our alpha testers. Springing out of her chair, Anna turns to Emika. "Chris will be fine?" She puts her hands on her hips. "How about Anna?" Touching her forehead and looking away, she continues her Broadway special. "Granted, I have no partner. But does that mean I have no blood in my veins?" she says, pointing at her wrist. Lifting her palm over her forehead, she asks, "Is there anyone who even cares about sweet, innocent Anna?"

Emika places her hands over her mouth, and her shoulders shake. My turn to be the thespian. I approach Anna and put my hand on her shoulder. "Honey, I was worried sick about you." Pointing at my broken chair, I lift my brows. "See?"

"Can I play the piano?" Chris asks, staring at his hands.

Emika snaps her fingers. "Why don't you all come over for dinner? Chris can play the piano, and . . ." She looks at Anna and presses her lips together.

I help Emika out. "Given Anna's dexterity for drawing, a straight line is progress."

Lifting her middle finger at me, Anna quips, "How about this for dexterity?"

(Vincent's living room)

Almost erupting in a peal of laughter, I'm inspecting Anna's sketch, a slice of pizza in my right hand. Hulk is salivating, standing on his hind legs, begging for a piece.

He gets down as soon as Emika calls him. "Come here, Hulky baby. Daddy is struggling with euphemism." She is struggling not to laugh.

Anna glares at Emika. "You and Vince are mean."

"And perfect for each other," Emika retorts, smiling.

Putting the sketch back on the coffee table, I say, "Not bad?"

"I thought so, too," Tabi confirms, nodding.

Tucking her hair behind her ears, Emika looks around and finally turns to me. "Seriously?"

Anna's face turns red as she shoots daggers at Emika.

Shaking my head, I give in to my laughter. Locking my eyes with Emika's, I reveal, "Last time, she drew something that resembled Mickey Mouse and called it Batman."

"Yeah!" Tabi snorts. "If you could call that Mickey Mouse."

Anna, standing up, takes away the sketches. "No more love for Vincent." She points her index finger at Tabi. "*Et Tu*, brute."

After handing little Nozo to her mother, Chris walks toward the piano. He wipes his forehead with a handkerchief, puts it back in his pocket, and sits on the bench. After thirty seconds of silence, he begins playing Pachelbel's Canon in D. He struggles to keep the notes from his left hand distinct from his right, but he knows the keys and the scales, which is the point of this Neurolink.

We all applaud as Chris concludes the three-minute piece in about four minutes. Exhaling deeply in relief, he stands up.

"You should bow," Emika instructs Chris.

Watching the six-foot-four Chris beginning to bend, Emika giggles and admits, "I was kidding." Then, she runs toward Chris and wraps her arms around his waist. Emika has now fully become part of our team again.

Ravi and Maddy have been quietly sitting, only giving customary laughs. Something's off. Ravi always checks up on Emika, and Maddy will do anything to keep Nozo on her lap. But not today.

Nodding his head, Ravi cuts a dry smile. "Glad the code worked." That's not the response I was expecting from the head of R&D.

I sit on the ottoman opposite Maddy and Ravi. "What's up?" I ask.

Emika nudges Maddy's shoulder. "C'mon, tell him."

While Maddy hesitates to form words, Ravi moves to the edge of his seat and looks at me with a sad smile. "Maddy and I have been trying . . . but with no luck." Then, he pauses, taking a deep breath. "Could we—?"

I smile. "Yes. Wasim will be lucky to have you two as parents."

Astounded, Maddy widens her eyes. With her trembling voice, she asks, "How did you know?"

"I saw the way you looked at Wasim. I see it every day when Emika looks at Nozo." I hate to admit it, but Amara looked at me like that in the core.

Touching Maddy's hand, Emika assures her, "Told you he is perceptive."

Standing and taking my phone out of my pocket, I turn to Maddy and Ravi. "I have one question, though. If you had conceived, would you still want Wasim?"

Without a moment's hesitation, Maddy says, "Yes."

"I will ask Jean to start the paperwork," I say, smiling.

Tabi frowns. "Why don't we ever pay Jean?"

"I want to, but he wants to do it pro bono."

"Why?" asks Chris.

I stretch my arms, pick up Hulk, and sit back down. Scanning everyone's faces, I reveal, "He was friends with Luther and Rudy—two bullies who would beat me up, call me names—because my name sounded different. I was poor and an orphan, but they made me feel worthless until . . ." I shut my eyes—and see Akane wrapping that scarf around me, taking me to the doctor, giving me that tux, and calling me family.

You hurt me deeper than they ever did.

(Vincent's office)

Linda pokes her head around my office door. "Dr. Bose and Dr. Stevens are here."

Looking beyond her, I smile. "Come in, guys."

First, Ravi enters, then Maddy. Ravi is holding a framed picture in his right hand.

Turning back, Maddy speaks softly, "Come here, Wasim. Don't be afraid."

The wide-eyed little one, dressed in a navy blazer, khakis, brown shoes, and a tartan bow tie, slowly walks in. I go over to Wasim and lift him up.

Pointing at the frame in Ravi's hand, I ask, "What's that?"

"Wasim drew his family." Smiling, he adds, "It's for you."

Handing Wasim over to Ravi, I take the picture. My heart flutters as I point at the girl in the picture and glance at Maddy.

"That's Nozo," she says. "On her left is Emika, and then you."

Taking over, Ravi states, "On Nozo's right is Wasim, next to him is Maddy, and the last is me."

Taking the picture with me, I sit on my chair by the fireplace. Touching my shoulder, Ravi asks, "Everything okay?"

I look up at his face. My voice cracks. "I am a part of Wasim's family?" Squeezing my shoulder, Ravi nods. I run my hand over the colored sketch.

I get up, put the framed drawing in my bag, then wipe my eyes with my cuff. "I'm taking this home."

Taking Wasim from Ravi's arms, I look into his eyes. "You will do great things."

You are me.

I turn to Maddy and Ravi. "You guys hungry?"

"Yes," Maddy says.

"Let's collect Emi and Nozo and have lunch together." Rubbing Wasim's hair, I smile. "Let's make it Wasim's family time."

Ravi looks at Maddy for approval. "Of course."

"Let's collect Anna, Chris, and Tabi as well." Staring into Wasim's eyes, I smile. "Buddy, let's expand your family."

(Tabi's office)

Chris

Dodging the binders on the floor, Anna and Ravi sit next to each other on one of the two love seats while I occupy the other one.

Shutting her laptop, Tabi exhales, "Wow! A few days, and we will be beta testing."

Ravi asks Tabi, pointing at her two Pulitzers on the floor, "Don't you think these require better placement?"

"Fuck 'em." Tabi shrugs, reaching for her Starbucks cup.

Anna sighs, scanning the mess. "Stressed about the beta testing?"

"That! And Vandal." Fisting her hands, she says, "I wish the cops caught him."

There's a knock on the door, and Markus pokes his head in. Looking at Tabi, he asks, "You wanted to speak?"

"Yes, yes." Waving her hand, she instructs, "And close the door behind you."

After closing the door, Markus tosses his hair from his eyes. As he looks around, I speak up, rolling my eyes. "Emika and Vincent are not here."

Weaving around the binders on the floor, Markus sits on a solitary chair opposite Anna and Ravi and perpendicular to me. Tabi leaves her desk with her Starbucks cup and sits next to me.

Staring at Markus, Tabi begins, "We will soon begin beta testing. We want zero hiccups."

"I know." Markus shrugs.

Ravi smirks. "You sure? Because the way you stare at Emika makes everyone uncomfortable."

Rolling his eyes, Markus sneers, "You mean Vincent?" He sighs. "It's all about—"

"Listen, sunshine," Anna interrupts, lifting her finger. "We are all here because of him. We know your feelings are unrequited. Your constant ogling won't change anything."

"Unrequited?" Markus lifts his brows and smirks. "That's what she told you?"

Crossing her arms, Anna squints at him. "Go on. It stays in this room."

Exhaling slowly, Markus begins, "The company sent me to the airport to pick up Emika when she arrived in London in February 2024." He smiles. "I could not move my eyes from her." His voice cracks as he continues, "We began dating shortly after she broke up with Vince. Around April 2024, we decided to move in together."

Anna scoffs, smirking at Ravi and me. "Familiar pattern, right?"

Fuming, gritting his teeth, Markus asserts, "But then, the first of the obstacles came—Vincent's Senate hearing. She saw it live and delayed our moving-in plans."

"What was the next one?" I ask.

"Pregnancy," Markus admits with a broken smile. "She knew it wasn't mine."

Shit! This went pretty far. I just hope Vincent knows all this.

"How?" asks Anna, grinning at each of us.

"Nozo was conceived a few days before I started dating Emika." Narrowing his eyes, he opens his heart. "But I accompanied her to every doctor's visit." Sneering, he adds, "She was clear that I was not the father. So, she made me wait outside like a second-class citizen." Shrugging, he scorns. "What if my presence contaminates Vincent's high IQ offspring?"

Tabi hands him a bottle of water. He takes a few sips and continues, "And something happened in the middle of August 2024. Her mole disappeared, and she got an offer from Nardin Robotics. Like an idiot, I dropped her off at the airport for her interview with Nardin and her meetup with Vincent. She didn't even look back once she cleared security." Staring at the pile of binders and books on the floor, he sighs. "I kept standing there like a moron."

After taking a few more sips of his water and wiping his mouth with his cuffs, he continues, "Then, she was back. But she wasn't the same. All she wanted was to raise her daughter. Still, I took her to the hospital when her water broke on November 15. And all my hopes ended when she laid her eyes on Nozo." He sneers. "If Nozo had different colored eyes, maybe Emika and I would've had a shot." Glancing at Tabi, he continues, "But I supported her through childbirth, picked the little one up from daycare . . ." He stares at us helplessly. "I became a convenient nanny she called a friend." Sniffling, he asks, "Why can't I be Nozo's father? I powdered the rashes… changed the diapers." He scoffs. "Emika kept saying she wanted to move past Vince. I don't know if she couldn't or wouldn't. Maybe she lied about that to keep using me as a nanny." He stares blankly at Tabi's bookshelves. "I often think there may be a place where I met her before Vincent did. I keep looking at her . . . because of the possibility of that life." Scanning our faces, he sighs. "I won't stare anymore."

Tilting her head, Anna asks sympathetically, "Why did you come here? Were you following them?"

He shuts his eyes as if trying to remember why he is here.

What answer are you constructing? What are you hiding?

Then, he opens his eyes and gives us all a sad smile. "Maybe my love surpasses my self-respect." Shaking his head, Markus gets up and turns to Tabi. "Anything else?"

"Nope."

As Markus leaves, I breathe out all the air I am holding in. "What a clusterfuck. Do you think Emika still has a thing for this guy?"

Anna cracks her knuckles. "Can't say." Then, she takes a deep breath and says, "Markus today is worse than Vincent was when Emika left him."

Shaking his head, Ravi asks, "Does Vincent know? What'll happen if he finds out?"

"He won't do anything irrational like before," Anna replies, shrugging. Ravi touches Anna's wrist. "Irrational?"

Staring at her manicured fingernails, Anna shakes her head. "I asked him why he would suddenly buy a Taycan. Guess what he said?"

"He likes fast cars," I say.

Anna brings her hand to her forehead and reveals, "He said, 'Emika moved on from me to Brad in a matter of days. I can, too—zero to sixty in three and half seconds.'"

"Wow!" Ravi exclaims, lifting his brows.

Anna lifts her brows. "Yep! Not the response from 190 IQ points." Sighing, she adds, "He doesn't feel that about Emika anymore. He accepted her for all her flaws." Anna stares blankly at the floor. "It's different with Akane, though. Her words hurt Vince deeper than what Emika did in 2024."

"But he doesn't show it," I comment.

Anna stares into my eyes. "That's because he is distracted with Quantum World . . . and Nozo and Emika." She gives me a dry smile. "I love Nozo and am happy to see Vince getting into a new rhythm. And I love us around Emika. Unlike Akane, she is more like us . . . but I miss the childish Vince around Akane. The unbridled joy in his eyes. Akane connected Vince with his lost childhood." Dabbing her moist eyes with her sleeve, she says, "Sorry."

Ravi puts his arm around Anna. "It's okay."

Pointing at the door, I change the subject. "Did you guys notice how Markus shut his eyes to answer Anna's question?"

"Which one?" Anna asks.

I roll my eyes. "When you asked if he was following them."

Snapping her fingers, Tabi says, "Yeah! I saw that. Like he was trying to make some shit up."

(March 2027—Vincent's home)

Vincent

We are having a fake martial arts fight, which Nozo believes to be real. She is dressed like a ninja in an outfit picked up by her loving mom. Looking up at me, she takes a forward stance.

Furrowing her eyebrows and lifting her soft fists, she sneers, "Papha going down."

Resisting laughter, Emika, acting as the referee and Nozo's coach, whispers in her protégé's ears, "You can beat him, *Nozo-chan*. Go for his legs."

"*Hai*," declares Nozo, clenching her tiny baby teeth beyond her rosy, red lips.

I see Hulk napping on his buffalo plaid plush bed ten feet away.

Hey, bug, are you getting old? You're just eight. I don't believe all that nonsense of dog to human age conversion. You're my pup, my boy. That's all. Don't. Ever. Leave. Me.

Nozo runs at me, huffing and kicking my ankle. Raising her eyebrows, Emika signals with her hands for me to fall.

Holding my ankle, feigning to be hurt, I grunt in pretend pain and fall to the floor. "Oh, I can't move. I'm sorely defeated."

Then, I lie down, squinting to see Nozo's reaction.

With her arms in the air, Nozo stomps. "I win, I win."

Emika sits on the floor next to me, covering her mouth with her hands lest Nozo sees her smiling. Hulk comes and licks my ears while Nozo nudges me with her foot.

"Papha, wakey, wakey." Through my slightly opened eyes, I see Nozo looking up to her mom and nudging me more. "*Me o akete*, Papha."[72]

Emika touches Nozo's head. Nozo's voice cracks as tears fill her eyes. "*Me o akete, kudasai*, Papha." Grabbing my robe, she digs her head into my chest and sobs.

---

[72] Open your eyes, Papha.

That's it. Placing my hands on her soft back, I sit up. I wipe her tears with my thumb. "I am fine, Nozo." Crumbling her brows, she hides her face in my chest again.

I kiss Nozo's head. "Can I see a smile?" I ask.

"No." She shakes her head while keeping it against my neck.

Pulling her head back gently, I kiss her forehead, nose, and cheeks. "How about now?" I lift her, bring her belly to my mouth, and blow a lethal raspberry tummy tickle.

Uncontrollably, Nozo yells, "Ahhh!"

Turning to her doting mother, I announce, "We have a soprano in the family. She can hit the octaves for 'Queen of the Knight Aria.'"

While Emika laughs, covering her mouth, I bring Nozo to my eye level and wipe her nose with my sleeve. Deeply exhaling, I ask, "Can we have some breakfast now?"

Wrapping her tiny, chubby arms around my neck and tilting her head, she says, "Okay. Mum will sing."

Sighing, Emika rolls her eyes.

Half of Emika's lap is occupied by my head and half by Hulk. She runs her hands through my hair and Hulk's fur while watching a documentary on Egyptian mummies on our home theater system. Nozo, dressed in a puffed sleeve frock, has fallen asleep in my arms and is drooling onto my robe.

Massaging my scalp, Emika says, "Hey, Maddy and Ravi wondered if we could arrange a playdate between Nozo and Wasim before things get crazy with beta testing. Ravi bought Nozo a Lego set."

I nestle my head deeper into her lap. "Sure. Can I also play?"

"What?" she asks, affectionately pinching my cheek.

I look up at her. "I never had a playdate. Nozo gives me a glimpse of what could have been my childhood if I'd had one." I clasp my hands together. "Can I, please?"

She kisses my forehead. "Yes." Then, she kisses my nose. "Yes." Finally, kissing my lips, she whispers, "Yes."

It's time for Nozo to go to bed. Emika's voice faintly reaches my ears amid the sound of me loading the dishwasher.

"A little help, Vince!"

I rush upstairs. Emika is sitting on the floor, by *the starry night wall*, with her knees folded and her hands covering her mouth. Nozo, dressed in her Totoro pajamas and Kiki hairband, is casually wrapping her mom with toilet paper. Hulk is helping her with the roll by chasing after it.

Getting down on my knees, putting a hand on Nozo's shoulder, I ask, "What are we doing to Mum?"

"Mum is a mummy," she explains, lifting her tiny chubby index finger. *Okay, let's tire you out.*

I draw her close. Raising my eyebrows, I say, "You know what?"

"What, Papha?"

Signaling Emika to get ready, I tell Nozo, "Mummies become ghosts."

"Huh?" Nozo asks, her eyes widening.

Freeing herself from the toilet paper, Emika stands up. "Who do I smell? Is it Nozo? She smells delicious." Furrowing her brows, she approaches Nozo. "*Kimi no chīsana Hana o tabemasu.*"[73]

Covering her nose, Nozo screams, "Ahh! Mum will eat my nose!"

As Emika chases her screaming daughter and Hulk chases Emika down the hallway, sirens of several police vehicles and the red and blue lights cutting through our glass walls halt our play. The sky flashes lightning, turning all the surroundings purple, followed by thunder, resonating through the floors and making all the chandeliers shake. The lights flicker. Nozo and Emika cover their ears. Emika lifts Nozo and rests her head on her shoulder while I walk to our front door. Opening the door, I count five police cars. Beyond them are two G-wagons, Edward's finest stepping out of them. Edward is directing them.

A Black police officer introduces himself, extending his hand. "I'm Douglas Tyson, Chief of Police."

My heart thumps. Are Emika and Nozo in danger?

Shaking Chief Tyson's hand, I ask, "What brings you here?" I point at the G-Wagons. "Why are they here?"

---

[73] I will eat your tiny nose.

Over the thunder, I hear Edward shouting at his men, circling his hand. "I need men every four feet around the property." He raises his voice. "Am I clear?"

"Sir, yes, sir." As the soldiers behind him encircle our property, Edward approaches me.

With awe, Chief Tyson mumbles, "I need those guys in my force." Turning to me, he says, "Someone identified you as family."

"Identified?" My throat goes dry. Breathing anxiously, I look beyond Chief Tyson and speak to Edward. "What's going on? Where's Philip?"

"He's on sight."

My hands are shaking. I don't want to voice what I'm thinking, but still, I ask, "What sight?"

Edward touches my shoulder. "You better come with us." He points his finger at Chief Tyson. "You need to have at least ten officers inside the house. Be gentle with them. If the dog barks, don't dare to touch him."

"Certainly, sir."

As a dozen officers enter our home, I go in with them. Kissing Emika and Nozo, I tell them, "I will be back soon."

Emika gulps. "Don't do anything stupid."

"Papha?" Nozo asks.

Kissing Nozo again, I tell her, "Listen to Mommy."

She frowns but agrees. "Okay."

CHAPTER 14

ASHES

"Freak! I rue the day I met you"
—Anna

March–April 2027

Vincent

SITTING IN THE FRONT PASSENGER seat of the G-Wagon, I rub my hands, shape them into a cup, and blow into them. Glancing at me, Edward raises the car temperature to seventy-two.

"Sorry about that," he says.

"Thanks." I breathe in the warm air and then ask, "Where are we heading?"

"You'll know," he responds with a cracking voice.

The thunderclouds move away, revealing a sky bright with constellations. As we turn right and ascend, bits of soot land on the windshield. What the fuck? The sky quickly changes from crystal clear to smoky, the color changing to brown and burgundy, then slowly to red and yellow. The smell of the air inside the car changes to something stifling. Edward hits the brakes after turning the G-Wagon sharply to the right. I jolt, first left, then forward, and brace my hands on the dashboard.

Lifting my head, I shut my eyes tight to block out the blinding blue and red lights of a dozen police cars and the yellow rays of the ambulances. I cover my ears to shut out the blaring sirens and the human voices yelling into radios.

Slowly, I turn to Edward, removing my hands from my ears and opening my eyes. I grind my teeth. "What did Vandal do?"

Touching my shoulder, Edward presses his lips together. Wiping the corners of his eyes, he says, "I'm sorry."

My heart almost beats out of my rib cage. "Is it Tabi?" Shutting his tear-filled eyes, he shakes his head. I breathe out a sigh of relief; his adopted daughter is fine. Why would I even think such a thing?

Getting out of the car, I cough as my lungs fill with the stuffy air. My eyes burn from all the soot. Walking forward, waving my hands to clear the thick smoke as I go, I hit a yellow line of barricade tape. Squinting, I see the source of the smoke—a crashed vehicle, upside down, engulfed in fire. I see a group of firefighters deploying a high-temperature-resistant fire blanket over the car while four fighters spray aerosol into the fire. So, it's an EV.

My pulse races. Anna, Chris, and Ravi all drive EVs. I can't make out the model from where I'm standing. One door is split from the car, and the roof is squished into the chassis. The entire road is plastered with rubber bits from tires, shattered glass, and bits of metal reflecting the police and ambulance lights. Recognizing the odor beyond the burning metal and rubber, my breathing becomes frantic, and my skin crawls. It's the smell of burning flesh.

Looking to my left, I see Anna in her Yale sweats, sobbing, her head on Chris's chest. I let out a breath. Those two are safe. Chris is staring into the fire, his eyes glowing against the yellow reflection of the fire. He is not blinking. With one hand on Anna's head, he wipes his eyes with his other. He is holding something battered. Next to Chris, sitting on the ground, is

Tabi. Her hands are shaking as she tries to pump her inhaler. Touching my chest, I exhale in relief. These three are safe. Beyond them, I see Chris's Jaguar and Anna's Polestar.

So, is it—? No.

My heart starts pounding, and I can't seem to catch a breath.

Noticing me beyond the smoke, Chris calls out, "Vince?"

"Yes," I respond, wheezing.

Leaving Chris, Anna runs to me. Tugging my lapel, her eyes flooded with tears, she screeches, "When will he stop? What does he want?"

My throat closes up as I begin to recognize the make and model of the battered car. Looking down at Tabi, I ask, "Where is Ravi?"

Lifting her trembling hands, she points at the destroyed car. Chris hands me a battered, burnt license plate. RAVI-007. My hands begin to shake, and I curl them into fists. I grit my teeth as tears flood my eyes.

(2017–University)

"Hello?"

"Dr. Bose, this is Vincent. And I have Anna and Chris with me. Is this a good time to talk?"

"Dr. Abajian, please call me Ravi. I understand if you can't offer me the job. I know visas for international students are getting more and more difficult. I just want to let you know that I love your team and wish you all the best."

"You're right. Work visas are tricky. That's why the finest immigration lawyer in the state will get in touch with you."

Raising his voice, Ravi asked, "What?"

"Tell me, Ravi, does $200,000 a year work for you?"

"You will not regret this, I promise. I will work very hard. How can I thank you, Dr. Abajian?"

"How about by calling me Vincent?"

(Back to the present)

I feel the blood rushing to my head. I lift the yellow barricade tape, grinding my teeth and whispering, "I failed you."

As I duck under the barricade, a police officer intercepts me. Placing his hand on my chest while reaching for his handcuffs, he orders, "Stay back."

"Get out of my way, officer," I warn.

"I will shoot you, sir, if you take one step forward."

I would like to see you try, you low-IQ piece of shit.

I feel a surge of strength as my arteries begin to throb. Grabbing the officer by his collar and belt, I toss him about ten feet behind me.

"Son of a bitch," he shouts. And then, I hear the cocking of about twenty guns, all pointed at me.

"Please, don't!" Anna screams. "I have lost enough tonight."

And then, another voice orders, "If I even hear the clicking of another trigger, I'll make sure that all you can do for the remainder of your lives is flip burgers."

I know the voice and its conviction. Dressed in his overcoat and scarf, Philip points his hands at twenty police officers. "Lower your weapons. Now!" Everyone is dressed in their pajamas except Philip. Why? Is he returning from somewhere?

Philip limps toward me with his walking stick. His pace quickens as I'm about to snap my fingers. Moving his arm forward, he shouts, "No! You cannot bring back the dead."

I fall to my knees, defeated, and my tears drip onto the asphalt. "He was my little brother. I failed him." I form a fist and punch the glass- and metal-covered ground. Grinding my teeth, I hiss, "I'm worthless. It's all my fault. I pushed Vandal." I stare at my hands as the intreton in my body pushes the metal shrapnel and shards of glasses out of my skin. The cuts heal immediately, leaving no scars.

Grabbing my shoulder and shaking it, Philip says, "Get a hold of yourself."

I look up into Philip's face through tear-soaked eyes. "What did Ravi ever do to Vandal?"

Tabi sits next to me and holds my shaking hands. She has yet to speak a single word. Staring into her eyes, reflecting the blue and red lights of the emergency vehicles, I ask, "Maddy knows?"

She hugs me tightly, with every morsel of her strength.

Breathing into her shoulder, I only manage, "No. No."

I have to be better than David Kruger and Philip for Wasim. Emika and Nozo will accept him. They will. Moving my head from Tabi's shoulder, I tell her, "Send someone for Wasim. He can't go to the orphanage twice." Touching my chest, I declare, "Emi and I will adopt him. Nozo will have a brother."

Tears drip from her eyes and reach her chin as Tabi stares at me blankly. Her lips quiver as she turns her head to the shattered vehicle.

"No." I shake my head, then her shoulders. "No."

She lifts her hand about three feet from the ground. Her voice cracks as she whispers, "Just three, like Farid. Three innocent lives." Tugging me by my lapel, she grinds her teeth. "Why?"

I stand up abruptly. It becomes clear what Emika meant; I would just open the doors to the core at the right moment, with nothing dragging me. I won't let my memories of Akane impair my task anymore.

Looking at Anna, Chris, Philip, and Tabi, I warn, "Stay back." Running toward the ash, the fire, the ruin, I snap my fingers.

Before I'm swallowed by the core, I hear Philip shout, "No!"

(Core)

Chronos's voice reverberates through the core as he states, "Welcome, Time Corrector. It's been a while."

Ignoring his reception, I float inside the tourbillon, going toward the door marked "Ravi." Beyond the gate, Ravi reads *Jataka Tales* to Wasim while Maddy gently runs her fingers through the little boy's hair. Tears surge in my eyes as it finally sinks in that all three are dead.

Upon seeing me, Maddy and Ravi come and hug me.

"I failed you," I whisper, clasping my hands together in front of me.

Engulfing my hands with his, Ravi tilts his head and smiles. "Failed? No. I could not have asked for a better family than you. I forgot how abusive my mom was, how neglectful my father was." He looks at Maddy and Wasim, and his eyes light up. "I wouldn't even have them without you. Thank you, Vincent."

I point at Wasim. "But he deserved to live." Looking at Ravi's smiling face and Maddy's forgiving expression, I state, "You all deserved to live."

"It's not your fault," Ravi assures me, placing his palms against his cheeks. "But can you do us a couple of favors?"

"Anything."

"I had already asked your friend Jean that"—he pulls Maddy toward him—"the proceedings from our joint properties and investments go to Amara's Tree of Life."

"Why?"

Maddy touches my shoulder. "Why not?" She points at my heart, saying, "That place shows what's in here."

"What's the other request?"

Smiling, Ravi says, "Spread our ashes in the Columbia River. Keep the urns at Amara's Tree of Life."

"Okay." My voice breaks. "Anything else?"

As my tears roll down my cheeks, Ravi hugs me tight. Pulling his head back, he locks his eyes with mine and smiles. "Live your life with Emika and Nozo." Shaking me by my arms, he says, "Don't spend your life hating someone you loved all your life. At least hear Akane out." He pulls me back for another hug and whispers, "I couldn't have asked for a better mentor, friend . . . brother."

And then, he lets go of me.

Walking back through his doorway, I reach the main grounds of the core. At the top of my lungs, I yell, "Where are you? Show yourself!"

The future me, wearing the plaid suit Emika gifted me, appears. My blood rushes to my head. Tugging his lapel, I demand, "Who is Vandal?"

Removing my hands, he says, "I can't tell you. You must find out yourself to unlock your full powers."

"And keep waiting as he slaughters those I love?" I grab his throat. "Why? What's the point of power?"

He croaks, "You to fight the real enemy. And you need that power to know about all the turbulences in Philip's life."

I let go of his throat, leaning on his shoulder for support. "Is it worth getting the power?"

Shrugging, he smirks. "I wouldn't be here if it were." He snaps his fingers and makes the whole core disappear.

(Back to reality)

On my knees, I screech, "Come back, you worthless orphan!"

"Who's he talking to?" Anna asks Philip.

While Tabi helps me stand up, Philip explains, "His future self."

"What?"

A policeman, holding a battered box, walks over the shattered glass and metal and approaches Philip. "We found remains of a bomb. It was detonated remotely. We will send it to our forensic, sir." He lifts the charred box smelling of burnt plastic. "This was a Lego set, sir, and a wristwatch."

I walk to the police and collect the box and the watch. "Wow! What else can you tell us, Sergeant?" Pointing at the fire, I ask, "That's fire?" Pointing at the emergency response team loading three burnt bodies into a vehicle, I ask, "Those are dead bodies?" Then, I point at the child's body. "Sergeant, do you know who that child was?"

Looking into my "scary" eyes, he gulps. "No, sir."

"That child was me." I continue glaring at the policemen. "It's funny . . . the moment I thought I caught a break, the moment I had parents, you and your moronic force let Vandal kill me." Narrowing my eyes at him, I ask, "What have you been doing since the last murders? Handing out speeding tickets?"

Emika was wrong. Catching Vandal is my job.

Wheezing, I place my hands on his shoulders. "Listen to me carefully," I hiss between gritted teeth. "If any harm is done to Anna, Chris, Tabi, my Emika, my little Nozo, my Hulk, Amara's Tree of Life, or any more of my family, I will wipe your entire force from this reality."

The sergeant jerks his face back and sneers at my threat.

"You think I'm joking?" Snapping my fingers, I create a spark that transforms into a small core the size of a volleyball. Luminous intreton marks appear on my skin.

"Vincent, no!" shouts Philip, his eyes wide.

The police take their guns from their holsters and aim them at me. I don't even recognize my laugh as it comes out of me; it's cruel and sinister.

Spreading my arms wide, I yell, "You think bullets can harm me? Try it!" My voice is so loud it shakes the ground, lifting all the shattered glass, metal, and rubber.

Philip gestures with his hands for the police to put their guns down.

The sergeant's face turns pale. Chris's eyes are wide, moving between the core in my hand and me, as Anna and Tabi cover their mouths in disbelief.

"Don't disappoint me. Protect every person I mentioned," I demand, glaring at the sergeant.

He stammers, "Y-yes, Dr. Abajian."

(Home)

I am holding a picture of Ravi, Maddy, and Wasim in my left hand. Emika took it the day Wasim gave me that sketch. In my right hand is Wasim's sketch. Ravi's shattered Audemars Piguet Royal Oak is on the coffee table. I haven't slept. Emika hasn't left my side, nor has Hulk. Nozo is in her room. Emika hasn't spoken a single word. She is waiting for me. She knows everything from Anna, Chris, and Tabi.

My sight gets blurry as I look into the three pairs of eyes in the photograph, staring at me, smiling, reminding me how I failed them. When Vandal killed Altaf and Miguel, I should have asked Philip to protect Anna, Chris, Ravi, and Tabi. I was supposed to give a safe home to Wasim. My tears drop onto the frame and slide down the glass. My eyes fall on Emika's untied shoelaces. I place the photo and the sketch on the coffee table as I bend down to tie the laces with a Berluti knot. My hands shake.

Gently, Emika places her hands over mine. I lift her hands and kiss them. Lifting her hands, I kiss them.

Gazing into her warm eyes, I confess, "It's all my fault."

Wrapping her arms around me, she whispers, "No."

"You shouldn't be with me."

She tightens her grip. "Shut up." Then, she pulls back and cups my face in her palms, giving me a broken smile.

I know you're setting your loss aside. You, too, lost someone who called you his little sister.

Tilting her head, she says, "Take a shower. Tabi, Anna, and Chris will be here any minute."

(Breakfast)

The shock has rendered us speechless. The only sounds in the room are from chewing and silverware clattering on plates. Emika ordered food for everyone, including the police and Edward's men. Anna leaves her seat and sits next to Nozo.

She touches Nozo's cheeks and says, "I love you, baby."

"Huh?" little Nozo asks, looking up at her wide-eyed.

Holding Nozo's hand, Anna looks at us. Her lips quiver as she says, "Come closer, all of you." Pushing our chairs back, we gather around Anna and Nozo like a team before a match. Emika picks up Hulk, too. Anna says, "We don't know who is next. But I just want to say I love you all before it's too late."

I take a deep breath. "Vandal is next. I have made sure. All he has to do is hack us."

They all turn to look at me. "What?" Tabi asks.

"Follow me." I look at Emika. "Give Nozo some activities in her room. She doesn't have to hear our debates."

(Time cave)

I didn't want anyone to see this, but things have changed. Pointing at the one-hundred-screen mammoth, I say, "Ludwig, Athena, show us Enigma."

The screens all change to black, and all the MAC addresses of the first one thousand helmets we manufactured appear—ten per screen. All are green except for two that are yellow and four that are red.

Anna, Emika, Chris, and Tabi stare at the screens, eyes wide and mouths gaping. Shaking Emika by her shoulders, Anna asks, "You didn't know?"

Emika shakes her head, still staring at the system. "I've been to this room but never saw this." Her lips wobble as she points at the screens and asks, "Are those MACs?"

Taking a deep breath, I admit, "Yes." I point at the yellow MACs. "Those are Ravi's and Maddy's minds—currently inactive." Then, I point at the red ones. "Those are the minds of you four—active."

"Active, as in?" Anna asks, shooting daggers at me.

"The Mind monitors all your activities—the network you access in and out of any computer. Therefore, I will also know if anyone hacks into you." Shrugging, I confess, "Sorry."

"Vince!" Emika screeches in disbelief.

Chris puts his hand on my shoulder as I sit in my chair. "How did you do this without us knowing?"

"I have clearance above all of you. Sorry. I had no time to debate."

Chris's eyes bulge out. He shrieks, "You have what?"

Fuming, Anna comes over and grabs my lapel. Scrunching her lips, she grumbles, "You never considered us your equals, did you?" She tightens her grip. "How could you transform The Mind—*our* invention—into a virus?" Shaking me, she demands, "How could you betray us? Were you spying on us the whole time? You creep!"

As I look at Anna in disbelief, Emika charges in and removes Anna's hands from my lapel. Emika's face turns red as she yells at Anna, "You think he did it for fun? To spy on you?"

Pulling her wrists from Emika's grip, Anna glares at her. "You agree with him?"

"How could you support this?" Chris demands, placing his hands on Emika's shoulders. "Is this who we are? Spies?"

Nostrils flaring, Emika shrieks, "Catching Vandal is a moral responsibility!" She points at the screens. "Now, we have the tech to do it."

"At what cost? This is not moral!" Chris shouts, shaking Emika.

Emika winces in pain as she tries to remove Chris's hands from her shoulders.

My patience erodes. Grabbing Chris's arm, I grind my teeth. "You are hurting Emi."

"Sorry." Chris removes his hands from Emika's shoulders. Glaring at Emika, he says, "Clearly, you support Vincent. Well, then, it's you two versus us three."

Tabi breaks her silence. "Sorry, Chris. I'm with Vincent on this one."

"What?" Chris glares at her.

Tabi scoffs, "You think we could have gotten Dick Graham while being ethical?" She pokes Chris's chest. "You would support me if you lived in agonizing pain all your life."

Chris narrows his eyes at her. "And you are an authority?"

"Really? What's your pain?" Touching her cheeks, she starts to mock Chris. "Oh, no! My parents didn't attend my graduation. They don't call me on Thanksgiving." She points at herself, voice trembling, "Try living one day in my shoes. One second, I was fetching water for my siblings, and the next, everyone was vaporized." She pulls my sleeve and glares at Chris. "Try one minute of his life—wondering why he was dropped at an orphanage and bullied every day. Try living with the memories of all the time correctors." Moving to Emika, she takes her hand and continues, "Wanna try her? Living a fragmented reality, where she can't even piece her life together?" Wheezing, she scowls at Chris. "Your pain is a luxury we would love to feel."

Chris clenches his jaw. "Well, then. Maybe you shouldn't be with me."

"She doesn't need you." Emika frowns at Chris, holding Tabi's hands. "We have lots of rooms."

Getting inches from Emika's face, Anna snarls, "Fuck all that! The Mind is our invention. We did it as a team. And you don't see anything wrong with how"—she points her finger at me and continues—"he sabotaged it?" Waving her hand in front of Emika's eyes, she asks, "Are you blind?"

Putting her hands on her hips, Emika scoffs, "I'm blind? Our invention?"

Fearing an even uglier turn, I implore with joined hands, "Emi, no."

"Shut up, Vince." Pointing at me, she glares at Anna. "When he was in a slump after Elise died, how many things did you, Chris, and Ravi invent?" Tapping her chin, she mocks, "Umm . . . let me think . . . oh, that's right! Zero." She shakes her head. "What's your idea of invention? Bingo! Let's wait till Vincent invents something, and he will put our names on it when we file for a patent. Quantum World is Vincent's brainchild. Neurolink is his idea. So, why would he ask you two before converting it into a tracking device?"

Anna shrieks at Emika, "Bitch! We should never have hired you! Should have never brought you to this place after the—"

I feel blood and intreton rushing to my head. My eyes burn as I stare at Anna and shout, "Shut up! Do not call her that. Nothing is her fault."

Each of the hundred screens blinks, the lights flicker, the chairs roll away, and Anna is thrust back four feet, falling on her backside. I look at my hands, and the green intreton marks appear.

Rushing toward me, Emika takes my hands and asks, "Are you okay?"

Before I can answer, Anna blurts out, "Freak! I rue the day I met you." Then, she covers her mouth in disbelief, struggling to put the words back. Her eyes are wide and wet.

I stare at Anna blankly. My voice trembles. "What?"

You saw me through Elise, Emika, and Akane. I was there for all your heartbreaks. You were there the day I learned of Kruger's death, and you were the first to know that Emika broke up with me over the phone. There has been no one else I trusted more than you for over a decade. I love you like I love Fred, Krista, and Sasha. And you let this one action define who I am? You rue the day I told you, "Let's out-publish and out-invent your adviser?" The adviser who almost ruined your life, rendering you unemployable?

Doubting her own words, Anna takes a step toward me, but she stops as she looks at the monitors. Deciding to live by her words, she wipes her eyes. Then, she grabs Chris's hand.

"Let's go. From now on, Vince is just our CEO—the lone genius. He made that all too clear." She scans Emika from head to toe, saying, "I don't know who you are."

They both walk out of the time cave, slamming the door and leaving it open. As she leaves, Anna tells a police officer, "Don't waste your efforts on Vandal. The real villain lives under this roof."

Falling to my knees, I stare at my hands as the intreton markings disappear. I knew we would debate and argue, but I didn't expect this. Sitting next to me, Emika holds my hand. Tabi remains standing, puffing, unable to grasp that Chris just walked out on her.

I look at Emika. "I wouldn't have spied on anyone."

"I know," she says gently, wiping my eyes.

Touching Emika's wrist, I feel her racing pulse. "Your temper . . . Are you okay? It's like the concert night all over again."

"No one talks to you like that."

"Yep," agrees Tabi, her arms crossed.

Emika and I stand up. She rubs Tabi's back while I tell her, "Chris doesn't know any better."

Her eyes are still wide. Grinding her teeth, she mutters, "Then he should have shut his piehole."

(Columbia River)

Emika

Nozo is gripping my fingers tightly as we walk toward the bank of the Columbia River. I am looking down, avoiding tripping over any rocks. Vincent is just a few feet ahead of me, carrying the remains of Wasim in his left hand and Ravi's in his right. The urns are made of silver; I picked them. Vincent couldn't.

Today, I drove the G-Wagon. My Vince couldn't. Behind me is Tabi, holding the remains of Dr. Madison Stevens. Anna and Chris are waiting at the bank, and close to them are the police, who are entrusted with protecting them. The wind lifts my hair, and my black dress whips around my legs.

Pulling my hand, Nozo looks up. Her eyes are teary from the chilly breeze. Shivering with wet eyes, she says, "*Samui desu, mama.*"[74] Today, she is not asking for candy.

---

[74] I'm cold, Mama.

As I tighten her Burberry parka, my phone rings. I know it's Akane—again. She has been trying to reach Vincent for the last two weeks since the news about Ravi, Maddy, and Wasim spread through the media. Vincent asked me to ignore her. I don't want to argue with him, not in his state. I reject the call.

Gomennasai, Akane-san.

We all reach the bank. Everyone is silent. The water burbles as it hits the shores, cascading over the rocks. The birds tweet around us, welcoming the spring. We are done with this lengthy, murderous winter. Going to the bank's edge, Vincent and Tabi place the urns on the ground. I take Nozo near Vincent. Holding her tightly, I say, "Nozo, say goodbye to *Ravi-san, Maddy-san*, and Wasim."

"*Mata ne,*[75] *Ravi-san, Maddy-san*, and Oo-sim," she murmurs.

Kissing her forehead and wiping the corners of my eyes, I praise her. "Good job. Always *mata ne*, never *sayonara*."

"*Hai.*"

Vincent, Tabi, Chris, Anna, and I hold Wasim's urn. As Anna's hands touch Vincent's, he promptly retracts them, muttering, "I'm a freak, re-member? Shouldn't touch; I might infect you." Then, staring at the ashes, Vincent says, "See you later, little one. Never forgive me."

Anna's lips tremble at Vincent's self-accusatory words. She extends her hand toward Vincent's shoulder but stops as soon as her gaze meets his bloodshot eyes. There were no overlapping hands with Maddy's ashes, as the urn was larger.

The wind picks up as we all get closer to the bank, uncapping the final urn—Ravi's. As we start pouring, the view becomes hazy, tears blinding my eyes.

Goodbye, Ravi. Goodbye, Onii-san.

Instead of reaching the water, some ashes land on the riverbank rocks, and bits get stuck to Vincent's black suit jacket. Setting the urn on the bank, Vincent opens his coat without a second's hesitation and starts to wash it in the water while murmuring, "I'm so sorry, Ravi. I know all of it should go to the river." Rubbing his eyes with his shirt sleeve, he mumbles, "I promised you."

---

[75] See you later.

Dropping his jacket on the ground, he untucks his pristine white shirt, creates a pouch, and stuffs it with the ash-smeared rocks. Collecting one stone after another, he keeps mumbling, "No, no. I can't fail this time."

I can't watch him like this. If there's a God, they better stay out of Vincent's way when he catches Vandal and rips him apart. Anna, wiping her eyes, joins him in collecting the rocks.

Hesitantly, she approaches Vincent, pleading, "Let me come close to you, please." She extends her handful of stones and says, "Please, for Ravi." Then, she drops the ash-smeared riverbed rocks into Vincent's shirt—not white anymore but with stains of gray, brown, and ash, from anger, resentment, and, above all, love.

He releases the rocks into the river, removes his shirt, and washes the remaining ashes into the river water. Sitting in his undershirt, his shoulders begin to shake, and I can hear the words through his cracked voice.

"Goodbye, my little brother."

This is the Vincent underneath the arrogant genius—the vulnerable soul I love. He blankly stares into the water, watching the currents take away the remains of what was Dr. Ravi Bose.

As I walk toward him, Nozo turns to the right and pulls Chris's trousers. Tilting her head back sharply to look up at him, she asks, "I'm not your favorite?"

Sniffling, Chris looks at me. I nod, and he gently picks up Nozo. Hugging her tight, he says, "Always and forever."

Placing her index finger on Nozo's palm while staring at Vincent, Anna assures her, "My favorite, too."

As Tabi and Chris avoid eye contact, he sets Nozo back down. Nozo, pointing at her father, asks me, "Why is Papha crying?"

Kneeling to reach Nozo's eye level, I kiss her cheeks. "He is missing *Ravi-san*."

"Where is *Ravi-san*?" she asks, tilting her head.

Sitting on her knees, touching Nozo's shoulders, Anna explains, "Ravi is everywhere. He is watching over us. He just doesn't have a body right now."

"Oh."

"Go and wipe your papha's tears." Anna kisses Nozo's cheeks. "Tell him what I told you about *Ravi-san*. Hey, but don't tell him I told you. Okay?"

"*Hai.*"

"Now, go on."

While little Nozo runs toward her father, shouting, "Papha, Papha...," Anna turns to me. First, she tries to touch my shoulder, then she retracts her hands, folding her fingers into a fist, and presses her lips together.

Staring into my eyes, she says, voice quavering, "Vince loves piping hot ramen when he is cold."

"Thanks," I say before turning away.

Shaking Vincent's shoulder, Nozo points at the water and the sky. Vincent's eyes follow her hands. Then, he hugs her, looks in our direction, and nods.

After a few more long moments, Vincent stands, the sun now behind him. He ties his wet shirt and jacket around his waist and places Wasim's and Ravi's urns in the crook of his right arm. Holding Nozo's hand with his left, he looks at us.

"Emi, Tabi, it's getting late."

Grabbing onto Maddy's urn, turning away from Chris, Tabi stands up. "Let's go."

After placing Nozo into the car seat next to Tabi, Vincent asks, "Can I drive?"

"Sure."

"We will keep the urns at the orphanage." Pressing the ignition key, he asks, "Can we have the ramen with the kids there?"

"Sure. The kids would love to see you," confirms Tabi.

I squint at Vincent. "Wait, you heard the ramen part?"

"I'm a freak, remember?" he mutters, clenching his jaw.

Some wounds are too deep. I don't know how much more you can take. Everyone breaks, despite their resilience. I want to be with you if you ever reach that inevitable point. I just don't want to be the cause of it anymore. I love you.

He catches my gaze and wipes my tears with his thumbs. Then, picking up my left hand, he kisses my fingers and gently says, "I love you, too."

Can you hear my thoughts?

(Vincent's living room)

Tobi

Philips's men have set up about one hundred tatami mats for Vincent to cut through. As he cuts them in a single stroke, the men replace the mats. Philip is standing nearby, with a stopwatch in one hand and a walking stick in the other. The *thwacking* sound of Musashi's *katana* cutting through the tatami travels through the air, passing the rapidly budding cherry blossoms fifty feet away and piercing through the thick floor-to-ceiling glass wall.

Every day, I miss my birth parents, Farid and Amina. But that loss forged the path that led me to an older brother like Vincent. Ironies.

Hulk follows Emika and sits next to me as Emika hands me a cup of *genmaicha*. Holding her mug in both hands, she stares at Vincent, shaking her head.

Softly, she whispers, "Please rest." Sitting on the sofa beside me, Emika asks, "Why is he practicing *Tameshigiri*?"

"Vandal is a trained fighter who has injured Vince several times."

Her eyes widen, and she covers her mouth. "What?"

"Don't worry. Vandal ends up being in worse shape, I assure her. And Vincent heals almost instantly."

"I see." She takes a deep breath. "I'm nervous about tomorrow."

"You will do fine as the new head of R&D," I say, touching her shoulder.

Touching my hand, she says, "I didn't think Chris and Anna would vote in my favor."

"No one doubts your ability as a scientist. Plus, both Vince and Philip were on your side."

Squinting, she turns to me and asks, "Why didn't Vince involve Philip in his plans to catch Vandal?"

"Beats me." I shrug. "But he doesn't do anything without reason."

Outside, Vincent is sitting and catching his breath, holding the *tsuka*, the *katana*'s blade resting on the ground. As one of Philip's men fires a blank, Vincent jumps up with shocking speed, using sparks from his left hand to thrust himself forward. He kicks three tatami mats, then cuts ten of them—all in under one second.

"Did you see that? Wow!" I exclaim.

But Emika frowns. "Yes. He is killing himself."

Touching her shoulder, I assure her, "He'll be fine." Then, taking a deep breath, I say, "There is something I need to tell you."

She smiles. "Sure."

"Markus still loves you."

Emika's eyes widen. "Wait, you know?"

"We all do. Ravi did, too." Pressing her hand, I say, "It's none of my business, but does Vincent know?"

Closing her eyes, she admits, "Yes. And he told me everything about Akane." She opens her eyes and looks at me. "But Vince doesn't have any contempt toward Markus. He said that whatever I did between February 2024 and October 2026 was none of his business." She takes a sip of her tea and then smiles. "I have no contempt toward Akane, either. He wouldn't be the Vincent I love without her."

Hesitantly, I ask, "Assuming you'd never met Vincent, would Markus have played a greater role in your life?"

Shrugging, she says, "Perhaps." Looking at the setting sun and Vincent's silhouette, she smiles. "Though, I think a part of me would always look for Vince without knowing what or who I'm looking for. Even if I were content with my life." She closes her eyes, breathes deeply, and then opens them again to look outside. "I'm grateful to be in a reality where our paths crossed at the perfect moment. It's a fragmented reality. It hurts, and it's confusing." Smiling, almost lost in her thoughts, she adds, "But I wouldn't trade it for anything."

(March 29, 2027)

Emika

It's the eve before beta testing. I tiptoe into Vincent's time cave.

Accidentally stepping on an open notebook, I look down only to see that the entire floor, other than a small perimeter around Vincent's chair, is covered with white notebooks filled with handwritten MACs and equations. Vincent takes a couple of dot stickers, writes 879 on both, and then attaches a yellow string and a green string to the wall. Unaware of my presence, he stares at his one hundred monitors and scratches his head.

Tucking my hair behind my ears, I sit on the floor to examine the equations in the notebooks. I haven't seen these equations in my ten years of education in mathematics across Kyoto, Oxford, and Caltech. He made them up! I shouldn't be surprised.

Looking up, I inspect the wall. There are two pins at the center—one for this lab and one for Quantum World. These two pins are surrounded by five hundred pins above them and five hundred below them, each corresponding to one beta user and one helmet. What are the green strings for? Are they depicting the traffic between Quantum World and the beta users? The yellow strings run between this lab and the beta users. Some strings are attached with dot stickers numbered 1 through 879.

"Ludwig, get me the info from screen 88."

"Ah. Those are beta users 880 through 889. The Mind is ready, and all the codes are in place. Do you want to know the identity of the users?"

Vincent sighs, exasperated. "Once again, no. The less I know about them, the better." He then writes the number 880 on two dot stickers and attaches them to the strings, mumbling to himself, "I'm not a creep. I don't care who you are. Unless you get hacked, that's all." Going back to his chair and rocking his entire body, he keeps repeating, "I'm not a creep. I'm not a freak . . ."

Anna, what have you done to my Vince?

Getting up from the floor, I go over to his chair and swivel it toward me. Next to his keyboard is a glass box encasing Ravi's shattered watch. Carved into the wooden base underneath the glass are the words, "My biggest failure yet."

Looking up, Vincent asks me, "Am I a creep?"

I bring his head against my chest. "Shut up."

"I will catch him, right?" Vincent asks, wrapping his arms around my waist.

"Yes." I pull back to look straight into his eyes. "I will be here till you finish up. About a hundred more, right? Then let's eat. We can order in, or we can cook together. Whatever you want."

"Okay." He agrees.

"You need to rest."

He keeps repeating, "I need to rest, I need to rest . . ." Staring at me helplessly, he asks, "What if I become creepier while resting? How can I stop that?"

Pulling his head to my chest again, I run my fingers through his hair. "Shhh."

(April 5, the fifth day of beta testing—Emika's office)

Philip looks around my office and smiles. "Vince met his match in organizing. Who is a bigger neat freak?"

"I am. He is more organized, though."

Sipping the matcha I made him, he looks outside. "Vincent wants me to infuse Musashi's sword with intreton. He wants to hurt Vandal with it."

Leaving the window, he limps across my office toward me, using his walking stick, somehow not spilling his tea. "How can he be so sure of catching him?" Tilting his head, he locks his piercing eyes with mine. "What's he up to?"

Vincent doesn't want anyone to know what he is up to. He regrets telling Anna and Chris. But why would he hide it from Philip? Is it because he is our biggest investor? I can't reveal what Vincent is up to, but maybe this will do.

"Vince took Ravi's loss very personally. As always, he blames himself. And it doesn't help that Vandal knows him somehow."

"So, you know."

"Yes, I have seen the *shuriken*. Vincent thinks that maybe someone has altered Vandal's memories."

His hand holding the teacup trembles. "I'm sorry you have to deal with all this."

"How can I help him?" I ask, tucking my hair behind my ears.

Philip's face lights up, and he says, "Maybe he needs to be around those who helped him through the first loss. His first set of siblings."

I lift my brows. Why didn't I think of that? "Thanks. I will call all three. I'll make it a surprise for him."

Gripping his derby handle tightly, Philip stares at the floor. Then, with his face scrunched, he looks at me. "You may want to call her, too."

"Why?" I ask. "It's her loss that Fred, Sasha, and Krista helped Vince through, right?"

"With only the three of them present, it reinforces Akane's absence and her derogatory comments. That, on top of Ravi's death . . ." Philip lifts his finger. "Vincent needs to face Akane and hash it out. This could be the only opportunity."

I sigh. "I see."

Philip sets his teacup down on my desk. Then, taking support from his cane, he goes to the door.

Before he leaves, I ask, "You haven't met Akane, right?"

His lips wobble as he confesses, "How can I? I ruined her life. And, in the process, I ruined yours, too."

Meeting his gaze, I say, "Vince doesn't blame you."

"I know. That's what separates him from me."

After Philip leaves, I return to my desk and pick out a framed photograph of Ravi, Maddy, and Wasim. The same one we have in our house.

Why did you have to go? I miss you. Among the three, you were the kindest.

(February 13, 2024—AI lab at the uni)

I shut my ears tight as Anna's voice echoed through the whole lab as she screamed, "How could you?" She shook me by my shoulders. "You made Vincent buy that house. Then, you cheated on him. And now, you're leaving the day after tomorrow?"

Chris squinted at me. "So, you won't finish your contract?"

"I want to get away from all of this. This place reminds me how he is hiding things from me." Looking at Anna, Chris and Ravi, I declared, "His constant texting with Tabi and ignoring me . . ." I covered my face with my palms to hide my tears.

Removing my hands from my face, Ravi turned to Chris and Anna. "Give her some space."

Pointing at me, Anna protested, "But she—"

"Guys, please. You're hurting her." As Anna and Chris left the lab, Ravi sat on his knees, holding my hands. "You think getting away from all this will clear your mind?"

"I think so," I said, sniffling.

"All right, then. Don't worry about the contract." He pointed at this watch. "It's late, and you need to pack." He placed his hand over mine and asked, "Can I drop you home?"

I wiped the corner of my eye. "I'll Uber."

"Shut up."

(February 13, 2024—The parking lot of Emika's townhome)

Stopping his car in front of my townhome, Ravi turned to me and touched my shoulder. "Don't be a stranger."

Tears welled in my eyes as I hugged Ravi. "I will miss you all."

"Call Vince before you go?" He looked into my eyes. "He deserves that much, right?"

"Yes." Sobbing, I asked, "What am I doing?"

He shook his head and smiled. "If you need anything, just call me. Okay?"

(Back to the present)

I called Vincent the next afternoon, and Nozo was conceived that night. My tears drop on the photo, and I gently wipe them off. I hold the picture against my chest.

Goodbye, Ravi. Goodbye, Onii-san. *Vince will catch Vandal—whatever it takes.*

My office phone interrupts my thoughts. Susan—Ravi's assistant, now assigned to me—is on the other line.

"Dr. Calimaris and Dr. Washington are here."

"Send them in."

Coming inside, they sit next to each other on the two-seater. I have to be calm. Sitting on the chair opposite, I ask, "What do you want?"

Anna looks at Chris, and he nods. She takes a deep breath and says, "I may have overstepped."

Anger rushes through my body, but is this an olive branch? So, tilting my head, I scoff. "You think?" Narrowing my eyes and placing my elbows on the desk, I lean toward them and ask, "What do you think Vince would have done if one of you took Ravi's place?"

"The same," Chris admits, swallowing hard.

Turning to Anna, I ask, "Then how could you?"

When her eyes tear up, I leave my seat to retrieve a tissue box, handing it to her before sitting back down. Sobbing through a wad of tissues, Anna asks, "Will he forgive us?"

I sigh. "Unless one is Akane, Vincent doesn't hold grudges. Yes, he will forgive you. But he will not forget it." Shaking my head, I say, "So, what do you want from me? I have a busy day."

(April 12, 2026, the last day of beta testing)

Vincent

The music room at Amara's Tree of Life is furnished. Pushing Nozo's stroller in, Hulk trotting alongside us, I see the whole room is now varnished with mahogany wood panels. The Shigeru Kawai is the centerpiece next to the fireplace. The walls are lined with shelves full of trumpets, violins, cellos, trombones, acoustic guitars, and electric guitars. There are six rows of ten chairs.

Touching Tabi's arm, I say, "This is beautiful."

"Your Emika's work. She chose every single instrument."

"She never said a word."

"Doesn't surprise me. She's not a credit seeker."

Looking around, I ask, "Where is she? She took my phone and disappeared."

I wanted to take her out tonight to celebrate the completion of beta testing. But she asked me to come here, instead. I fold my palms.

Ravi, I wish you were here. You would be proud of your little sister.

The wooden floor gently shakes with the pitter-patter of fifty children—shoes, crutches, and the screeching of wheelchairs. Turning back, I see all the children dressed in formal wear. Coming into the room, they all take a seat. Each of them is wearing a microphone. What is Emika planning?

My Emika appears in a yellow and white lace dress, walking toward the piano in untied sakura-printed converse. She kicks off her shoes and sits on the piano bench. Then, she takes out origami paper and folds it into a bird. Locking her eyes with mine, she solves the Rubik's Cube sitting on the piano in under a minute, without even looking at it. That's some muscle memory! Setting it back on the piano's surface, she signals at someone, and the room darkens. As she cracks her knuckles, one light shines on my Emika. Tabi takes Nozo from her stroller and sits, placing her on her lap. I follow suit, putting Hulk in the chair on my left.

Gently, Emika starts to key the piano. I don't recognize this adagio. How? I know all of them. This one hints at something different—not Western classical but classical, nonetheless. Staring at me, Emika teases me with her wink and her keying. As she changes the movement, I recognize the tune—it's Pink Floyd's "Comfortably Numb." I can extract any song from any introductory notes that aren't even attached to the piece. Shaking my head, I smile at my failure.

You are a maestro, Emika. Piano was your true calling.

Closing her eyes, she begins to sing. "Hello, hello . . . Is there anybody in there?"

I don't believe in magic outside my ability to bend time and alter reality. Still, her velvety voice, paired with her playing, is nothing short of my ability to change reality.

The light shimmers around her as she ends the verse with, "Can you show me where it hurts?"

Then, her keying meets a male voice, singing, "There is no pain you are receding." As the light shines on the man, my jaw drops. Fred? He walks toward my Emika as he continues to sing. "A distant ship smoke on the horizon." Standing behind her, he closes his eyes and concludes his verse with, "I have become comfortably numb."

Emika starts back in. "Okay, okay, okay . . ." Fred's voice joins hers. But there are others, too. The light shines behind Emika's shoulders, where Krista and Sasha stand, singing in unison, "Just a little pinprick." Sasha winks at me.

I turn to Tabi and whisper, "Who planned this?"

"Who do you think?" she responds, rolling her eyes. "They were rehearsing all day."

"Where are they staying?"

"The guesthouse. Since yesterday. Your house from this moment on." Looking at her watch, she says, "I have to be somewhere." After handing Nozo to me, she leaves.

Emika, Fred, Krista, and Sasha conclude the verse with the lines, "Come on, it's time to go."

Then, fifty children begin the chorus from the back. "There's no pain you are receding."

I don't care if they are out of tune. Surrounded by the little Vincents and Tabis, I don't feel like a freak. As the chorus ends, Emika adapts David Gilmour's famous guitar solo into keying on the Shigeru Kawai. She crisscrosses her hands, closes her eyes, and smiles. This keying could convince the most stubborn of cherry trees to bloom.

Concluding her music, Emika stands up. Then, she, Fred, Sasha, and Krista bow to the children, Nozo, Hulk, and me. Emika blows a kiss at me. As I walk toward her and my siblings from school, Ayesha, Farouq, and Mariya intercept my path.

Smiling and looking at me with her right eye, Ayesha hands me a small box. She points back at the piano, saying, "Those two ladies taught us to bake a cake."

At this moment, I don't see any struggle in Ayesha's scarred face.

"Emika said you are sad," Farouq comments.

Walking close to me on her prosthetic legs, Mariya smiles and points at the box. "So, this cake is for you. If you feel sad, Vince, come here. We will make you a cake." She smiles up at me. "Anytime."

As I place the cake on a chair, my vision gets blurry. Kneeling, I spread my arms. "Come here, all of you." As I hug them, I kiss their little heads. If sharing whatever little these kids have with me brings them joy, then maybe I am not a freak.

(Vincent's home)

Looking at Fred, Krista, and Sasha, I say, "Please stay with us for a few days. April 15 will be a beautiful day in our backyard."

"That's the plan," Sasha assures me.

As I walk toward my study, Krista asks, "Where are you going?"

"To find Vandal."

"What's he saying?" Fred asks Emika.

Emika tells him, "I will explain in a few minutes." Then, she comes to stand in front of me. "Here," she says, handing me back my phone. "Sorry."

Bringing her close, I kiss her lips softly. "I still don't know why you took it."

She shrugs, her lips curling mischievously.

Tucking her hair behind her ear and running my thumb across her cheek, I ask, "Wanna help me catch Vandal?"

"I think you got this one," she says, winking at me. "I will instead enchant your friends with tales of your ability as a time corrector."

(Time cave)

As I enter the time cave, I wonder, *Why are the lights on?*

Then, I see Anna sitting in my chair and ordering Chris, "No, no, that one, you dumbfuck."

Sitting on the floor, Tabi glares at Anna. "Hey, be nice to him."

Anna has a pen in her mouth, and her glasses are on top of her head. All three are in their pajamas. What are they doing here? Wasn't I a creep and a freak?

I clear my throat. "Ahem!"

Anna tilts her head and furrows her eyebrows, pulling her glasses down to her nose. "What the fuck were you thinking, marking the inbound and outbound traffic with the same colored strings?" Pointing at me, she turns to Chris and Tabi. "Presenting the big genius from MIT." Then, she looks at me and grumbles, "You thought you could do all of it alone?"

Fighting a smile, I confess, "I didn't want to." So, that's why Emika took my phone away—so I wouldn't know when someone walked into my time cave.

"Can we stay here for a few days?" Chris asks. "Emika said we could."

Smiling, I walk over to them and touch Chris's shoulder. "Sure. It's her house."

Anna wraps her arms around me. "I am so sorry."

"It's okay," I say, running a hand over her apricot-smelling hair.

"It's not." Her voice trembles. "I will be more careful with my words."

I kiss her head. "Please don't. I insist."

She pulls her head back. Frowning, she asks, "Why?"

I grin. "I like my Anna—careless, childish, and sinister."

"Idiot."

Whispering into her ear, I ask, "On April 15, during *hanafubuki*, if I say to you, 'It's time,' will you do something for me?"

"Time for?" Then, she squints at me. "What's *hanafubuki*?"

Vandal

Let's call Dina.

"Hello, Hank."

"The Jaeger that Mr. J built is awesome."

"Hank?"

"Yes?"

"Why did you make me hack the beta testing? Mr. J doesn't even know, right?"

"He doesn't. He just wants Vincent's powers. But I have to destroy Vincent's legacy—Quantum World, Neurolink. Do you think people will stick by him once his legacy falls?"

"He has a family. He does a lot of good." Dina's voice quavers. "He is very kind. He takes care of orphans." She sobs, "And we have already killed so many. Can't we just stop?"

I grit my teeth. "We, too, had a family. We will stop after this."

CHAPTER 15

REVELATION—STAGE 1

"Admit, you hate me. Or at least ask me why I did what I did."
—*Akane*

April 13, 2027

<u>Vincent</u>

I T'S SPRING OF 1991.

Touching her chest, Akane concludes, "Moe." Then, she announces with pride, "I hide, and you seek."

No surprise there. Crumpling my brows, I complain. "When you start with me, you become 'a,' and I become 'tiger.' But when you are 'eeny,' you combine 'a tiger' for yourself." I glare at her. "That's why you always hide."

Crossing her arms, she looks away. Shrugging, she says, "Okay, then. *Asobimansen.* I won't play with you."

Oh! She is angry. What if she doesn't talk to me?

Nudging her shoulder, I say. "Sorry."

Her eyes instantly brighten. "Okay. Forgiven." She smiles and waves her hand. "Count to one hundred, then look for me." Lifting her finger, she furrows her brows. "Count slowly."

"Okay."

Before she goes, she ruffles my hair and kisses my cheek.

"Huh?" I ask.

Rolling her eyes, she quips, "Silly."

As I face the library wall, her footsteps fade. After counting to one hundred, I enter the hallway. Standing still, I am torn between searching the art room and the cafeteria.

Where are you? Why do you always hide? Why do you always win? One day, I will hide. That'll teach you.

I pick the cafeteria. As I walk around, peeking under the tables, the spring wind forces the cafeteria's balcony doors to open. Outside on the railings, I see a robin chirping.

Do you want me to follow you?

As I cross the empty cafeteria, the wind blows again, stinging my eyes. I close them. A heavy hand presses down my shoulder, and I open my eyes again. Looking up, I see a grown man smiling down at me. He has my eyes.

"Who are you?" I ask.

"I am you from 2027."

"Where is Akane?"

He swallows hard. "There is one place you can always find her. Close your eyes and count to three."

I do as he says, then slowly open my eyes. Staring at my hands, I see I am not eight anymore. My perpetual calendar wristwatch shows it's April 15, 2025. This is not Montagnola. I stand in front of the *ema* display, wearing a bespoke blue suit over a black cashmere mock neck sweater.

Sifting through all the *emas*, I wonder, *Where is it? You said we would stand the test of time. Liar.*

As tears flood my eyes, I hear a faint, trembling voice over the wind.

"Looking for this?"

Before I can turn my head around, the sound of "Clair de Lune" starts ringing in my ears.

Opening my eyes, I shout, "Akane!" before realizing where I am. Then, shaking my head and removing the comforter, I get up. That was weird. Why would I ever look for that *ema*? Fuck that *ema*.

Looking at my watch, I see it's 7:30 a.m. on April 13. Emika once again extended my alarm by two hours.

Walking into the kitchen in my pajamas and robe, I see the Michelin two-star chefs are on breakfast duty. I smack my lips at the scent of freshly made bread, the sizzle of bacon frying, the essence of creamy scrambled eggs, and the smell of morning coffee on my Kalita Wave. They all tantalize my senses. I inhale deeply. Emika, with her hair pulled back in a clip, carefully notes a recipe for avocado pancakes from Sasha, a specialty at Thyme & Cumin. After pouring myself a cup of Jamaican Blue Mountain and pulling out a chair at the breakfast counter, I turn to Emika.

"I have the recipe. Sasha learned it from me."

Glaring at me, Sasha lifts her middle finger.

Krista is baking chocolate and caramel cookies; the aroma is infectious. Nozo, in Kiki's outfit, is holding a broom in her left hand. Pulling Krista's apron with her right hand, she asks, "Cookies?"

Leaning down to fix Nozo's Kiki hairband, Krista says, "In a bit." Then, she kisses her cheeks.

Before Krista stands up straight, Nozo tugs her apron again. "Now?"

Krista widens her eyes at me. "Exactly like you!"

After switching the TV on, Tabi sits at the breakfast counter next to Chris, and he rubs her back.

"Can I get a little . . . you know, to go with the second cup?" Fred asks me, having finished his first cup of coffee.

Rolling my eyes while walking to the bar, I ask, "Scotch, Bourbon, Irish, Canadian, Japanese?" while

"It's not even eight in the morning," Anna says, scrunching her face at Fred.

Walking toward the bar, I grin. "He likes to start early."

Picking a twenty-one-year-old Balvenie single malt for Fred, I return to my place at the breakfast counter, overlooking the pink sakura. Two more days to *hanafubuki*, when the petals will fall like pink snowflakes—an unparalleled beauty.

After a few moments, the TV interrupts breakfast with a breaking news segment.

"Pinnacle Financial Group has been hacked," the anchor announces. "We have with us the CEO, Megan Millar . . ."

The mood in the room quickly changes to complete silence as I lean toward my cell phone. "Ludwig, was Megan a beta user?"

"Ah, yes, Vincent. User number 912."

"Run Enigma on Megan's helmet."

Clapping her hands, Anna grins at me. "Chop chop, Vince, Chris, Tabi." Forming a fist, she squeals, "Got you, MOFU."

I take a few sips of my coffee as Nozo pulls my robe and asks, "Papha, what is MOFU?"

My hand grabs my belly as I spit my entire mouthful of coffee on the breakfast counter. Anna, Fred, Chris, and Tabi all catapult away from the counter. Emika throws me a roll of paper towels while glaring at Anna, who is biting her nails in embarrassment.

The rest hide their laughter behind tightly pressed lips, and Krista distracts Nozo with the announcement, "Nozo, hon. Cookies are ready."

Clapping, Nozo runs after her, forgetting the question.

After wiping the counter, as I'm about to get up, Emika pushes me back into the chair. She points her finger at Tabi and orders, "Nobody is leaving yet. We will all eat as a family. It takes about an hour for Enigma to scan every network." Squinting at me, she asks, "Right?"

"Yes, ma'am," I say, eyes down.

As we all gather to eat, Anna drums on the table impatiently, repeating, "We will, we will catch you."

Closing my eyes, I take a bite of bacon, avocado pancake, and eggs. The symphony of flavors and textures gets interrupted by the flapping of wings outside the window. Turning, I see the robin on the grass. I click my tongue.

Scanning everyone's faces, I ask, "Who called Akane?"

While Fred, Krista, and Sasha stare at each other, Emika admits, "I did. Philip said I shouldn't leave her out." She points at Fred, Krista, and Sasha and adds, "They agreed." Then, she frowns at me and tilts her head. "Wait, how did you know?"

Rolling his eyes, Fred quips, "Probably that pigeon he sees."

"Robin," I correct him, glaring at him.

Emika squints. "What robin?"

"Some bird that only Vince can see," Sasha mumbles with her mouth full of bacon and avocado pancake.

Reaching for a buttered toast, Krista tilts her head. "Wasn't it a sparrow?"

"*Robin*," I clarify, exasperated. Pushing my chair back, I stand up.

Washing down his thick-cut bacon with his scotch-infused coffee, Fred grins. "Imaginary. Might as well be a baby dragon."

Before I can react to Fred's wisecrack, Nozo spreads her arms and says, "Papha, I want a baby dragon."

I walk over to her and kiss her head. "Sure."

Anna, Tabi, and Chris all get up, too. Emika glares at me. "Where are you going?"

"Breakfast is done." I shrug. "Time to catch Vandal."

Turning to Anna, Chris, and Tabi, Emika asks, "Can you handle the program without Vince for an hour?"

"Of course," Anna says, shrugging.

Pointing at me, Emika instructs, "You will change, take a shower, and pick up Akane."

"Why, what happened to Michisato and Masato? And her Maybach?"

Standing up and putting her hands on her hips, Emika says, "I don't know. But you will settle your differences outside. And when you two come in here, you better be well-behaved." She kisses Nozo's head and stresses, "Like my Nozo." She points her finger at me and asks, "Are we clear?"

"Yes, ma'am."

Smiling mischievously, she removes her hair clip, lifts her arms, and ties my hair. Tapping her chin, she turns back to the group and points at my head. "Sasha, Krista, like this?"

While I scowl, the morning light shines on Emika's warm eyes. Winking, Krista explains, "Yep. Shave the beard, and Vince will turn into a pretty girl."

Placing her right hand on my shoulder, Emika gleefully puts her left hand on my face, her index over my mustache, and the remaining three on my chin. "I can see that." Hugging me, she observes, "Without the beard, you are the spitting image of Amara." Covering her mouth, her shoulders shake uncontrollably while she comments, "Nozo's Papha is a pretty girl." Her eyes squeeze into two lines of lashes.

I should have brought a scarf. The outgoing winter is grasping for straws with its last bit of chilly weather. I lift my lapel and blow into my folded palms, waiting for the engines of the Gulfstream 700 to stop spinning. Slowly, the whirring of the blades gives in to the beauty of spring—the chirping of birds, the gentle spring breeze of returning leaves. As the door opens and the stairs descend, my phone vibrates. It's Anna. My heart thumps. Have they caught Vandal? So soon?

"What's up?"

"There are so many networks. Do we need to go through all the subnets?"

"No. Just the unique Identity Class A internet addresses and traceroute them all. Leave the obvious ones out, like shopping investments and such, and concentrate on inbound traffic. See if anything stands out. If something does, then look for the subnets. Okay?"

"Yes, but. . .""

The door of the Gulfstream 700 beams up. And, like every time I see Akane, she emerges as light. She descends the staircase, putting on her shades and fastening her trench coat over her white jumpsuit.

From the phone, I faintly hear, "Vince, Vince . . ."

As my heartbeat peaks, I tell Anna, "I'll call you back," and then I hang up. I can't look away. The part where I thought the sakuras' beauty was unparalleled—scratch that.

Kimi wa boku no hikari desu[76]. *Shut up, Vince. You are nothing to her—just a media whore. But then, why is she here?*

---

[76]   You are my light

She comes close to me as two flight attendants load her luggage into the trunk of my G-Wagon. Removing her shades, she hugs me. Her tears reach my sports jacket shoulder as she sobs, "I am so sorry for Ravi and Maddy. And the little one they adopted."

Unwilling to return the embrace, I keep my fisted hands in the pocket of my jeans. Walking away, I open the passenger door for her.

As we leave the hangar, she scoffs, "What? You can't even hug me?"

I keep quiet. As my sight gets blurry, I wipe my eyes with my cuff. I grind my teeth so she can't see my trembling lips. Looking at her Gulfstream through my rearview mirror, I start to drive out of the hangar.

Undoing her trench coat, she throws it in the back seat, next to Nozo's car seat. Glancing at me, she comments, "Papha removed Masato and Michisato from my service using his power as the board chairman. I brought shame to the Egami name by publicly admitting my love for Sawano." She sniffles. "He won't forgive me for calling you what I did. He avoids me at meetings and parties. He leaves before I enter." Shaking my arm, she demands, "Say something." She takes a deep breath and whispers, "Admit, you hate me. Or at least ask me why I did what I did." Wiping the corner of her eye, she insists, "It's me. Your Akane."

I move to the side of the road and slam the brakes, and we both jolt forward. Glaring at her, I sneer, "My Akane? Wow! Which one? The one who promised me something by the *ema* stand? Or the one who swapped my face with Sawano's? The one who found me after thirty-three years, or the one who called me a media whore?" Gasping, I admit, "I don't give a fuck about your reasons . . . you didn't need to slander my name like that." I grind my teeth. "Do you know what it takes to build your name from nothing?" *I wasn't privileged like you…I came from nothing.*

She presses her lips tight and shuts her eyes to hold back her tears. "So, you do hate me."

Wiping my eyes, breathing hard, I let out every single feeling I had been bottling inside. "I can't hate you, even if I say so. And I tried. But you must win, right? Like the hide and seek games?" I glare at her with tear-soaked eyes. "So, there you have it. I hate you. Happy?" My voice cracks as I declare, "I hated you when I first saw you."

Her eyes widen. "Vince?" she says, covering her mouth in disbelief.

Tears run down my cheeks as I take a breath. How could I say that? And why am I not stopping? My head throbs.

"I hated you when you played the violin for me and when you tied that scarf around me. I hated you every time we shared an ice cream bowl. I hated you when you were by my side all day and night as I recovered. I hated you when you left me and when I spent thirty-three years waiting for you. I hated you when you came back."

Unfastening her seat belt, she wraps her arms around my neck to rescue me from myself. Gripping me tightly, she assures me, "It's not your fault."

"I hated you when we went to Copenhagen," I say, breathing hard.

"It's not your fault."

My voice softens, yet I declare, "I hated you when you lied in Kyoto." Why can't I stop myself?

"It was not a lie. It still isn't. Nothing is your fault."

Tears leave the confinement of my eyes. "Then why did you say I was just someone from your past? Why did you call me a media whore?" Shaking her, I demand, "Why did Ravi die?"

She wipes my tears with her thumb. "You will catch Vandal. And you are not just someone from my past." She says gently, giving me a broken smile, "*Kimi ga subete desu.*"[77] Closing her eyes and taking a deep breath, she says, "Now, let's go home. I'd like to meet our little Nozo." Pausing, she swallows hard. "Your Emika." Opening her eyes, she sniffles. "And everyone else." She presses the ignition button, bends her head, and rubs her fingers across her cheeks, wiping her tears away. "*Saa iki mashou.*"[78]

As I drive, she looks out the window, still sniffling. "I can restore that photo album," I offer.

She takes my hand and kisses my fingers. "Thank you. That's all I have of us. If I were not here, I would visit Kyoto on the fifteenth and look at that *ema.*"

My phone rings as I am about to reach for Akane's hand. I ask, "Can I take it?"

"Sure."

I accept the call. "Yes, Anna?"

---

[77] You're everything.

[78] C'mon, let's go.

"I'm s-sorry."

"What?"

"Vandal is an insider."

My heart races as I ask, "Who?"

"We were thorough. We checked and checked. The subnet address points to the network diagnostic lab." Sobbing into the phone, Anna screeches, "I hired her, Vince."

"Her?" I ask, keeping my eyes on the road. "Who runs that lab?"

Gasping, Anna shrieks, "It's Frida."

"Vince, it's Emi." Akane looks at the car speakers as soon as she hears the name.

"Go on."

"During the dinner at the conference, she had something spherical in a jute bag. It could have been the helmet." Then, she adds, "*Gomennasai, Akane-san.* We are in the middle of catching Vandal."

Waving her hands in dismissal, Akane smiles. "No worries."

The sweet Frida? You think you know a person.

"Is Tabi around?" I ask.

"Yes," says Tabi.

"Use your channels to create an APB on Frida." I form a fist. Fuck! Frida?

What made you like this? Are you the killer's sibling? I am sure the man in the video has at least two siblings.

I'm getting another incoming call. "Guys, Fred is calling. Can I hang up for a sec?"

"Sure," says Tabi, and then she hangs up.

I answer Fred's call. "Yes?"

"Hi, Akane. Is Vince being a jerk?"

Staring at me with moist eyes, she swallows the tremble in her voice. "He is incapable of that."

"Is that why you called?" I ask, shaking my head impatiently.

"No. Nozo was showing us her digital album."

"And?"

"There is a blond guy with Emika and little Nozo. The title of the picture is 'My little family.'"

"It's Emika's ex—Markus." I scrunch my face as I take off on an almost empty expressway. "Markus even works for us. It's fucked up shit, man."

Crumpling her brows, Akane stares at me.

"I get it. Except . . . I think he has a different name."

My grip on the wheel tightens. "What?"

"I know that face, those blue eyes. Does he jerk his head to move his hair?"

"Yes," I say, my breath coming faster. "So, who is he?"

"Rudy's brother, Hank. Why did he change his name, and what happened to his twin sister?"

"Mercedes, engage autonomous mode." Lifting my hands from the steering wheel, I massage my temples.

Nudging my hand, Akane asks, "Everything okay?"

"It will be now." But I never uttered the word "Vandal" to him. "Fred? What's the name of his twin sister?"

"Dina."

Dina, are you who I think you are?

"Did Dina have a middle name or an alias?"

"Let me ask Krista or Sasha. I think Dina was enrolled in a club with them."

"Vince, Sasha here. Dina's name is Dina F. Von Stein, and her brother is Hank M. Von Stein."

Grinding my teeth and forming a fist, I punch on the wheel. "Fuck!"

If only I had paid attention to people's faces in school. My head throbs. If only I had invited them to our Thanksgiving, their cover would have been blown. Ravi, Maddy, and Wasim would be alive.

"Fred?"

"Yes."

"Get Emika and Tabi. Please."

Markus! That's why Vandal never attacked us when we were all together. You couldn't hurt my Emi and Nozo. But what have I ever done to you? Where are you?

Helplessly staring at Akane, I say, "I have to catch him."

"You will," she says, touching my hand.

"Vince, it's Emi. I've heard." She sobs into the phone. "I should have suspected Markus's broken nose . . ." Her voice cracks. "I got Ravi and Maddy killed. Little Wasim died because of me. What have I done?" she cries.

"Everyone in the house is safe because of you," I assure her. Clenching my jaw, I command, "No one leaves the house till he is caught. Am I clear?"

"Yes," confirms Tabi.

"But you are not here," Emika shrieks. "What if—?"

Akane leans toward the speakers. "Nothing will happen to your Vince, Emika. I promise you."

I hang up abruptly and say, "Mercedes, call Anna."

"Vince? I heard," says Anna, jabbering.

"Leave the time cave. Please be with Emika." Breathing hard, I continue, "She blames herself, so all six of you be close to her and Nozo. Give her company. Keep her mind off Markus. Can you do that for me? Please?"

"Sure." She hangs up.

Akane dabs the corners of her eyes with her fingers. Faking a smile, she says, "You love your Emika."

She did not replace you. Across all my realities, I will pick no one but you. But I don't regret the twisted path that led Emika to me. And yet, despite your denial in the media and my stubbornness, deep down somewhere, I want to return to how things were with you.

I take a deep breath.

But then, everything oscillates back when I look into Emika's warm eyes and pick up my Nozo. There is only one answer.

I hold Akane's hand and look into her eyes. "I am just doing my best."

"*Wakarimasu,*" she says softly.

I check my watch—10:55 a.m. The roads are mostly empty. Markus could have attacked my house before Emika came back, though. Why didn't he? Who is pulling his strings?

"Mercedes, call Philip."

"Vince?" asks Philip.

Grinding my teeth, I blurt out, "Markus and Frida are Vandal. Their names are Hank and Dina."

"Markus as in Emika's ex? Who are they?"

"My juniors in school, from Montagnola."

"How did you find out?"

"I knew they'd hack us, so I created a trap."

His voice gets somber. "Get home safely."

"Thanks." I hang up.

While the car is still in autonomous mode, I turn to Akane and ask, "So, where were we before Anna called?"

Smiling, she says, "Me, being in Kiyomizu-dera on the fifteenth, at the *ema* stand."

"What's there?"

"Us. Forever," she says, swallowing.

As I watch Akane, darkness engulfs the sun. Strange. It was supposed to be sunny all day. The road starts to shake, and my two-ton vehicle wobbles. Earthquake?

Suddenly, Akane looks up, unhooks her seat belt, wraps herself around me, and yells, "Watch out, Vince!"

A chained flail shatters the windshield, pierces through the safety airbags before they can even deploy, stops the car in its tracks, and lifts it, the wheels still spinning. My face and hands are peppered with shards of glass and intreton bits. Squeezing my eyes shut, I shake my head to clear the screeching and beeping in my ears. My heart pounds. A high-pitched ring pierces through my ears, and I cover them with my hands. As the sound ceases, I shake my head. Where is Akane? As the car turns the front side up, I see two intreton-alloy spikes from the flail have pierced through the roof and are keeping the car hanging. My heart stops when I see the third one. It has sliced through my Akane's right shoulder. Her white jumpsuit is covered with blood and shards of intreton.

No! No! No! You can't leave me again.

Hyperventilating, I undo my seat belt. Gripping the hand bar, sitting on the dashboard, I get close to Akane and put my hand under her nose. She is breathing. She is alive. I have to get her to Dr. Lee before it's too late. How? Can I suit her up and use the core? I look at my bracelet. Fuck! It's smashed. Even if it weren't, she couldn't survive the core, even with the suit. Okay. Let's stabilize her first.

One step at a time, Vince.

I tap her cheeks. Her eyes are heavy, but she manages to open them.

"I got you." I have to risk pulling her out. But she might bleed to death…but, if I don't, the intreton in the spike will poison her. My voice trembles. "It will hurt, but I need to pull you off the spike." Tears flood my eyes as I slide my left hand into her mouth. "Bite my hand when it hurts. Now, breathe."

Wrapping my right arm around her waist, I start pulling her out. She screams in pain and bites into my hand as tears stream out of her tightly shut eyes and more blood flows from her shoulder. Blood leaks from my hands where her teeth break the skin, but I can't show my pain.

"You are doing great. Keep biting."

Gentle, Vince. Gentle.

Finally, I pull her free. Opening my jacket, I cover her wound tightly. Her eyes close. Abruptly, the car starts to shake. The glass from the windshield separates from its frame, falls, and shatters on the ground below us. I fall to the back seat, my back cracking from the impact. Looking up, I see a chained flail attached to a two-story-high, manned Jaeger. As my left hand heals from Akane's bite, I form a fist.

You will pay for this, Vandal.

Who made that Jaeger for him?

I climb back up to the front. The screech of the machinery echoes through my ears, making it hard to think clearly.

Think, Vince. Think. Eliminate all the noise. What did you do when Vandal attacked the railway system?

Yes, I covered Akane with an intreton shield. I have to cover both of us. But I can't use my hands. I have to keep the pressure on her wound. Suddenly, there's a blinding light. How is my whole body covered in sparks? My hands, legs, and chest are glowing, bright as lightning. I did not even snap my fingers to create the sparks. The intreton envelops both Akane and me.

The sparks must have hurt Vandal's eyes because the flail swings wildly, dislodging from my car. As we fall, the intreton shield encasing Akane and me, drops out of the gap left by the windshield. Akane and I land safely on the asphalt. The car smashes to its rear, and Akane's luggage springs up from the trunk and into the air. One of her bags rips open; it's full of toys for Nozo. Nozo's car seat is smashed to bits. The car I bought to keep my Emika and Nozo safe is now hanging by its rear wheels, stuck on the guardrail. The sirens and horns of emergency vehicles blare through the air. Vandal's intreton-powered Jaeger picks up the shell with Akane and me still inside. Vandal squeezes the grip, trying to break the intreton casing. Bits of metal from the Jaeger's claw crush against the shell and clatter to the road. Sweat drips down my forehead. What if he breaks it? I need help.

I screech at my phone, "Ludwig, call Philip."

Philip answers, "Vince?"

"Vandal is attacking us!" I shout. "Get your X60 here now! And bring the sword."

"Got the signal from your bracelet—already on my way!"

The Jaeger lifts our shell to the eye level of the machine's operator. Markus. Hank. Vandal. Our eyes lock as I press my jacket harder against Akane's wound.

You better hope she comes out of this alive. If she doesn't, I will take one organ out of your body each day while keeping you alive—one for each tragedy you caused.

The Jaeger drops us. As the shell hits the ground, Akane's blood squirts from her wound and sprays on my face.

Hugging her tight, I whisper, "Help is on the way. Just hang in there."

Vandal keeps stomping on the shell as the metal of the Jaeger's feet dents, with nuts and bolts sprinting out and dropping on the road. He stops and then screeches the chain flail tearing through the asphalt concrete on the street, igniting sparks. The battery pack in my G-Wagon catches fire. As Vandal lifts the chained flail, hoping to smash the shell, I call Philip.

"Just a few more minutes, Vincent. On the X60."

Vandal strikes his flail against the shell. The blasting noise and the shrilling pitch pierce my eardrums, but I can only shut my eyes as my hands are pressed to Akane's wound. Shards of intreton from the flail get stuck to the surface of the shell as Akane starts coughing up blood.

"She doesn't have a few more minutes!" I shout, sobbing into the phone. "If something happens to her, I will fuck up this world."

"I hope it doesn't come to that."

As Philip and Edward pull us in and close the latch, I drop the intreton shield surrounding Akane and me. Dr. Lee and three of his assistants rush toward Akane.

Placing his palm against my cheek, Philip asks, "Are you hurt?"

"I am fine, but . . ." I point at Akane, at a loss for words.

Attending to her wounds with intreton patches, Dr. Lee turns to me. "I can stabilize her. She has lost a lot of blood . . ." Stammering and staring into Philip's piercing eyes, he assures me, "Yes. She should be out of danger in six to ten hours."

Looking at Akane's beaten, tattered body, covered in blood, I try to slow my breathing. Turning to Philip, I ask, "Can this X60 fly to Tokyo in less than ten hours?"

"It can do it in five." Pressing my shoulder, he smiles. "Good luck changing her reality."

I lift my brows. "Wait, you read my mind?"

He smiles. "No. I saw this future. You're changing her reality and the outcome of many things." He sighs. "I can't read your mind any longer. Reading your mind would be like staring into the sun." Removing my broken bracelet, he says, "You won't be needing this anymore. You don't even need to snap your fingers. You can summon the core with your mind."

So, this is the power Vincent from the future talked about, the power that meant I wouldn't need the suit and would have the ability to defeat the real enemy. Who is that? What's the outcome of changing Akane's reality?

Philip touches my shoulder. "Soon, you will be the most powerful time corrector, an extension of the core. Chronos made a perfect choice." As he takes in my bloodstained shirt, his eyes well up. "I am sorry," he says softly. Then, he hands me Musashi's sword. "Infused with intreton."

Walking to the emergency hatch, I say, "I need a parachute."

Opening the door, Philip lifts his voice to be heard over the wind's roar. "You don't!"

The wind whips around me as I yell, "Keep the cage ready!"

And then, I jump.

After a few seconds of being thrust forward by the plane's velocity, my body succumbs to gravity. No parachute, my ass. I am free-falling. I can't even keep my eyes open.

Philip, you old fuck. In a few seconds, I will be smashed to bits.

No. I have to see my Emi, be with my Nozo, play with my Hulk, and free Akane. This can't be the end. I love my life. Wow, I have never thought that before. I look at my hands; my body drops upside down through the air.

"C'mon, how do I create turbulence?"

Suddenly, my body starts glowing like a falling meteor, and my head is the brightest part. My hair and head are shimmering white, and the rest of my body shines blue with white sparks. Gliding through the air now, I stare at my glowing hands. Looking up, I don't see the sky we see from Earth. I see wormholes—dark objects spiraling by the shimmering surroundings, colors like my sparks. The whole sky lights up in a number system I have not seen before. This must be the quantum time. So, the core is Earth's connection to quantum time, and I am its keeper and corrector?

But why would I get this power when Akane's life hangs by a thread? I grind my teeth. I don't have a moment to lose.

"Ludwig, navigate me to Hank Von Stein."

After creating turbulence and going through the core, I enter a car junkyard in the middle of a desert. Removing the *katana* from its *saya*, I walk between the rows of rusted cars stacked one over the other.

Looking at the parched land, devoid of trees and smelling the stench of rubber and rust, I ask Ludwig, "Where are we?"

"Ah. Very close to Las Vegas."

The two junkyards of human civilization—this place and Las Vegas. A slight, scorched breeze hits me, spinning sand and dust. As I walk, I hear a thud synchronizing with my walking. I grin.

My breathing gets quicker, and blood rushes to my head as I shout, "Come out, come out! Show yourself."

The stacks of cars start jiggling. A rusty sedan smashes into the ground just two inches ahead of me as I jump back and throw an arm over my eyes against the dust.

"You gotta do much better than a Datsun," I sneer.

Every single car starts dropping to the ground, throwing sand onto my face. Shutting my eyes, I smile. I can predict the movement of each vehicle. I dodge them all without even looking. I open my eyes; it's all dust.

Coughing, I say, "That's better."

Let's bait you.

I continue, "Keep hiding, you coward. You are as worthless as your brother."

A loud thud reverberates through the ground behind me. Sand, shards of metals, and rubber fly by my body. Turning back, through the dust, I see the Jaeger, its eyes glowing.

Inserting the *saya* into my belt loop, I grip the *katana*. Rage boils in my veins as I yell, "You better stay in there. Else you won't have a fighting chance."

He walks toward me—each step a thud, each a memory of what he did to Akane, Ravi, Maddy, Wasim, everyone. Opening the jaw of the Jaeger, he jumps out, bracing himself with his left hand as he hits the ground. He has a massive axe in his other hand, nearly as long as he is tall. Shoving the axe into the ground, he stands up.

Pointing at the axe, I grimace. "It's too big for you."

As the dust clears around him, I see his arms, chest, and thighs have straps, each connected to a glowing switch attached to his chest. Each belted strap has four syringes filled with liquid intreton.

You stole these from Philip's island?

He pushes the switches on his chest, and his veins start to bulge. As he swells larger and larger, I have to keep lifting my head higher to see him. He must be eight feet now. The belts snap as his muscles grow, his skin rippling.

Forming fists, he screams in pain, "Ahhh!"

Yeah, fuckface, your bones can't support that frame.

Huffing, he looks at me and grins. Then, he kicks his heavy Jager sideways, and it flies fifty feet, landing on a few junk cars and smashing them. Looking back at him, he spins the axe in his hand and grinds his teeth.

"C'mon," he growls, his voice deep, saliva dripping from his mouth.

Then, he smashes his free hand on the ground, the force generating a pulse that rattles the ground, shaking the cars and making their alarms go off. Dust whirls around us, and I cover my eyes with my arm.

As the dust and the pulse hit me, a power surge flows into my hands, sparking with strength. Bending my left leg, I swing the *katana* in an arc over my head. I square my body, ready to attack. Gripping his axe, Hank heaves it, swishing it through the air, and charges me. As sand flings up around us from his feet thudding, he strikes me with his axe, first a forward thrust and then a backswing, both at lightning speed. Blinding sparks fly as my *katana* blocks his axe. Our eyes meet—his blue eyes going wide with fear. Aiming for my head, he strikes, grunting. Holding the *tsuka* with my right hand and the back of the blade with my left, I push back Hank's axe.

He won't give in as he pushes harder on his axe, forcing me backward. I let his axe come within two inches of my face. Then, breathing out, I shove him away. He catapults backward and crashes into a pile of cars. As soon as he lands, more cars from the surrounding piles fall onto him, burying him under rusted metal.

Wheezing, I wipe the sweat from my forehead. Metal screeches and groans heavily as Hank pushes himself out from under the pile. He walks toward me slowly.

Five feet away, he raises the axe high and yells, "You killed Rudy!"

"No." I grind my teeth. "Though I could have if I wanted to."

His eyes well up. Wiping them angrily, he shouts, "You killed my mom and dad! You turned us into orphans!"

"Lies!" I yell from the bottom of my lungs, but he still doesn't listen.

Glaring, he circles around me. He takes an arching swing with his axe. As I dodge, he grabs my shirt with his other hand. Dragging me by my shirt, he picks me up and turns me upside down. Groaning, he lifts me over his head and then smashes me to the ground, and I lose my grip on my *katana*.

Kicking the blade away, Hank brings his massive foot down on me. My body bends to his kick. I feel the stinging pain of my ribs cracking before the intreton mending them. Groaning, I spit blood and intreton from my mouth. He lifts his other foot, going for my ribs but then stops. Why? Doesn't matter.

I take the chance to swiftly turn sideways and roll away. Picking up some dirt, I throw a fistful into his eyes. As he grunts in pain and brings his hand to his eyes, I rush to stand, pick up my *katana* and toss my ruined shirt away. Enough.

My skin and hair glow with intreton sparks. Glaring at me, Hank grips his axe tighter, preparing for another strike. I see him in slow motion. I don't even need to predict his moves. Lunging at me, he aims three successive blows. I dodge his first easily, and the axe blade misses my nose by an inch. I can even move my head away before the air from the axe's motion reaches my eyes. Lifting his axe, he goes for the back of my head, but I dodge again. He aims for the top of my head the third time, but the axe blade meets my *katana* as I swing over my head, just in time.

I take a deep breath and surge forward with all my strength, shoving him away with my *katana*. I smirk—my turn. I can feel my *katana* becoming an extension of my arm. After centering myself, I make about twenty attacks in less than a second, each slicing through Hank's flesh. Blood and intreton gush out.

He falls to his knee, gasping for air. And still, he doesn't give up. Taking support from his axe, he tries to stand. I slice his ankle by throwing the *katana* from my right hand to my left. Grunting, he falls to the ground with a deafening thud, throwing dust and dirt up. As I watch, intreton flows from his ankle and heals his wound. He laughs like he laughed when he burned and murdered Miguel and Altaf.

"You are not the only freak."

Suddenly, he lands the axe from his position on the ground, and I evade it by an inch. As his arms swing by, I grab his right hand and crush it against my waist. Inhaling deeply, I jump to the side while still holding his hand, snapping his elbow joint. He screams in pain, shutting his eyes. Before the intreton can mend his joint, I spin my body in a full circle, swinging my *katana*. I sever his right wrist from his arm. Blood and intreton spray all over, splashing against my skin.

Groaning in agony, on his knees, he stares at his severed appendage, holding his right arm with his left hand. As he reaches for his detached hand, I lunge forward and pick it up.

"It's mine," I say with a smirk.

Grinding his teeth, he snarls, "Bastard."

Without access to the intreton in his veins, his severed hand reduces to its normal size. I grab him by his hair. Locking my eyes with his, I clench my jaw.

"Tell me, did you laugh when you killed Ravi? When you murdered Maddy and took the life of an innocent boy?" I bring my *katana*'s blade to his throat, shoving it one centimeter into his flesh. If I kill him, I won't find out who is behind all this.

Exhaling, I create turbulence and then kick Hank into it. Now inside the core without his suit, intreton spurts out of his body. He writhes in pain. Lifting his head by his hair, I stare into his blue eyes. I see flashes of what he's been up to.

You killed Elise? And all those poor souls with her? The Kauffmans and Max? Who kills a dog? I never called Rudy a vandal. Although he was one. Who fucked you up? I see a man in a mask . . . Dina stretches her arms out and calls out, "Please, Mr. J. Leave Hank alone."

Unable to breathe in the core, clutching his throat, Hank gasps. Extending his hand, he pleads, "Kill me."

Putting the tip of my *katana* on his throat, I sneer. "Why did you hesitate to break my ribs a second time?" Shaking his chest belt, I shout, "Who is Mr. J? What does he want?"

With his eyes shut, he mumbles, "My memories . . . all jumbled here. Mr. J . . ." Then, he passes out.

"Ludwig, create the shortest path to Philip's prison."

(Philip's hold)

On the floor, Hank is still unconscious. I hand Philip the severed hand, saying, "Sew it, throw it, I don't care."

Collecting the hand gingerly, Philip says, "Akane is out of danger. I will now transport her to Japan."

I sigh in relief. "Thanks."

He touches my shoulder. "You need a shirt."

(Vincent's home)

I open the door to my home with shaking hands. As I walk in, all eyes fall on me in Philip's shirt, peppered with my blood and intreton. Their faces are blurry through my eyes, soaked with tears, blood, dust, and grime. It's been a long day, and it will still be longer. Hulk runs over to me. I pick him up, and he licks my face. I stare back at everyone.

Please don't ask me anything. I need a moment.

It's 9:00 p.m. Earth time on the West Coast—still April 13.

Everyone begins to speak at once.

"How's Akane?"

"Are you okay?"

"Did you catch him?"

"Can we go home now?"

I don't care who is saying what. Putting Hulk on the floor, I say, "I need a moment." Then, I go upstairs to my bedroom.

Unbuckling the *katana* from my waist, I drop it on the floor. I sit on the edge of the bed, covering my eyes. Jumping on the bed, Hulk sits beside me, placing his paw on my thigh. I know what I must do. Warm hands touch mine and remove them from my eyes. I see Emika staring at me.

Smiling against the warning of all my muscles and the fiber of my soul, I manage, "You couldn't have known."

"It's not about me." She touches my face gently. "I am ready when you are."

I stare into my shaking hands. "I would have gladly lived my life, wrongly convincing myself she hated me—that we did not matter." Grinding my teeth, I whisper, "But she came here to die. She says she'll keep doing it."[79] Tears drop from my eyes. "Now, it has come to this. I have to erase Vince from her."

Emika goes into the bathroom, starts running a bath, and returns. As she unbuttons my shirt, she inhales sharply. "What's that?" she asks, pointing at my torso.

"Vandal's footprint." Puffing, I admit, "He could have killed me. But someone wants me alive."

Pressing her lips together, she takes off my tattered shoes and removes my socks, sobbing quietly as she does so. Unbuttoning my trousers and pulling them off, she instructs, "Stand up." Holding my hand, she leads me to the bathroom. "Get in," she says, pointing at the bathtub.

The jacuzzi tries to relax my muscles and convince me that better days are on the horizon. Lies. Kneeling beside the tub, Emika massages my hair with shampoo and washes it out with a hot water stream from the detachable shower head. The blood, dirt, grime, and metal bits wash away, leaving the memories of love, resentment, and hatred behind. As my breathing turns to sobs, Emika stops the water flow.

Touching my head, she asks, *"Nani?"*

Looking up at her, I say, "Hank killed Elise and over two hundred people in the plane. He killed Dr. Kauffman, her husband, and . . . Max."

---

79 As mentioned in Chapter 1 of this book.

I am not using Markus's name to dissociate your mind from the guy you loved. Maybe you still do.

Her lips wobble. Touching her hand, I say, "Don't blame yourself."

She takes a deep breath, pretending to disregard my comment, and hands me a towel. "Can you dry up?" she asks, bottling her feelings.

"Yes."

As she walks out of the bathroom, she says, "Good. I'll put together your outfit."

A few moments later, wiping my head with the towel, I walk to the suit valet, where a bespoke blue suit and a black mock neck cashmere sweater hang. It's one of the suits made by the Andersons. I saw it in my dream this morning.

Pointing at the suit, I turn to Emika. "You said you'd return those."

Touching my wrist, she uses all her will to smile. "And I would have if I didn't know any better."

"Didn't know what?"

"What it's like to live with a hasty decision." Gripping my wrist, she adds, "I made several of those in 2023 and 2024. Once I buried my anger, I regretted my thoughts, words, and actions."

I love you, Emi. I put on my trousers and sweater and ask, "Is Nozo sleeping?"

"You want me to wake her up?"

"Nope."

Gently, I open Nozo's door and tiptoe near her crib. Bending down, I kiss her forehead, chubby fingers, and tummy. Lifting the blanket, I kiss her little toes.

If I am not back, then just know that Papha loves you.

As I leave the room, she asks in a sleepy voice, "When will you be back?"

"Soon."

"With my baby dragon?"

"Of course."

Closing the door behind me, I see Emika sitting on the floor, weeping, her hand covering her face. Sensing me, she looks up.

"No one knows where Frida is," she says.

Taking her right hand in mine, I help her stand and then bring her head to my shoulder. "It's Dina," I remind her, running my hand over her hair. "I will find out where she is and who is behind all this."

She pulls her head back to look at me. "How?"

"I will be in the core for two days."

Her eyes widen in fear. "That's too long. Will you be okay?" Touching my face, she whispers, "Just say yes."

I kiss her head. "There is a folder in every cloud drive called 'Just in case.'"

Pushing me, she looks at me with her wet eyes. "No," she sobs, lips trembling. Her voice becomes firmer as she lifts her finger and repeats, "No."

Giving her half a smile, I say, "If I get delayed beyond April 15, you will find details of every invested dollar in that folder." I pull her close and stare into her eyes, absorbing every last detail. "It's all yours. Nozo's trust fund is there, too."

She punches my chest and then fists my sweater. "No."

As we climb down the stairs, everyone stands up. I scan their faces. "I will redo forty-five years, which will take me two days. Emika will fill you in."

They all start looking at each other in confusion. And then, the questions begin.

"When will you be back?"

"Which forty-five years?"

"Where is your bracelet?"

"Can you not go?"

"How is Akane?"

"Don't you need a suit?"

"Does Philip know?"

I lift my hand. "Please." The room grows silent. "I will cover this house with an intreton shield."

With his brows up, Chris asks, "Why?"

Sighing in exhaustion, I explain, "If I don't, your realities may change, even if the core selects the path of least resistance." I kiss Emika's head. "I don't want her reality to change again. If I don't meet her . . . our Nozo will cease to exist." Even the thought makes it hard to breathe. "If I don't meet Emika, Quantum World won't exist." Looking at Fred, Krista, and Sasha, I say, "If I don't cover this house with intreton, you will all forget

Akane . . . and I want you to remember her, though she won't remember us if I succeed."

Fred smiles. "Us, we understand." Then, he scoffs. "But good luck making her forget you."

Wrapping her arms around teary-eyed Emika, Sasha assures her, "Vince will be fine."

"Good luck," Krista says, kissing my cheek.

Bringing her close, I whisper, "Emika will break as soon as I leave. Please be with her."

"You needn't have said it," she whispers back.

Anna is tapping her foot, waiting for her turn. Rolling my eyes, I address her doubt before she can voice it. "If I don't come back by the afternoon of the fifteenth, Philip will remove the intreton covering, and you can leave."

Frowning, she asks, "How did you know my question?"

"The freaky creep knows," I tell her, winking.

Tabi and Chris take turns hugging me. Emika wraps Akane's scarf around me.

"Why?" I ask her.

Pulling me close, she sobs, "It might get cold."

And then, I let her go and walk out the door. Closing my eyes, I let pulses of sparks come out of my body, slowly covering 100 Summit Drive, layer upon layer, like a labyrinth of crystals made of lightning. I look up at my work. Yes, that'll do. Our home, now separated from reality, will stand the test of time.

I see everyone in our home staring out at me from the windows. A gate resembling a wormhole surrounded by numbers of quantum time glowing white-blue opens up before me. I turn back and wave.

Emi, I am sorry I won't be with you when you break. But I will be with you for the remainder of my life if I return.

(Powder room)

<u>Emika</u>

Locking the door to the powder room, I stare at my face in the mirror. I had kept everything bottled for hours, waiting for Vincent to return with Akane. It's trying to crawl up from my stomach. It's choking my throat.

My hands shake, and I gasp for breath.

You were faking it all along, Markus. The dates, the nights, your touches, your kisses. Damn, at first, I even hoped Nozo was yours. When you said you loved me, was that a lie? I slept with a murderer. You almost killed my Vince. Was meeting me, loving me, all a ploy to get to Vince? But you didn't need to do all that. Tell me, what is my role in this treachery? You made me an accomplice. Why did you kill Elise? An attached Vince wouldn't have left her, and none of this would have happened.

My face turns red as the veins in my forehead bulge.

How could I even think of replacing Vince with you? I wish I had never met you, Markus. You murderer, liar, creep. How dare you put your filthy hands all over me? You killed children, and I let you come close to my Nozo. You killed a dog, and I let you near Hulk.

I can't seem to take a breath. Sitting with my legs folded up, I lay my head on my knees and tighten my arms around my legs. I slept with someone who electrocuted two people and made a video of it. I slept with the person who killed Ravi, Maddy, and Wasim.

Wasim was just a child, like Nozo. You couldn't even spare a child? I want my Vincent to rip you apart slowly.

My lips wobble.

And when he does that, I won't even shed a tear for you. Do you hear me? I don't care what made you like this.

Then, I stand up again and lean against the marble vanity sink.

No, I won't cry for you.

Breathing hard, exhaling in absolute anger, I swipe my hands across the counter, throwing the porcelain soap dish, the perfume dispenser—everything—to the floor where they all shatter. I curl my hands into fists and squeeze my eyes tight, but tears still slide out.

"No. I won't shed a tear for you." Hitting the vanity, I screech, "Fuck you!" As my voice echoes in the powder room, I hear a knock on the door.

"Are you okay?" asks Krista.

Quickly, I flush the toilet and turn on the faucet. Wiping my eyes and clearing my throat, I say, "All good. Be right there."

CHAPTER 16

REVELATION—STAGE 3

You have always hidden, and I sought you. That reality has to change. Today,
it's my turn to hide, and I don't want you to seek me until you are safe
—Vincent

Across Timelines and Realities

(April 14, 2027—Egami residence)

Vincent

"I HAVE NO CHOICE." I DIG my nails into my palms, clenching my jaw, trying to hide my feelings about Akane not remembering me.

Shaking me by my shoulder, Theresa shrieks, "Extract yourself? How could you? She woke up looking for you."

I fall to my knees. Looking up at Akane's parents through my teary eyes, I give in. "I don't want to do this . . . but I have to. It's my fault."

Kneeling, Theresa brings my head to her shoulder. As my tears wet her cotton yukata, she runs her fingers through my hair. "Why do you always blame yourself?" she asks.

I wish I knew. Maybe because I am the common factor for everything that's gone wrong? Pulling away and standing up, I state, "I need to give you something." Reaching into my pocket, I pull out the five-carat Kashmir sapphire ring Philip helped me procure. Sniffling, I hand it to Masayoshi. "I will be back in two days, but it will be 1987 in your time. Your realities will change." Pointing at the ring, I state, "But this will jog your memory."

He smiles, though his eyes tear up as he shows the ring to Theresa. Then, they both look at me in confusion.

Giving them a helpless smile, I touch my chest. "I would have given it to her under different circumstances." Gripping Masayoshi's hand, I insist, "Keep it where only the three of us will know. Somewhere you don't need to access every day, but that has been with you for a long time."

Theresa leaves the room and returns with a Japanese gold dust-encrusted lacquer box with hand-painted sakura blossoms on the lid. "This is a family heirloom—a gift from Emperor Hirohito," she explains.

I put the ring inside the box and then cover it with an intreton shield. I explain as they stare in amazement at the sparks from my fingers, "This will make it reality-proof. Only I can open it. And when I do, it will jog your memory of the future from a different reality." My voice cracks. "This reality."

Touching my hands, Theresa asks, "Why do you love her so much?"

"She was by my side when she could have been anywhere else." I sniffle, my eyes welling with tears. "She was my home when I was an orphan."

You are still my home.

Pulling my scarf, I add, "She tied this around me when she didn't have to."

Touching my scarf, Theresa looks at Masayoshi. "She always wore that since she was five. But we don't remember who gave it to her."

"That's right," confirms Masayoshi.

I walk toward the door. Turning back, I smile. "See you in two days but forty years in the past, when Akane will be just five, and I will be older than you."

(Core)

My hands are shaking, and my forehead is dripping with sweat as I stand outside the door marked "Akane." This door towers above all the other doors. I can't see the top, even tilting my head back ninety degrees. I smirk. Its stature is no challenge. If I can bring myself to this point—erasing myself from her—nothing is a challenge. I turn the doorknob.

As I enter, the door transforms into a scarlet *torii* gate. Right in front of me is a red, arched bridge—a *soribashi*—with crystal clear water underneath, gurgling in the current. Around the bridge are trees radiating with fall colors—red, orange, and yellow. The leaves are gently shedding, slowly covering the lush green floor with autumn colors as they fall.

Over the bubbling of the water and the whistling of the wind, I hear the sobbing of a child. A little girl is sitting next to a dead cherry tree. She is the one sobbing. I know that voice, that hair. She is my Akane, only nine years old. She is wearing a bespoke gray overcoat over a floral dress and crimson shoes—the same outfit she wore when she left for Berlin. Beside her is the sketch I drew for her, and she is knitting something that looks like a stuffed toy.

I sit next to her, and she turns to me. Her moist eyes glow as she asks, "*Anata wa dare desu ka?*"[80]

"*Tomodachi desu.*"[81] Then, pointing at the stuffed toy, I ask, "What are you knitting?"

My heart aches as she hands me the toy. It's a plush version of me when I was about eight. My voice trembles as I ask, "Who is he?"

Taking the toy back, she hugs it tight, shutting her eyes. Then, opening her tear-filled eyes, she whispers, "*Watashi no* Vincent. I am lost, and I miss him."

I wipe her cheeks with my pocket square. "Lost where?"

"I went to see a clock, and now, I can't wake up."

---

[80] Who are you?

[81] A friend.

"What do you want to do when you wake up?" I ask, kissing her forehead.

"I'll find Vince."

Shutting my eyes, I swallow hard to hide the tremble in my voice. "Where?"

"Here," says Akane.

She sounds different. Opening my eyes, I see an adult Akane, radiant as ever, dressed in a pink floral kimono with a burgundy obi. I am sitting on a raised platform opposite the *ema* stand near Kiyomizu-dera. It's spring. The dead cherry tree has come alive, the sakura has bloomed, and the petals are gently filling the ground with what she so lovingly told me were pink snowflakes.

She offers her hand. "Come with me."

As I take her hand, the sky lights up with fireworks—yellow, green, blue, and red, like gigantic, luminous flowers, as far as my eyes can see.

Looking back at Akane, I say, "This never happened when we were here."

Squeezing my hand, she smiles. "In my mind, it did."

Endless rows of *torii* gates spring up from the petal-covered ground. It looks like that *Fushimi Inari Taisha.*

She points at the *torii* gates. "These are my memories." Sniffling, she wipes her eyes. "Can you guess what's common in them?"

"No," I lie.

"I know why you are here." She clasps her hands together and pleads, "Can you not do it? It's not worth living without knowing you."

I place my hands on her shoulders. "A second's delay, and I would've lost you. I can't take it anymore. I can't relive the past thirty-three years." Sniffling, I stress, "I won't."

Reluctantly, she smiles. "Well, it will be my love versus your will."

"And what's driving my will?" I retort, giving her a half-smile.

Taking my hand, she says, "I will only take you to just a few *torii* gates." She shrugs. "Maybe you will change your mind."

She takes me through the first *torii* gate. Beyond the *torii*, she opens a door, where I see little Akane and little Vincent sharing a bowl of ice cream. There's a memory screen between them and us, something only I can pass as a time corrector.

Akane reveals, "This memory kept me going when I was in the turbulence in one reality and in a coma in another."

Pointing at the surroundings around the young versions of us—pink cherry trees, white flurries, bright autumn, and lush green summer grass—I ask, "What's all this?"

She dabs the corners of her eyes with her fingers. "Preserving the memory across seasons." Looking into my eyes, she says, "Oh! Don't cry yet."

Pulling me by my hand, she takes me through another *torii*. I see little Akane practicing her violin with Fred, Krista, and Sasha in the audience.

"Why am I not there?" I ask her.

"It was the surprise composition for your birthday." Putting her hands on her hips, she rolls her eyes. "You being there would have ruined it." Her lips tremble as she smiles at the scene. "It wasn't easy to mix notes from Zigeunerweisen and Meditation to make 'Happy Birthday.'" Her eyes brighten as she nudges me. "At the final moment, when I played it for you, I did not realize what I felt—I was only nine—but I knew I wanted to be with you all the time."

Pulling my hand, she says, "Come." She takes me through another *torii*, one among the thousands I see now. Through this one, I see myself lying on the infirmary bed, Akane holding my hand and resting her head on it.

Pulling her kimono sleeve, I ask, "What's going on in your mind?"

"That was the first time I prayed. I couldn't believe how someone would just come to listen to my violin, despite broken ribs and blood gushing from his nose."

"It wasn't just the music," I confess. "But I didn't know what it was until much later."

She locks her eyes with mine. "I just couldn't bear to see you shivering." She touches my scarf and says, "So, I wrapped this around you." She sniffles. "When I first saw your large, green, and blue eyes in 1989, you looked like someone from my past, an adult—someone who gave me the scarf in the first place." She shakes my shoulder and admits, "I think I may have called him silly." She stares at me and adds, "But I have no concrete memory of this. Neither do my parents."

Then, she pulls me to another *torii*. Inside this one, I see an eight-year-old Akane sitting in the bedroom of the Mandarin Oriental Penthouse in London. She is weeping, holding a stuffed toy resembling me. The room is dimly lit, and it's raining outside. Masayoshi wraps his arms around her while Theresa, climbing down from the bed, sits on her knees.

Holding little Akane's hands, Theresa asks, "How about we bring him with us next time?"

The sun peeks through the window as Theresa nudges Masayoshi's hand. "Say something, Masa."

Little Akane looks up. "Papha?"

Masayoshi visibly melts, kisses his daughter's head, and confirms, "Vincent *wa kazoku desu.*"

As Akane's eyes light up, the room transforms into a spring cherry tree garden.

"This is how I felt that day," adult Akane explains, gesturing at the changing scene. "The next day, I asked Papha to buy you that blue tux."

Pulling my sleeve, she takes me through another gate, leading to the exact moment she returned to me—radiating in her blue jumpsuit. The falling snowflakes turn pink and transform into cherry petals as I come out of my door. She is also surrounded by red and yellow fall foliage against a spotless, white winter backdrop.

Touching my shoulder, Akane tells me, "When I saw you that day, I felt the beauty of all four seasons." She takes a deep breath. "Brace yourself."

Then, she pulls me to another gate. Beyond the memory screen, she is on a video conference with Fred, Krista, and Sasha.

Resolutely, the Akane beyond the door says, "I've made up my mind. I will ask him on April 15."

Leaning toward their respective screens, Fred, Krista, and Sasha request in tandem, "In Copenhagen?"

Turning to me, Akane in kimono squints. "Why did they insist on Copenhagen?" She points at the memory. "Those three wouldn't tell."

I take her hands and look into her eyes. "I wanted to ask you on the same day—the day we wrote the *ema*. But then, you left me in tatters."

"I was shattered, too."

I scoff, "Really?"

You moved on rather quickly.

She pulls my hand. "Come with me."

At this gate, I see Akane in her maroon suit, sitting on the floor with a bottle of Screaming Eagle 1991 cabernet. She is murmuring to herself.

"I have waited so long and can't wait any longer. We will have a house in the US and one in Japan. Will you marry me, Vincent?" She puts a hand behind her ear. "I'm sorry, what?" Shaking her head, she asks, "You can't? Why? You knocked up a girl? Wow! And you thought she was me?" Her tears drip from her chin. "*Omoshiroi.*" Her shoulders shake as she looks up. "Look what you've done to me, Vince."

I place a hand over my heart, feeling a sharp pain. Taking a breath, I put my palm against the memory screen.

She squints and asks, "Is that you, Vince?" She stands up and comes close to the memory screen. She can't pierce through it, but I can, yet I am hesitating. "Where are you? Please come to me," she says, rushing around the room, looking around all the corners.

The Akane standing beside me pulls my sleeve. "Why didn't you come?"

"You told me not to," I scowl.

Shaking her head, she admits, "I didn't mean it. Ever."

Then, she pulls me to another gate. Pointing at the memory, she reveals, "My worst memory." She bends her head. "I am sorry."

Beyond the memory screen, I see Akane and Sawano staring at a camera as the television show host asks, "So, your friend Vincent is a struggling businessman and media whore?"

Turning to Akane, I ask, "Is that what you think I am?"

She is silent, yet she digs her nails into my palms. Removing my hand, I say, pointing at the memory screen, "I will ask her."

As soon as I walk through the memory screen, the Akane in the studio looks away from the camera and stares into my eyes. Sawano can't see me; it's not his memory. Akane lifts her brows and tilts her head.

What are you looking at, Akane? Come on, answer the question.

Sawano, without realizing what's happening, wraps his arms around Akane and says, "*Hanashite o kudasai,*" pointing at the camera.

Running her fingers under her eyes, Akane pushes her tears in. She cracks a broken smile and speaks in a shaking voice. "Yes, he is sort of a media whore."

I turn away and walk back through the memory screen. Here, Akane says, "I knew I saw you."

Grabbing her shoulders, I demand, "How could you replace my photo with Sawano, even if you love him?"

"*Gomennasai.* Because in Kyoto, you said, 'Attached, unattached, this silly is always yours.'" Tears spill from her eyes. "That's not fair to Nozo or Emika." Her voice breaks as she confesses, "I tarnished your name by a smidgen to make you forget me, to make you stop texting me . . . maybe even hate me, so you would become what's needed for Nozo and Emika." She locks her eyes with mine. Blinking her tears, she admits, "Sawano means nothing to me."

"What?"

She shows me the inside of her Tokyo apartment by taking me to another *torii* gate.

Clicking her tongue, Akane says to Sawano. "*Ima nani?*"

"*Sumimasen, demo daisuki desu,*" he mumbles.

Grinding her teeth, she yells, "*Daisuki desu? Omae wa bakadeska?*" As she stands, the cord to her satin robe comes loose. Bending his head, Sawano takes a peek.

Fisting my hands, I turn to the Akane next to me. "How dare he peek like this?"

"Perv," she says, shrugging.

Holding her robe, Akane screams, "Get out! Before I chop you to pieces."

Sawano wipes his forehead and collects the duffel bags.

Taking off my belt, I cross the memory screen and hit Sawano's leg. As he trips, the Akane wearing the kimono giggles, while the Akane in the penthouse narrows her eyes as I quickly leave the scene.

Tapping her chin, Akane mutters, "I always wondered how he managed to trip." Then, she asks, "Why did you do that?"

"I don't want anyone to look at you like that," I say, shaking my head.

Winking, she asks, "You got jealous?"

I look into her eyes. "I never stopped loving you . . . I tried, though." Taking her hand, we sit by the *ema* stand, residing in the core through her memory. "But I have to do this. You were the target for the April 13 attack."

"What?"

"Someone who knows how you feel about me knew that you'd throw yourself over me to save me. I can't let that happen. I almost lost you." I shake her by her shoulders. "I can't take any more risks."

She tugs my lapel and glares at me. "It's not for you to decide how I live my life."

It is for me to decide; you are my Akane. I have to persuade you in a different direction.

I grip her wrists. "You told me you woke up from a coma in an unchanged world in terms of acceptance, right?"

"So?" she asks, still glaring at me.

Gently removing her hands from my lapel, I say, "Imagine what you can do if those years are given back to you. You can be an inspiration in a country plagued by patriarchy and monoethnicity. Show them what Akane—a brilliant, biracial girl—can do." I touch her cheek. "With time in your hands, you will be the CEO of Egami—no more threats from your worthless cousins, whose only qualification is possession of a dick." My lips wobble, and I press them together tightly to control the tremble in my voice before continuing, "There'll be just one difference. You won't know your Vince until I know you are safe from Vandal." I bring my thumb and index finger together. "But that's a tiny price."

She leans over me. Narrowing her eyes to slits, she shrieks, "Tiny?"

"You wouldn't even know it." I kiss her forehead.

Her shoulders shake as she sobs, "Not. Fair."

"I know." I must promise something in return, something that's unlikely to happen. Got it. Wiping her tears with my thumbs, I say, "Okay. If we meet and you realize who I am, I will return the memories to you."

She wraps her arms around me. "What about the photo album?"

"That, too."

As I begin to walk away, she pulls my hand. "What?" I ask, turning back.

"If I ever remember you, I will look for you by the *ema* stand every April 15."

My voice quivers. "Okay."

I can't conceive why that date will be relevant after today.

As I cross the *torii* gate in front of the door marked "Akane," she says, "You know I can't leave this door to stop you, right?"

I turn back to her again. "Yes."

"If you made up your mind, why did you come and speak to me?"

"Because I love you."

Her voice cracks. "Can I kiss you?"

"Since when do you ask?"

She runs to me, locking her lips with mine. Her tears wet my cheeks.

I can't cry, Akane. If I do, I can't do what I must.

I wrap my arms around her waist.

I don't wanna let you go, but I have to.

Pulling away, she looks up at me. "I won't wish you all the best."

"Noted."

Beyond her, I see every version of Akane I have known—the one who first came to my class, the one who played violin, the one who tied the scarf around me, the one I shared ice cream with, the one who called me family, the one who prayed for me, the one who left, the one who came back, the one in Copenhagen—each brighter than the last. But the one who shines the most is the one in the floral kimono by the *ema*.

You won't make it easy for me, will you?

As I open the door, she says, "One last time. *Anata o aishiteimasu.*"

I look into her eyes. "*Watashi mo itsumo.*" Across all realities.

Then, I quickly close the door behind me. Breathing hard, I sit by the door and press my hand over my thumping heart; it has had enough. It's screaming, *Don't do it.*

Beyond the door, Akane's voice whispers, "Don't go."

But I have to, even if I don't want to. No matter the consequences.

You have always hidden, and I sought you. That reality has to change. Today, it's my turn to hide, and I don't want you to seek me until you are safe.

I scoff. This is what it has come to. Touching the door, I say, "Farewell, my love." Rasping, I absorb all my emotions and doubts.

My phone vibrates—a message from Philip.

Philip: She is safe in Tokyo. Resting. Good luck.

Me: Thanks.

There's no going back now. She will wake up to a different reality—where she is the CEO of Egami and doesn't know who I am. Now, how can I take myself out of Akane? Where do I begin? I am everywhere, in every corner of her mind. Every memory leads to a tapestry of more memories, leading to only me. How did it all start?

I wipe my eyes with my sleeve. I have to create turbulence inside this core, which will engulf all of Akane from here. But this turbulence may leak out of the core. I can't do this alone.

A wrinkled hand appears before me, and a voice deep enough to shake mountains says, "I will help you."

Grasping the hand, I stand up and ask, "Why, Chronos?"

"How can I not?" he admits. Then, he bangs on the floor with his scythe three times.

Zeus with his thunderbolt, Hades with his spear, and Poseidon with his trident appear. Hitting his spear on the ground, Hades says, "We will help you contain it." There are no smirks on their faces today.

My entire body starts to shine a brilliant white-blue. I can see the past and the future all converge. Bringing my hands together, I combine the sparks. I extend my arms, bringing them together and then expanding them again. The sparks create a deep white noise that resonates through the entire core. It pierces my ears, but I can't stop.

Chronos's scythe, Zeus's thunderbolt, Hades's spear, and Poseidon's trident multiply and create an impenetrable wall of weapons. The sparks touch them, then bounce back to me, and I make them bigger and denser. The light pierces my eyes, but I don't need to shut them. I see the entire quantum time inside this turbulence. I turn toward the door bearing the name synonymous with my life. I direct the whole ball of sparks, and they penetrate the door. My heart is punching my rib cage. The turbulence needs to reach every corner of the room, every memory of Akane linked with me. The force of the turbulence is pushing me back. Putting my left leg behind me, I bend my right leg and brace them both.

Grinding my teeth, I shove with everything I have. "How long?" I ask Chronos.

"A little bit more. Don't give up."

The turbulence stops, and everything goes still. The white noise turns to utter silence. Looking at my hands, I see strings of sparks change to luminous ropes.

"Pull!" Zeus shouts.

I tug the ropes of sparks, and the door and the room shatter into millions of pieces. Then, each piece becomes a part of the ball of sparks, increasing it to twice my size. As I walk close to the sphere, I see no Akane in it; it's all me through her eyes. Images of me from the first time she saw me in Montagnola to right before Vandal attacked us are orbiting around the *ema* stand surrounded by an endless number of cherry trees. That's her subconscious mind? Me?

Why? What have I done to deserve this?

As I touch the sphere, it starts shrinking. I pick it up when it gets to the size of a tennis ball. Its luminance rivals what it represents—Akane.

Looking at the gods, I wipe my eyes and say, "Thank you, gentlemen."

"Never thought you'd go through with it," Hades admits.

Holding the orb against my chest, I give him a broken smile. "Neither did I."

As I absorb the sphere into me, my skin glows. I fall to my knees and stare at my glowing hands. My tears, now the color of my sparks, drip into my palms. I look up at Chronos blankly.

Shutting my eyes, I form fists and yell, "What have I done? How could I do this?"

For the last five months, I wished she had never come back. How can I even think like that about her? Grinding my teeth, I punch the ground. It shakes and cracks, and the white-blue intreton underneath erupts like magma. I turn to Chronos and his sons.

"Look what I did, guys. I spent thirty-three years of my life just waiting for her." I strike the ground again, and more intreton erupts. "She finally found me . . . and in return, I destroyed all of it. In seconds." I stare into my trembling hands and then look up at Chronos and his sons. Clenching my fists, grinding my jaws, I ask, "What power is this? That removes the loved ones from me." I screech, from the bottom of my lungs, "Answer me? " Striking the ground, I scoff, "My life is now a cosmic joke without her." Chronos and his sons inch closer to me. Staring at Chrono's teary eyes, I demand. "Why did you pick me?"

Touching my heart, still glowing with Akane's memory, Chronos says, "That's why."

"I want none of it."

"That's another reason," Hades explains.

Lifting both my hands, I smash them against the ground. "I want none of it!" I keep hitting the floor as the intreton underneath mixes with the intreton in my tears. Defying gravity, the droplets rise. I keep looking at them with my eyes wide open, my mouth agape. Tilting my head back almost ninety degrees, I see the gravity-defying intreton converging into a mushroom cloud above us. And it stays like that.

As I stand up and exhale in relief, Zeus, touching Poseidon's and Hades's shoulders, says, "Any moment now."

Any moment what? My heart pounds with dread as a crackling sound emits from the intreton cloud. Lightning breaks from the cloud. The streaks combine, more streaks appear, and then they merge again. My eyes widen with wonder and fear.

I turn to Chronos. "What is this?"

Moving his index finger across the endless sky within the core, he reveals, "It's the chain reaction of time across realities."

Every streak joins and forms a blinding white flare, and I shut my eyes. Earsplitting thunder follows, and I fall to my knees, covering my ears. The blinding white light flashes behind my closed eyelids. I can feel the pulse of deep thunder as it thrums through my entire body. Slowly, I open my eyes and see my reflection on the intreton over the cracked floor. My eyes glitter in emerald green, and my hair is as white as the lightning I just saw. Shaking my head, I again see Vincent as I know him.

So, this is the power Philip and future me foretold?

Standing up, pointing at the intreton cloud, I ask Chronos, "What just happened?"

He puts his hand on my shoulder. "For over two years, you have been creating short turbulences inside the core for your journeys." Pointing at the cloud from my turbulence, he states, "This one was different—too long . . ." Locking his eyes with mine, he starts again. "Remember when you asked what caused the turbulences in the lives of Victor Constantin and Oliver Journe, and I said action in the future?"

Bringing my hand to my mouth in shock, I ask, "I caused it?" I touch my chest and look at the cracked floor. "Like, right now?"

"Your sorrow . . . an action in the future created a rupture across time, space, and reality. The path from different realities crossed, and turbulences occurred. I couldn't reveal it when you first asked me after freeing Emika." Bending his head, he says, "You are one with the core now—an extension of each other. You are the most powerful time corrector since Arne and me."

So, this is the outcome Philip talked about just before I jumped from his plane? He knew all along, yet he did not stop me. Why?

❋

(Reality 1, 1970)
(Le Mans Arena)

Victor Constantin

The crowd goes mad with thunderous cheers, whistles, and applause as Porsche ends the dominance of the Ford GT40. I spread my arms in joy, yelling, "Yes!"

My beautiful Amara throws herself into my arms. Tilting her head and locking her Turkish-blue eyes with mine, she asks, "Why are we happy?"

"Porsche won."

"So?"

"It's Oliver Journe's team. The guy who bought my painting." Holding her hand, I ask, "Hey, wanna go near the winning team? Maybe we can catch a glimpse of Mr. Journe?"

"Sure."

As we start to dodge through the crowd and move toward the winning team, the sky darkens, and white-blue lightning strikes from the clouds, followed by the deepest thunder. I cover my ears. What kind of thunder is that?

Staring at the sky and pulling my sleeve, Amara says, "Let's get back to the hotel. We can thank him later."

"You're right."

"What time is it?" she asks.

I look at my Speedmaster. "It's not ticking." I keep winding the watch, tapping on the hesalite case. My heart almost stops. This watch signifies my love and career. I touch Amara's cheek and say, "You go back to the hotel. Let me see if I can find a watch technician."

❋

(Hotel lobby)

"Keys for Victor Constantin, please?"

"Please sign here," instructs the concierge while opening the register.

Wait, whose name is above mine? Oliver Journe?

A group of people shouts, "There they are!"

I see the Porsche team surrounded by fans, journalists, and photographers. Taking the key to my room, I rush toward the crowd. Touching a man's shoulder, I ask, "Do you know where Oliver Journe is?"

Smiling, he points at the elevator.

As the elevator is about to close, I stretch my hand out and shout, "Wait!"

Someone inside holds the door as I rush toward it, dodging three people and almost tripping. Why can't I move anymore? Looking over my shoulder, I see a spiral wind that glows white and blue—the color of the lightning an hour before—coming toward me. I fall and try to crawl away as my legs and waist crumble to ashes. I try to grab the pieces and put them back, but as I stare at my hands, they wither away like ash in the wind.

Closing my eyes, I whisper, "Amara, I wish I had one more minute with you."

(Reality 2, 1969–1980)

(1969—Yvon Lambert Gallery)

Oliver Journe

I am standing before the painting titled *Ressuscité du feu et des cendres*. The woman depicted looks so familiar, but I don't know her. I tap my chin and smile. Maybe if I buy the painting, then I'll meet her.

(1970—Le Mans)

As I join the drivers in spraying champagne, the sky darkens suddenly. We all look up, seeing white-blue lightning. What time is it? I look at my Rolex Daytona. The seller said it would never stop if I kept wearing it.

I show the watch to my friend. "Can you believe it?" I quip. "Horological excellence, indeed. All the hype . . ."[82]

Against the backdrop of the thunderous cheering, he shouts, "There is a watch repair shop nearby."

(Accident)

Pressing the clutch, I move to fifth gear. The Porsche roars as I breathe in. The sky darkens, and beneath the clouds, lightning appears—the same color as the day we won at Le Mans. Damn, I never collected the watch. As I look ahead, the road bends. I have never seen this road before, but I was here just yesterday.

The sun hides behind the mountains, and everything turns dark. I shut my eyes against a pair of high beam headlights. Where did they come from? I press my brakes hard . . .

My face is wrapped in gauze, and I am lying in an emergency vehicle. Through the open doors, I see my car and an upside-down Saab in flames. The flashing blue, red, and yellow lights of emergency vehicles mix with their blaring sirens, overwhelming my senses. I shut my eyes and cover my ears.

"Please relax your facial muscles, sir," a nurse tells me. "The burned tissue will never heal otherwise."

---

[82]   The word Rolex is derived from Ho**ROL**ogical **EX**cellence.

(Hospital)

Hammering on the bedside table, stretching my jaws as much as I can, hurting to the point of tearing the healed skin, I yell, "Bring me a mirror!" A nurse rushes in and hands me a handheld mirror.

I look into the glass. As I touch my face, tears stream from my eyes. I am nothing but a fragment of what I was.

Touching my shoulder, the head of the Porsche race team assures me, "We will pay for restorative surgery, Oliver."

"I don't need it," I say, grinding my teeth. "This is a constant reminder of who is responsible." I form a fist. "One day, I will find who did this to me." Calming my breathing, I ask the team head, "Who are the other accident victims?"

(Prague Astronomical Clock)

As I push Iman's wheelchair, she turns to me and smiles. "Why do you wear a mask to cover your burns? There is no shame in showing your scars, Oliver."

"I know. You're right."

I keep saying, "Please excuse us," as I continue to push Iman's wheelchair through the crowd. People part, and I see the back of Philip Nardin. Ten more feet, and we will be in the front row. Wait. Why can't I push her wheelchair?

Turning back, Iman asks, "What's wrong?"

My leg muscles bulge as I push as hard as I can. "I can't move the wheelchair. It's stuck." Looking up, I see that same lightning—white and blue. The people behind us start shouting in panic.

"Help us!"

"What's happening?"

In front of us, Philip Nardin remains indifferent. He is so deep into fixing the clock, unaware of what's happening. As if he is in a different reality from us. Pulling my face down to her, Iman kisses me. She smiles against her tears.

"I guess this is it. I wish we'd had a long life together."

And then, a white-blue spark sucks us in.

(Current Reality—1970)

Philip Nardin

As I unlock the store's door, the owner of the patisserie next door asks, "Did you see the race yesterday?"

"Nah. I was out of town. But it's nice to have a new champion. Who knows if Porsche will win again?"

I sit in my chair, open the desk drawer, and glance through the offer letter from JLC. I sigh.

"Some dreams don't convert. I am doomed to die in this horrible place."

Wake up, Phil. There are job orders. What do we have?

A Rolex Daytona and an Omega Speedmaster. Owners: Victor Constantin and Oliver Journe.

I've heard these names before. Where? I close my eyes and press my temples in pain. Damn migraines.

(Back to the core)

Vincent

Bringing my hands to my head, I widen my eyes in horror. "So, I am the architect of all these destructions?"

Dodging Chronos, Hades, and Poseidon, future Vincent comes forward and touches my shoulder. He assures me, "I wouldn't use those exact words."

"I ruined the lives of Victor and Oliver," I say, my voice shaking.

"Unknowingly," he reassures me, pressing my shoulders. "Your action needs no justification."

Removing his hand, I lunge back. "Philip did so much for me, despite what I did to him. He deserves all my powers."

Smiling, he admits, "He did." Squinting, he says, "But don't jump to conclusions about the powers. In a few minutes, you will know a lot more." His eyes glisten as he says, "There are a few more doors you need to visit. Beginning with this one." He points to the one on his right, marked "Emika."

Looking around, I ask, "Where is Estrid?"

Estrid peeks out from behind future Vincent. Then, she comes forward and, standing on her tiptoes, kisses my cheek.

Holding her hand, I ask her, "Please don't enter Akane. Please let her be." My voice trembles. "There has to be some rationale behind my accidental crime. Her freedom is the reason by which I can justify everything. Please."

Estrid wipes my tears. "You think Akane loves you because I was in her?"

"No?"

"She was already looking for you when I found her," she tells me. "I never entered her or decided to stop searching for Arne."

"How could she be looking for me?"

Pulling my scarf, she says, "Maybe it's this."

"It's hers."

She tilts her head and smiles. "Is it?" She turns and walks away.

"What do you mean?" I yell after her.

(Emika's door)

Beyond the memory screen is a hospital room. The date on my wristwatch changes to reflect the reality of the room—November 15, 2024, Nozo's birthday, and the day Akane returned.

As Markus leaves the room, Emika stares at Nozo and smiles. Pointing at Markus, she whispers, "A few days here and there, and he could have been your papha." Kissing Nozo, she smiles. "I wanted him to be your papha."

Maybe that's the life you always wanted, and I got in the way.

As I cross the memory curtain, she turns to me. Her smiling lips contradict her teary eyes. "I am sorry for breaking up with you and letting someone else take your place. I thought you moved on, so I didn't stay on August 15." I wipe her eyes. Placing her hand over mine, she says, "I was standing at the crossroads."

I touch her head and smile. "You are never an imposition. Just hang in there. When the petals fall, I'll be back home—just a day for me but two years and five months for you."

Before leaving, I turn back to her. "Emi?"

"Yes?"

"The crossroads. . . it will always plague both of us. But can we work around it?"

"I want to."

✺

(Von Stein twins' door)

I enter the door marked "Von Stein Twins." My watch shows it's the year 2000. Beyond the memory screen, I see a little nine- or ten-year-old child on a bed, writhing in pain. His entire body is connected to tubes, pushing intreton into his veins.

A masked man orders a masked doctor, "More intreton. He can take it."

"Please, Mr. J, leave Hank be," a little girl pleads, tugging the masked man's trousers.

That's Dina—the nervous Frida.

Mr. J slaps Dina, and she falls, holding her cheek. Pointing his finger at little Dina, he says, "Never interrupt me, you little shit."

Hank wiggles in pain, trying to free himself. "Leave Dina alone. Push more intreton. Just don't hurt her." His mouth starts to foam as he says, "I beg you, Mr. J, I will do anything for you."

"That's my good boy." Mr. J rubs Hank's head. Turning to a nurse, he instructs, "Give my favorite Dina some cinnamon candies." Then, glaring at the masked doctor, Mr. J orders, "Intreton. Now."

As the doctor adds more intreton, Mr. J puts a helmet on Hank. "This will put you to sleep and alter your memories. You will wake up believing Vincent killed your brother. He bullied you in the dressing room, which cascaded into killing your parents. And he will refer to your brother as a vandal."

I can get in there and save the two kids. But I have made too many changes to the realities already. This would break time. Fuck! I'm so sorry, Dina and Hank. Maybe you are right to hate me.

✳

(The door marked "Crossroads")

What if Emika's reality changes again because I removed Akane's memories of me? Yes, the intreton around my house protects her reality, but what happens when I remove it? She is linked with the core, unlike anyone else in that house. I must jump-start the past.

Opening the door marked "1992," I rush to Philip. Touching his shoulder, I tell him, "Using my navigation tech, can you travel to Montagnola in the summer of 1992? You will find the nine-year-old Vincent sitting outside Headmaster Kruger's office. Remind him of his mission. And bring up the name Emika."[83]

"Mission? Emika?" he echoes, squinting at me.

Smiling at how young Vincent will ask him the same questions, I explain, "Emika will be Akane for a long time. The mission is to free her." As my eyes well up, I warn, "Bring Emika up when little Vincent laments about Akane. Don't mention the mission; he has to put that puzzle together himself."

"On it," Philip says. Then, he leaves.

I press my temples. Is this how all of it began?

I seek out Philip from the door marked "2024." I instruct, "NASA and DoD will contact you. Ally with them to build a supersonic jet. Call it X60."

---

[83] Chapter 18 of *The Winding* (Book 1).

"Why?"

"It will save someone precious."

"Who?"

"Just trust me on this."

I unlock the door marked "Time right now." I seek out the oldest Philip. I put my hand on his shoulder.

"Thanks for saving Akane. I couldn't have reset her timeline without you." Breathing hard, I admit, "And without that X60."

He smiles, and I can tell it's fake, probably hiding his anger. "Of course. I had to. Maybe as penance for what I did in 1991."

"I don't blame you."

"You should."

"You had your reasons. I know now," I say as I reach for the door.

Frowning, he asks, "What else do you know?"

Behind my back, I curl my hands into fists, and my nails dig into my palms. I, too, fake a smile. "We'll meet again, outside the core."

"Are we forgetting something?" Philip asks, stretching his hand out.

I smirk. "Nope."

(Central core)

Finding Chronos waiting for me when I get back to the core, I ask while catching my breath, "What caused the turbulence in Alexanderplatz?"

Lifting his finger, he scowls. "Your guess is correct."

"What are my powers?" I swallow hard. "Does it justify the cost?"

"Ludwig, prepare a path to the Egami residence in 1987."

(1987—Egami residence)

Masayoshi peeks outside his door and is startled upon seeing his injured security personnel groaning on the ground around me. Pointing at them, he asks me, "How did you do this?"

"I had training," I say, touching my broken jaw as it heals.

He squints. "You look familiar. But from where?"

Grimacing at his innocence, I say, "There's a box from Emperor Hirohito that you can't open. Can you bring it here?"

His eyes widen. He motions for me to enter and then says, "Wait here."

A few moments later, Theresa and Masayoshi bring the box and hand it to me.

I break the intreton lock with a delicate flick, open it, and take out the Kashmir sapphire ring that has now traveled across time. As Theresa looks at the ring, her eyes get wet. Then, she looks at me.

"Vincent?" she shrieks in joy, then clasps a hand over her mouth.

"Yes. Currently older than both of you."

She picks up the ring and hands it to me. "Please take it."

"I have no use for it," I say, shaking my head. "But I do have two requests. Failing to meet them will put us back to where we are again."

Joining her hands, Theresa agrees. "Anything. You saved our Aka-chan."

"Not yet. You will not take Akane to Berlin to see the clock in Alexanderplatz. Philip Nardin will invite you, and you will deny it. Am I clear?"

"Done." Masayoshi nods. "And?"

Taking a deep breath, I hesitate. This is not easy. "Akane will not go to Montagnola," I finally say, sniffling.

Theresa's voice trembles as she asks, "Why?"

"She must not meet me until April 15, 2027."

As I turn to leave, Theresa grabs my hand. "Do you want to meet her today?"

"I shouldn't," I whisper, my voice cracking.

As I open the door, I hear the sweetest voice, rivaled only by my Nozo's. "*Anata wa dare desu ka?*"

Tears drip down my cheeks. How can I not turn back? Wiping my eyes, I look back to see all the lights in the room seeming to shine on a five-year-old girl. She walks toward me as I fall to my knees.

Touching my face with her tiny, chubby hands, she repeats, "*Anata wa dare desu ka?*"

"*Boku wa . . .*" I pause, holding her hands, and try again. "*Boku wa* nobody *desu.*"

She tilts her head. Then, she smiles and squeezes her eyes into two thick lines of eyelashes. She points at my tears and asks, "*Nobody-san,* are you silly?"

"*Hai, so desu.*"

Stretching her eyes wide, she turns to her mom. "*Ooki na midori to aoi no me,*"[84] she exclaims, pointing at my eyes.

"*So desu yo, Aka-chan.* Large, green-blue eyes," concurs Theresa softly.

Akane turns to her doting father. "*Samui desu, Papha,*" she says while rubbing her arms with her hand.

Taking my scarf, I wrap it around her little neck and her arms. "*Atatakai desu ka?*" I ask.

"*Hai.*" She nods. "*Arigatō gozaimasu, Nobody-san.*"

I stare into her warm eyes. "The scarf is yours now." Standing up, I rub her head and then turn to her parents. Wiping my eyes with my cuff, I explain, "Now, you know where she got the scarf." I bow to them. "I will take your leave. Remember the promise."

As I am about to exit, I hear little Akane asking her mom, "*Kare wa dare deshita ka?*"[85]

I turn back and see *Theresa-san* wrapping little Akane in her arms. Against her wishes, she gathers her will, locking her eyes with mine. Resting her head on Akane's tiny shoulder, tears streaming from her eyes, she says, "He is nobody."

I nod and give her a broken smile.

---

[84] In the reality where Vincent and Akane were classmates, she made this observation. This is mentioned in Chapter 2 of *The Winding* (Book 1).

[85] Who was he?

Turning back to me, Akane smiles. She grips her scarf and says, *"Anata o wasurenai."*[86]

"You will always be family." Masayoshi says, bowing.

I bow back and then take my leave.

So, Akane's memory of getting her scarf is forged from a different reality from when I met her in Montagnola. She kept looking at me in school and saying, "Found you." That must be why she said, "Perhaps I knew you before I knew you," when she returned. Is that how it all started? Is that why she called me family, because of what Masayoshi said? The realities are cross-wired. And my giving little Akane the scarf only happened because Emika tied it around my neck before I left for the extraction. That scarf is looped across realities.

---

[86] I won't forget you.

CHAPTER 17

HANAFUBUKI

". . .You are my constant across all realities."
—Akane

April 15, 2027

(Amari residence)

Vincent

LOOKING OUT THE GLASS WALL, I watch the lone cherry tree slowly shedding its petals—the promise of a beautiful spring. The tree's shimmer is at the mercy of the sun's ability to break through the labyrinth of clouds hovering over Kyoto. Yet, it's determined to shine.

In the living room, Hiroshi and Siri Amari are sifting through the gifts I got them. Signed Pink Floyd albums—*The Wall*, *Wish You Were Here*, *The Dark Side of the Moon*, and *Atom Heart Mother*.

Hiroshi, squinting through his reading glasses, asks, "These must be rare and expensive."

"It's nothing, really, *Hiroshi-san*," I say, waving my hand dismissively.

Placing the albums on his piano, he joins me by the glass wall. "You are not here to ask for my daughter's hand?" he asks, scratching his bald head.

"Why would I ask you?"

"It is customary in our culture."

"Ah. Customs." Frowning, I ask, "Is it also customary to chastise your daughter for things beyond her control?"

He bends his head as Siri covers her mouth with her hand, her eyes wide with surprise and indecision. Should she praise me for standing up to her husband in a patriarchal society or throw me out for impregnating her daughter and forgetting about her? I wouldn't care if she threw me out; I don't need any courage to stand before anyone. If I can erase myself from Akane, then I fear no one but myself.

But Siri comes forward and touches my arm. "More *ocha*, Vincent?" she asks.

I bow. "No, thank you. But your tea is better than Emika's." Winking at her, I say, "But I won't tell her."

She smiles and pats my arm.

Hiroshi-san points at the Pink Floyd albums. "Then why impress me with those?"

"I don't need to impress anyone, sir." Clearing my throat, I clarify, "Emika once told me that you and *Siri-san* met at a Pink Floyd concert. So, those albums are just a little reminder of the resulting miracle—your daughter." Scoffing, I stress, "Emika is nothing short of a gift, yet you never realized that." Walking to the front door, I turn back. "Growing up, you were my favorite pianist and conductor. But then, I heard another pianist, who is far more talented than you and has an incredibly kind yet confused soul."

Hiroshi stares into my eyes. "Who is this pianist?" He knows the answer, but he wants to deny it.

I open the door, and a gust of wind breezes over my hair. Looking back at Hiroshi, I declare, "Your daughter, sir."

Falling to his knees, Hiroshi Amari, the maestro, starts to cry. "That's all I ever wanted," he confesses, his voice cracking. "Her music was a gift from God."

"*She* is a gift, whether she's a musician or not. I wish you knew her and witnessed the beauty in her flaws, too." I tap my chest. "Because I did, and she's perfect."

My music icon looks up at me helplessly. Standing up, he takes me by the shoulders and asks, "How can I mend this?"

I smile at the maestro. "Call her and tell her you will always be there for her when she needs you. Be there for her, even when she says she doesn't need you.[87] That's all she needs—kindness, patience, and tolerance. That's all anyone needs."[88]

(Kiyomizu-dera)

My job is done, and I must head home. But something pulls me back, and I find myself in the same spot I was in last year. I climb the stairs leading to Kiyomizu-dera. I can't even keep my eyes open against the wind; my jacket is flapping around me, and my trousers are pasted to my thighs. I keep going, though; I have to know something.

Under different circumstances, I would have given that ring to Akane today. Before Vandal attacked us, Akane told me she'd be at the *ema* stand on April 15. I'd asked her what was there. "Us. Forever," she said. But that was a different reality. Did the *ema* stand the test of time and reality?

A *torii* gate stands between me and the main shrine. The wind intensifies as I near the entrance, changing direction, hitting my face sideways as I cross the *torii*. I take a step back, and the gust changes course again. Now, I stand with half my body on either side of the *torii*. The wind hits me at a

---

87 Vincent tells this to Jean in *The Winding* (Book 1).

88 Vincent told Emika to be kind, patient, and tolerant toward her parents in *The Winding* (Book 1).

perpendicular angle. Is this a gateway to a crossroads of reality? Then, two children run past the gate, unscathed.

My shoes scuff against the ground as I walk toward the *ema* stand. There is no one by the *ema* stand. A crowd of about a hundred people, mainly young boys, and girls, are busy taking selfies with someone, perhaps a celebrity. They are fifty feet from the raised courtyard of the prayer chamber, all talking in Japanese. If I try, then I can decipher what they are saying. But my mind is elsewhere. My eyes are fixed on the *ema* stand surrounded by breathtaking cherry blossoms—situated outside the courtyard but brushing on the *emas*. A few petals gently fall on the ground next to the *ema* stand. The diffused sun through the clouds creates a golden and pink hue around the cherry trees, making everything sparkle. I collect a few fallen petals and put them in my jacket pocket.

As the crowd gets denser, I walk within an inch of the *ema* stand. Two days back, when I woke up, I thought, *Why would I ever look for that ema?* Now, I am sifting through all the plaques, looking for the red one among the yellow ones. It would easily stand out if it were here—as Akane does. But I am a fool, still scrutinizing each plaque, hoping it's there, just hidden, hoping our promise stood the test of time. Wasn't it me who wanted to burn that *ema* down a few months back? So, why am I hoping it's here, in a reality where Akane never met me? As my heartbeat slows, I realize the lie. I give up and sit on the raised courtyard.

Stand the test of time, you said. Liar. A lie that made me want to fail at my mission.

Why am I finding it so hard to breathe?

I should be delighted that you are not here looking for me. I hid, and you never found me. I should be happy our paths never crossed. Even if they did, my memories of a life where you didn't know me would take time to develop. It's been just two days for me but forty-five years for you.

I stare at my hands—so utterly skillful at deleting myself from the only person who mattered to me for the longest time. I force a sad chuckle. Tiny water droplets fall on my palm. Why would I cry? I grind my teeth—I shouldn't feel this way. I succeeded. That's all that matters. Vincent: 1, Love: 0. Vincent: 1, Akane: 0. Why are my shoulders shaking?

With my right hand, I hold my left shoulder. "Stop shaking."

Then, a robin lands next to me and stares into my eyes. After a few moments, it flies away.

I hear a voice rise above the crowd's din—an infectious, smiling tone, like the first note of Consolation No. 3.

"One more picture . . . yes, sweetheart, you can be anything you want if you work hard . . . okay, let me sign your notebook . . . of course, I will be here next year on this day. I am always here on this day."

And then, someone asks, "Why do you always come here on this day?"

I won't look. It must be a lie. She can't be here; the *ema* is not here. She saw me only once—when she was five, at that. She can't remember me. I can't have failed. This love . . . all it does is hurt. But it's also undeniably beautiful. A piece of me wishes I had failed.

No, you can't have failed, Vince.

But she is alive, unscathed. So, I did succeed.

The voice pierces through the wind, the crowd, and the symphony of cicadas boosting the golden hour. "This is a special place, on this day... Can you excuse me now? It's getting late, and there is someone I must meet." The sound of soft footfalls gives in to the spring breeze.

"Found you," says the voice etched so deeply into my mind and heart that even the thought of removing it would be a fool's errand.

I inhale sharply. How can I not turn? Piercing through the clouds, the sun shines on a face unfazed by an altered reality as if the setting sun was waiting for this very moment. She is wearing the pink floral kimono with the maroon obi, like last year and in the core, but with one difference; the scarf is tied around her neck. In her hands is the red *ema*. It can't be.

As our eyes lock, she holds up the *ema* and asks, "You are looking for this, right?"

I see no anguish on her face—only the smile of someone who has lived their life in contentment. But, as she comes closer, I see her eyes flicker with tears.

After hanging the *ema* where it belongs, she sits on my right. "So, is it Vincent or Mr. Nobody?"

My heart grows almost unbearably heavy. "Vince." Pointing at the receding crowd, I look into her warm, curious eyes. "So, you are an icon now?" My voice cracks as I whisper, "I did not fail."

Wiping the corners of her eyes, she says, "No, you didn't. But it wasn't easy . . . with fragments of a life unlived."

"I am sorry."

She looks down and scoffs. "By the time I was twenty-four, I had been engaged twice. But I could never love those guys for who they were. And I did not even know what I was looking for." Snickering, she adds, "And when you are an Egami, you don't know if those guys love you or your money." She raises her eyes. "I was only interested in three things: knowing the fragments of my life, violin, and learning how to run our company." Shaking her head, she smiles. "My music education at TUA was insufficient for the third, so I enrolled at Harvard."

Harvard? That was where she was in my dream. My hands begin to shake, so I clasp them together firmly.

Touching my arm, she reveals, "I first saw you at a debate on AI, Harvard versus MIT. After you smashed your opponents, I made sure I learned your name." She locks her eyes with mine. "Those eyes, that name, the memories . . . I couldn't put them together. You looked like a younger version of the man who wrapped this"—she gently runs her fingers over the scarf—"around me. I think I said '*Anata o wasurenai*.'" She takes a deep breath and then confesses, "From that moment on, I stalked you. I always hid my face under my hoodie. But then, one day, you almost caught me. It was a cold autumn morning, the leaves falling, and you chased me from a cafeteria. As I turned back to look at you, my hoodie dropped." Swallowing hard, she whispers, "And I ran away."

I reach for her hands but then hesitate, curling my hands into fists instead.

So, it wasn't just a dream, after all—just the memories of a reality that hadn't formed entirely in my mind.

I stare into her eyes. "Why didn't you come to me?"

Sobbing, she asks, "And say what?"

"I don't know," I reply, sighing.

My memories from MIT now intersect three realities. The first two have the same impact on me—whether she was lost or in a coma from the turbulence. The third one is where I never met her, yet I could not forge any meaningful romantic relationships because I was missing someone I hadn't met.

Squinting at her, I ask, "What did you do?"

"I called my parents, threatening that if they didn't explain, I would remove myself from the Egami Corporation." She wipes her eyes and smiles. "They were in Cambridge the next day." From the pouch of her obi, she takes out a Kashmir sapphire ring. "They explained everything. That you came from the future and tied this scarf around my neck. The importance of this place. The significance of this date." Her eyes widen as she says, "I could not believe those words, so I had to come to see the *ema* for myself." She covers her mouth. "How can something from 2026 exist in 2008?" Her voice cracking, she admits, "So, I learned to live with memories of a life unlived from the future."

Then, she stands up and walks toward the cherry trees.

I follow.

Spreading her arms, she twirls, letting the pink petals fall on her. "Papha told me not to meet you until today. But every year, I'd come here on this day to find you. I'd stare into the *ema*, hoping to see you, rehearsing what I would say to you." She looks at me and adds, "I took an oath that I wouldn't wear that ring until I found you."

"So, wear it."

She puts the sapphire on the ring finger of her right hand, then tilts her head and smiles. "I know you are attached." She cuts a dry smile. "The one who links me with my memories of the future is not mine anymore. Right?"

I don't answer.

Yes, I am. And it hurts. I am torn; there is this life with Emi and Nozo, and there is the one with you across all realities. But I must keep my promise to you, the one I made in the core.

I take a few steps toward her until we are inches apart, her kimono brushing against my suit in the breeze.

"What?" she asks.

"Can I touch your hands?"

Lifting them from her sides, she says, "Yes."

I take them in mine, her skin warm. "Close your eyes. I will give you back our memories. You will feel a slight tickle. Keep hold of my hands, or else you will faint, okay?" I take a deep breath. "Ready?"

"Yes."

Her eyes are closed, and she has an enchanting smile on her lips. As the sparks from my fingers encircle her hands, her smile gives in to a slight tremble, then a frown. Tears form at the corners of her eyes and slowly trickle down her cheeks.

I am sorry for the pain residing in the beauty.

The sparks retract as the memory transfer is completed. Pulling her hands away, she falls to her knees. I sit on the ground beside her.

Her voice quavers as she calls out to me, "Silly? *Watashi no* silly?" She places her palms on my cheeks and says, "There isn't anything more beautiful." Then, she frowns. "I understand keeping me away from Berlin. But why would you tell Papha to keep me away from Montagnola?" She tugs my lapel. "*Naze?*"

I take her hands from my lapel and hold them. "Across every alternate reality, Vandal would attack you. And I would extract you and, in the process, ruin lives going back to the 1970s. This was the only way to stop it." Squeezing her hands, I stress, "I had to end the cycle of destruction and ruin beyond this life. None of this will repeat beyond the end of my life."

She squeezes my hands back. "You gave me those twenty years I'd spent in a coma. I am the CEO of the entire Egami Group." Lowering her eyes, she reveals, "Yet, in their eyes, I am still a *hafu*. How is citizenship dependent on race, Vince?"

"I don't care what they think."

"What?" she asks, raising her eyebrows in surprise.

"I don't care if the world changes." Kissing her hands, I confess, "I lied to make things easier. All I want is to live in a reality where you are alive, even if I am irrelevant to you."

"Why?"

Against every good judgment, I say, "Because I love you."

Her eyes fall on her blue ring. Wiping her tears, she asks, "If things were different . . . Would we stand a chance?"

My voice cracks. "I'd have room for no one else." As she raises her eyes, I point at the *ema*. "And that must count for something."

A gentle breeze lifts my hair. Wrapping her arms around my neck, Akane kisses my cheek. Locking her eyes with mine, biting her bottom lip, she says, "I should stop here."

The breeze passes, and my hair falls back into place.

Swallowing hard, she looks down. "Thank you. You gave me back twenty years. I owe everything to you—"

"Shut up."

Quickly shaking her head, she presses on by asking, "Is there anything I can do?" She looks up, taps her chin playfully, and asks, "Hmm . . . You want the scarf back?"

"Keep it," I say, smiling. "If you ever find me shivering, you can wrap it around my neck."

"So, there's nothing you want?"

Staring into her eyes, I say, "You can answer a question for me."

"What?"

"What have I done to deserve your love?"

She shakes her head. "Silly. It transcends reality." Then, she takes my hand and kisses my knuckles. "The selflessness in erasing yourself from me...so that I am safe and I get my lost years back." Our eyes lock as she confesses, "But in the altered reality, when you saw the five-year-old me shivering, you risked it all by wrapping the scarf around me." Her voice cracks. "You are my constant across all realities. You cannot truly erase yourself from me." She cups my cheek. "When you transferred my memories, I realized that your acts in this reality and the previous one made me always say, 'found you.'" Gripping my lapel, she confesses, "I love you."

"Me too, always." My heart gets heavy with the thought of living in a reality where we can't be together.

She touches my face gently. "If you want to see me, use the core." Tilting her head, she smiles. "And one of these days, I will drop by to see your family."

"Once, you called me family," I whisper.

"I still do. You are. But things . . ."

I bring her head to my shoulder and kiss her hair. "I know."

Then, we both stand. As I begin to walk away, I turn back to look at her. Against the ground's lanterns, the setting sun shines its last light on her face. Standing by the *ema* stand, she once again takes out the *ema*. Bringing it to her lips, she whispers something. A warm wind brings her voice to my ears.

"*Anata o aishiteimasu*, Vince."

Fifty feet away, I whisper back, "*Boku mo itsumo.*"

I don't know if she heard me. But she lifts her eyes from the *ema*. She reluctantly waves her hand as the wind lifts her hair around her face. Nodding, she wipes the corners of her eyes.

I can snap my fingers and be anywhere I want, choose any reality I want, and still feel out of place if you are not there.

I wave back, whispering, "*Jaane mata ne.*"[89] Lowering my hand, I form a fist, swallow my tears, and start my journey home.

(Vincent's home)

Emika wanted me to settle my differences with Akane before setting foot in our house again. Before Vandal attacked us, I asked Akane why she would go to the *ema* stand. It took two full days for me and forty-five years for Akane to answer that. But now, Akane and I understand each other perfectly.

I stand in front of my door with a baby dragon plush pillow in my right hand. I stare at my empty left hand. It's April 15. Some of us were supposed to be in Copenhagen today, including Akane—especially her. Do I regret this twisted path leading to 100 Summit Drive? I don't know.

Curling my fingers into a fist, tilting my wrist, I look at the time—7:30 a.m., according to the watch made by Philip Nardin. I don't want to startle anyone. I tap my watch.

"Athena, disable all alarms."

Lifting my hand, I absorb all the intreton surrounding the property, putting it back into reality. It's too cloudy for a hopeful spring. Maybe we won't witness *hanafubuki* today.

Silently, I open the door. Inside, my Emika is sitting at the piano, playing "*Emika no uta.*" She is still in the Raindrop prelude.

Who are you trying to reach?

I take two more steps forward, and it becomes all too clear. Emika is clad in my MIT sweats. I don't deserve to be missed like this. Hulk is by her feet, gently mouthing the untied shoelaces of Emi's sakura-printed

---

[89] So long.

converse. Lifting his eyes, he glances at me and then goes back to chewing his mom's shoelaces.

My Nozo is sleeping with her head on Tabi's lap and her legs on Chris's. Tabi is the custodian of Nozo's Kiki hairband, tied around her arm, while the broom is resting against Chris's right foot. Across from them, Anna is glued to her cell phone. Krista and Sasha are taking food from the fridge. Fred is sniffing every bottle in the bar, mumbling to himself, "Hmm, that could be my next."

With her hands on her hips, Krista glares at Fred. "What's the point of choosing, since you will sample everything, eventually?"

As she turns her head, she notices me. Her eyes brighten. She opens her mouth wide and pulls Sasha by her apron. They are about to yell my name, but I bring my index finger to my lips. Frowning, they cross their arms.

Emika is still engrossed in her piano, but everyone else's eyes are on me now, though they keep their mouths shut. Gently lifting Nozo's arm, I place her baby dragon under it. She coos in her sleep. Looking around at everyone, I put my hand over my heart and bow, conveying my gratitude for staying and caring for Emika, Hulk, and Nozo these two days. Walking over to the piano, I sit next to Emika on the piano bench. Tears well in her eyes as she opens them. As she lifts her hands from the keys to take out my pocket square, I put my hands down, taking the reins of the music seamlessly as though we are the same pianist.

Resting her head on my shoulder, she whispers, "I dreamed I couldn't reach you, and I didn't know you. I was playing this piece to find you." While I move through the Raindrop prelude to Chopin's Ballade No. 4, Emika nestles her face into the crook of my neck and asks, "If I can't find you, will you answer me if I play this song?"

I kiss her head. "I'm home, right?"

"*Hai*," she whispers.

"Keep playing," I tell her. "I'll be right back."

When I stand up, I feel a slight tug on my trousers. Looking down, I see the innocent smile that makes every ordeal tolerable. Holding her new acquisition with her tiny, chubby hands, Nozo says, "Thank you, Papha."

I pick her up, and she rests her head on my shoulder, yawning. Rubbing her back, I say, "Anything for you."

Handing Nozo to Chris, I walk to the mantel, touch Akane's violin, and then pick up the photograph of us having ice cream. Looking at everyone's curious faces, I state, "I need five minutes. Alone."

Shaking my shoulder, Sasha demands, "Is everything okay?"

"Yes," I tell them, my voice cracking. "Five minutes. Please."

With the photograph in my left hand, I walk upstairs. Hulk leaves his safe place under the Steinway and follows me. With each step, the masterful strokes of Emika's fingers on the piano become fainter. Crossing through the bedroom, I enter my walk-in closet. Letting Hulk in, I lock the door behind us and sit on the floor with my back against the door. I bring the photograph to my chest.

You lived through time and reality. I hope we do, too.

I stare into the picture, seeing how Akane looks back at me—not at the Vincent next to her but at *me*. My tears drop on the glass. While I wipe them off the frame, Hulk licks them off my face.

Touching his head, I assure him, "You have seen me like this before."

My breathing quickens as I open the back of the frame. I flip the picture. Akane's writing is on the top left—"*Watashi to Watashi no*" in *hiragana*, "Silly" in English, followed by "*Vu~incento*" in *katakana*. I gently touch her delicate penmanship. Just below that, in English, Krista had written, "Akane and Vincent, sitting in a tree . . .", and it was signed by Sasha and Krista. In the farthest corner is Fred's signature. I can picture him rolling his eyes when asked to sign it. Inserting my hand into my jacket pocket, I retrieve the sakura petals. Turning the pocket inside out, I get all of them out. I cup them in my hands and bring them near my face as sun rays shine through the skylight, making the petals shimmer.

You are the witness to the ema *standing the test of time. Right?*

I place all the sakura petals on the back of the photograph and then put the frame's backing on again.

So, now, be witness to what's in this picture. Can you make them stand the test of time?

I lift my cuff and replace Philip's watch with the Roger Smith Series Five. Through the closed door, I faintly hear that Emika has moved to the final part of Nocturne, Op. 9, No. 2.

Taking my phone out, I say, "Ludwig. There is an unattached drive in my time cave. Can you attach it to my network?"

"Done."

"Now, retrieve the folder, 'Akane & Vincent' from my cloud drive archives. Restore it across all attached drives and send a link to Akane's cell."

"Done."

Less than a minute later, my phone beeps with a text notification from Akane.

> Akane: Thank you.
> Me: Just keeping my promise.
> Akane: That's all I have.
> Me: It can't be all. You are an inspiration . . . I saw it. So, live your life.
> Akane: You, too. I know you are standing at a crossroads, but don't ignore what's right in front of you.
> Me: *Mochiron.*

What's in front of me?

What do you mean, Akane? What have I ignored?

I sit with my legs folded, my elbows on my knees, and my head in my palms. My hands are trembling. Am I cold? Sweat is trickling down my neck. Am I hot? When the future affects the past, I thought I could take it. And I did. But, in the midst of all this, I am losing myself. I can't grasp reality—the present.

Show me, Akane. What have I ignored? Nothing makes sense when all the futures and pasts are happening simultaneously, and I see them all. I don't know what I'm missing.

I open the closet door and let the light from the bedroom windows come in.

The sound of Emika's playing stops for a moment, and then she starts a new song, her voice accompanying the piano this time. As she begins, I hear, "*Haru no kaze . . .*" The clouds beyond the skylight break, and the sun rays touch all the bespoke suits Akane had made for me—the ones I wanted to discard. Emika has put them back and neatly placed them just the way they were. A sunbeam shines on the edge of my cufflink drawer.

Is that what you want me to see, Akane?

I stand up. Opening the drawer and sifting through the contents, I look for something whose existence I had almost forgotten. And there it is—hidden among the letters I exchanged with Akane, Fred, Krista, and Sasha, concealed beneath over fifty pairs of cufflinks, collar stays, and watch band extensions. I pick up the little box and place it in my pocket. Leaving the closet, I look outside through my bedroom window. The petals have begun to descend, slowly dancing before reaching the ground. Blossoms that were together will wither away in solitude. But not today—not in this house. It is April 15, after all.

Holding the photo frame to my chest, I look down. "Hulky, let's go." He stands up, wagging his tail, shaking his whole body.

Downstairs, I put the photograph on the mantel and touch Akane's glowing face. Through numerous refractions, the golden sunlight infused with the pink tone of the sakura from the backyard shines on Emika as she weaves magic with the piano. Three years back, when I first witnessed the *hanafubuki* in my backyard, my heart desired this very moment. I must watch this miracle before me and wait for her to finish this song.

After she keys the final stroke, she stands up, bows before the small applauding crowd, sits back down, and casually starts playing Handel's Passacaglia. I head to the bar and take out a bottle of Yamazaki 55. I pour four ounces into a glass and chug it all. The ensuing burn on my tongue and throat hides the subtle woody flavor from the Mizunara oak casks. I press my lips together and shut my eyes. Fuck liquid courage. When I open my eyes, everyone—except Emika, Nozo, and Hulk—looks at me.

"What?" I ask, shrugging. Pointing at the sakura while keeping my eyes on Emika, I distract them. "Just look at the beauty." They all head toward the glass wall and the backyard, except Emika. She keeps playing, augmenting the beauty outside. Staring at her, I say, "It takes me back to exactly three years ago when I recorded that video and my cold hands were seeking your warmth."

Emika stops keying and quickly turns her head. "*Nani?*" Her voice shivers.

I walk over to her, take her right hand, pull her away from the Steinway, and guide her to the ottoman by the sectional. "Please sit," I say.

Hulk jumps up first, leaving half the space for Emika. She sits with her legs crossed and then pulls the sleeves of my MIT sweatshirt down over her wrists. Staring at the undone shoelaces of her converse, I take her feet and tie her laces into a Berluti knot. She tucks her hair behind her ears.

Tilting her head, she gives me a smile. "When will you teach me that knot?" Lifting her brows, she emphasizes, "Hmm?"

"What if I don't?" I stare into her warm eyes. "How about, in this life, I keep tying that knot?"

She bites her lips, and her eyes widen. "Huh?" she asks softly.

Looking away from her, I raise my voice. "Anna. It's time."

Turning back, Anna leaves her place by the glass wall. From the top of the mantel, she lifts a photo frame encasing a picture of Ravi, Maddy, and little Wasim and stands close by, facing Emika and me. Then, she cups her hand around her mouth and shouts, "Hey, the trees are not running away."

Everyone moves from their stations by the glass wall and encircles Emika and me. Nozo is on Chris's lap, and Tabi has been chosen to hold onto the baby dragon.

"What's going on?" Emika asks, looking around at everyone.

Clearing my throat, I say, "Several things have gone wrong, bending time and altering the reality that led you into my life the first time. When I met you, I was so happy." I sigh. "Then, you left."

"I'm sorry."

Taking her hands, I continue, "When you came back, my life was flawless." I bring my index finger and my thumb together. "A minor imperfection is what it took to make it perfect." Smiling at her, I ask, "Do you remember what you told the realtor about us?"

She smiles back at me. "That we are a work in progress with beautiful potential."

"Do you still feel that way?" I ask, staring into her eyes.

Her voice softens as she admits, "We are past potential."

I look away for a second, turning to Anna. She nods. Reaching into my pocket, I take out a small box. As I open the box, Emika's eyes brighten.

"In that case, would you terribly mind wearing this?"

She gasps and brings her hands to her mouth. "I dreamed of this very moment," she breathes. "When did you get this?"

"The day I got your Cartier Tank."

Yes, I concealed my feelings, even when you left and the months after you returned.

Leaning toward her, I say, "If you don't like it, just know that Anna picked it."

Glaring at me, Anna starts, "Mother—" But then, she looks at Nozo and remembers her previous faux pas. "Ffff."

Wiping her eyes with her sleeves, Emika turns to Anna. "Thank you. It's beautiful." Then, she collects Nozo from Chris. Kissing Nozo's chubby cheek and pointing her finger at me, she asks, "Hey, do we love this papha?"

Nozo's entire face lights up as she smiles. "Yes. He gave me baby dragon."

Looking into my eyes, Emika declares, "Well, how can I say no to that?" Then, she gives me her hand. "Put it on me." After placing it on her finger, she wraps her arms around my neck and whispers, "I love you."

I kiss her neck, scented with amber, vanilla, vetiver, and sandalwood. "I love you, too."

Apparently, the group's applause is not enough for Fred. "What a sorry bunch." Tapping Emika on the shoulder, he asks, "You were born in 1991, right?"

"Yes."

Walking to the bar, he fetches two 1991 Moet Chandon Dom Pérignon bottles. Chris brings the champagne glasses while Krista, Sasha, and Tabi admire Emika's new acquisition.

Anna touches my shoulder. "Learn to be happy, idiot," she whispers. "I don't know what you went through, but there's no one like your Emi."

"I won't argue that."

While Fred and Chris start pouring drinks for everyone, Anna pulls me up from the sectional. After collecting her drink and fetching me one, she raises her glass. "To Emi and Vince."

"To Emi and Vince!" everyone choruses.

Anna closes her eyes and takes a deep breath. When she opens them again, her eyes are moist. "To Ravi, Maddy, and Wasim."

We lift our glasses. "To Ravi, Maddy, and Wasim!"

Krista sits on a barstool and asks, "I don't want to rain on this joy. Vince is my brother. I couldn't be happier for him, Emika, and little Nozo. But . . ." Her voice cracks as she trails off.

Embracing Krista, Sasha finishes her thought. "But how is Akane? We've been meaning to ask you that since you came back." She looks at Emika. "I'm sorry."

"I take no offense," Emika assures her. She also turns to me and says, "Tell us."

I chug my entire glass of champagne. Then, I take another half-finished bottle and drink it to the last drop. I inspect everyone's faces—the curious, the skeptical, the worried.

Taking a deep breath, I explain, "She is fine. She never went to Montagnola and was never sucked into the turbulence."

As everyone sighs in relief and the Montagnola trio hug each other, I add, "Despite everything, she remembered me." Shaking my head, chuckling, I admit, "So, I gave back her memories. She remembers all of you."

Smiles erupt on the faces of Fred, Krista, and Sasha, and they all laugh happily.

But I can't join them. Instead, I stare at my shaking hands. "Nothing surprises me anymore. After what I have learned . . ."

"What?" Emika probes, touching my cheek.

Scanning the room, I ask, "Can someone open a puzzle or Lego box for Nozo? She can't hear this."

CHAPTER 18

REVELATION—STAGE 4

"Vince and I are forging links to this infinite movement
of causality… he is just better than me"
—Philip

April 15, 2027

(Underground of Philip's residence)

Philip

STEPPING OUT OF THE ELEVATOR, I look up, stretch my arms wide, and breathe in. Smirking, I spin my walking stick in my hand while humming, "The lunatic is in the hall, the lunatics are in my hall." No more walking sticks after today—goodbye, pretension. I frown; it gets a little worse when I reveal it. Beyond the crystal cage, I see Hank's wrist perfectly attached to his arm, except for a bloodstained bandage.

Circling his cage and grinning, I point my walking stick at his wrist. "Dr. Lee is exceptional, isn't he?"

"So, you're the man in the fedora hat?" Hank asks, baring his teeth.

Bowing, I admit, "Guilty!" I frown, pointing at the uneaten food. "Gai's food is good enough for you? Expecting Michelin star treatment in jail?"

Hank raises his defeated eyes. "Jail? Vincent saved Akane, right?"

Pouting, I retort, "Aww! I am so sorry." Furrowing my brows at him, I remind him, "Yes, you failed that, but you attempted. And what about Elise? The other victims with her? The plane crash in Japan? The Kauffmans?" I chuckle darkly. "The DA and the SA will have much fun with you."

"I did whatever Mr. J asked of me! So did Dina." Getting down on his knees, he pleads, "I will take all the blame if that makes you and Vincent happy." He clasps his hands in front of him. "But can you protect Dina from Mr. J? She is bright . . . just misguided. She had potential—not like me."

I sneer. "Very well."

"Thank you." Then, he stands back up and presses his temples. "My memories?" he asks. "Didn't Vincent bully me in the changing room?" He shakes his head, confused. "Why does he sound kind?"

"Because he *is* kind, like his mother. But, tempered with streaks from the darkness . . ." Winking, I clarify, "possibly from his father." Bending my head, I explain, "Your hatred is formed from a doctored memory. That memory has been disappearing since Vince became one with the core. He can now delete any doctored memories of his choosing."

At this revelation, Hank sits back down. "Mr. J played us?" he exclaims. Then, he looks up at me helplessly. "Can't you or Vincent catch Mr. J?"

I laugh, clutching my cane with my right hand and holding my stomach with my left.

You are too naive.

"Ah. Why do you think we haven't caught him?" Squinting at him, I ask, "Who is Mr. J?"

"Someone who took care of Dina and me." Breathing hard, Hank states, "Like a father."

My shoulders shake with laughter. "Father?" I jeer. "No, he didn't give two shits for either of you." I swallow hard.

Maybe he should have. They were just children…what have you done, J?

"I want Mr. J to admit that," Hank screeches.

"Very well. Ask him." I spread my arms. "He is right here."

With wrinkled brows and mouth agape, Hank yells, "Where?"

Turning to the elevator, I say, "Edward. Dr. Lee."

Edward exits the elevator and comes toward me, tying a tourniquet around my arm. Dr. Lee pushes liquid intreton. After injecting a bit, he stops.

I glare at him and order, "More."

Trembling, he thrusts the whole piston in. I smirk. I don't need to hook up to a machine. I got my powers directly from the time corrector, Vincent.

As the intreton settles, my veins throb. Dr. Lee and Edward have seen it a thousand times. But Hank's jaw has dropped. As tears trickle from my eyes, I use all my strength to create a spark—perhaps the last residual power I have after Vincent became one with the core. The spark circles wider and makes a door to the core.

Looking back, I smile. "So long."

My face burns and heals simultaneously as soon as I enter the core. I fall, holding my face until the tissues heal my fifty-year-old burn. Holding my derby handle, I try to stand up. The intense pain from damaged nerves shoots down my left leg. Losing grip on my cane, I fall back to the floor. I can feel my pulse in every vein as I roar.

"Ahhhh!" My eyes bulge, my teeth bare, and my jaws clench. I throw up blood and intreton, gasping for air. As the pain recedes, my breathing evens out. Slowly, I stand, using the cane for balance. I take a handkerchief from my trouser pocket and wipe the blood and intreton from my face.

Then, taking out the mask from my jacket pocket and unfolding it, I leave the core and enter the world of Edward, Dr. Lee, and Hank.

With his hands shaking, his fingers pointed at me, Hank stutters, "It— it can't be." As Dr. Lee puts on his own mask, Hank howls at him, "You pushed intreton in me?"

My voice is muffled as I tighten the mask. "If I were anyone else, Vincent would have caught me. The trust blinded him." My voice cracks as I admit, "Such a good . . . boy."

Touching my chest with my left hand, I declare, "I am Oliver Journe. You know me as Mr. J." I grit my teeth. "Vincent took everything from me. I am a monster of his making." Grinning, I point at Hank. "And you are mine."

(1984—Orphanage, Paris)

The warden pointed at the crib. "The child with the unusual eyes."

Standing over the crib, I looked into the baby's eyes. Then, I immediately jerked back. Those eyes were not just unmistakably Amara's. They also gave me a flash of my past life. My hands shook as I grabbed the edge of the crib.

"I need a minute," I told the warden.

Picking up the baby, I rested him in the crook of my left arm. Giggling, he grabbed my right index finger. At that moment, a blinding spark appeared—so bright I had to close my eyes. When I opened them again, I saw a man in his forties standing before me. He had the same piercing eyes as the baby I was holding. On his wrist was the exact watch I was making.

"Who are you?" I asked, my eyes wide.

He pointed at the baby. "Him."

"What?"

"I am the time corrector—Vincent Abajian. Find David Kruger, the headmaster of a boarding school in Montagnola. I should be raised under his guardianship."

Squinting at him, I asked, "What will I get in return?"

He grinned. "I will tell you the future, and you can plan your business accordingly—where to invest and such." Lifting his finger, he added, "If you do well, I will let you enter the core directly. I will also give you some power to alter realities."

I did not know what he was talking about, but he grabbed my right hand, and sparks transmitted from his hands to mine.

Grimacing, he warned, "Don't get greedy."

(Back to the present)

As I pace around Hank's cage, he turns his head to follow me. "With each installment of sparks from Vincent's hands to mine, it became clear that I wanted to share in all of Vince's power or have it all for myself." I stop walking and look straight into Hank's pale eyes, pressing my temples. "As if someone was whispering into my ears, 'Is that all you want? To be a caretaker to Vincent's throne?'" I move my hand from my head and flutter my fingers. "The words kept buzzing—like a lunatic in my head. So, I went to the core, using the power Vincent had gifted me, and spoke with Chronos."

(1990—Core)

"The power cannot be shared." Chronos shook his head. "But it can be transferred entirely after the time corrector completes all three phases of power."

"What three phases?"

Raising his index finger, Chronos revealed, "Getting the spark." He lifts another finger. "Unlocking the core. This is when Vincent can transfer parts of his power. The Vincent from the future already transferred some to you when you saw him in 1984." Raising the third finger, he said, "The last is becoming one with the core. He can then transfer all his power." Frowning, he stressed, "But only if he wants to."

"Why would he want that?"

Chronos shrugged. "Guilt, maybe. Or if he believes someone else is better suited than he is."

"How can Vincent get it?" I asked. The prospects made my heart drum with joy.

"Escalating tragedies."

(Back to the present)

I tap my chin. "The tragedies wouldn't happen if I raised Vincent. Yes, an orphan he had to remain. What else?" Looking at Hank, I say, "I found myself split—one who wanted everything for my little Vincent and one who wanted him to get the power and be so disenchanted with it that he would willingly give it away." Tilting my head, I admit, "As Philip Nardin—busy building an empire of trillions—I couldn't do either. So, I had to mesh with them in the core."

"Them?" Hank asks.

"Going back to the core, I found Oliver and Victor." I grind my jaw. "It wasn't easy, keeping them separate." Staring into the throbbing veins in my wrist, I confess, "I can't tell Philip from Oliver and Victor." Catching my breath, I reveal, "whenever I transform, I need my walking stick for a couple of days."

Giving Hank a dry smile, I say, "It is the omnipresent Victor in me who attended Vincent's graduation, provided his university's endowment, and asked Edward to adopt Tabi. The boring stuff." I lower my voice. "As Philip Nardin, I couldn't harm Vince because he helped me build my empire with intreton-c." Grimacing, I touch my face. "It burns . . ." Sensing the shooting pain in my leg, I groan, "It hurts to be Oliver Journe . . . but I had to do this to begin my work. The words of Chronos, 'Escalating tragedies,' kept ringing in my ears."

Grinning with pride, I confess, "In my quest to bring Vince to his final power stage, I caused the events necessary to get him through the first two levels." Spreading my arms, I look up and announce, "I did it all."

(Late fall, 1991—Montagnola)

Before closing his door, I reminded David Kruger, "I want those bullies reprimanded."

"I'll do my best," he assured me.

Leaving the building, I transformed myself into Oliver Journe. It was raining, and I saw little Vincent rushing to the music room in the distance. I knew from the future that he was going to meet Akane. Three bullies—I knew they were Rudy, Luther, and Jean—were running toward Vincent. With my walking cane, I intercepted them. Should I stop them? I grimaced—no fucking way. I wanted them to do more. So, I added fuel to the fire.

Taking out a small travel bottle of whiskey and a pack of smokes from the jacket pockets, I asked the boys, "Want some?" As two of the three boys stretched their arms up to grab them, I lifted them out of reach. "On one condition."

"What? What?" asked Luther, jumping with his arm stretched, trying to reach my hand.

"I'll do anything for those, mister," admitted Rudy, smacking his lips.

The third boy, Jean, hesitated, grabbing Rudy's shoulder. "We shouldn't. What if Mr. Kruger finds out?"

I watched Rudy and Luther beat Vince within an inch of his life, less than fifty feet away, while Jean stood on guard.

What if he dies?

I didn't know if it was pity for Vincent or fear of not getting my powers, but if I hadn't tapped my cane loud enough for Jean to yell, "I think I see Mr. Kruger," that would have been the end of my boy.

I waited until I saw Vincent get up. He pressed a hand tightly to his broken ribs and held his bloody nose with his other as he limped to the music room. I fell to my knees, banging my cane on the ground. How could I have done that to a child? My Amara's boy, no less. In a puddle on the sidewalk, I saw my reflection. I was Philip Nardin again, not Oliver Journe.

"Please forgive me, Vincent. I love you, but I can't help it," I pleaded. "I made those bullies, yet I wanted Kruger to punish them." I put my hands over my ears. A lunatic was in my head.

(Back to the present)

"That beating did not unite Vince with the sparks. How could I create a new tragedy?" Raising my brows at Hank, I smirk. "In Kruger's words, I found hope. He went on and on about how the sweet Akane tied that scarf around Vincent. And how she never left his side when he was in the infirmary." I chuckle. "And then, Kruger told me the most fantastic story. During a rehearsal in their dorm room, Akane threw herself between Vincent and Fred."

Gritting his teeth, Hank punches the crystal wall. "What did you do?"

"I went to the future and found a 3D hologram invention Vincent was working on." Tilting my head, I smile. "I used that to make an image of Vincent on November 15, 1991."

✸

(November 15, 1991—Berlin)

The Egamis accepted my invitation and watched me repair the World Clock at Alexanderplatz. I knew what I had to do to make little Akane get sucked into the turbulence. As the 3D image appeared in front of the clock, shouting, "Help me!" Akane dropped a plush toy that somewhat resembled Vincent, sprinted from the safety of her parent's arms, and rushed toward the image. Then, I created a blasting spark using Vincent's powers, taking in more people, including Akane's parents. I made it all look like an accident.

✸

(Back to the present)

Edward hands me a glass of water. After taking a few sips, I clarify, "Of course, Vincent accidentally changed that reality when he freed Emika. But still, the way little Akane ran toward Vincent's image showed what he was to her." I bat my eyes. "Aw! Innocent love." Handing the glass of water back to Edward, I reveal, "And it worked. On November 23, 1991, when Kruger told Vincent about Akane's disappearance, he got his first spark."[90]

Hank's eyes widen, and Dr. Lee's face pales in horror. But Edward is unfazed; he knows what resides under Philip Nardin's skin.

Pointing my cane at them, I ask, "You think I am heartless?" I pound the walking stick on the floor. "I. Am. Not. Heartlessness would have been to stop and let the cruelty of sucking that beautiful child into the turbulence become meaningless. So, I kept on." Grinning, I continue, "I knew Akane would throw herself over Vincent to save him again on April 13, 2027. Poor thing didn't even know she was the target." I snap my fingers. "But first, I needed to create the perfect enemy to attack her." Pointing my cane at Hank, I ask, "Who killed Rudy?"

Grunting, Hank punches the crystal wall of his cage. "Vincent!"

I chuckle. "Wrong. Masquerading as a doctor, I broke into the infirmary and snapped Rudy's neck."

Hank's eyes widen, the horror of this revelation rendering him speechless.

"I made you believe someone bribed the doctors and Kruger." Snickering while shaking my head, I reveal, "It was perfect timing! Paying Kruger for Vince's upkeep while you and Dina were waiting outside."

"What else did you do?" Hank growls.

I wink at him. "The usual." Lifting my thumb, I say, "Planted narcotics in your father's casino." I raise my index finger. "Bribed the police to kill him and make it look like suicide." Lifting the third finger, I deliver the final blow. "Replaced your mother's antidepressant pills with cyanide."

Falling to the floor, Hank surrenders to hopelessness. "My entire life is a lie." Raising his red, wet eyes, he asks, "You staged everything?"

"The sex traffickers during your parents' burial were real." I shrug. "If I hadn't come, Dina would have been sold to the Russians or the Middle East, and you would have been thrown into the trash after they took out your eyes, your heart, your kidneys—the useful shit." Pointing the cane at Hank, I say, "You owe your lives to me."

"No!" Hank shakes his head and glares at me. "Was Emika your plan, too?"

---

[90]   Chapter 1 of *The Winding* (Book 1).

I grin. "Somewhat. I learned she was instrumental in Vincent's second power phase. But I had to dispose of Elise before Emika could come into play." Turning to Edward and pointing at his intreton-c powered legs, I ask, "What do you think of Lombard and Dick Graham?"

"Vile," the otherwise calm Edward snarls. "They took my legs . . . Tabi's family."

I snap my fingers and then point at Hank. "That's why I asked you to bribe Bangalore officers to loosen one canister. Lombard canisters weren't all that bad, but without the leaked canisters, I couldn't bait Vincent into seeing their evil and convince him the canisters were rubbish." Grinning, I rub my hands together. "He fell for it. And he blamed corrupt Dick and Lombard for the whole mess." Spreading my arms, I laugh. "That was an exceptional performance in the Senate. After that, I took revenge for Tabi and Edward and destroyed Lombard. With Elise gone, Vincent's path to Emika and the second level of power was clear." Groaning in pain, I press my temples.

"Are you okay, sir?" Edward asks, putting a hand on my shoulder.

"Yeah," I say, panting. "Vincent is in my head, reading me. It's only one way now . . . so, I get all the headaches." As I try to steady my breathing, I continue, "It's funny, though—what Vincent told me when he brought up Emika."

(Vincent's home)

Vincent

Touching my chest, I gasp for breath. Emika rushes over to me and rubs my back. I turn to her kind face. "I wish it were that simple—that Elise died, and you came." My voice trembles. "When I told Philip to remind me of my mission in 1992, I shouldn't have . . ."

"What?" Emika probes gently.

Tucking her hair behind her ears, I confess, "I shouldn't have revealed that Akane was inside you. He figured out that my resolve to set you free would lead me to unlock the core." Holding her hand, I stare into Emika's eyes. "And he planned the whole conspiracy around Elise accordingly, taking full advantage that the past and future have no meaning in the core." I sigh. "Elise being a money launderer and her father being corrupt added fuel to Philip's ambition. Before I saw him in 1992, he attended my graduation in 2001. Hearing my plea to return Akane, Philip used my navigation tech from 2024 and the power I gave him to enter the core as Oliver in 2001."

Squeezing Emika's hand, I continue, "There, he convinced Chronos to grant my wish for Akane to be returned. Chronos can find anyone in the core. Thinking that Oliver, as Philip's shadow, had my best interests in mind, he took the nine-year-old Akane from 1991 from her chamber in the core and merged her with the almost ten-year-old Emika of 2001." I cup Emika's cheek. "That merging made you pick the violin over the piano." I confess, "My wish ruined your life."

Kissing my hand, Emika assures me, "No."

Bringing her close, I kiss her forehead. Then, resting my chin atop her head, I look around the room at everyone—some are breathing hard, some are drinking, and some are wiping their tears.

Philip

Punching the crystal wall, Hank demands, "Which happened first? How can you talk about freeing Emika in 1992 when she was merged with Akane in 2001?"

"They happened simultaneously, you moron! Vince and I are forging links to this infinite movement of causality." Sighing, I admit, "He is just better than me."

Hank groans, pressing his hands to his head, "You and Vince ruined Emika's life."

"An unruined Emika would have never batted an eye at you," I sneer. "My entire space project was created to earn Vincent's trust." Spreading my arms, I declare, "$150 billion is nothing compared to becoming the master of realities and time. But there was no intreton in that spaceship—except the fuel." Forming a fist, I reveal, "All the intreton is mine. I knew it would be handy when Vince took away my powers. And he did—yesterday, in the core, when he did not transfer any powers to me." Staring at my hands, I groan, "My powers are leaving me."

(Yesterday in the core)

Extending my hand, I asked, "Are we forgetting something?"

He smirked. "Nope."

I knew my cover was blown. But Vincent did not harm me. He just quietly left the room. I kept running toward all the versions of Vincent post-2024, but they all kept vanishing as I neared them. Out of desperation, I ran to the littlest Vince in his bassinet.

Rocking the sweet child while gasping for air and hope, I asked, "Hey, little one. How about spark?" Without a spark, the snapping power is useless.

Vincent's voice boomed through the ceilings, the walls, and every corner of the core. I covered my ears, yet his words pierced them.

"All the power is mine, Philip. You will soon lose your ability to snap."

(Back to the present)

I tighten my grip on my derby handle. "I knew this day would come, but going back to 2024, I did things differently when he became the time corrector."

"How?" Hank asks, breathing hard.

My eyes well up. "During our chess sessions and car races, I saw what life would be if I had a son." I clear my throat. "Maybe it's Victor in me, but I wanted to give Vincent a choice. If he agreed, he wouldn't have to be one with the core, and he wouldn't have to remember Emika."

"What plan, sir?" asks Dr. Lee.

Spreading my arms, I look up, imagining the possibilities. "Commercializing alternate realities." Smiling, I reveal, "Plan A."

Vincent

Sitting on the sectional, Anna asks, "What commercial application? Why?"

Taking a deep breath, I explain, "So Philip, Oliver, and Victor can coexist in the same reality but also separately." I touch Emika's face. "So you don't have to choose between Markus and me. You can have both."

"I will never want that," Emika says, tugging my lapel. "I will never pick him over you."

I know better. I know you wanted Nozo to be his.

Philip

I look at Edward, Dr. Lee, and Hank. "As such, he wouldn't allow such application. So, I had to earn his trust by pushing him to the edge." Fisting my left hand, I chuckle. "With one hand, I asked Dina to hack JPX." I fist my right hand. "With this, I stopped the trades and saved Egami Enterprises and Akane from embarrassment." Pointing at Hank, I sneer, "I made you create the airport fiasco in Southeast Asia, and I convinced Vincent to keep Akane away. When Vincent wanted to grant Akane some power, I convinced him that would be detrimental to her. I was earning his trust, and I could tell he was leaning in my favor." I spread my arms. "I played the genius, Vincent, like Itzhak Perlman fiddles the Soil Stradivarius." Frowning at Hank, I shout, "But then, you had to do the Seattle theatrics! Why?"

"I know you asked Dina to give Emika the dinner pass . . ." Hank's voice trembles. "Since Emika laid her eyes on Nozo, I tried to stop loving her...but I failed. Terribly." He stares into his trembling hands and clenches his jaws, "On the day of the conference, jealousy took over my thoughts... and I couldn't bear the thought of Vince and Emika in the same place for too long. So, I had to do something."

Knocking on the crystal wall, I yell, "Your theatrics convinced Vince not to commercialize an alternate reality. If you hadn't been stupid, I would have convinced Emika to move on and leave Vincent with Akane. And you would have had another chance with Emika." I grind my teeth. "You made me move to Plan B—reviving Vincent's memory and driving a wedge between him and Akane." Staring at Hank, I scrunch my face in disgust. "Your actions ruined your pathetic, mediocre, middle-class dream—family, hatchback, small house...Yuck!" Grimacing, I ask, "How is the thought of Vincent and Emika being together forever sitting in your mind?"

Hank's eyes well up as he murmurs, "What have I done?" Raising his teary eyes, he frowns at me. "Then why did you offer her a job in 2024?"

"I was conflicted; I wanted Vincent's power, but I wanted him to be happy," I admit, my voice shaking. "You and Emika reached a plateau after her pregnancy, so her coming here wouldn't change anything."

"Really? Hank scoffs. "Would Vincent feel the same about Akane if he'd been with Emika when Akane returned?" Pounding on the wall, he demands, "Would he have erased himself from Akane after I attacked her?"

"Yes! It doesn't matter who Vincent spends his life with. Akane is his cosmological constant." Lifting my finger, I clarify, "Akane is the key to his power and existence."

Glaring, Hank asks, "So, Vincent doesn't love Emika?"

I roll my eyes. "Of course, he does. But that has no bearing on his power as a time corrector. His love made him free her on August 13, 2024. It also freed Akane." I smile. "Emika's rejection of the job offer only made things easier. Two years of romance between Vince and Akane meant a deeper heartbreak." Lifting my finger, I reveal, "When Vincent went unconscious, after I absorbed all the intreton on August 30, 2024, I . . . I . . ." Touching my chest, I force a laugh. Why is it hurting?

Pushing past the pain, I continue, "I deleted his entire call log from before and his chats with Emika that day—and her contact details. Eliminating every bit of Emika from his life." I smirk. "When Akane came along, I helped him acquire the Kashmir sapphire ring, the Stradivarius violin." Lifting the cane above my head, I raise my voice. "I escalated Vince's dreams to their peak." Knocking the cane on the floor, I screech, "Imagine the drop. Imagine the pain of the escalating tragedies." I touch my cheek. Tears? Why? I quickly wipe them away.

Turning to Edward, I say, "I knew the exact moment Vincent became one with the core would fracture my realities." I tap my chin with a finger. "Should I let it happen? I'd be an artist like Victor. Fuck that. Or a glorified mechanic like Oliver. Who wants that? Should I just be a watchmaker like Philip was destined to be?" Spreading my arms, I declare, "No. Being this—the wealthiest, most powerful man in the world—is fantastic. So, I planned, even if it meant Vincent took away my powers."

Looking at Hank, I bend my head and acknowledge, "You did so well . . . electrocuting Miguel and Altaf and burning Ravi and his family to ashes. Ravi's death was the perfect stage to bring Akane back." I scrunch my face. "But you got a little carried away, trying to break the shell where Vincent and Akane were or almost killing Vincent in your duel." I scream from the bottom of my lungs, "Escalating tragedies!"

Vincent

Their faces become blurry against my tears. As Emika rubs my back, I continue, "That evening, Philip was not there to support us. He was there to inspect Vandal's killing of Ravi, Hank's murdering of Maddy . . . and . . ." Touching Emika's loving, anxious face, I say, "Sorry . . . and Markus's slaughtering of little Wasim." As her lips tremble, I bring her head to the nook of my neck, whispering, "None of this is your fault."

I stare blankly at the floor. "I wondered why Philip needed a cane, but my trust blinded me. If I only took a deeper look at him in the core . . . we could have avoided this all." Curling my hand into a fist, I hiss, "He played well. Making Vandal break into his island facility and then hack into Stellarcloud meant we wouldn't suspect Philip."

Emika raises her brows. "Then why were Edward's men and the cops here that night? Wouldn't they know Markus wouldn't attack here?"

"Theatrics," I scoff. "To remove Markus as a suspect."

Tabi brings her hands to her mouth. Stammering, she asks, "Dad knows everything?" Tears stream from her eyes as she loses hope that her adoptive father is innocent.

I lower my eyes. "Yes."

Philip

Shaking my head, I chuckle, "That gullible Emika. I asked her to call Akane, and she did."

"Do you know what that did to her?" Hanks yells at me.

"Nothing more than realizing she fucked a psychopathic killer." I smile at the missed possibilities. "It would have been perfect. In saving Akane from the brink of death and erasing himself from her, Vincent became one with the core. But, from the guilt of realizing his act ruined the lives of Victor, Amara, Oliver, Iman, and countless others, he would transfer the power to me. Then, Vincent's bitterness would have driven Emika away." I point my finger at Hank. "And maybe, she would find comfort in your loving arms." Shaking my head, I say, "I don't let sacrifices go unnoticed. I'd have given Vincent fifty percent of Nardin Industries and pumped hundreds of billions into Quantum World. That would have been the perfect Plan B."

Vincent

I hold Emika's hands. "Philip's perfect plan relied on me not knowing Markus was Vandal. But, driven by jealousy and anger from a doctored memory, Markus had to destroy my legacy by hacking Quantum World. However, he did not have the heart to remove his photos from Nozo's album. That changed everything."

Emika touches my face. "I would have never left you for Markus, even if I didn't know who he was. No matter how bitter you became." She assures.

(April 15, 2027)

<u>Philip</u>

Banging on the cell, glaring at Hank, I shriek, "But you had to ruin it! You made Dina hack The Mind and fall right into his trap. With your covers blown, Vincent knew where to look in the core and learned the true identity of Mr. J. He found out who I truly was."

"Vince would have figured it out, anyway!" Hank yells, pounding on the crystal wall. "Maybe not the day of the hacking . . . but a few days after, maybe."

I shake my head in disgust. "He would have given his powers to me by then. Without access to the core, all he would have known was that Markus was Vandal. He could have never linked you to me."

And I would have killed you and Dina to show Vincent that I cared for him.

"That's all you care about. Yourself." He looks at his hands. "I killed for you . . ." Gasping for breath, he says, "All my life, I blamed someone who had nothing to do with my suffering." His voice trembles. "You made me kill children." Looking up, he stares into my eyes. "Was it easy for you?"

I punch the crystal wall as I demand, "Easy? Was it easy to train you for over twenty years to fight Vince? And prepare Vince for almost three years to fight you?" Knocking on the floor with my cane, I ask, "You think finding a foster family for Dina was easy?" Grinding my teeth, I lean toward Hank. "You thankless piece of shit. Do you know how much it cost me to make your suit, that Jaeger, train you to use the core, use Vincent's navigation techniques, and make intreton-piercing shurikens? Paying for your and Dina's education?" I catch my breath while leaning against the crystal wall. "How much it cost my health to transfer my snapping power to you?" Shaking my head, I sigh. "I should have trained Dina; she's so much better."

Standing up and pounding on the crystal, Hank howls, "What have you done to her?"

Vincent

I walk toward the console table by the front door. Opening a drawer, I take out the battered bullet Tabi gave me three years back, holding it with my thumb and index finger.

"It was not Edward who shot Dick Graham. He hit the fuselage tank of the G400." Lowering my brows, I continue. "Frida's adoptive family—the Chaturvedis—agreed that she'd spend the summers with Edward." I turn to Tabi and reveal, "You are the daughter Edward loves, but Dina is his true protégé—a master sniper and hacker. Hank was just the muscle."

I shake my head at my own stupidity. "Philip fooled me into thinking his supercomputers and satellite links were aiding him in catching Vandal. But those were Dina's tools to attack JPX, hack airports, reroute planes." Forming fists, I snarl, "I trusted Philip. But it was all lies."

Philip

Turning to face the projector across from Hank's cage, I say, "Let's move to Plan C." Clapping my hands, I activate the projector, and an image of my island emerges. "Look closely. There are over a hundred Amphi tanks, Falco planes, and more than ten thousand super-soldiers injected with intreton, ready to kill and die at my command."

Hank stares at the projections in sheer horror. "All these to fight Vince?"

I shake my head. "Of course not." Lifting my brows, I consider it. "Or . . . maybe?"

My cell phone vibrates inside my jacket pocket. Looking at the name on the screen, I smile in anticipation. "Time to test Vincent's strength."

Sliding my finger across the screen, I answer. "Yes, Dina?"

"I have the d-d-drone in place," she stutters.

"Dina, don't listen to him!" Hank yells. "Mr. J is Philip Nardin."

I glare at Hank. "She knows."

Hank sinks to his knees, hopeless with the realization of his stupidity, naivety, and betrayal.

"Wait about ten minutes and then deploy the payload."

"What if he stops it?" she asks.

"Then we will know the extent of his powers."

"If I deploy the payload, you will let Hank go?" Dina pleads. "Let us be tried in court. Please, sir, free us. We will take all the blame. Please?"

"Of course," I say.

No fucking way.

"Over and out."

Shaking his head, Hank cries, "You won't set us free."

Five of Edward's soldiers enter the room. Turning to Edward, I say, "Release Hank."

As the crystal cell opens, Hanks steps toward me. "Why did you let Vincent capture me?" he asks.

I gesture for Edward's men to surround Hank. "So that you don't become a rogue. I can use you again. I wanted Vince to do my work." I smirk. "And he did." Smiling at Hank, I say, "So, no, I won't free you."

Edward's men grab Hank's neck and make him kneel on the floor.

I turn to Dr. Lee and point at Hank. "Prepare him to join the rest of the soldiers." Taking my mask off, I throw it on the floor. The burn marks are gone. Lifting my thigh, I shatter the cane. I spread my arms and smile. "Goodbye, pretension."

Edward's men chain Hank with intreton-powered cuffs. As they shock him with tasers, he writhes and screams in pain. They drag him away. Before they leave the room, Hank manages to turn back and glare at me, his eyes full of lost childhood, betrayal, and defeat.

I fall to my knees, tears slowly dripping down my cheeks. Touching my chest, I rasp, "What have I done? Dina and Hank were just little kids. They looked up to me, like a father . . ." I stare at my bloodstained hands. "Look what I did . . . there were so many innocent lives in those flights . . . children." I sob, "I killed children." As my hands begin to shake, I fold them into fists. "I am sorry, Vince, my boy. With my own hands, I ruined your life. Emika, I am the real culprit. I am sorry, Akane. I am sorry, Elise, Ravi, Maddy, Wasim." Helplessly, I look up at Edward. "There is no redemption from this, right?"

"Afraid not, sir."

"We must move forward, then," I murmur. "What were you thinking, Vince, giving me the power when I picked you?" My voice trembles as tears continue to stream from my eyes. "I am not you. I am the people I despise—power-hungry, corrupt politicians. I despise me." Sobbing, I hum, "The lunatic is in my head. The lunatic is in my head."

Edward touches my shaking shoulder. "Sir, what made Vincent share his powers with you?"

"It was his way of thanking me." I smile brokenly as I state, "He is a good boy, my Vince. He shared his powers and overrode the reality where I was a mere watchmaker." Looking up, I stare at Edward through my teary eyes. "Look what I did in return."

"Please forgive my curiosity, sir . . ."

"Go on," I say, sniffling.

Helping me get up, he asks, "Wouldn't someone like Vincent simply erase himself to stop all this?"

I shake my head and shut my eyes. "I knew he would. So, I devised the perfect countermeasure."

"Which is?"

I bring my shaking hands to my mouth. My voice cracks with horror and shame. "There are some things even I am too ashamed to admit. There's no excuse . . ." I press my temples. "Vincent knows."

✺

Vincent

Falling to my knees, I stretch my arm out before me and spread my fingers. "Stay back, please." My voice trembles. "After realizing I was the source of all these problems, I wanted to erase myself."

Bringing her hand to her mouth, Emika sobs, "No."

"I stopped when I realized what Philip, as Oliver Journe, did to my mother when he anticipated I would do this. And what he would continue to do." Grinding my teeth, I explain, "He'd use my snapping ability and navigation tech to masquerade as Oliver and rape my mother repeatedly to neutralize any attempts to erase myself, so I'd be eventually born. Born from rape." I slam my fists on the floor. "He was that suitor—Oliver Journe."

Wheezing, I stare at my shaking hands. "I enabled him to rape my mother. Philip is my biological father. All my skills and tastes come from

Philip, his shadow, Oliver, or his echo, Victor." I point at Philip's painting of Amara above the mantel. "Imagine her life. She was loved by Victor, raped by Oliver, and nursed by Philip in her final days. All three are the same man, converging from different realities. The greed surrounding my power made Oliver do it. It's all my fault."

I wipe my eyes. "And I blamed Amara for dropping me at the orphanage. She did nothing wrong . . . I shouldn't be born." Grinding my teeth, I strike the floor again, my skin glowing with intreton. The floor cracks as I confess, "How could I defend a rapist in the Senate?" I look up at everyone's faces. Their eyes are wide with shock at my revelation and the glowing intreton. Pounding my chest, I rasp, "The one who funds our firm ruined Emika and killed Ravi, Maddy, Wasim, and Elise. The one who paid for my schooling almost killed Akane." I hang my head in defeat. "There is no coming back from this."

I look at my reflection on the glass wall. My hair glows like silver fire, and my eyes are as bright as gleaming emeralds, my entire body lighting up like the core. Everyone's faces grow pale.

I turn to Anna. "You were right . . . I am a freak."

Anna's lips wobble as she whispers, "No."

Before anyone can say anything more, a whirring sound pierces through the clouds and reaches my ears.

I smirk. "Bring it on," I say, standing up and spreading my arms wide.

I don't need to move this house from reality. The second hands of every clock and watch in the house slow and eventually stop, then reverse. Everyone in the room becomes still, then slowly moves backward. The falling pink snowflakes, defying gravity, lift back to the blossoms, where they promise to stay together. Another lie.

(Philip's island)

Dina

Their home is on my screen. Dr. Abajian, Emika, Nozo, and Hulk—four innocent lives. My colleagues and schoolmates are there, too. I hold the joystick. My hand is shaking. Sweat is dripping onto the red button. Mr.

Nardin saw me see him change from Mr. J to Philip. He threatened me, "One word, and I will kill Hank." I know he won't release Hank. But he will instantly kill my brother if I don't do this. I have no one but him—someone who will throw his life away for me.

Dr. Abajian, please save everyone. Though I knew you were innocent, I had to do all this. That's why I sweat and pant when I see you and anyone close to you. I know you will never forgive us, but please save your family.

I want this to stop.

Die, Dina. Die. Press the button, Dina! Kill them all, then kill yourself.

Shutting my eyes tight, biting into my cinnamon candy, I press the button with my thumb. What have I done?

Little shit, Dina, what have you done?

There is no coming back. What have I done to deserve this life? It was only yesterday that I was just eight.

I open my eyes and look at the clock, but it's stopped. What? How is it reversing? Why can't I move? How are my tears trickling up? The drops transform into spheres and move up around my face. My thumb moves away from the button, and my hand slowly lifts up. The cinnamon candy in my mouth pushes between my lips and reenters the wrapper. Tears that had collected on my glasses clear up. Then, suddenly, everything resumes, and the clock starts again. I feel a nudge on my shoulder. My heart stops as I look to my side.

I stutter, "D-Dr. Abajian?"

He puts a hand on my shoulder. "It's Vince." Pointing at the joystick, he says, "Don't do it. You are better than this."

Standing up, I look away from him. My tears trickle down my cheeks and splatter on the desk. "I am not better. You don't know who Mr. J is." I confess, "I hacked the Neurolink." Wiping my tears, I admit, "Hank let Mr. J experiment on him, so he doesn't hurt me instead . . . I hacked JPX so Mr. J would stop torturing Hank." I sob, "He is more than a twin; he took care of me like a parent . . . Mr. J forced him to attack Dr. Bose. He said he'd kill me if Hank didn't do it."

He brings my head to his chest, comforting me. "Shhh. I know everything." Rubbing his hand on my back, he soothes me. "I am sorry for everything."

I pull back and look at him in shock. "You are sorry? You should never forgive me. Anna, Emika, and Chris will never forgive me."

"Maybe they won't," he says, touching my hand. "But I have."

Wiping my eyes, I ask, "Can you save Hank?"

He looks straight into my eyes. "Hank crossed the limits of my generosity." He lifts his finger. "But I won't attack him unless he provokes me."

"Why?"

His voice cracks, and he swallows hard. "Because somewhere in her heart, buried deep down, Emika still loves him. That's why." He touches my shoulder. "Keep working for Philip. He must never find out that we had this conversation."

(April 15, 2027—Vincent's home)

Vincent

The clocks resume.

"What did you mean when you said, 'Bring it on?'" asks Fred.

"Nothing." I smile. "Dina just deployed a missile at our house."

Crumpling her brows, Sasha screams, "That's nothing?"

Emika sprints toward the stairs, screaming, "Nozo, Hulk! Get down now!"

"Get in the cars now!" Tabi orders everyone. Her eyes are about to bulge out.

I raise my voice and wave my arms. "I have stopped it."

"How?" Emika lifts her brows in shock. "You were here."

(Yesterday in the core)

Vincent

"What are my powers?" I asked. "Does it justify the cost?"

Chonos smirked. "It never justifies the price." Gripping his scythe with both hands, he explained, "You can invert, forward, and stop time. But do it only for a few minutes. That's all you need." He brought his thumb and index finger together. "A tiny smidgen of asynchronicity between Earth time and Universe time." He winked. "And when you do, it will seem to everyone that you are in different places."

"Does Philip know the specifics?"

"No, but he will stop at nothing to get a sense of your power."

I squinted at him. "What will happen if I extend it longer than a few minutes?"

He looked into my eyes. "A reset."

Scoffing, I asked, "Answer me this. Why did you choose me?"

"The tussle between you and Philip will lead to something far greater than what the job of a regular time corrector would entail." He took a deep breath before he continued, "It will create a different world for everyone except . . ."

"Except?"

His eyes wet, he said, "I am proud of you."

(April 15, 2027—Vincent's home)

<u>Vincent</u>

Staring at the retreating sparks, I say, "If I'd had this power sooner, I could have saved Ravi, Maddy, Wasim. I could have reversed time and wouldn't have had to change Akane's reality." Grinding my teeth, I growl, "Haven't I had enough?"

Fred, Krista, Sasha, Chris, Tabi, and Anna come closer to me. They hug, kiss, and hold my hands, assuring me that none of this is my fault. Lies again. A few steps away, by the glass wall, shimmering against the sun-infused pink *hanafubuki* behind her, Emika stares at me.

Sobbing, she asks, "What's a reset? Why did Chronos say, 'except'?" Everyone turns to her, but she keeps her gaze locked on mine, her eyes wide with worry. "What will happen to you?"

I finally understood what the future me was doing with the *tanto* in his hand the day I freed Emika. Breathing in, I press my lips together and fake a smile to hide my sorrow. "We'll find out."

The *Time Corrector* will return . . .

www.ingramcontent.com/pod-product-compliance
Lightning Source LLC
Chambersburg PA
CBHW020009120726
47903CB00004B/1199